Operation Deep Strike:
An India-Pakistan Covert Ops Spy Thriller

Rahul Badami

Book Title: Operation Deep Strike
Book Author: Rahul Badami

Published by Rahul Badami

First Published 2017

ISBN-13: 978-1976202407
ISBN-10: 197620240X

Rahul Badami asserts the moral right to be identified as the author of this work.

Principal Characters

Ops Team
Armaan Ahmed
Baldev Bakshi
Roshan Gupta
Hitesh Vohra

Indian Administration
Jagdish Inamdaar, Prime Minister
Gen. Vishwajeet Singh, Director General, DIA
Shikha Tiwari, Head – Advanced Warfare Systems, DIA

Pakistani Administration
Mian Fateh, Prime Minister
Sohail Akhtar, Divisional Director of ISI
Gorbat Khan, CTD Inspector, Quetta
Fazal Darzada, Balochi leader

Acronyms

AFS – Air Force Station

AWACS – Airborne Early Warning and Control System

BARC – Bhabha Atomic Research Centre

BMD – Ballistic Missile Defence

CIA – Central Intelligence Agency

CTD – Counter Terrorism Department

DG – Director General

DIA – Defence Intelligence Agency

DRDO – Defence Research and Development Organisation

ELINT – Electronic Intelligence

ETA – Estimated Time of Arrival

EXFIL – Exfiltrate

FATA – Federally Administered Tribal Areas

GES – Ground Exploitation Station

GPS – Global Positioning System

GR – Grid Reference

HUMINT – Human Intelligence

HVT – High Value Target

IAF – Indian Air Force

IGP – Inspector General of Police

INFIL – Infiltrate

INS – Indian Naval Ship

ISI – Inter-Services Intelligence

ISRO – Indian Space Research Organisation

KP – Khyber Pakhtunkhwa

LTRA – Long Term Resident Agent

LZ – Landing Zone

NCA – National Command Authority

NDS – National Directorate of Security

NOTAM – Notice to Airmen

NVG – Night Vision Glasses

PM – Prime Minister

PMO – Prime Minister's Office

POK – Pakistan-occupied Kashmir

R&AW – Research and Analysis Wing

RPG – Rocket-Propelled Grenade

SAM – Surface-to-Air Missile

SAT – Satellite
SIGINT – Signal Intelligence
SITREP – Situation Report
SLCM – Submarine-launched Cruise Missile
TEL – Transporter Erector Launcher
TTP – Tehreek-e-Taliban Pakistan
VR – Virtual Reality
WSB – Weapons Storage Bunker

Prologue

Hunza Valley, Gilgit-Baltistan, Pakistan
Bang!
Abdul knew he was about to die as soon as he heard the gunshot.
Bang!
The second gunshot was as loud as the first, reverberating in the tiny hotel room. Abdul watched in horror as his security guard who had opened the door crumple down on the floor. Two small holes blot red on his beige uniform. The body lay motionless.

Dead.

Abdul couldn't see the assailant. He was in one corner of the hotel room and the half-open door blocked his view of the killer outside the door who had shot his guard.

This also meant that the assailant hadn't seen him. Yet. He only had a second before he too would be gunned down.

Abdul's eyes darted around the room searching for an escape route. The window. It was open. It was the only way. But he hesitated.

"He should be in here." He heard shouts beyond the door.

Abdul glanced back. The assailant walked past the door. Abdul could see him now. A smoking 9mm was in his hand, the face masked by a black cloth. Only the eyes showed. Dark. Furious. Deadly. The killer's gaze burned with such intensity, Abdul felt his soul shiver.

"There." More men poured into the room. All masked. All of them carried weapons.

Abdul had seen enough. His decision was made.

He turned and jumped through the open window.

He fell through fifteen feet and landed on the snow-covered ground. His room was on the first floor of the hotel and the snow cushioned the impact of his fall. He was alive, but he wasn't safe. Abdul scrambled to his feet and ran. He wasn't sure where he wanted to go. But he wanted to get as far away from the hotel as he could.

He hurried through the snow filled path, his boots trampling through the wet snow making it difficult for him to run. But he had to run, his life depended on it.

Abdul looked back in the dim glow of the moon. His pursuers had also jumped through the window and were after him. They were relentless. And they were catching up. He willed himself to run faster.

To one side of the path was a small snow-clad hill. He clambered towards it, his breathing laboured. Once at the top, he paused for a moment to catch his breath. The snow-capped mountains looked magical under the moonlight. In the distance, he could see the Attabad Lake, the youngest lake in the world. The moon reflecting off the still water was a sight to behold. But none of the beauty held any value for Abdul. He desperately searched for a place to hide. But the open hillsides didn't have any.

Abdul had decided to take a small vacation to keep away from the pressures at work. As a missile engineer working on numerous projects for the Pakistan Army, he received very few leaves. Little did he know when he planned his vacation that it would turn out this way. A few minutes back, there had been a knock on his hotel room door. His guard had opened the door and the nightmare had begun.

Abdul had immediately guessed who they were. Terrorists. He wasn't sure why they were after him. But it didn't matter. He didn't want to stay to find out.

He looked down the hill. There were six of them at the foot of the hill. Three continued sprinting on the path parallel to the hill, and the remaining three spread apart as they climbed up the hill. Towards him.

Abdul realised he was going to get boxed from all sides. He waded through the knee-deep snow. Slowed down by the flakes that sunk under his weight. The three men on the foothill below raced past him on the even path and were now approaching towards him from the side.

The first of the pursuers was only a few feet behind him, swinging his sub-machine gun; his eyes resolute and intent. Abdul wondered why they hadn't shot him yet. A dread of terror filled the pit of his stomach as a new realisation struck him. They wanted to torture and kill him.

As he ran, the tip of his boot landed unevenly on the wet snow. His feet slipped back, propelling his upper body forward and he found himself falling. He landed flat on his face. The moist snow momentarily blinded him. He scrambled frantically to get up, but a powerful foot plunged itself in the small of his back. The wind went out of his chest as he got pinned to the ground.

Abdul raised his face to look at his assailant. "Please, no," he begged.

The assailant just laughed and kicked him hard in the side. A streak of pain sizzled through his abdomen. He whimpered in agony. The other five terrorists had now reached the first assailant and they stood laughing, jeering at his helplessness. They all had their guns trained on him.

Abdul clutched the side of his body and looked up at the terrorists with horror.

Was this how his life would end?

Chapter 1

India-Bangladesh International Border

"Approaching target zone. Switching to Night Vision."

Roshan Gupta's heart thudded like a pneumatic hammer. The blood vessels in his ears throbbed, echoing his fears. The night was dark; the light from the half-moon inadequate. The visibility extended to only a few feet. He peered through the darkness. The shadows of the trees and the waist-high grass appeared like enemies lying in wait.

Roshan slid down the visor attached to his ballistic helmet. Immediately his world changed to white and green. The jungle looked bright and sunlit; the visibility had improved drastically. He could now see till far in the distance. The only gripe was that everything in the visor showed up in various shades of green. The visor was fitted with Night Vision technology.

Roshan looked around in a slow circular arc. His heart eased out with each beat. There was no unnatural movement; the forest was quiet except for the ambient sounds. An occasional frog croaked in a nearby swamp, crickets chirped in the trees and flies buzzed around his ears. He swatted them away.

"Keep a sharp lookout, boys." Armaan Ahmed, Roshan's group leader of the covert mission whispered as he slithered through the grass a few feet ahead of him.

Roshan mentally acknowledged his superior's order and scanned the jungle one more time just to make sure. He didn't want to make any mistakes. This was the moment he was waiting for a long time. An exceptional service record during his tenure in the Army wasn't enough for him; he hungered to do more. Now as part of the Defence Intelligence Agency, it was the first time he was involved in a 'strategic' operation. This was the next level stuff for pros, he told himself. It was his first mission with the DIA and he wanted to prove himself.

He looked at his team members. There were four of them and he, Roshan Gupta at twenty-six years, was the youngest of the group. Armaan Ahmed, the group leader and Baldev Bakshi were experienced veterans; both in their forties. Their exploits during the Kargil war were legendary. The fourth member Namit Seth was their tech guy. His primary role was to give technical data during the planning and operations stage. His secondary role was to provide backup. In other words, he would take out the targets himself only when needed.

They had received intelligence that a group of six top-level ISIS-affiliated terrorists based ten kilometres inside Bangladesh planned to carry out a major terror attack across the border in India. The sources said that the terrorists were scouting recruits for their attack. The Director General of the Defence Intelligence Agency had ordered a cross-border operation and the task was assigned to their group.

During the mission briefing, Namit told Roshan he didn't remember the last time, he had to provide backup to Armaan and Baldev. The veteran duo were enough. They could each pump out four headshots in less than two seconds. It was Roshan's first covert ops and he was glad he had a strong team.

They had been airdropped close to the border and then quietly sneaked through the dense jungle and crossed the border and made their way to the target zone ten kilometres away. Now close to the target zone, they had slowed down, wary of alerting their adversary.

Roshan heard Baldev whisper at his side. "Target at eleven o'clock, one hundred metres ahead."

Roshan looked at the direction indicated by Baldev and saw a small clearing ahead. He could make out a man standing guard among the green shapes. Behind him, the dark outline of a tent was visible. Roshan squinted through the scope of his Dragunov SVD sniper rifle and the man's profile zoomed up.

"Target in my sights, One." He addressed Armaan. "Waiting for your order."

"Let's close in." Armaan said.

They crouched slowly among the undergrowth taking care to stay below the waist-high grass. The moon was behind the clouds and it was pitch-dark. The six hostiles were battle-hardened, but Armaan had said that the darkness and the surprise factor would work in their favour.

Roshan parted the grass and observed the tent in the clearing that housed their target. They were thirty metres from the tent. Armaan gave a hand signal and they stopped. He waved Namit to spread right, and Baldev to approach from the left. Roshan watched both of them sneak in opposite directions through the grass leaving Armaan and him alone. He focused back on the guard. The man hadn't noticed their approach.

Armaan gestured to Roshan and pointed towards the terrorist. Roshan realized that Armaan was telling him to go ahead for the kill. Armaan was giving him the privilege of initiating the operation as well as testing his skills at the same time. Roshan already started to like Armaan's leadership. The best way to learn was to be tempered in the fires of experience. And Armaan wanted to know if his nerves were made of steel. He would not disappoint Armaan.

Roshan took a long, deep breath and visualized his previous experiences. He had been in impossible situations prior to this and had survived. Taking a headshot in a quiet jungle with a cool breeze waving through his hair? He could do it with his eyes shut.

Roshan looked through the scope of the Dragunov SVD. He could see flies buzzing in a circle above the guard's head, appearing like white flying specks in the green haze of the night vision. The Dragunov was equipped with a suppressor and custom-made subsonic bullets that kept the noise to a minimum. Roshan held his breath, focused the red dot on the man's head and gently squeezed the trigger. A silenced spit emitted from the Dragunov and the recoil shuddered in Roshan's palms. A spurt of blood erupted from the man's head and he slid down to the ground, dead. Roshan turned his sights to the tent. There was no movement. He roved his sights in a wide arc and scanned the general area. The tent was silent; the crickets still chirped undisturbed in the night.

A pause of two seconds. Then Armaan gave him a hand signal. *Move to the tent.*

They sprinted through the trees and made their way

across to the tent. Roshan's pulse quickened with each step they took in the direction of their objective. *This was the moment of reckoning.*

Armaan had mentioned during the briefing that the slightest mistake could ruin a mission. He wondered if they should have waited a few more seconds before approaching the tent. What if the terrorists had woken up and were waiting for them? They could be walking into a trap. And he would be killed in his first covert mission.

But it was too late to back out now. He saw Armaan switch to his handgun as they ran. Roshan also pulled out a silenced Glock 17 from his holster. The Glock was better than the Dragunov for close quarters combat. They were approaching the tent, its canvas door rolled down to prevent the chilly night wind from entering. They stopped in front of the tent. Roshan's pulse thundered as he levelled his Glock at the tent expecting an ambush. But Armaan was calm; he raised three fingers and wordlessly counted down.

Three. Two. One. *Go.*

Armaan ripped the tent door open with a swift jerk and rushed through. Roshan closely followed behind gripping his gun tightly, his heart about to explode with the adrenaline rush of imminent battle. The next couple of seconds were a blur as he quickly looked around and found the terrorists sleeping on the ground. He dimly registered that the faces matched the Intel they had received. Roshan's hands twitched with the nervous energy of a combat situation as he pulled the trigger twice in rapid succession hitting two terrorists straight through the head. He heard three spits at his side and turned to look. Armaan had finished the rest of them.

Roshan glanced down at the bodies. All five terrorists were dead. Each sported a bullet in their head. It was a textbook kill. Swift, silent, and effective. The rush of blood swirled down. He felt no emotion at their deaths. They were out to kill innocent people. It was either the six of them or the sixty or so that they would kill. For him, the choice was easy. He felt no compassion towards terrorists who masterminded the deaths of defenceless, common people.

"Good job." He heard Armaan say. Armaan had a smile on his face.

It took a moment for Roshan to realize that they had accomplished their objective. Armaan's words made his chest swell with pride. The mission was complete.

His first mission.

He had played on the pro level and had succeeded. This was the beginning of something new. Only a fraction of soldiers made it this far. Roshan took a deep breath. He had proved himself good.

"Thank you," he replied.

Armaan glanced at his watch. "Let's exfil out of here."

They came out of the tent to find Baldev approaching them. "All quiet. Let's go," he said.

Armaan looked around. "Where's Namit?"

Boom!

A thunderous explosion nearby lit up the jungle like daylight. Roshan's eyes widened in horror as he saw the black outline of a figure, arms and legs splayed in mid-air silhouetted against the dazzling white background of the blast. The body swooped through the air and fell right in front of them.

Roshan's blood turned to ice as he recognized the motionless figure lying in front of him. It was Namit.

He was dead.

Namit had gone around to circle the tent, and had probably stepped on a landmine or a tripwire. Roshan looked over him; the eyes were still open. He had died instantaneously.

Lights switched on in the distance. Roshan peered through the scope and saw that it was a small village and men were emerging from a couple of houses half a kilometre away. Faint shouts could be heard as the people looked at the smouldering remains of a tree near the tent that was still burning. The light from the burning tree illuminated their presence. More people streamed out from their houses. As some of the villagers raced in their direction, Roshan realized that they held guns in their hands. They looked like either the sympathisers of the terrorists or their recruits. It didn't matter.

They were an immediate threat.

"Let's move. We will be swarmed in a few minutes." Baldev broke into a run. Armaan followed him.

Roshan started to join in. And then he stopped. He looked back at Namit's corpse. They couldn't leave him behind.

"Roshan." Armaan ordered him, "Follow us."

Roshan hesitated. "But sir, we cannot leave Namit here."

Armaan stopped and turned to him. "Our mission was to eliminate the terrorists, and not to rescue a dead comrade. Can't you see we will be overwhelmed if we stay here? One dead is better than four dead. Now follow me, and that's an order."

Roshan stared at the lifeless figure on the ground. He couldn't bring himself to abandon Namit. It didn't matter that he was dead. "No, sir. I cannot. I will carry him."

"Fool, you are jeopardizing everyone's lives. I will deal with you later." Armaan turned and raced towards the border.

Roshan turned his thoughts to Namit. He bent down and lifted his six-foot frame and propped it on his shoulder. His colleague's body plus the weight of his rifle and backpack crushed him. He straightened himself with difficultly and trudged between the trees trying to get away from the area as quickly as possible.

The shouts grew closer. Roshan glanced back and could see flashlights bobbing their rays up and down in the night, a couple of hundred metres back. They were gaining on him. He hurried his pace weaving through the trees; the calf of his legs burning under the impossible weight. The path was uneven and rocky and he was at a definite disadvantage.

Roshan sneaked a quick peek behind him. The pursuers were only a hundred metres behind. He estimated there were a dozen of them. And he was alone. They would be onto him in less than a minute. He felt a tug in his foot as he rushed past two trees. His balance swayed as his foot got entangled in a root and he fell heavily onto the ground with Namit's body falling besides him.

Roshan frantically scrambled behind the cover of a

tree, but it was already too late. The enemy closing in had heard him fall. Shots whizzed all around him. The flashlights directed their rays in his general direction. Roshan couldn't let these vermin win. He brought around his Dragunov and trained it on the hostiles. He took careful aim from behind the tree and squeezed off a burst of shots. A couple of the terrorists fell down.

But it was a mistake.

He had given away his exact position. The enemy now alerted to his location got in behind the cover of the trees. And they started firing at him. The bark of the tree shredded as bullets relentlessly pounded it. Roshan was completely pinned down. He couldn't return fire without risking being shot at.

He was trapped.

Roshan crouched behind the tree and waited for a break in the firing. Suddenly, he saw a movement in the periphery of his vision. One of the men had made a wide arc and had raced to a position parallel to where he was, only a few metres away. He understood immediately; the firing had been a ruse. He had been pinned so that he would be distracted and their colleague could take him out.

The black eyes of the terrorist signified death. So did the AK-47 in his hands.

Roshan knew he had only a fraction of a second to correct the situation. He swivelled his gun in mid-air to shoot down the adversary.

But it was too late.

The terrorist's AK-47 barked twice. Two bullets thudded into Roshan's chest and crunched through his ribcage. A white hot pain seared through his chest. The Dragunov flew out of his hand, and his body slammed against the jungle floor.

The terrorist walked closer, the AK-47 outstretched in his hand. Roshan watched with trepidation at the barrel hole of the AK-47 pointed right between his eyes.

He was disarmed. There was no escape. He waited for the bullet to come out from the barrel and end his life.

"Burn in the fires of hell, infidel." The terrorist growled.

A sharp gunshot echoed in the night.

Chapter 2

Roshan awoke with a jolt.

His heart shuddered in his chest and sweat poured down his hairline. He looked around in the darkness. He was in his bedroom. He glanced at the radium hands of the bedside clock. It was four am.

He had been dreaming the same dream again.

He looked down at his chest and fingered the area where he had been shot. The wounds had healed, but the memories hadn't. It had been months since that fateful night on the Bangladesh border when he was nearly killed.

Roshan remembered how it happened.

It was Armaan who had returned after calling Baldev back. Armaan had shot the terrorist with a single bullet to the head before he could kill Roshan. Together Baldev and Armaan had then unleashed a fury of gunfire against the remaining terrorists.

Roshan had stumbled in his wounded state as he picked up his gun. He gritted his teeth against the pain and used his blood-soaked fingers to chamber a fresh ten round magazine. He squeezed off a shot at the terrorists, and then another. The gun recoiled wildly in his arms; he couldn't control the aim in the condition he was in. By the time he had downed one of the terrorists, the fight was over. Armaan and Baldev had mowed down the others.

Armaan looked around at the terrorists, ensuring that they were dead. He then turned to Roshan, the anger unmistakable in his eyes. "Soldier, what was our mission?"

Roshan gasped as he tried to keep his voice steady, "To kill the designated terrorists."

"You nearly failed our mission. Your insubordination almost cost us our lives. What do you have to say in your defence?"

"I did," Roshan struggled against the pain in his chest, "what I thought was right."

"You are not here to think." Armaan's voice cut like steel. "You are here to follow orders. My orders. You'll answer to the DG for what happened tonight. Baldev," Armaan gestured to Baldev, "you help Roshan, I'll take care of Namit."

Armaan and Baldev then carried Namit and Roshan through the jungles back to base. It was a treacherous journey through the jungles and swamps, but they made it. The doctors looked at Roshan's wounds and told him that it would take a long time to heal, but he was lucky that the bullets hadn't passed through his lungs or heart.

Roshan spent many days in convalescence in a military hospital while his wounds healed. Most of the time was spent in retrospection of his first mission. Baldev had met him in the hospital, but Armaan hadn't. Baldev told him that they could have come for Namit later; Armaan was more concerned about the safety of his team. As a group leader, he had already lost one of his men, and he didn't want to risk the rest of their lives. It was also the reason Armaan took the decision to fight against the pursuing group of terrorists; as he couldn't let Roshan face them alone.

Roshan felt gratitude towards Armaan, but simultaneously felt guilty with himself. He had been carried away with bravado, when the mission required stealth. He remembered the soldier's creed was to follow orders. He cursed himself for his stupidity. He wanted to impress Armaan, but had ended up hospitalised for months instead of doing more field ops. His decisions had made him a liability for the team. No wonder Armaan had been so angry with him. He promised he would do his utmost to follow his leader's orders the next time.

The alarm in his mobile buzzed. It was 4:30 am. Roshan swiped across the mobile screen to turn it off. His thoughts returned to the picture of Armaan castigating him for his actions. He would be meeting Armaan on their next operation. His chest tightened as he wondered how Armaan would treat him after their previous experience. Would Armaan want him back? He hoped that Armaan would have forgiven him by now. In retrospect, his actions were an utter embarrassment. Roshan prided on his discipline, and he had let the emotions of the moment override his discipline.

No. He wouldn't let Armaan down again. If Armaan allowed him for another mission, he would ensure never to disobey his orders.

Ministry of Defence, South Block, New Delhi, India
Shikha Tiwari stood up from her desk with a frown. She couldn't concentrate. It had been thirty minutes since she had been working on a whitepaper with the topic 'Responding to Cyber Attacks during Wartime'.

And she was stuck.

Shikha looked over from her cabin to the team sitting in the cubicles, and a momentary smile replaced her frown. They were part of the Defence Intelligence Agency attached to the Ministry of Defence and she was proud of the work she did. While the armed forces worked at the borders, her team worked behind the scenes to ensure that any enemies' malevolent designs were thwarted. Shikha had been part of the pilot team when the DIA had been created way back in 2002.

She had worked assiduously and her intelligence and skills were recognised with multiple promotions over the years. She currently led her own team as the head of Advanced Warfare Systems. They were tasked to find cutting edge solutions to military challenges.

Intelligence agencies historically relied on HUMINT – human intelligence – the information gathered through human assets primarily through espionage. However, with the advent of computers and technology SIGINT and ELINT rose to prominence. Signal Intelligence and Electronic Intelligence were obtained by 'listening' into the enemy systems to gain knowledge of their plans. And based on the Intel received, they would develop solutions. From cyber-security to satellite reconnaissance, they were involved in all fields imaginable.

Shikha frequently liaised with the DRDO and the BARC for many of their top secret projects. And she took great satisfaction in making a small contribution to the massive organization that was the Ministry of Defence.

"You seem to be distracted." Tanmay Mehta walked towards her.

Shikha looked at Tanmay. He was a veteran of their

team. They had worked together for many years and had a professional respect for each other. She realized what had sidetracked her from her work. She looked down at the screen at the half-finished whitepaper she'd been creating.

"It's nothing." She mumbled.

Tanmay shook his head. "I've seen you working. Once you start, you never leave anything half-way. Something bothering you?"

"Yes, actually there is," she could tell it to Tanmay. He would have his own opinions and she wanted to know what they were. "It's about today's meeting with the PM."

"Ah!" Tanmay brought the word out as if he understood everything. Shikha wondered if he understood. His next words confirmed that he did indeed. "You don't like him, do you?"

Shikha nodded. "I don't like the way he talks." The Prime Minister was newly elected. He had previously been the Chief Minister of Uttar Pradesh and had helped garner a majority of seats in the all-important state, propelling him into the Prime Ministerial seat. He had a habit of being outspoken on all matters, and was decidedly a right-wing hardliner.

Tanmay said, "He speaks controversially to make an impact and sell himself. And the media gobbles it up." He paused. "We will come to see who he really is in today's meeting."

"That's what I am afraid of." Shikha said. "It's a defence security review. The moment we talk about defence, we have to talk about Pakistan. And you know his opinion on Pakistan."

"Pakistan must be shown a clear mirror of their doings." Prime Minister Jagdish Inamdaar spoke to the people assembled in front of him.

Shikha gripped her chair tightly in an effort to refrain from speaking. She looked around at the twenty or so people that sat around in the oval shaped meeting room. The three Chiefs of Staff, the Defence Minister, the Defence Secretary, the National Security Advisor, the R&AW chief, and a handful of core team members, everyone was nodding to Inamdaar's suggestion. While Shikha was no pacifist, she didn't appreciate the aggressive undertones of what the PM was implying.

The Defence Security review meeting had started with the three Chiefs of Staff apprising Inamdaar of the current border scenario followed by the achievements and challenges of their respective forces. Then the Defence Minister had talked about the roadmap for the Ministry of Defence. It was during the R&AW chief's discussion on external threats, specifically the threat from Pakistan's non-state actors that Inamdaar interrupted.

"I say," Inamdaar continued, "we need to find a way to end this nuisance on our western border. We give them Most Favoured Nation trade status, and they give us terrorism. They give us Kargil and Mumbai attacks. And each time we are in reactive mode. My predecessors allowed things to drift along in inertia. I will make things happen." He smashed his fist on the mahogany table.

"PM sir," the Defence Secretary said, "it is not just the threat of terrorism, but Pakistan is balancing its military capabilities in the nuclear arena. They know they can never win a conventional war against us, so they have launched a war of attrition where our army personnel are ambushed by non-state actors and their bodies are mutilated. They think we won't attack because they have the Bomb. They consider our reticence to be our weakness."

Inamdaar shook his head, "We have to figure out a way to resolve this. We cannot allow Pakistan to hold us to nuclear ransom. We have been looking for a diplomatic solution for ages and haven't found any. We need a military solution on the cross-border terrorism."

The Defence secretary shook his head, "A military solution is unthinkable against a nuclear-armed state. Pakistan has employed a full spectrum nuclear deterrence from low-kiloton Tactical Nuclear Weapons as a response to our Cold Start doctrine, to now being a Nuclear Triad with the recent trial of their Submarine Launched Cruise missiles. It's impossible."

Inamdaar straightened in his chair, "I do not want to hear the word 'impossible' in this room again. I need answers on how we can mitigate the nuclear risk and uproot the terrorism threat."

The R&AW chief joined in, "The nuclear risk is escalating by the day. Till recently, they could deploy their warheads only from missile silos or via aircrafts, which we could easily track with our Airborne Early Warning and Control Systems posted at the international border. But with the sea-based nuclear capability, we now have no idea from where and when their submarines will launch nuclear attacks, if they ever decide to pull the nuclear trigger. If they launch missiles from a submarine in the Bay of Bengal, our AWACS at the border become redundant. In addition, I have received credible information that Pakistan is covertly working on a top-secret military facility that will help them leverage their sea-based nuclear capability."

Shikha's ears perked up at the information. She looked around and saw that everyone's gaze was fixed on the R&AW chief. He said, "I can see that I have got your attention. Here's what our team has found out…"

The R&AW chief spoke for a few minutes. A hush descended on the gathering as he finished. Everyone was numbed by the information shared. Inamdaar spoke first.

"Do we have a confirmation that this Intel is genuine?"

"Yes," the R&AW chief replied, "Satellite data confirmed what my agents in Pakistan found out. The facility in question indeed exists."

"Do you have any proposals about what we should do?" PM Inamdaar asked.

"I spoke with General Singh before coming to the meeting today on our possible responses." The R&AW chief said, "General, would you like to share your thoughts?"

General Vishwajeet Singh, the Chief of the Army Staff nodded, "Before I elaborate on my ideas, I would like to talk about history. In the eighties, when the nuclear programs of both our countries were under wraps, we were approached by the Israelis. They wanted our support to scuttle the Kahuta nuclear plant. The Israelis had already destroyed a nuclear reactor in Iraq and they wanted to do the same in Pakistan. At the end of months of deliberation, the Kahuta attack never happened. But, and this is the point I want to stress, what if we had gone ahead and bombed the Kahuta plant?" He looked around the table to ensure that he had everyone's attention. "Would we have a nuclear Pakistan today? Would we have a state that belligerently harbours UN-designated terrorists including the likes of Osama Bin Laden and Masood Azhar? No. The past gives us the answers for the present. If we don't do anything now, we risk a situation that will grow worse by the day. And that is why I suggest that we take a leaf out of the pages of our Israeli friends and do something that we should have done decades earlier. We send a team in and neutralize this secret facility."

"That's insane." Shikha interrupted. "It will lead to war."

Everyone turned to look at her. Shikha's cheeks reddened as she became conscious of being the object of everyone's scrutiny. She could still hear her words hung in the air. The silence was palpable and the stares of everyone in the room unnerved her. She had been shocked at the overtness of the General's plan. But now she felt like biting her tongue off for interrupting her boss.

"Lead to war?" General Singh bored his eyes into her. "We are already in a state of war for decades now. Haven't you heard of Siachen? Thirty plus years, and probably the longest military standoff ever."

"But," Shikha fumbled for words, "this will only escalate the conflict. We should pursue diplomatic avenues. We got our independence through non-violent means. Not via a war. War is the last option that we should consider."

"War is simply diplomacy by other means. We have tried enough options; some people only understand the language of a gun." The General spoke with the ruthlessness of someone who had experienced multiple battles in his lifetime. "And as far as our independence is concerned, I suggest you read up on our history. Even the British were forced to leave India after we fought with them."

"Folks," Inamdaar looked at his watch, "we can deliberate on our options later. Let's take a break for lunch. I think the next point of discussion is Responding to Internal Threats. We will reconvene in thirty minutes."

Chapter 3

Shikha stared at her plate in the basement canteen. She had tried to eat the *thali* but the food felt tasteless in her mouth. Her mind was still at the meeting, cursing herself for opening her mouth.

"You asked a valid question, Shikha. Don't feel bad about it."

She moved her eyes from the plate to see Tanmay looking at her closely. He had also been present at the meeting, but he had been prudent enough to keep his mouth shut.

"I shouldn't have said anything at all. It felt as if everyone there was out baying for blood, except me. I am not a pacifist, but this is not how we should go about things. The General will probably fire me for speaking out of turn."

General Vishwajeet Singh, the Chief of the Armed Staff was also the Director General of the Defence Intelligence Agency, and oversaw multiple teams including Shikha's. The post of the Director General of the DIA was rotated between the three Service Chiefs and currently Vishwajeet Singh was at the helm of affairs.

"You are needlessly worried. General Singh doesn't like yes-men around him. And I don't think the others do too. I am sure people appreciated hearing a counter opinion of the situation."

"You think so?" Shikha's dread went down a few notches and she realized she was extremely hungry. She gobbled down a *kachori* and looked at Tanmay.

"I am sure of it." Tanmay said. "In fact, now everyone in the meeting will remember you for taking up a stand."

Shikha wasn't convinced. "But what did the General mean when he said that I should read up on our independence?"

Tanmay smiled. "Did you ever wonder why we didn't get our independence in 1942 during the Quit India movement, or in 1945 after World War II ended? Why the year 1947?"

Shikha thought about it and shook her head. "I don't know."

Tanmay cupped a hand to his mouth in a dramatic gesture as if he was about to reveal a big secret and leaned in towards Shikha. "This is top-secret. The war in 1946 against the British gave us our independence in 1947."

Shikha shook her head, and laughed it off. "What war? There was no war with the British if I remember my history lessons in school."

"Ah, but there was one. The Naval Uprising of 1946."

"Wait. Are you saying, we fought against the British before independence? Why isn't this mentioned in the history books?"

"There are many reasons. But it all started a few years before in the early forties when the British proposed a deal with India. India had long been asking for *purna swaraj*" – full independence – "from the British and the Quit India movement was part of it. The British said that they would give us independence, only if we agree to give our soldiers to help them fight Nazi Germany. The British promised us our freedom after the World War ended. Our leaders agreed and a staggering twenty-five lakh soldiers volunteered to fight on behalf of the British. So we fought and in 1945, the war ended. But our troubles didn't end. India was the crown of the British Empire, and the Brits didn't want to leave it. They wanted to milk India as long as possible. The twenty-five lakh soldiers returned home, but still no independence."

"The British rulers went back on their word." Shikha said.

"In 1945, after the war was over, they gave a watered-down proposal wherein trade and defence would still be managed by the British Raj with no timelines for complete independence. The proposal was rejected outright. The simmering resentment against the British rule grew manifold. In February of 1946, it reached a boiling point. In Bombay, the naval crew were suffering from substandard treatment. They asked for better food and accommodation and their British officers ignored their request. The crew mutinied and took the ship to the waters. Using wireless communication sets, they informed the crews on other ships in the harbour as well as sailors on ports across India. The news of their abject treatment travelled faster than a viral Facebook post, and soon sailors from Karachi to Calcutta had gone rogue in support of their Bombay brethren. Ten thousand sailors participated in the uprising. They put up the Tricolour on the ships and threw aboard anyone who resisted the uprising. On the ground, in Bombay, British establishment buildings were ransacked and the Tricolour was hoisted atop them."

Shikha leaned in. "It must have been quite a spectacle."

"Yes, imagine a British gentleman and his milady, the cream of Bombay society driving their plush cars in the middle of the road only to be stopped by a boisterous mob of angry Indians. And ordered to get down from the car and then shout '*Jai Hind*' loudly."

"I cannot imagine."

"I laugh whenever I try to picture it. Those elite snobs surrounded by the revolutionaries would have positively crapped in their imperial undies. After the British left India, PM Clement Attlee later confessed in British Parliament that there was no way they could hold on to India if the soldiers didn't support them. Ten thousand sailors were involved in the uprising. It was a fraction of the twenty-five lakh soldiers that the Britishers looked with trepidation as a potential lynch mob. They were completely surrounded by Indians everywhere. It would have taken only another spark to rouse the Army too."

"So, they had their tail between their legs?"

"Not quite, they shot their own ships to curb the agitation. Leaders like Gandhi and Jinnah condemned the rebellious act, and requested the mutineers to desist. Sardar Patel personally came down to Bombay and told the sailors to stop fighting. And they did."

"Why did Gandhi and Jinnah side with the British? They should have sided with the revolutionaries."

Tanmay took a sip of water and placed the glass down. "There were already talks in place for a peaceful transfer of power from the British government to India for many years. Both the leaders rightly thought that supporting the revolutionaries at this stage would undermine the political solution for India's independence and could lead to anarchy post-independence. The uprising ended in just five days, but it was enough for the British to realize that the tide had turned. The writing was already on the wall. They had to move out."

"But why doesn't anyone speak about this uprising? Why don't our history books mention this?"

"It's for the same reasons I mentioned earlier. The Indian leaders feared anarchy. After the uprising was quelled, more than five hundred sailors were court-martialled for misconduct. They weren't allowed to join the Navy even after Independence. They were patriotic freedom fighters, but we erased their names from history. Some say it was their fight that paved the way for our freedom; others don't agree.   But it was definitely the final nail in the coffin."

Shikha thought about what she had learned in school and then compared it with the information that Tanmay had shared with her. It was incredible how much of what you learned as a child became a part of your truth. She realized there were many sides to each story. Each more surprising than the other. She looked down at her empty plate. She hadn't even realized she had been eating throughout Tanmay's discourse.

Tanmay continued, "If we hadn't fought, who knows how long it would have taken. The British held on to Malaysia till 1957 and kept sending troops to the Middle East for even longer. General Singh is right. Some people only understand the language of a gun. Peaceful words make us appear meek."

"And," Shikha asked, "is that the reason the General wants a war? A quick and messy solution to a long agonizing problem."

"He talked about a military solution, and that's different from a conventional war. You know, we have been hearing about non-violence for so long, it has become ingrained in our psyche and thought process. We cannot think of any other solution, and it always ends in the argument that we won our freedom through non-violence, so we should pursue peaceful methods in all situations."

"So, you agree to the General's plan? You agree to an overt attack that will bring us war."

"I agree only to the observation that we should pursue all available options."

"It's the same thing. How can we send our soldiers to Pakistan without worrying that Pakistan won't declare a war that may escalate into a nuclear conflict?"

"Isn't Pakistan doing the same thing? They send their terrorists to attack our cities, infiltrate our military bases and behead our *jawans*. Do they ever wonder: India is a nuclear power; maybe we shouldn't provoke them so much? It's time to call their nuclear bluff and show them that two can play this game." Tanmay looked at his watch. "Let's go. The meeting resumes in five minutes."

"... and that is how we will respond to missile attacks on our territory." General Singh looked down the table at his audience as he finished his talk. "Any questions?"

Shikha kept her eyes on the documents in front of her. She wasn't sure if she was going to ask any more questions today. She and the others had provided their briefs to the PM and the Defence Minister apprising them of the status in their respective departments. She had listened as others asked questions, and was surprised when Tanmay stood up to ask one.

"Sir," Tanmay started, "I am a member of the Advanced Warfare Systems and my question is to the group at large. We create Ballistic Missile Defence programs, but our systems aren't tested as per a real-world scenario. We talked about using our BMD systems to shoot down incoming missiles, but we aren't sure how effective they are."

Shikha nodded to herself. Tanmay had shared his concern with her earlier. The Ballistic Missile Defence or BMD in short was deployed to prevent enemy missiles from striking on targets within India by shooting them down in mid-air using missiles. Someone had used the analogy to describe the BMD system as stopping a bullet with another bullet.

The General stared at him. "You are contradicting yourself. You say your lab created the BMD missiles, but you aren't sure if they work."

"No sir, what I meant was that our BMD systems were given the green signal after few successful tests. But the tests didn't represent a real-world scenario."

"Explain yourself."

"In the tests that were conducted, a target missile was launched in the air, and then our BMD missile was fired. It tracked the incoming target missile and shot it down. Technically, the BMD missile succeeded, but in a real-world scenario, our enemy won't send a single missile at us, they will send a dozen missiles at once. We should be testing with multiple missiles instead of one during the testing stage."

"Why don't we do that?" Inamdaar enquired.

"It's because of budgetary reasons. We will require multiple target missiles and equal number of BMD missiles to shoot them down. And that will cost a lot of money. Moreover, no BMD system in the world is one hundred percent accurate. In a real-world scenario, we may not bring down all of the incoming missiles. Between reloading our missile defence systems and the short travel time to target from neighbouring countries, we may reach a missile saturation point, beyond which the BMD systems may get overwhelmed by the superior number of incoming missiles."

"Do we have a solution for this?" Inamdaar asked.

"We are testing some prototypes, sir." Tanmay said. "I am expecting a breakthrough soon."

"Good. Keep me in the loop." Inamdaar turned to the others. "Next item on the agenda is a Leaders-only meeting. I would request everyone else to clear the room. Thank you for attending."

Shikha grabbed her papers and followed Tanmay and the others as they filtered out of the meeting room. Once outside Tanmay whispered, "So what do you think of our new PM?"

Shikha frowned. "Too early to take a call."

"General Singh, I would like to know more about the plan you spoke of earlier today."

General Vishwajeet Singh glanced at Inamdaar. The top-level leaders-only meeting had touched upon various mission-critical items during the two hours they had been discussing. It had been a productive meeting and the General had been pleased when the PM had agreed to most of the items on his long-term roadmap for the Army.

"The plan to neutralize the sea-based leg of Pakistan's nuclear triad?"

"Yes, I want to know how realistic it is."

The General saw everyone was curious to hear what he had to say. He trusted the men he had under his command, and he knew that they would achieve any objective he would set out. He spent a few minutes outlining the plan he had in his mind, and explained why it would be successful.

"It will be a straightforward op. If you give your permission, I will deploy my team on this mission."

"You have my permission. Go ahead. I need results. We have allowed Pakistan to bully us for far too long. It's time we show them a mirror of their doings."

"Thank you PM sir, you will get the results you want."

Chapter 4

"So, you understand what you have to do, Armaan?" General Vishwajeet Singh, the head of the DIA as well as the Chief of Army Staff looked at him.

"Yes sir, I do." Armaan thought about the plan that the General had just outlined. It was a bold and audacious plan, and a lot depended on what they would find once they reached Pakistan. But Armaan knew that he could pull it off.

As a member of the Defence Intelligence Agency's covert ops unit, he had been to Pakistan multiple times for undercover activities, sometimes staying for weeks to complete his objective. Their activities were almost all black ops that never saw the light of the day. Their unit was so secretive that it didn't even go by a name. The General had once told Armaan that he had an understanding with the Chief of the Research and Analysis Wing. To protect the DIA team and keep its activities anonymous, everyone was told that only the R&AW team carried out operations outside the country. It suited Armaan perfectly. He didn't care about accolades or being in the limelight. He was only interested in completing the mission.

This would comparatively be a short stint.

The General echoed his thoughts. "It would be a quick job. In and out. This mission is critical though. I have told the PM that we will accomplish it."

"Sir, you can count on me. I promise I will come back only after the mission is completed."

"Excellent. I know you have always delivered results."

Armaan asked, "What about the team?"

"Baldev will be there with you as usual. Roshan Gupta too."

Armaan shook his head as he heard the name. His brow darkened as he remembered the op in Bangladesh. "Isn't there anyone else? He screwed up the mission last time."

"I checked the mission report, and his actions were understandable. I then went over his service record. He has a list of commendable achievements to his name during his stint with the Army. He deserves to be on the team."

Armaan couldn't argue with the General, so he changed the subject. "What about Namit's replacement? I will need a tech for the plan you have outlined."

"Hitesh Vohra is the name. You will meet him later today. There will be four of you. We will keep in touch via satellite relay. Your call sign is Markhor."

"And the op code?"

"Operation Deep Strike."

The Sukhoi Su-30MKI screamed as it took off from the tarmac and rocketed into the open skies above Hindon Air Force Station. Armaan watched it till it disappeared into the horizon. He always felt reassured by the sight of the titanium birds protecting India.

The Hindon AFS was located some thirty kilometres east of New Delhi. Sprawled over an area of fifty-five square kilometres, it was known as the largest airbase in Asia. Its proximity to the capital ensured that in the event of a sudden war, New Delhi would receive air support in under five minutes against any hostiles.

"Do you have any questions about the mission?" General Singh asked.

Armaan watched the rows of C-17 Globemasters pass by as they drove past them. Their destination was a four-storey glass building up ahead. They were seated in the rear of a car and Armaan turned his gaze towards the General.

"Why can't this mission be done just by Baldev and myself?" he asked.

"I thought we had already discussed this." General Singh said. "You know we need backup and tech for our mission."

"I don't want a bunch of rookies spoiling my mission." Armaan still couldn't get over the fact of how Roshan's insolence had nearly messed up the Bangladesh mission and endangered everyone's lives.

"First off, they are not rookies." General Singh spoke in a cold voice. "Their past record is exemplary. And secondly, it is not *your* mission. You have been selected by *me* to lead this mission. If you are not happy with your team, I can replace you with another group leader who will be happy with the team."

Armaan glared at General Singh. *How could the General think of replacing him?*

He was a veteran of countless military ops from Kargil till date and had received multiple awards. There was no one better than him for covert operations. The General may be his boss, but he couldn't simply dismiss him from the mission.

"You won't find a better leader than me." Armaan spoke in a haughty tone. He didn't care if he annoyed General Singh, but he wanted to make a point. The vehicle slowed to a stop in front of the entrance of the building. The driver kept the engine idling waiting for them to disembark.

"Maybe I won't," the General looked at Armaan with a steely gaze, "but, I can ensure that you won't lead any future missions if you think of your own requirements as greater than that of the team or the mission. I will give you two choices. Either my mission with the men of my choice, or you can stay in the vehicle and it will take you back to the office and I will tell Baldev to lead the mission."

Armaan's face turned red in anger as General Singh spoke. He couldn't believe what he was hearing. The mission was important to him and that was why he didn't want newcomers to goof it up. Why couldn't the General understand that he considered the mission important enough not to leave it to inexperienced soldiers? He couldn't trust the young whippersnappers to do the job right. As a soldier, the mission was paramount to him, even if the General didn't understand his side of the story.

Armaan was one of the most experienced veterans of the DIA's covert ops team. He had to be on the op. It was up to him to ensure that the mission succeeded despite rookies like Roshan and Hitesh. As the leader, he could control the mission, and ensure they wouldn't screw up their jobs. The General couldn't see that Armaan shared the same objective of seeing the operation succeed. He would go on the mission, and keep the new scouts on a tight leash and ensure the mission was accomplished.

"So what's your answer?" General Singh had already exited the vehicle and watched him through the window. "Are you coming for the mission, or are you staying here?"

In response, Armaan sprinted out of the car and violently slammed the door shut.

The General led the way as they walked through the doors and went up the stairs to a conference room on the first floor. Three men were already waiting for them. At six feet and six inches, Baldev Bakshi was the tallest in the room. Armaan felt relieved by his presence. They had been together on countless ops. His face always had the hint of a smile. It contrasted with the bulging muscles that stretched through his shirt and gave an aura of raw power. He had the strength of a bull and Armaan had witnessed hapless adversaries crumble when they encountered Baldev.

Armaan flitted his eyes to Roshan Gupta. He was reminded of the debacle in Bangladesh. A wave of resentment flooded through him. He turned away to look at the only stranger in the room and assumed that the unknown person was Hitesh Vohra, the replacement for Namit.

The introductions were brief and the General came to the point straightaway.

"Gentlemen, you know why you are here. We are on a covert ops mission. I have given the operation specifics to Armaan, and he will give you the complete details of the mission at the right time. A Globemaster is waiting for you outside. It will take you to Jamnagar. Your eventual destination is a top-secret facility in Pakistan. No missions assigned to us are easy. This won't be any exception. But I know you will accomplish this through stealth and skill. Any questions?"

"What's the mission duration?" Baldev asked.

"It shouldn't take more than twenty-four hours."

"Will we get schematics of the facility?" Hitesh asked.

"Yes. Armaan will share the details." The General waited. When there were no further questions, he continued. "Good luck, boys. This mission is very important, and the directive comes right from the top." He paused to make sure the significance of his words sunk in with the team members. "I am counting on all of you. I know you will do well."

The meeting over, they exited the building and walked out onto the tarmac. A massive Boeing C-17 Globemaster III was waiting for them, its turbofan engines running. The General stood outside and the four of them entered in through the cargo bay door. The co-pilot was waiting for them, a flight manifest in his hand. He looked at them in surprise.

"Just the four of you?"

Armaan looked inside the enormous cargo area of the Globemaster. They looked puny compared to the immense empty compartment that could lift a payload of nearly eighty tons and carry even main battle tanks and helicopters inside the monstrous belly of the aircraft. He nodded at the bewildered co-pilot who looked as if he had been expecting four hundred passengers instead of four.

"Yes, just the four of us."

"Wow, you must be pretty important. The plane has been refuelled and is ready for take-off. Wheels up in five minutes."

"Thank you."

As the cargo bay door closed, Roshan spoke up. "I was raring to get back into active service during my months in convalescence. Excited to be here."

Armaan cut him off, "Don't get too excited. We are on a crucial mission. I would appreciate if you don't botch up anything this time."

Roshan hung his head. "Yes sir, I won't."

"Good." Armaan looked at the others. "I'm in charge now. And don't you forget that."

The others said nothing. Armaan leaned back in his seat, and felt the wheels rumbling under him as the Globemaster raced down the runway and then took off in the afternoon sky.

A few hours later they landed in Jamnagar AFS in Gujarat. As Armaan stepped off the Globemaster, he surveyed the rows of fighter jet planes that lined up at the side of the runway. The Air Force Station located near the Gulf of Kutch was the westernmost air base in India, not counting Naliya AFS a hundred kilometres northwest. Close to the Pakistan border, the jets could race to Karachi in a few minutes.

But they wouldn't be going on a jet.

Armaan looked around and spotted a chopper pilot waving to them. Next to the pilot was a HAL Dhruv helicopter. The transport for the next leg of their journey. Armaan walked over along with the team and got inside the chopper and it immediately took off.

"Are we going to Pakistan via a chopper?" Baldev asked.

Armaan shook his head. He watched as the helicopter traced a route along the Gulf of Kutch and then head for the open waters of the Arabian Sea. The wind whipped a spray of seawater in his face. He felt the tangy taste of saltwater in his mouth. "Look outside, where do you think we are going?"

Baldev looked at the endless sea that reached up to the horizon. They were going west, instead of north. "Are we going to land on a ship?"

Armaan smiled for the first time. He could see dark clouds raging in the horizon. A storm was brewing in the west. And they were headed right towards it.

His lips curled up in a sadistic grin. "Even better. We are going to attempt a near-impossible landing on a sub in the middle of the sea."

Chapter 5

The crew of the diesel-electric attack submarine INS Khanderi were intent in their purpose as Captain Mangesh Khurana gave the order to launch the periscope. They were approaching the target area of the rendezvous. The submarine raised itself to periscope depth and held steady.

Captain Khurana looked through the periscope. The waves tumbled along the surface of an angry sea. He could picture the swells splashing around and making a loud noise on the surface. No doubt it would be windy as well. His face registered a grim picture. It was going to be a difficult drop.

It wasn't everyday that they had a mid-sea drop. He was an experienced sailor, and even then he had only witnessed a handful of these missions. He had received the orders twenty four hours ago to approach the rendezvous point at full speed. Their team had traversed around five hundred nautical miles since yesterday. They had kept their side of the bargain. Now, they just had to wait to collect the 'package'.

Khurana twisted the periscope through a complete three-sixty degrees and confirmed there were no ships in the nearby vicinity. It surely wouldn't do to raise your submarine only to have it crash against a merchant ship, or worse, an enemy ship. He gave the all-clear to the Officer of the Watch.

"Raise her to surface."

As the ship rose, Khurana kept looking through the periscope around the surface. The area that they had selected for the rendezvous wasn't part of typical marine trade routes and it was perfect for a clandestine meet. The sea was deserted; only the pulsing waves crashed around as the submarine broke through to the surface.

He glanced at his watch. Three minutes to go.

He nodded at a junior officer. "Open the hatches."

The junior officer at the Bridge opened up the hatch. Captain Khurana ascended to the Bridge and peered through the hatch. It was worse than he expected. A torrential downpour of ice-cold rain lashed across his face. He swiped the rain off his face and gazed across towards the horizon in the east. The rain made it hard to see. A crack of lightning sizzled through the sky illuminating the entire sea for an instant. It illuminated a flying speck in the distance. He heard the faint roar of the HAL Dhruv helicopter as it approached them. The heli swayed laterally as it was buffeted by the strong winds. But the pilot seemed to manage well.

"That's our package."

Another lightning struck the sky followed by an ominous roar of thunder. Khurana shook his head. Four soldiers dropping down to his submarine hanging by a thin rope in this weather. Who would be crazy enough to volunteer for this? But he had his orders. He would ensure that the transfer was smooth.

"All right crew. Let's get ready to welcome the visitors."

Two men went up through the hatch and stood on the sail. They signalled to the helicopter crew using high-powered flashlights.

A rope ladder was lowered with a weight attached to one end, so that it would keep steady. The ladder swung in a circle around the submarine as the pilot frantically tried to align the rope ladder right over the hatch.

The waves crashed with a resounding force against the submarine's hull. The sky was grey and threatened to strike them with another bolt of lightning. Khurana craned his neck through the submarine hatch and looked at the helicopter; it's silhouette barely visible against the dark sky. It was up to the helicopter pilot now, his submarine was at standstill. Well, as still as it could be under the circumstances.

"Don't wait for the pilot to align his helicopter. Just grab the rope if it's within your reach." He told the two men on the sail. They both nodded.

The helicopter lowered itself a few feet more to counter the swing of the rope ladder. It worked. One of the men grabbed the rope and fastened it against the railings. He waved to helicopter crew.

High above the submarine, the man in the helicopter gave the thumbs-up. A moment later, a figure dressed in black emerged from the door and got ready to get down the ladder. He looked down at the ship and made the slow descent down the treacherously swinging ladder. Both the men on the submarine gripped the ladder to reduce the swing.

The soldier clung tightly as he made slow but steady steps down the ladder. It took him a few minutes to traverse the length of the ladder and place his feet on the firm steel of the submarine. The crew assisted the soldier down the hatch. The Captain looked up as the second soldier made his way down. A few tense minutes later, he joined his colleague inside the submarine.

As he approached, Captain Khurana thought his face looked familiar. He looked closely at the second person. He knew the guy.

The tall soldier took the Khurana's hand in a firm handshake. "Captain, I'm Armaan Ahmed."

Of course, Khurana remembered. Colonel Ahmed, the brave heart of the Kargil war. The man was a legend. Khurana wondered what mission he was onto. He could be sure of only one thing. Whatever, it was, no one could stand between him and his target. He was the perfect guy to rely on for any mission.

Two down, two to go.

"Captain?" the sonar technician's voice interrupted his thoughts. His voice had a tinge of concern on it.

The Captain turned around. "Yes?"

"We have an unidentified contact bearing zero-two-three. Range is ten thousand yards away."

"Is it moving towards us?" Khurana asked.

The technician answered the unasked question. "No, not directly towards us, but it's going to pass three thousand yards from our position. I don't think it has detected us. We are at standstill, so no propeller noises; though if it gets closer, our profile could be picked up on their sonar."

"All right. Keep a track on it. I want to know the moment it changes course or speed."

"Yes, Captain."

Khurana looked up at the helicopter. The third person was readying himself for the transfer. While he had told Sonar to keep an eye on the unknown contact, the situation made him uneasy. He knew that Naval

Command would have let him know if there were some friendlies in the area. For a moment he debated whether to risk it; there was no sub quieter than the Khanderi. The Captain had previously been assigned to the nuclear-powered submarine INS Arihant during its sea trials. Even if the Arihant stopped, the reactor had to keep pumping coolant which gave off an acoustic noise that could alert subs in the vicinity.

But the INS Khanderi was dead quiet when at a standstill. It ran on air-independent propulsion which meant that it made no noise when the propeller was stopped making it perfect for coastal assignments. Plus the ship could stay underwater for weeks if needed. But the Captain shook off the thoughts. He would observe discretion.

Their submarine was sitting still in open waters. If the unknown contact, definitely a hostile detected their submarine, they were a sitting duck. One torpedo would be all it would take to sink them. There would be no chance for them to close the hatch, start the engines and get it up to enough speed to get out of torpedo range. He called out to his sonar.

"Has the contact changed its bearings?"

"No, Captain," the sonar technician said. "It will pass by us in around twenty-five minutes."

There was no getting around it. Things would become too tight if they stayed around. He had to make a decision in the next five minutes. As he wondered what to do, he realized the decision was straightforward; safety reigned paramount. All the lives on the submarine were his responsibility; and he wouldn't risk it.

"Colonel Ahmed, we will have to abort the drop."

Armaan straightened to his full six feet three inches and frowned darkly. "Why?"

"There is an enemy submarine in the vicinity. We will have to move out quickly." Khurana didn't like the idea of aborting the mission, but there was no way they could get the drop completed before the other submarine was onto them. He hoped that Armaan would understand the situation.

"No way, Captain. Not without my men." Armaan replied.

Khurana's ears perked in disbelief. He had never been given such a curt reply in all the years he had captained the ship. An angry tinge of red shaded his cheeks.

"Colonel, I don't think you understood the gravity of the situation. We are moving into a potential hostile situation. We have to abandon the drop."

"The other two men will take around ten minutes to come into the submarine. I recommend we wait until then."

"But by then the enemy submarine will be right upon us. We will be detected the moment we start our engines."

"We should risk it. I cannot accomplish my mission without my full team."

Khurana found the man impossible. He snorted in anger "Listen here. On this submarine, I give the orders."

"Yes, and your orders were to assist *me* with the drop. Our mission cannot be compromised under any circumstances."

Khurana shook his head in exasperation. "But wouldn't your mission be compromised if our submarine is torpedoed?"

Armaan stopped. "Yes, it will. What do we do then? My men are still up there."

"We move out of here to our backup rendezvous point. And then complete the drop."

Armaan looked up through the hatch for a long moment. "Give the order."

Khurana relayed the orders and it was communicated to the helicopter crew. Five minutes later the hatch was closed and they were back in the depths moving towards the backup rendezvous point. He still kept an eye on the unknown contact. They were moving away from the contact, and its speed and direction hadn't changed. He breathed a sigh of relief. They hadn't been detected.

He watched Armaan who was pacing back and forth in the cramped space, clenching his fists and muttering to himself. Armaan glanced at his watch and asked Khurana, "How much time do we have?"

"It will take another twenty minutes to get to the secondary rendezvous point."

Armaan simply grunted and resumed his pacing. Khurana saw the eyes of the crew on the impatient 'guest' and knew he was a bad influence on their well-disciplined team. The quicker he could get Armaan to his destination, the easier it would be for him. *I wouldn't miss him. He may be a legend, but the fame has gone to his head.*

Half an hour later, they reached the secondary point. The submarine surfaced again and the hatch was lifted open. It was raining heavily as the helicopter appeared overhead. A thundering boom echoed in the horizon. The rope ladder was lowered for the second time, but the weather had worsened, and the ladder couldn't be controlled. It was swinging in maddening circles around the submarine, just outside the reach of the frustrated submarine crew.

As the crew kept trying, Khurana watched the impatient Armaan resume the pacing that he momentarily stopped while the submarine had ascended to the surface. The muttering increased with every passing minute that the rain-soaked ladder stayed out of the hands of the hapless crew.

"What are those nincompoops doing? We don't have all day while they play catch."

Khurana was about to say something when the Comms Technician said. "Sir, the pilot has said that he is low on fuel. If he can't drop the two others in the next ten minutes, he will have no option but to return to base."

"Tell him we understand the situation. We acknowledge –"

"Oh no, you don't." Armaan interrupted in a harsh voice. "Tell him I want my men down here immediately. The pilot can crash in the Arabian Sea for all I care."

Khurana gave a hard stare at Armaan and then turned to the Comms Technician. "Tell him we acknowledge the situation."

He turned towards Armaan. "I think it bears reminding that I give orders on this ship. Now, go and sit in the Captain's quarters while we recover your team in the next ten minutes. And that's an order."

Armaan opened his mouth to say something, but he closed it and wordlessly turned around in the direction of the Captain's quarter. Khurana stared at his retreating figure in disgust. *I don't know what he thinks of himself.*

Khurana turned around and walked over to the hatch opening. "How are we doing?"

"We've got hold of the rope ladder and the first soldier is on his way down."

"Excellent." Khurana said. He motioned to the Sonar. "Are you picking up any activities in the neighbourhood?"

"None sir."

Khurana rubbed his hands. It was the first good news in a long while. They could now get the other two men without event. Patience, he told himself.

A few minutes later, both men were safely dropped onto the sub. They lowered themselves into the hatch and shook hands with the Captain. The helicopter took off, and the hatch was closed shut.

Armaan returned. He had a begrudging smile on his face. "Thank you Captain for your help."

Khurana nodded. "I know how to execute my responsibilities. Now, onto the next step. I was told by Naval HQ that you would let me know your destination once your team was on board. So where do you want to go?"

Armaan handed over a sealed envelope.

Khurana took the envelope and went over to his desk. He unsealed the envelope and glanced at the contents. It was as he expected. They were to chart a course for sector Pandora. He handed over the coordinates to the Navigator. "What would be the ETA?"

The Navigator glanced at the coordinates, and replied after a moment. "Six hours."

Chapter 6

Roshan opened his eyes and adjusted them to the dim light of the submarine. His back felt stiff from sleeping in the cramped guest quarters. He carefully emerged out of the steel cased bunks and stretched himself. He had been woken up by the voices coming in from the Control Room. Roshan glanced at his watch. It was two am. He had been asleep for four hours. It was enough for him.

They should be near their destination by now. He looked at the other bunks. Two of them were already empty; only Hitesh was lying in his bunk sleeping soundlessly. Roshan tapped him. "Wake up."

Hitesh woke up immediately. "Have we reached the insertion point?"

"We should in a few minutes. Come."

They went over to the Control Room. The hub was abuzz with activity. Roshan located Armaan and Baldev in a corner talking amongst themselves and went over to them. Armaan noticed them. "Roshan, Hitesh, we will reach the insertion point in fifteen minutes. I have discussed the details of the exit with the Captain. The submarine will surface twenty-five kilometres off the coast. We will be using a motor boat to reach the shore. Do you have any questions?"

"Yes." Hitesh said. "How are we going to find transport once we are on the shore?"

Armaan snorted. "Are we on the shore yet?"

"No, sir."

"Then ask me when we reach there. You have a habit of jumping the gun, Hitesh."

"Sorry sir." Hitesh replied in a humbled voice.

"Does anyone else have another stupid question?"

There were none.

"Okay. I will let you know once we surface."

Hitesh and Roshan retreated to one side of the Control Room as Armaan and Baldev resumed their conversation. Roshan watched Hitesh sigh inwardly and felt sorry for the poor fellow.

Hitesh said, "I don't understand. He asked for

questions and I had one. Why request questions if you don't want to answer them?"

Roshan placed a hand over Hitesh's shoulder. "I don't know. Maybe he's stressed out about the mission. I have heard about him. He led men bravely into battle, and been shot twice in combat. There's a lot we can learn from his experience."

"Yes, I know all that. But for once I would appreciate that he would respect me as a team member."

"I suggest you stay out of his way for some time. Don't speak unless you are asked, you know?"

"I'll do that. Thanks Roshan."

Roshan nodded, but deep inside, he didn't like Armaan's attitude. This person didn't look like the Kargil hero who had broken through enemy ranks and taken up combat posts. The intensity was still there, but the direction wasn't. He acted like a know-it-all who patronized his team members.

Roshan hoped that the coming days would prove him wrong.

Baldev watched Roshan and Hitesh leave beaten down by Armaan's tongue lashing. He had winced through the entire conversation, but didn't speak out. He didn't want to embarrass Armaan in front of the duo by speaking out of turn. He squeezed Armaan's shoulder.

"It's Namit, isn't it?"

Armaan looked at him for a moment and then turned away.

"Armaan, I have known you for fifteen years. Maybe more. We have worked on the craziest missions together. You've cared for me like a brother. And you know, I've done the same. We have been on two missions since Namit died, and in both I saw an emotional intensity in you. As if the mission was something personal for you. You didn't treat me any differently, but I wondered. And now, ever since Roshan and Hitesh have come onto the team, I'm seeing the extent of the change in your behaviour. Why? This is not who you are. This is not how you treated Namit or others when they joined your team."

Armaan looked back at Baldev, but he didn't say anything. The monotonous conversation of the submarine crew in the Control Room filled in their silence. Finally Armaan spoke.

"When I went to Namit's wife to offer my condolences, she accused me of failing her husband. I can still picture her; her eyes were streaked with tears and her voice cut through to my core. I am to be blamed for what happened."

"Namit's death was a freak accident. You can't blame yourself."

Armaan shook his head. "As the leader of the team, it was my responsibility to ensure everyone's safety. I failed."

"You're being too hard on yourself. If you had truly failed, the General wouldn't have given you this mission."

"As a leader, I've to be hard on myself. Namit died under my command."

Baldev was not making any headway to counter Armaan's line of reasoning. "We have seen our share of death through the years. What changed?"

"I can't take away the image of Namit's wife, her bloodshot eyes accusing me of failing in my duty. I look at Roshan and Hitesh and I wonder if I will lead them to their deaths, or will their incompetence lead to mine. Sometimes I wonder if it's best I go all alone. Better not to trust anyone, or let anyone else trust you."

"You are wrong about them. Roshan and Hitesh are proud to be on this team. They competed against a hundred other capable soldiers to be part of the DIA. They know the dangers. And so did Namit. It didn't stop him from joining the team and going into Bangladesh. And Namit would have wanted you to continue. You are disrespecting his memory with such thoughts. If not, for the landmine, he would have been here with you, on this very mission."

"Only to die now or later." Armaan spoke in a stiff voice. "I'll prevent that from happening even if I have to go solo."

Armaan stood up and walked over to the Captain leaving an exasperated Baldev wondering what to do next.

"We should reach the coast in an hour."

Roshan shivered in the biting cold of the open sea. They were huddled together in a motorised inflatable dinghy. The temperature had dropped drastically and the howling wind ripped through his jacket freezing him to the core. He looked back at the submarine. Only the black outline of the submarine could be seen against the cloudy grey sky as the submarine slowly sunk in the waves.

The thunderstorm had ended, but the dark clouds still hovered above them threatening to spill over any moment. Nevertheless, Roshan was thankful for the cloud cover. Visibility would be low and it would help his team make their insertion into the coast easier.

Roshan felt a tug in his gut as the boat made its way north. If there were any patrol boats around, they would be in trouble. He pulled out his binoculars and glanced around but the sea was devoid of any ships. Only the low humming of the motors gave them company as he looked around with a wary eye.

"We will be landing on Makran coast." Armaan said. "The place I've selected is uninhabited and there will be a very low probability for us to be detected."

"Makran, eh," Baldev said, "good choice."

Roshan nodded as he listened. The southern border of Pakistan was mostly horizontal and ended into the Arabian Sea. The provinces of Balochistan and Sindh bordered the coast. Makran was located in Balochistan.

Armaan said, "The General asked me and I told him that Makran is a good insertion point into Pakistan. The coastline is long with many miles of uninhabited shoreline and hills adjoining the shore. It should shield us from prying eyes.

Baldev steadied the rudder and looked at Armaan. "Do you have any assets in the area?"

"I have a contact here that will help us move inland."

Baldev smiled. "Knowing you, I'm not surprised you planned in advance. I know you have a habit of keeping the cards close to your chest, so I didn't ask earlier. This contact; is he one of ours?"

"No. He's a mercenary. I recruited him last month when I was here. He spouts about his ideology, but deep inside he simply wants money and will sell out to the highest bidder."

"You were here last month?" Baldev asked.

"Yes, on a solo mission. But we will talk about it another time. I can see the shore up ahead."

Baldev ripped out his binoculars and scanned the shore. "I don't see any signs of life."

"We will move in closer and then turn off the motor and paddle down till we reach the shore. I don't want anyone to hear us come in."

Half an hour later, they had reached the coast. Roshan's eyes swept the area. The shore was simply a few metres of brown mud that stretched in an arc from west to east. In front of him, beyond the meagre shoreline, his view was blocked by small rocky hills that stretched into the distance.

Armaan and Roshan took positions along the shoreline and acted as lookouts while Baldev and Namit gathered the equipment from the boat. The sky was full of dark clouds with dawn still an hour away. After safely placing the equipment on the shore, they shredded the inflatable dinghy and drowned it out of sight.

"Let's move out. We will be rendezvousing with our contact four kilometres from here off N10 highway."

They quietly made their way through the hills grateful for the natural cover. Each of them constantly kept looking around aware that discovery at this point would threaten the mission before it even started.

No one spoke, and everyone walked in silence. They made their way through shallow valleys, crossed over the hills till finally Armaan who was in the lead raised his hand indicating the group to stop. Roshan peered over Armaan's shoulder and saw a wide grey strip that marked the Makran Costal Highway.

"There's an abandoned garage on the side of the road. That's our rendezvous. Roshan, you go first and scout the area."

Roshan nodded and then moved forward and crouched behind a large boulder near the road. He scanned the length of the highway. There was no movement of any vehicles. Then he sprinted to the rear end of the garage. It was a dilapidated shed with a broken roof and without a door. He glanced in and confirmed that there was no one inside, except for the remnant junk of vehicle motors and axles. Dust had piled up everywhere. It didn't look as if anyone had been in recently. He signalled the all-clear to Armaan. They scurried to his side.

Baldev looked around. "For a highway, this place is deserted. Do you know when our contact will arrive?"

Armaan looked at his watch. "He should have been here five minutes ago."

Baldev said, "You mentioned he is not one of ours. Do you think he can be trusted?"

"Do you remember our mission in Afghanistan? Always remember Rule Number Two."

Baldev chuckled. "You and your rules."

"Those rules have saved my life on countless occasions. And yours as well, when you were with me. Don't forget that."

Roshan was curious. "What is Rule Number Two?"

Armaan quoted solemnly, "Never trust anyone."

Roshan thought about it. In a profession of skulduggery and double-talk, who could you trust upon apart from yourself? "That makes sense. Especially in our profession. And what is Rule Number One?"

Armaan was about to answer when a bright headlight illuminated the dark highway. Roshan instinctively gripped his weapon tightly.

"Everyone," Armaan ordered, "stay in the shadows. You'll be my backup in case we run into a problem. I will see who it is."

Roshan, Hitesh and Baldev retreated in the cover of the garage while Armaan stood alone by the side of the highway intently looking at the approaching vehicle.

The vehicle came to within twenty metres and then parked to the side of the road. The headlights extinguished and the doors opened. Four men emerged and walked up to Armaan. The men were heavyset, bearded and covered in shawls to protect themselves against the early morning chill. One of them spoke.

"Welcome to Pakistan. I hope your trip went well."

But Armaan's eyes didn't register the greeting. "Where's the stuff I asked for?"

"It's in the van."

"And our transport?"

"It's on its way."

Armaan nodded and a faint smile creased his lips. "How are your people doing?"

"Oh, they are surviving, but we Balochis have seen worse. We are happy with whatever support you give us." The Balochi leader looked around. "Where are your guys?"

Armaan signalled with his hand and the remainder of his team assembled. "This is Fazal Darzada. He's the local Balochi leader."

The Balochi glanced at the newcomers. "Only four of you?"

"It's enough for our needs."

"Good." The Balochi suddenly whipped out a gun that was hidden in his shawl and pointed it at Armaan. "Grab them." He commanded his colleagues.

Roshan watched in disbelief as four guns were pointed towards them.

Things didn't look good.

Chapter 7

Islamabad, Pakistan

"Sir, you need to see this." PM Mian's secretary handed him a dossier.

Mian Fateh rubbed his sleepy eyes and cursed his job. It wasn't easy being the Prime Minister of Pakistan. It was three am in the morning, and his entire day had been spent on just one thing.

Early in the morning at around nine am, he had received an alert that there had been a bomb blast at the Gwadar port. Twenty people had died in the blast, and another forty were wounded. Bomb blasts were commonplace in Pakistan and he knew that the Counter-Terrorism Department would look into it. He hadn't given it much thought till an hour later when the Chinese Ambassador to Pakistan had called him. One Chinese national had died in the blast and the Ambassador requested, in fact insisted that the PM personally look into the matter and punished the culprits responsible.

The PM had then excused himself from all non-essential meetings of the day and had met with the Head of the Counter-Terrorism Department and asked to be provided with hourly updates on the Gwadar attack. So far, no one had claimed responsibility for the blast.

Mian took the dossier and plopped it on the desk. He wasn't sure if he had the patience to wade through it. He knew his secretary would have gone through the dossier and highlighted the critical points of the report for his consumption. But today his brain was overloaded to the point of exhaustion. He couldn't bear to read another word that referenced Gwadar.

"What does it say?" Mian asked his secretary. It was best if he listened to the highlights.

"The modus operandi of the attack suggests that the Lashkar-e-Jhangvi is involved. It is not dissimilar to their previous attacks."

PM Mian nodded. "Anything else?"

"The Lashkar-e-Jhangvi operates from across the border in Afghanistan. Our intelligence sources have noticed an uptick in the chatter between different terrorist cells across the Af-Pak border. It's not just the Lashkar but even the various factions of Al-Qaeda are communicating with each other."

The PM had never understood the love-hate relationship between the different terrorist groups. One day they were friends, the next day they were sworn enemies. Most of the current terrorist groups had fractured from the original Taliban and the Al-Qaeda, and had decided to remain separate. Based on what he heard, it seemed that they were regrouping together. "So, the intelligence community thinks that they have patched up their differences. Why?"

"The report surmises that the Gwadar blast was just a start. They could be planning something big."

Dasht-e-Margow, Southern Afghanistan

Shafiq looked around him in the faint light of the early dawn. It was still dark, but he could make out the faces of his comrades lying down in the sand, deep in slumber. In a few minutes, they would all be fully awake, ready for another day.

Shafiq watched his commander Malik through the open door of the tent. Malik was already up in the freezing cold and was talking with the guards on the night watch. Shafiq took off his blanket and grabbed the trusty AK-47 that he kept with him at all times. He checked the barrel to ensure no sand was clogged in it. He removed the chamber and checked the bullets. Satisfied, he cocked the weapon and got to his feet.

Shafiq straightened his *khet partug*, the traditional *shalwar kameez* dress common in Afghanistan. He surveyed the barren area. They had camped in five tents under the shadow of a mountain. Each tent housed ten of them. The tent was made of brown canvas cloth that matched the surroundings. If one looked from afar, the tent would be camouflaged among the huge rocks that lined the foot of the mountain. It was also a perfect cover in case a spy satellite observed them from the sky. It would not be able to distinguish the tent from the ground.

But there was a very low probability of that happening. All around them, the brownish yellow ground was barren with no trees or sand; only rough rocky ground everywhere. It was a bleak place. He grinned, Dasht-e-Margow, *the Desert of Death*; the name fit very well with the desolate surroundings.

Shafiq relished the cold biting breeze of the early dawn. It stung in his face, and rippled through his body. An average person would freeze in this weather, but he admired the power of his body to resist the cold. He took a stroll through the perimeter of where they were camped. The guards were smoking weed; they were to be relieved at first light. He walked up to them as their conversation with Malik finished.

"How did the night go? Did you guys fall asleep?"

"Shafiq brother, you know we always stay alert. Even a rat won't slip past us."

"Good to hear that. Did anything unusual happen during the night?"

"No. It was a quiet one."

Shafiq nodded. "All right. Just don't snore in the middle of the training today."

The guards chuckled as Shafiq moved forward watching the dirt road that curved along the mountain. He preferred interacting with the men to get a feel of things on the ground rather than hearing it from someone else. He didn't expect anyone to know where they were, but he had learned to expect the unexpected. They were part of the Lashkar-e-Jhangvi group and they conducted most of their operations along the Af-Pak border.

Dasht-e-Margow was their backup location, where they could regroup and plan out their forthcoming missions. They would take long arduous runs through the rocky desert. It had become a set routine. Four hours of runs every morning, were followed by lunch and a short nap; and finally capped by weapons training.

They didn't know what their next mission was, but everyone was talking about it already. It again became a subject as they sat in small groups during breakfast.

"We've been training here for two months already." Shafiq overhead the comment. "When are we going to see some action?" The speaker asked.

Shafiq looked up. Zia had asked the question to

their leader Malik. Shafiq shook his head. *Meddlesome Zia*. Always complaining and butting his big head into everything. He simply couldn't keep his mouth shut.

"The training is very important. We need to be ready." Malik replied.

Shafiq listened with curiosity. Rumours were rife that the upcoming mission was going to be huge based on the extended training routine they went through every day. He wanted to know when the mission was going to be launched.

"I've been hearing that from day one, but so far, all we are doing everyday is endless running and shooting. My hands are itching for revenge against the infidels. So when are we starting to move out? I'm tired of doing the same old crap day after day." Zia raised his voice.

Shafiq wondered if Malik would get angry at Zia's outburst. Shafiq considered Zia to be a deranged psycho. His father and brothers were butchered during the incessant wars that had sprung up ever since the Soviet army had turned up in Afghanistan during the eighties. His father had died fighting the Soviets, and brothers had died in the rebel wars. Since then Zia considered the entire world his enemy. There was no saying what he would do next. Shafiq couldn't understand why Malik didn't rein him in; or simply get rid of him.

Malik spoke in an even tone, "I don't know when our mission starts. We will be informed by our senior leaders. Till then, we have been told to keep training."

"I won't do the training. I am only interested in the mission." Zia declared in a petulant tone.

Malik said nothing. Instead he reached inside his robe and pulled out a pistol and pointed it at Zia's head. "You have the brains of a camel. Now I give you two choices: you will be dead before the mission, or you will stay alive and do the training as well as the mission."

Zia looked around for support; but everyone's eyes were hostile. "Zia, listen to our leader and stop this nonsense," one of the men said.

Zia seemed to evaluate his options and realize he didn't have any. "I'll do the training." He finally spoke.

"Good." Malik put away his gun. "Does anyone else have any doubts about what our superiors are planning?"

There were none.

"Excellent. Brothers, I am not sure what is being planned, nor when the mission will be executed, but we should come to know soon –"

"Someone is approaching," one of the guards shouted.

Everyone's eyes turned to the path along the mountain that provided the sole access to their hideout. It was an open jeep with a solitary driver.

"Relax everyone," Malik said as some of them grabbed their weapons, "He is our messenger." Malik walked over to the approaching jeep. The jeep stopped next to him.

Shafiq watched the messenger and the commander speak, wondering what they were talking about. Maybe their mission would start shortly and this was the message the messenger had bought.

Shafiq finished his breakfast quickly knowing that the commander's conversation would be brief. He wanted to be ready for whatever the commander had to say. The others also finished their breakfast and started talking amongst themselves.

"What do you think they are discussing?" One of the men asked.

"I think we'll get new orders. And possibly a date to move out," Pasha, a veteran of their group replied.

"You could be right, Pasha. You are, most of the time."

"I know. Okay the messenger is leaving. We will know in a minute." Pasha said, as Malik saw off the messenger. As the dust trailed off from the departing vehicle, Shafiq realized that the messenger had unloaded half a dozen large crates from the jeep. The guards were bringing them to the camp under Malik's instructions. Shafiq had no doubt it contained their arms and ammunitions.

Weapons were their group's bread and butter. Without weapons, they would be unable to wage their holy war. Most of their well-wishers had dwindled in the decade since 9/11, but some of their ardent supporters still existed who funded them generously with weapons.

Warlords in central and east African countries, rebels in Syria and Yemen were their current sponsors. These people took the opium raised in the poppy fields of Afghanistan and in return provided them with money and guns.

Malik had a thin smile as he walked across to the group, followed by the guards. "Brothers rejoice. All our training will now stand in good stead. The messenger has sent word from our superiors. We are to move out tomorrow."

A chorus of excited shouts answered him. Malik continued.

"We've been waiting for long. Only a few hours more. Nothing is more valiant than a sacrifice doing Allah's deeds. If we are martyred in our mission, we will be granted Paradise."

The cheering grew louder.

Malik raised his hand to indicate silence. "Now men, there will be a change in our training regime. Today, we will be going to the top of the mountain."

"The top of the mountain?" Pasha asked.

"Yes," Malik said. "We are going to do some shooting practice there. Using this." He flipped open one of the crates. Inside were a dozen RPG-7s.

Shafiq found the request odd. They rarely did shooting practice with Rocket-Propelled Grenades. Their supply of RPGs was scarce and used only in combat. Plus the idea of trekking up the mountain and then shooting at targets didn't make sense. He wondered what to make of it as some of the men went to the ammunition crate, and the others queued in a line in front of their leader ready to march up the hill.

Shafiq shrugged it off as he clutched his gun and joined the others. He had orders to follow.

Chapter 8

"But why?"

The words involuntarily escaped from Roshan's lips. One of the Balochis jabbed a gun in his back. Their weapons had been taken from them. They were defenceless.

"Why you ask?" Fazal Darzada looked at Roshan. "Let me tell you why? You guys only give us lip service. You use us because it suits your own convenience. You use the word 'Balochistan' only to irritate the Pakistani government, nothing more. You couldn't care less about us."

"That's not true, Fazal." Armaan said. "We help you because your government doesn't listen to you."

The Balochi leader turned his gaze at Armaan. "Do you really have our best interests at heart? No, you use us because you hate the Pakistan government, just like us. Beyond that, we have nothing in common."

"We are not enemies, Fazal."

"And neither are we friends." The Balochi replied. "In fact, it's because of you guys that we face the most problems. You create problems and the government holds us responsible." Fazal thumped his fist on his chest to emphasise his point. "Us."

Roshan looked around. The highway was deserted; they could make a dash back to the beach, but with the weapons pointed right at them, they wouldn't survive for more than a few feet before being gunned down. He looked at the Balochi leader. "So what happens now?"

"You will answer my questions, and then I am going to hand you over to the police."

"The police. Why?"

Fazal jabbed the butt of his AK-47 gun into Roshan's shoulder. "I said I will ask the questions."

"Don't you hurt him." Armaan said in a quiet, yet intense voice. "Or else, you will pay the price."

Roshan was surprised to see Armaan stand up for him. Since the time they had met at Hindon, Armaan had acted curt with him. He wondered if under the brusque exterior, Armaan really cared about his safety.

Then another thought struck him. Maybe he was more concerned about the integrity of the mission than about him.

"Hmph. Look at me. I am scared." Fazal scoffed "From where I see, you are at gunpoint. So, don't make any stupid moves or think of doing stupid things. You have to pay for what happened at Gwadar."

"Gwadar?"

"Yes. Gwadar. You guys attacked Gwadar port and the Army arrested and killed my people. We are innocent, but no one believed us. You will be our evidence."

"I don't know what happened at Gwadar, but none of us are involved in it."

"Lies." The Balochi leader roared. "You Indians are keenly interested in seeing Gwadar burn. Now tell me how did you plan the attack?"

Armaan said, "Fazal, you have to trust me. We had nothing to do with it."

"Really? What makes you think I will believe you?"

"There are many groups who are against the Gwadar port. We may be the first that will come to your mind, but surely, do you really think we are the only ones? Gwadar has become a competition to other ports nearby, like Chabahar and Dubai ports."

"So? What's your point?"

Armaan pressed on. "What if a billionaire businessman in Dubai seeing a loss in his trade paid a few mercenaries to sabotage the Gwadar port? A single bombing and trade stalls due to fear."

Fazal mumbled. "Be that as it may, but I still don't believe you."

Armaan said, "Fazal, you've known me for some time. You know this is not my modus operandi."

Roshan looked at Fazal, he seemed to have been softened by Armaan's logic, but Fazal asked, "What's stopping me from calling the police and having you arrested? I'll be able to prove my men innocent and have you indicted. It will be front page news. 'Balochi leader catches Indian spy.' Our rapport with the government will increase and they will give us reward money."

Armaan shook his head, "Sorry to burst your bubble, but will they believe your story? A suspect Balochi leader catching an Indian spy? I think the front page news would be more like 'Balochi leader *and* Indian spy caught by Counter Terrorist police.'"

"They won't trust you." Fazal retorted. "It will be your word against mine. A Pakistani's versus an Indian's."

But Armaan was unruffled by the threat. "You said what's stopping you from having me arrested? I'll also ask: what's stopping me from giving you away as an accomplice? I will simply state that we've known each other for a long time. You only betrayed me because you were not happy and wanted more money from me. I will hold you equally responsible for the anti-national activities going around here."

Fazal growled, "You remorseless swine."

Armaan shrugged, "It's the only way to survive." He patted Fazal on the shoulder. "Let's be reasonable about this. Two thieves cannot play cop. The Pakistani government is not your friend. It won't help to make enemies out of us too. You need help and support. We are giving you that. So let us go our way, and you can go your way. What do you say?"

Fazal's colleagues spoke with him in the Balochi language. He talked with them for a minute and then turned to Armaan.

"All right. We will let you go. You can take your weapons and get lost."

Armaan smiled. "Thanks brother. You wouldn't regret it."

Fazal handed the guns to Armaan. "I'm already regretting it."

One of the Balochi men retrieved a case from the van and handed it over to Fazal. Fazal opened it in front of Armaan.

"Here's your stuff. Four mobiles with local sims and four National Identity cards. You can put your photos on the Identity cards and pass off as a local. But it wouldn't stand scrutiny, so don't show it unless someone asks for it."

"What about our transport?"

"It should have been here by now. Though honestly, I wanted to pack you off to the authorities in it." Fazal chuckled and then turned serious. "It seemed like a good idea at that time."

A beam of light lit up the dark road for the second time. "There's your ride." Fazal said.

Roshan looked at the vehicle that had just turned into view far off in the distance. A moment later another vehicle's headlights followed the first.

"Who's the other one?" Roshan asked.

Fazal replied. "It's not one of ours. This looks fishy. You guys get out of sight. I will let you know when the coast is clear."

Roshan and the others took cover in the deserted garage. He watched through the cracks of the wooden walls of the garage as the two vehicles came in. The first vehicle was driven by a bearded person wearing a shawl, not unlike the other Balochis. But it was the second vehicle that closely followed the first that took his breath away.

It was an Army jeep. Four Pakistani army men with weapons in their hands scanned the area as they drove in. Both vehicles stopped right behind Fazal's van. The Army men came out and accosted the Balochis, guns trained on them.

"What are you guys doing here in the middle of the night?"

Fazal sneered at them. "It's none of your business."

"That answer will only earn a bullet in the head for you. I ask again; what are you doing here?"

"We are going to the shore to earn our daily bread. We are fishermen."

One of the Army men pulled the driver of the second vehicle by his collar and brought him in front of Fazal. "This guy said a different story. He said he was to wait back there and wait for you to signal him to come in. Not something the average fisherman would do."

Fazal didn't answer.

The Army man pointed his gun at Fazal's head. "Talk or die."

Roshan sitting in the shadows of the garage whispered to Armaan. "What do we do?"

"I have a two-step plan." Armaan had an intense look in his eye.

"What's that?" Roshan asked.

"The first step is that we kill them..."

"I like the plan already." Baldev interrupted.

"And?" Roshan enquired when Armaan hadn't elaborated on the second part.

"The second step depends on the success of the first. Baldev you take the one on the left, Hitesh you take the extreme right. I will take the second one, and Roshan you take the third from left. I want a clean headshot. No mistakes, no second chances. Are we clear?"

The other three nodded.

"On my mark. Aim. Fire."

Their silenced weapons emitted four spits, and all four Army men tumbled to the ground, hit straight through their heads. Roshan and the others emerged from their hiding place and joined the Balochis.

Fazal nodded at Armaan. "You guys do have your uses, I would admit." He looked at the bodies. "But as always, I am reminded of the mess you leave behind. So, I am starting to regret the day I ever met you."

Armaan scrutinized the bodies. They had all been shot in the head; death had been instantaneous with minimum of blood spilled. As he expected, the uniforms were clean.

He beckoned the others. "Now for Step Two of my plan. Dump the bodies and take their uniforms. We can take their jeep and pass off as Army men."

Hitesh asked, "What if someone questions us?"

Fazal replied, "This is Pakistan; no one questions the Army." He made a thumbs-up sign to Armaan. "It's a brilliant idea; better than the van that I brought."

Armaan allowed himself a slight smile, "Coming from you, that's quite a compliment."

"I guess we are done here. Don't come calling again. You are a real nuisance." Fazal walked away to join his colleagues.

"You have a good day too." Armaan said.

The Balochis departed in the two vehicles. Roshan and the team busied themselves with the task of getting rid of the bodies before dawn emerged.

"Move it everyone," Shafiq heard Zia shout in the front of the group.

It had been an hour since they started their trek to the top of the mountain. They were halfway up the mountain winding through a narrow goat-trail, the pebbles crunched under their boots. The mountain they were climbing was part of a long range and from this height they could see the entire valley below. It was a cloudless day and sweat poured through Shafiq's hairline. The air was still and he tried focusing on the narrow path. They were going along a steep cliff and a false step here could lead to a fatal fall down the mountain.

Pasha cursed behind him. "What does that Zia think of himself? He is not fit to wipe Malik's shoes and now he is acting as if he is the leader of our group."

Shafiq chuckled wryly. "He seems to have forgotten that only a few minutes ago, he was against doing any training. And now he is ordering everyone around. I wish Malik throws him down the mountain."

Pasha said, "Malik won't do that. He has a lot of tolerance for Zia."

"Why is that?" Shafiq was curious. Shafiq had joined the group much later than Zia and Pasha.

"Zia's father and brothers fought alongside Malik. They were close friends. They would have wanted Malik to mentor Zia. It's a debt of blood."

"But Zia is a crazy demented fool." Shafiq said.

"Yes, but Malik knows that even a crazy person like Zia has his uses. In our previous mission, he charged blindly at the enemy and killed many of them. I was surprised Zia didn't get himself killed; he got away with a minor bullet wound. It looks like he's got a death wish, and was disappointed he didn't die."

Shafiq thought about it. Zia had no one to live for. Malik was channelling Zia's suicidal tendency into an asset for their group.

Pasha echoed his thoughts. "Malik is smarter than he looks. His focus is not Zia, but our mission. He will put up with Zia's eccentricities and use him to his advantage."

"We will rest here for five minutes." They heard Malik's command up ahead. They had reached a wide terrace on the side of the hill. The goat trail ended here and the summit was another two hundred meters of moderate climb. Malik beckoned Zia. "Zia, tie this cloth to that tree there." He pointed to a barren tree, its leaves shorn off and the tree appeared naked without the greenery to clothe it. Zia climbed the tree and tied the cloth made out of their tent canvas to one of the branches. He clambered down smiling with self-importance.

Pasha looked at Shafiq, "You see what I mean."

Shafiq sat on a rock and by force of habit disassembled and reassembled his gun. He flipped the safety lock on and off. He could do this in his sleep, he mused inwardly.

The few minutes of rest passed quickly and they resumed their climb to the top. Thirty minutes later they were on a rocky plateau that marked the summit of the mountain. They could see for miles around. Shafiq looked down at their camp, and its brown tents were invisible against the ground. There were few clouds around and the sky was a light shade of blue. The wind had picked up and it was welcoming after the exhausting hike. Shafiq inhaled deeply feeling the cold wind inside his lungs. It felt wonderful.

"You Shafiq," he heard Zia's belligerent tone behind him. "Stop loitering around and help us unload the RPGs."

Shafiq gritted his teeth in disgust. He turned around and saw Zia scowling at him. *How dare this fool tell me what to do?* He clenched his knuckles tightly to prevent himself from bashing Zia in the face. It would be unwise. Malik wouldn't be happy if there was infighting within the group. He glanced at Malik who made an imperceptible nod.

Shafiq thought about it. It wasn't worth picking up a fight with a scum like Zia. He relaxed his fists and walked past Zia without speaking a word.

"That's better. Now move it, you lazy slob." Zia said

Shafiq's ears turned hot with fury at the words. He

bristled at the remark. He turned around and was about to say something when Malik beckoned him.

"Shafiq, can you come here? I need your help."

Shafiq walked sideways, glaring at Zia. Zia smiled back at him, revealing a set of crooked teeth. Shafiq forced his gaze away, anger surging within him at the humiliation. He was an obedient soldier, and didn't deserve this treatment.

He walked up to Malik and said, "Brother, did you see how –"

Malik interrupted, "I saw everything. You weren't helping our brothers. Zia rightfully called upon you to help."

"But –"

"I don't want to hear anything further on this topic. Now," Malik gestured at the crate in front of him, "distribute two RPGs to each person."

"Yes, Malik." Shafiq replied in a subdued voice. He proceeded to pick up the RPG-7s and hand it over to the waiting men.

Malik walked over to the front of the group and waited till the launchers were distributed. "Now brothers, you can see the terrace below where we tied a marker to the tree." He pointed to the brown canvas cloth that was fluttering in the breeze. "That will be our target."

Malik walked around as the men looked at their target halfway down the mountainside. "At this height, when you fire, you have to take into account the speed and direction of the wind too. Pasha, you can try first."

Pasha took aim and fired. It missed the tree by only a couple of metres.

Malik nodded appreciatively. "That's good, but we have to become better. Hafeez, your turn."

Shafiq watched as one by one the men tried to aim and knock down the target. He was still fuming at the unfair treatment given out by Malik. It looked like Malik favoured Zia more than anyone else in their group.

Shafiq felt someone's eyes upon him. He looked sideways and found Zia looking at him. Zia's gaze was malevolent.

Chapter 9

"All right, here's the mission overview." Armaan said.

Roshan looked around the room. They were stationed in one of the numerous rundown motels that were littered alongside the N10. They had passed themselves as tourists from Karachi and the proprietor hadn't given them a second glance. Armaan had paid in cash, and the proprietor had handed him the keys and gone back to read his newspaper.

The walls of their room were frayed out and the paint peeled off at the corners. Some of the windows were broken and dust had laden on the tables and chairs. The room didn't look like it had been used in a while.

But Roshan liked it. It was isolated, and a little way down from the highway. Armaan had pointed at it as they drove east to an undisclosed location. So far, they only knew the outline of their mission. They had to infiltrate a top-secret facility. Only Armaan as the group leader knew the specifics and as per protocol he would reveal it only after reaching Pakistan. This place would be their base point. Armaan had grouped them around the table and Roshan and the others leaned forward in curiosity and anticipation.

"Have you boys heard of the Babur-3 missile?" Armaan looked around the table.

Roshan found the name familiar from his study of Pakistani military assets, but couldn't place it. Hitesh the analyst spoke up. "I am aware of it. Babur-3 is the submarine version of their land based cruise missile Babur-2. It is capable of carrying both conventional and nuclear warheads. With the induction of the Babur-3 missiles, and the submarines that will come from China, Pakistan will be able to complete its nuclear triad."

Armaan nodded. "Our target is to neutralize the Submarine-Launched Cruise Missiles. The SLCMs are a significant adversary to our Ballistic Missile Defence program. Our job is to locate them and render them ineffective."

Baldev gave a knowing look. "Ormara?" He asked.

Armaan nodded and then pressed a key on his laptop. The far end of the wall was lit aglow projecting the image from the laptop screen on to the wall. He pressed a few keys on the laptop and the image on the wall focused itself into a map filled with brown and blue representing a land close to the sea.

"Gentlemen, welcome to the sleepy coastal village of Ormara. Also home to the Jinnah Naval base. Right now we are around ten minutes drive from the naval base. Our Intel indicates that the Babur-3 missiles were inducted in the Agosta-class subs after their tests. And the inventory of the missiles are stocked somewhere on the base. Our job is to neutralize the cruise missiles by reprogramming them."

Baldev interjected. "Why don't we simply destroy them?"

"The orders come directly from the General. He wants to neutralize the weapons without making the Pakistanis aware of it. We will reprogram the missiles in such a way that the missiles will still work as described. The only difference is that once the missile is in mid-air, the online system will shut down turning the missile into a dud."

"How will we hack these missiles?"

"Using this." Armaan held out a small thumb-sized device. "This was created by the DRDO. We cannot hack the missiles from outside. We will have to be inside their military network to do this. First, we have to access the launch systems from inside one of their submarines and install a kill switch. The kill switch program will propagate through the network to the other subs. Next, we will need physical access to the missiles itself to sync the kill switch."

Hitesh interrupted. "So let me get this straight. We will force our way through a heavily guarded naval base. Enter inside a submarine, tell the crew to excuse us for a few minutes and hack the missile controls?"

Armaan smirked. *This guy is a greenhorn analyst, not a fighter.* "That's about right." He said.

"But how? The Pakistanis will see us from a mile away and capture us. It's impossible to succeed."

"It's impossible which is why I have been entrusted with this mission." Armaan paused. "And I intend to succeed."

"So how do you propose we infiltrate the naval base?"

"I studied the layout of the naval base. And you should too." Armaan turned to the wall and pointed at the satellite image. "Take a close look at the Jinnah naval base. The location was strategically selected by the Pakistan Navy."

The satellite map of the naval base represented a coastline with an inverted T landmass jutting out perpendicularly into the sea. Armaan zoomed in the image and the details became clearer.

"The Jinnah naval base looks like an upside down pick-axe. It is surrounded by sea on two sides. If you look closely you will see the southern end is horizontal and is actually a mountain. Its name is Hammer Head Mountain. On the eastern side you will see the docks of the naval base. The Hammer Head Mountain acts as a natural shield against hostile attacks. During the 1971 war, the Indian Navy launched Operation Trident and attacked the Karachi port and sank two ships and set fire to the entire port. It was a humiliating defeat for the Pakistan Navy. After that incident, the Pakistani naval brass realized that their entire Navy was located at only one port with no redundancies. To avoid this, they expanded their naval bases at other locations like Ormara and Turbat. The advantage at Ormara is that the mountain will protect the base from any kind of Trident-like operation in the future."

Armaan zoomed in the map further. It now focused on the eastern side that housed the Jinnah naval base and the outline of the docks could be seen clearly. "Now I would like to show you something interesting. Next to the naval base you can see the base of the mountain extending underwater into the sea. Do you see anything unnatural under the sea?"

"Eh. What's that?" Roshan heard Hitesh saying.

Roshan peered closely at the image and suddenly he realized what Hitesh was referring to. Just off the facility, the base of the mountain under the sea appeared to be dug in a direction towards the docks. The canal-like feature ended into a kilometre long wall constructed on the sea bed.

Roshan hesitated. "Is that a man-made structure under the water?"

Armaan nodded sombrely. "That is the entrance to an underground submarine pen. Our Pakistani friends have dug tunnels under the mountain to house their submarines without anyone coming to know of it. I wouldn't be surprised if the Chinese helped them with this. China has its own underground secret naval base at Hainan Island. Knowing the close ties between the Pakistanis and the Chinese, they would have shared their technical knowhow for creating them. My guess is that they are building submarines in there with Chinese help."

"Are you sure?"

"We will find out in a few hours."

"Pull to the side." Armaan instructed.

They had passed Ormara and continued east for another four kilometres. Armaan wanted to make sure that they were well out of sight of anyone questioning them loitering near the base. He had seen a cluster of buildings and decided that it was a good place to park the vehicle.

Baldev slowed down to a stop next to one of the buildings and turned off the engine. "I am ready." He said.

"Good." Armaan said. "Time for a radio check." He twisted his earpiece and spoke. "Markhor Three and Four, we are at infil zone. Do you copy?"

Hitesh and Roshan were at the hotel and would provide technical assistance during the op. They were on a secure satellite relay that could work from anywhere in the world.

Hitesh's voice came through loud and clear. "Copy that. Markhor One."

"Excellent. We will be at the base in sixty minutes. Request radio silence till then."

Armaan then turned towards Baldev. "Time for an equipment check."

Armaan quickly went through the list of items they were carrying.

He had FN F2000 Assault Rifles, Glock 17 pistols, serrated blades inserted inside a hidden lining in his boots, underwater diving equipment, and a waterproof rucksack that contained a laptop, clothes and spare magazines. They checked off the items one by one. Once he was satisfied, they got out of the vehicle. Armaan's eyes roved along the length of the road.

"Let's move." he said.

They passed by the buildings and continued towards the shore. It was rocky with dense foliage everywhere. They sprinted silently through the trees till they eventually reached the end of the clearing. The shore was right upon them. They donned their underwater suits and plunged into the water.

As the water engulfed him, Armaan felt his heart thudding through his suit. No matter how much field experience he had, no matter how many missions he had led from the front, the fear never went away. It was always there waiting for him to submit to it. But Armaan was aware of one thing. He dreaded the fear within himself more than the fear of the enemy. The enemy couldn't scare him until he succumbed to his internal fear. It was a daily fight that he fought and won every day, refusing to yield to the stress and overwhelm of his assignments. It were these qualities that made him achieve near-impossible missions.

They swam underwater keeping to the seabed as much as possible. The cobalt blue sea was clear and the visibility was good under the water. They swam among the fishes that zigzagged away as they approached.

A few minutes later, Armaan saw Baldev point ahead. The base was closer now. He had traversed half of the distance. There was only one ship berthed at the dock. Its hull was visible under the water. And next to it he could see a yawning black rectangle under the sea.

The entrance to the underground submarine pen. Our Intel was right.

Armaan stayed close to the seabed and made his way to the rectangular tunnel that was shrouded in darkness. He nodded at Baldev and then entered the pitch-black tunnel.

Armaan felt as if he was swimming blind. The tunnel seemed to stretch out for ever. He tried to take slow conscious breaths to prevent himself from getting panicked by the darkness. A few seconds later he could discern a faint light. After two hundred metres, the ceiling was lit by halogen lights spaced at regular intervals. He kept swimming till the tunnel opened in a huge cavernous opening.

Armaan stopped under the water and glanced at Baldev behind him. He pointed upwards with his index finger. Baldev nodded. They slowly rose to the surface. Once they broke the surface, Armaan looked around. The inside was unlike anything he had ever seen before. The place was huge. It was larger than two cricket stadiums placed side by side. The ceiling high over their head was lit up by hundreds of lights that illuminated the place brightly. The walls were painted white and a wharf-like structure outlined all four sides where it joined the water. There were five different docks parallel to each other and on four of them lay hulls of half-finished submarines. At least fifty people were working on each dock. Most of them were construction workers in beige uniforms. A few Navy officers distinguished by their white uniforms gave orders to them. The fifth dock housed a familiar submarine, the PNS Khalid. Maintenance crews surrounded it and a couple of officers supervised them.

Baldev took off his breathing apparatus and took in the scene. "Wow! This place is buzzing with activity."

"I can see that."

"You were right on the money. They are indeed constructing subs in here."

"Yes. The implications are disturbing. I wonder what will the General make of this." Armaan pressed a finger in his earpiece. "Three and Four, are you receiving the video feed?"

Attached to Armaan's collar button was a miniature camera, not unlike a mobile phone camera, but many times powerful. It was providing a live video via satellite relay to Hitesh and Roshan in the hotel.

"We are receiving the feed." Hitesh's voice came

into his ear. "I assume our target is the PNS Khalid."

"You assume correctly. We are going to get into the sub and check out their missile systems."

"But, how are we going to get past all these people unnoticed?" Baldev asked.

"We can't. So we improvise." Armaan said.

"How?"

"We do the opposite. We draw attention to ourselves."

Chapter 10

They moved to one end of the underground dock, far away from the bright lights in the centre. They unzipped their swimsuits in the relative darkness. Armaan opened his rucksack and pulled out the clothes and started donning them. Next to him, Baldev did the same. After wearing the clothes, he reached inside the rucksack and pulled out an officer's cap. They both now looked like officers of the Pakistan Navy.

Armaan made final touches to his uniform. "The IDs are in the pocket. I am a Commander and you are my Lieutenant." He pointed to the insignia on his shoulder that represented three golden stripes and a circle against a navy blue background. "Follow my lead and don't make any mistakes."

"I never do."

"Put the Assault Rifles in the rucksack. This is a delicate mission and we won't need them. We will keep the Glocks with us. Tie the rucksack to the post there and submerge it under the water. We don't want anyone inadvertently spotting our stuff."

Baldev did as he was told and then they made their way to the docks. Armaan walked purposefully followed by Baldev a step behind him. Armaan peered at the PNS Khalid. He had read the dossier on the submarine and knew its layout inside out.

The sub was imported from the French, its original name being Agosta 90B. At a length of two hundred and fifty feet, the submarine was on the shorter side and it required only a crew of thirty-six to manage it. The submarine hatch was open and a few of the crew were busy with their work. A couple of officers were stationed on the platform adjacent to the ship. They would immediately notice if he tried to sneak in.

If they confronted Armaan, they would immediately realize that he was an unknown face. And then the questions would start. A top-secret base like this would be known to only a few people, and these officers would know everyone associated with the project.

That left him with only one option.

And it was a dangerous option.

Armaan would tell the officers a big part of the truth. A truth so shocking that it would grab their complete attention and they would believe him immediately. But there was a risk. On the off chance that they didn't believe him; it could result in their arrest, torture and eventual death.

He had to be convincing. There was no other way.

Armaan strode over to the two officers engaged in a discussion and observed the insignias on their shoulders. They were both Lieutenants. It was good, he outranked them. He noted the ID and spoke to the officer who had broken midway through a conversation with his colleague to look at him.

"Lieutenant Mirza? I am Commander Makheja from Karachi." Armaan spoke in an authoritative tone that brooked no nonsense. "Are you in charge here?"

The man straightened and gave him his full attention. "Yes Commander. How may I help you?"

"I have come here to review the security of this base. And I don't like what I see."

"Begging your pardon sir, but we were not informed of your visit," the Lieutenant said.

"Yes, that's because I ordered them not to. I wanted to conduct a surprise check and see for myself how things stand. I will be honest, the security here is pathetic."

"Why is that, sir?"

Armaan mentally nodded to himself. *That's the way. Keep them unbalanced and on the defensive.* "I have received a report that there could be a possible security threat to the PNS Khalid. Possibly from Indian spies."

"That can't be possible."

Armaan continued as if he hadn't heard the Lieutenant. "I would like to know the security protocols you have set, and how you would respond to a breach in security."

"You can rest assured sir." The officer fumbled for words. "Our security protocols are of the highest standards. Everything from personnel security to data security follows a detailed validation process. We have had no incidents of a breach so far. That's a testimonial to the integrity of our security protocols.

Armaan grunted. "I'll be the judge of that. What about the crew members? Have you noticed anything out of the ordinary about them?"

"No sir. All of the crew members have been thoroughly vetted before they came aboard."

Armaan could see that the crew around the ship had stopped and started to glance at their way. He could see that the officer in front of him was trying hard to keep his composure. He tried not to steal a glance at Baldev whom he had warned to keep an impassive face.

"I would like to personally discuss with the Captain about this threat alert. Where can I find him?"

"He's inside the sub."

"Lead me to him."

The officer led the way across the gangplank onto the submarine. He climbed the ladder and went down the hatch, with Armaan and Baldev right behind him. Since the submarine was docked, the Captain was not available in the Control Room. The officer passed the technicians sitting in front of large screen displays into a narrow passage that contained berths on both sides and they eventually reached the Captain's quarters.

Captain Younis Yusuf's shoulders drooped as he read the internal memo on the screen. A few minutes ago, he had been happily looking forward to his retirement in a few days. Now, with a growing heaviness in his chest, he read the message again.

The message conveyed that his Navy pension would be delayed by a few months due to 'technical reasons'. The message further apologized for the delay and requested him to be patient.

Yusuf shook his head. Why me, he asked himself. How could he be patient? He had opted for an early retirement so that he could fund his daughter's marriage through his pension money. The marriage was only a month away. He had to arrange everything from *Dholki* to *Nikah* to *Valima* and now he wouldn't have the money to pay for the occasion.

His financial resources were meagre, and the only option left was to postpone his daughter's marriage.

Yusuf winced at the thought. His daughter had been looking forward to the marriage. She would be crushed. He wondered what would be the reaction of the groom's parents when he would request to postpone the marriage. Would they agree? Or, would they call off the entire thing?

As he stared at the screen, a thought struck him. What technical reason had delayed the pension? His retired colleagues had got their money without any hassle. Why him? Then he remembered how he had been outspoken in his views during the last quarterly meeting in Karachi. He had complained about the lack of maintenance spares for their ships and subs. While he hadn't directly criticized his boss, the questions implied that his superior wasn't on top of things. His muscles tensed as he remembered his superior's anger-splotched face as he talked about how their navy was in the doldrums. He hadn't given it much thought at that time. Now, as he read the message an umpteenth time, he had a suspicion that his outspokenness was the reason behind this delay. Did his superior decide to teach him a lesson for being too opinionated?

Yusuf wanted to call Karachi and confront his boss. This was not an ethical way to punish him. If he had a problem with Yusuf, he should have talked to him directly. Yusuf's fingers itched as he debated whether to call his boss. But he restrained himself in the end. He wasn't sure if his boss was behind this. His call could worsen their relationship.

The sound of footsteps broke his reverie. He turned around to see Lieutenant Mirza enter his quarters followed by two unknown men.

"Captain, these two gentlemen from Karachi wished to meet you."

Karachi? The name of the city reminded him of his superior. He looked at the two men. One was a Commander and the other a Lieutenant.

What do they want from me now?

Armaan watched Captain Yusuf as Mirza informed Yusuf the reason for their presence. The Captain's eyes grew wide as he listened.

"Tell me gentlemen, how may I be of service?"

"I would like to speak with you in private." Armaan said, looking at Mirza.

Mirza took the hint. "Please excuse me Captain. I have to check up on the crew." He turned and left.

Armaan watched him till he was out of sight and then spoke. "I have a suspicion about your Lieutenant. The security alert that we received; it could be him."

Yusuf's eyes blazed red. "How dare you assume that one of my best men could be a traitor?"

Armaan voice was low, but his inflection cut like steel. "Your man completely disregarded the protocols. When I arrived, he didn't check my entry logs with Port Security. He didn't verify my identity by calling up the Karachi base. All of it is very suspicious. I suggest that you keep a tab on him. He may be a mole."

Yusuf's anger didn't abate. "I agree that he has done grave dereliction of his duties. But it doesn't necessarily mean that he can be a spy for someone else."

"We have received intelligence reports of possible data breach on this submarine. I wouldn't be surprised if Indian spies are behind this."

"That's not possible. This submarine is not susceptible to hacking. It is in an isolated network."

"We are here to verify that," Armaan said. "My colleague and I wish to keep this a secret so that the knowledge of the breach doesn't get leaked if it's true. I want to review your crew logs, and your data logs. This is an order from Headquarters."

"Very well," Yusuf replied. "You can use the terminal in here. The crew rarely come in here."

"Thanks." Armaan nodded, and then gestured at Baldev. "You got this?"

Baldev nodded and sat in front of the terminal. "It will take me only a few minutes. I appreciate your help, Captain."

Yusuf looked at Armaan. "While you are here, would you like to check out our submarine?"

"I would love to," Armaan responded.

"Follow me then."

The Captain guided Armaan to the next room. A

couple of crew members were sitting in front of a console with their ears covered by headsets. "This is the Sonar room. The PNS Khalid has both bow mounted sonar as well as towed-sonar arrays that help us with anti-access and area denial A2/AD strategies. You should see the sub in action. We can repel any hostile forces."

Armaan looked around. "I have no doubt about that."

They moved over to the next room. Rows of torpedoes lined up both sides.

"This is where the true strength of our submarine lies, the Torpedo room. We have four bow 533mm torpedo tubes with a range of 20 kilometres..."

But Armaan was no longer listening to Yusuf, his eyes focused on the missiles kept next to the torpedoes. It wasn't what he had expected.

The missiles were long and painted in white colour with a grey tip. But it wasn't the colours that caught Armaan's attention; it was a small lettering in English embossed along the side of the missile that read *MBDA Exocet SM 39*.

Yusuf continued unaware of the turmoil in Armaan's head. "These are the Exocet anti-ship missiles. They have a range of fifty kilometres."

"I thought that the Babur-3 missiles would be used in the Khalid-class submarines. Is that not the case?"

The Captain ran his hand on the Exocet missiles. "I also thought so, but the Babur missiles were designed for the Vertical-Launch Systems in our newer submarines. The submarines are being constructed as you may have no doubt seen in the naval base, but not fast enough. The submarines should have been built by now, with the Babur integrated in them providing us with the long elusive nuclear triad capability. When the leadership realized that the subs weren't ready and we won't get a credible second strike via the Babur SLCMs soon enough, they asked us for our inputs. It was only during the testing stage that we came to know that the Babur wasn't designed for the Khalid-class subs. We needed an intermediate solution and the obvious proposal was to redesign the Babur to allow it to be launched from a torpedo tube instead of a VLS. The tests were successful, but the problem is the torpedo-launched missiles have resulted in a smaller attack range. After the tests, the missiles were sent to Sargodha for a rejig."

"Sargodha?"

"It's where they designed the original Babur as a Land-Attack Cruise Missile. The engineers over there are working with us to fix the missile range issue. I hope they will be able to help us quickly though I doubt it."

"Why?"

"I will be honest. Between the Army, Air-force and Navy, we are treated as step-brothers. Our budget is the smallest of the three. In 1971, the Indian Navy blockaded our ports and our Navy couldn't respond. We would have done better if there had been someone to champion our causes and give us better warfare capabilities. But the Army Chief only cares about his Army. Our priorities fall way down the line. But over the years I've learned to take things in my stride." Yusuf shrugged, "I think that's enough whining for today. Let's get back to my quarters."

Armaan said, "Yes, my subordinate should have found something by now."

Armaan followed Yusuf but his mind was preoccupied. Beads of perspiration formed on his forehead even though the temperature inside the submarine was cool. He felt the steel walls closing in on him. The Babur-3 missiles were not here. It meant that their mission was incomplete.

They had planned for both a software intrusion and a hardware interception. Baldev was working on the software end, but it would be of no use if they couldn't modify the hardware components of the missiles. With the missiles relocated outside of the naval base, their mission had flopped big time.

They retraced their steps back to the Captain's quarters. Baldev was sitting in front of the terminal. He turned at their presence.

Armaan said, "Did you find anything?"

"I checked the logs and there was nothing out of the ordinary. No patterns or anything suspicious to report. I suggest we check in at the base."

His words meant that the software part was done.

Armaan turned towards Yusuf. "I am sorry to have bothered you with this inconvenience, but it's my job, and we cannot take security lightly."

"No, that's fine. It's reassuring to know that none of my crew is involved in anything suspicious. I knew it from the start, but it's good to have someone give a validation. I will escort you outside."

"No thanks, Captain. We have taken enough of your time."

The Captain walked them back towards the hatch and Armaan and Baldev exited out of the submarine. They clambered down the ladder and walked across the gangplank. The two officers they had met earlier were busy conversing with a couple of crew members. No one gave them any attention. They quietly walked across from the submarine to the diesel station. Once they were behind the station and out of sight, Armaan looked at Baldev.

"Did you insert the program?"

"I plugged the device, and it did its work. Hitesh should be able to confirm. We now have to figure out where the missiles are kept on the base."

"I just spoke with the Captain. The Babur-3 missiles are not here."

"Not here?"

"No, it's been sent to Sargodha for further testing."

"Our mission is incomplete. What do we do now?"

"Let's first get our stuff and move out of here."

They found their rucksack undisturbed tethered to a string at the edge of the wharf. They untied it and donned their wet-suits and slipped quietly under the water to return the same way they had come in.

Chapter 11

Quetta, Balochistan, Pakistan

Gorbat Khan ran his fingers through his tousled hair absentmindedly as he looked at the computer screen. It had been a long day. Sure, most days as the Inspector of Quetta's Counter-Terrorism department were long, but today threatened to ruin his family life. Tomorrow was his son's tenth birthday and he had yet to buy him a present.

Yesterday morning, he had told his wife, he would surprise the boy with a PS4, but that was before the attack on Gwadar port.

Now, it had been thirty hours and he had not gone back home. He had spent most of yesterday at Gwadar completing an on-site investigation, going through surveillance videos and asking questions. So far, they had not found any leads yet. No organisation had claimed responsibility for the attack, but the politicians had already gone on air saying that it was the work of the Indian R&AW agency.

Gorbat looked up at the clock. Thankfully, it was showing the right time. It was five pm. He remembered being annoyed that the clock had stopped for weeks and no one had bothered to repair it. Finally, in frustration, he himself had taken it to the local watch shop to be repaired. Gorbat was a punctual man, and he needed to know the precise time throughout the workday.

The workday was officially over. He deserved a break. He needed time to relax and think with a clear mind. His men were still on the field searching for forensic evidence. He should call it a day. No one would chide him for leaving on time.

But it was hard for him to log off. His men weren't fully trained to do the work. They had a paucity of resources. For a province like Balochistan that was rich in resources, but perennially poor; the CTD represented the problems of the state accurately. Their department never had a dedicated trainer to train the staff on effective counter-terrorism strategies. They didn't have enough people to man the shifts, with most of the local talent being called to beef up the Punjab Counter Terrorism department. And most troublesome of all, they never had any significant budget for their routine work. Today, they had run out of petrol, and since they didn't get the transport budget last week, Gorbat had to pay the money out of his own pocket. *These people will turn our country into Somalia.* He banged his fist on the table in frustration.

The monitor blinked once and then went blank. It was yet another reminder of the doldrums their department was in finance-wise. When they had requested for computer equipment, they had been provided with end-of-life PCs from the Punjab CTD. The Punjabi team had received brand-new laptops, and the Balochistan police had received second-hand rejects.

Gorbat sighed as he reached behind the monitor and fiddled with the cable that was connected to the monitor port. The screen flickered back to life, but he knew that the dangling cable would switch off at the slightest jerk. He looked at the screen trying to remember what he was doing a moment ago. His overloaded brain couldn't respond back with an answer. He needed to switch off his mind. He looked at the clock again. It was five thirty pm.

Gorbat got up. It was the law of diminishing returns. After a point of time, the productivity wouldn't improve however much additional time he sat on the chair. He knew he had reached that point. He locked his computer and was about to get up when the desk phone rang.

He looked at the device wondering if he should pick it up. If he let it ring, they would call his subordinates and he won't have to bother with the call. But the ringing tone pierced into his conscience. He couldn't sit back while someone had called his number. If they wanted to speak with his subordinates, they wouldn't have called him. They needed his help.

I was never good at delegation. It's too late now.

Gorbat picked up the phone, "Inspector Khan speaking."

"Gorbat, this is Raza. I need your advice on something that's just come in."

Gorbat wondered what Raza wanted. He was the Inspector of the general police department. He had previously asked for help whenever they encountered a situation related to terrorists. "Raza, I was about to leave. Can we discuss this tomorrow morning?"

"Actually, this could be related to yesterday's Gwadar bombing."

Gorbat was suddenly all ears. Raza had spoken the magic words. Gorbat had been working for almost two days without a lead. He couldn't go home without at least knowing what Raza was talking about. Raza's office was in a different section of Quetta's police headquarters complex. He convinced himself that it will take only a few minutes. And it may probably turn out to be nothing.

It took him a couple of minutes to pick up his stuff and lock the door to his office. He exited out of the building and walked across to the adjacent building. A minute later he was seated across Raza.

"What did you find that you think could be related to the bombing?"

Raza pulled his desk drawer and handed a dozen photos to Gorbat. Gorbat went over the photos. It showed a motor and what appeared to be the remains of an inflatable dinghy. The photos were taken from various angles, and the background showed a muddy beach.

"What is this?"

"These photos were taken near Makola village on the Makran coast. One of the local fisherman's net got stuck under the water. He tried to pull it free and then discovered this. It's an inflatable dingy. Only the motor is intact. The rubber was shredded to deflate it and submerge it out of sight."

"How is this related to the Gwadar bombing?"

As an answer, Raza pointed to one of the photos. The photo showed a close-up of the motor. Gorbat followed Raza's finger. A small but distinguishable print read 'Made in India'.

"We had an attack yesterday, no one has reported about a missing boat, and we find a submerged boat a few kilometres from Gwadar."

Gorbat looked at Raza, "So where does that leave us."

"I have a pretty strong hunch that the boat came from India. It landed on the Makran coast. The crew sneaked over to Gwadar and bombed our port."

"The evidence is pretty circumstantial." Gorbat played the devil's advocate. He was excited, but he knew that hasty judgements were emotional and not logical. "That boat could have been submerged for months."

"It isn't. Look at the motor. It hasn't rusted. My guess it's been under the water for a few hours to a few days. That matches with the timeline of the bombing."

"It isn't much to go upon."

"And that is why I called you. We can prove nothing until we have captured the people behind this."

"Let's say your theory is right. But they couldn't have done it without local help."

"Do you suspect anyone?"

"In Balochistan? All locals are suspect here. But they don't have the resources for this." Gorbat thought for a moment. "Except for the tribal lords. I know one who is rumoured to be working with the Indians. And he is from Makola. Fazal Darzada."

A few minutes later Gorbat was back in front of his office opening the door. He switched on the lights and powered up his desktop. He studied the dossier for Fazal Darzada. He had been apprehended multiple times for inciting violence and sedition, but the charges were never proved against him.

Gorbat thought of asking the Makran police to follow up on the lead. But then, they could be hand in glove with him. He had to be personally involved. He twirled the paperweight on the table wondering what should be done. It was a flimsy lead, it could mean nothing. He couldn't waste an entire day going to Makran only to find out it was a dead end.

He sat straight. There was one thing he could do. He glanced at the dossier as he punched the digits on the desk phone. It rang for a few times before a deep voice answered.

"Hello?"

Gorbat said. "Am I speaking with Fazal Darzada?"

"Yes. Who is speaking?"

"This is Inspector Gorbat Khan from the Quetta Counter Terrorism Department."

There was a pause before Darzada replied. "Yes Inspector Khan, how may I help?"

"We found an abandoned boat from India on the Makran coastline where you live. I want to know where the Indians on the boat went." Gorbat had been in the field for a long time. He would know immediately if Darzada tried to evade the question.

The pause this time was longer. Just when Gorbat wondered if the line had been disconnected, Darzada spoke. "Some of my people saw four men with weapons on the Makola beach."

Gorbat's ears perked. "Why didn't they report this to the local police?"

"How do we know who those men were?" Darzada was indignant. "They could have been the local police themselves or the Army conducting some operations. Life is hard for us as it is, we don't want to make it harder by cross-questioning what the Army or police does."

"Do you know where they went?"

"Our people stay as far away as possible from people with guns. They fled away in terror without a backwards glance."

Gorbat thought about it. The chances of these people identifying the gun-wielding terrorists were slim. But after listening to the Balochi, he was now convinced that he had a lead. It was undoubtedly Indian spies, and they had infiltrated from the Makran coast.

"I'll be in Makola tomorrow. We can talk then. Good night." Gorbat hung up the phone.

Fazal Darzada got up from his chair and paced around the bedroom of his two-storey bungalow. The house was located on a twenty-acre estate. His was the only regal-looking house in the tiny village of Makola on the Makran coast. The others houses were ramshackle hovels where the local Balochis resided.

His father had lorded over the area and had taught the tricks of the trade to him many years back. The theory was simple. On one hand, blackmail the government that the people will rise in revolt if they didn't give him money to support the livelihood of the local Balochis; and on the other hand, complain to the local people about the government's apathy towards the Balochis and pocket a majority of the money. It was a fine balancing act and he had learned the art to perfection.

The local Balochis were simple villagers who didn't really care whether they were part of Pakistan or an independent state, but Darzada knew that perception was reality. So he used to stage frequent rallies whose audience were filled with his cohorts. And he used to talk incessantly on the injustices faced by the Balochis and repeatedly demanded for a separate nation. So far, the strategy had worked making him rich beyond measure, and with an indelible influence over the innocent Balochi people who still pinned their hopes on him.

But the association with the Indians was starting to turn into a problem. He was candid enough to admit that he did what he did for the money, and not for the Balochi cause. He would milk it for what it was worth and as long as he could. If the villagers didn't see it, that was their problem. Life was neither fair nor unfair. Life was simply going for what you wanted, and brushing aside everyone who stood in the way.

When Inspector Khan had called him, Fazal knew he was treading on dangerous territory. The inspector would be coming tomorrow and he had to be ready for his questions. He pulled out his mobile phone and spoke to one of his colleagues for a few minutes.

He ended the conversation by saying, "Call me once you are done informing the police."

Fazal hung up the phone. There was an easy way to disentangle himself from the situation. The solution was to lay the blame on the Indians. It was best if the police came to the conclusion by themselves. That way, the Balochis would never be questioned about their loyalty to Pakistan.

Chapter 12

"This is a goldmine." Hitesh excitedly looked at his screen.

Armaan looked at him. He couldn't share in the excitement. They had just returned back from the naval base. As far as he was concerned, the mission was a failure. They hadn't achieved all their objectives. Hitesh would be happy with the data they had extracted from the submarine files, but Armaan felt morose inside.

Hitesh continued, "It will take us weeks to sort out all this data, but so far it looks like we have hit the jackpot."

"Yes, but we didn't get to change the configuration on the missiles." Armaan looked out of the window. The Makran coastline spread out in the distance. If he was not on a mission, he would have been tempted to go down to the beach and laze around for hours. He shook the thought away. He had been chosen to deliver results, and by a quirk of fate, the missiles were not on the base.

Armaan had always prided on his abilities to deliver results. The mission had been a clean in-and-out exactly the way he had envisioned, but the critical objective hadn't been met. An emptiness gnawed at him, and he knew it to be the subconscious rebuke of a failed mission. The General had chosen him for this mission and he had let him down.

Armaan knew how critical this mission was. Millions of lives would be saved in the event of a war. And they would be able to decisively act against their adversaries. He slapped his hand on the window sill. It couldn't be. He shouldn't have failed at this mission. Too much had been riding on his shoulders. As he watched the cobalt-blue coast, a thought stuck him.

Who said the mission had failed?

Armaan realized that he had been thinking that the mission had failed already. His jaws set tight in determination. No, the mission hadn't failed. He could still salvage it. No mission objective was out of reach for him. He could achieve what an army of soldiers couldn't. He would resuscitate this mission from its death throes.

The General had given him the objectives. The General wouldn't care how he accomplished the mission. He wanted results.

And Armaan would give him the results he wanted.

He felt Baldev appear at his side. "I am sorry this mission went kaput. It's time to return home."

Armaan squared his shoulders. "No."

"No?" Baldev was perplexed.

"We will not leave without completing the mission."

"What are you talking about, Armaan? The mission is dead. Let's get back home safely before these guys find out what happened."

"No, we proceed to Sargodha and complete our mission there."

"That's crazy. We don't have the resources to do that."

"It doesn't matter. This mission is critical for the General. I can't give him no for an answer. As a leader, this mission is my responsibility and I promised him that I will execute it."

"But, do you realize what you are saying? We cannot go halfway through Pakistan searching for the missiles."

"We will do it. We have to do it. It's the only way."

Baldev shook his head, "We should at least consult the General about this."

"There is no need to bring the General into this. I am your mission leader and I give the orders. And this is an order."

Armaan glanced at the room and saw that Hitesh's and Roshan's eyes were on him. They had heard his argument with Baldev. So be it, he thought. It was best they understood who was running the show here.

Roshan said, "I am with you, Armaan. Let me know what to do."

Armaan nodded. It appeared that Roshan had finally learned his lesson after the Bangladesh fiasco. He looked at Hitesh waiting for his answer.

Hitesh shut down his laptop and stood up, "Yes, sir. I'll follow your orders."

Armaan glared at Baldev as if expecting him to rebel.

Baldev said, "I am coming, okay? And not because you are ordering me to. It's to protect you from yourself. You are like my brother. I'm seeing you go crazy, and I don't like it. I want to be there when you need me."

Armaan ignored his words and turned to Roshan and Hitesh. "The missiles have been shipped to Sargodha. We need to figure out where they went."

Hitesh said, "The Captain could be talking about the Central Ammunition Depot on Kirana Hills. It is a few kilometres away from the Mushaf Air base in Sargodha. My bet is that's where the missiles will be."

Armaan gave a grudging smile. *This kid may not be suited for field work, but he did have all the answers.* "Great. What do we know about that place?"

"Not much, the Depot consists of large concrete structures dispersed at the base of the hill. The structures may just be the proverbial iceberg tip, with some speculating that the weapons are stored in underground bunkers to protect them against a sudden attack by the IAF."

Armaan said, "Okay, so we have to get inside the Central Ammunition Depot, figure out which bunker houses the missiles, and access its systems."

"In a word, yes."

"I will figure out how we will accomplish that. Pack up your gear. We move out ASAP."

Gorbat looked at the wall clock. The time was seven-thirty pm and he was still in his office. He had spent the last thirty minutes reading and re-reading the file on Fazal Darzada. His mobile phone buzzed. He glanced at it. It was his wife.

"Did you get the birthday gift for Salim?"

Gorbat winced. He had completely forgotten about his son's birthday tomorrow. "I am leaving the office. I will buy it on the way home."

"Are you still in office?" Gorbat could hear the tone of disapproval in his wife's words.

"Yes, something came up."

"Okay come soon. We are waiting for you. Make sure you get the gift before the stores close."

"I will."

Gorbat again went through the motions of packing his stuff and turning off the computer. As he reached the door, the desk phone rang again. Gorbat stared at it wondering if it was Raza with an update. He picked up the phone.

"Inspector Khan speaking."

"Inspector Khan, this is Inspector Bugti from Makola village."

Makola, the name echoed in his ears. Inspector Bugti was the CTD representative attached to the Makola Police Station. "Yes, Inspector Bugti?"

"We found four dead bodies here. They have been shot."

It must be the Indians. "When did this happen?"

"We are trying to find that out. One of the locals found the bodies and called in. I have taken over the case as an incident of terrorism."

This was the evidence he was looking for. With Bugti in charge of the case, Gorbat's department would be rewarded for solving the Gwadar attack. He needed to be on site at the earliest.

"Keep the bodies in your custody. I am coming to Makola immediately."

As Gorbat turned off the lights and locked the office door for a final time, he realized that he had to make a difficult call to his wife.

It was evening and time for their prayers. Malik spoke the verses and the others joined in. After the prayers ended, Shafiq went over to his tent. Malik jokingly referred to it as their palace. Shafiq's 'palace' was nothing but a single worn bed that was too short to fit his tall body. Ten other similar beds were laid next to his. On the edge of his bed was a small locked chest. It contained all his worldly possessions.

No one was in the tent. Shafiq knelt down and took a key and unlocked the chest. A Colt pistol snagged off an American corpse, half a dozen magazine clips, and a much-thumbed copy of the Holy Quran stared back at him.

"Why do you keep that chest of yours locked?" Hafeez walked in through the door. "As far as I can see, there is nothing valuable in it."

Shafiq looked up and smiled. Hafeez was his next-bed neighbour. None of them had any possessions to speak of, except for the clothes on their back and the weapons in their hands. Apart from him, only a few others possessed bags most of which contained blankets and supplies of dry fruits. "It's of sentimental value to me. I know no one will take anything, but I will be upset if I lose these. It's my last connection to a world that once was."

Hafeez put a hand on his shoulder, "We all have lost a lot, which is why we continue to fight. We now have left nothing to lose. We will be victorious in our cause, or we will die trying."

Shafiq nodded solemnly.

"Come, it's time for dinner. Don't be late or Malik wouldn't like it."

Shafiq found the dinner to be livelier than that of the previous night. The menu consisted of *chapli kebab* and *naan*. They sat cross-legged in small groups on the ground. "People seem to be happier today."

"They would be, don't they?" Hafeez replied. "We had purpose, now we also have a deadline. Everyone is looking forward to what our leaders have in mind."

Shafiq looked around. Everyone was talking, mostly about the day's training and speculating about their upcoming assignment.

"What do you think our next mission is?"

Hafeez said, "It doesn't matter to me. My duty on earth is to kill the enemies of Islam."

Shafiq nodded appreciatively. Hafeez was right. They would get to know by tomorrow. He looked around. Zia and Malik weren't present with the group.

"Where's Zia?"

Hafeez looked around, "I don't know. Probably dead from all that talking and climbing."

Shafiq chuckled as he realized that even Hafeez disliked Zia, but then hardly anyone liked the blabbermouth. "Wishful thinking. But, it's not like him to miss an opportunity like dinner to talk about his great fighting abilities."

Hafeez glanced at Malik's tent. "Do you think Malik

may be training him to be the next in line for chief?"

A chill ran down Shafiq's spine. Today wasn't the first time he had a run-in with Zia. Zia and he had disagreements and arguments previously as well. It wasn't that Zia targeted him only; Zia was discourteous and rude to most of their group members. A person like him in power lording over their group was an unpleasant proposition.

"It could be possible."

Shafiq saw Hafeez frown at his response. Hafeez pushed his plate away. "You eat. I will take a look around."

Shafiq's eyes followed Hafeez as he strode to the commander's tent. He slowed down as he passed by, momentarily peeking inside and then continued strolling around the camp and finally returned to the table.

He sat down in front of Shafiq. "My hunch was right. Zia's in Malik's tent."

"What were they talking about?"

"I don't know." Hafeez said. "I couldn't hear them clearly. Malik's tone was low as he spoke with Zia."

Shafiq wondered at what Hafeez had said. Zia was the wrong man for the job. But then, they both could be assuming incorrectly. Zia and Malik could be talking about any number of things unrelated to their mission. He answered the unspoken question in Hafeez's mind.

"Only time will tell."

Chapter 13

Gorbat watched the jagged mountains of Balochistan rush past as he flew over them. From his vantage point atop an MI-17 helicopter, the landscape was full of mountains devoid of greenery. It had been an ordeal to get the helicopter assigned for the last-minute trip. He had gone to the top floor of the building that housed his department. The entire floor was the office of the Inspector General of Police. The IGP was alone in his office speaking on the phone.

Gorbat had decided it would be best that he made an in-person request to lease the helicopter. The CTD had only one helicopter for the entire Balochistan province. Gorbat still couldn't fathom the rationale behind the government procuring a single helicopter to cover terrorism in an area that spanned almost half of Pakistan. Gorbat waited till the IGP finished his call and then explained his request. The Inspector General tried to stonewall his request, but Gorbat was equally persistent.

"Why can't you go there tomorrow using one of our jeeps?" The IGP asked. "What's the need to leave right now?"

Gorbat said, "Sir, this is a matter of national security. The Indians bombed the Gwadar port. We still aren't sure how many of them came to our country, and if someone else from our end was involved. We need to track them before trail goes cold. An hour delayed is an hour lost."

"What evidence are you hoping to collect?"

"I don't know sir, but I know that I will find something."

"That doesn't reassure me. It doesn't justify utilizing a helicopter. Aviation fuel is expensive as it is."

Gorbat knew that he was getting nowhere. He had served under the IGP for many years. This was unlike him. He changed tactics.

"Sir, you can see my track record. I have closed ninety percent cases that were assigned to me. You can rely on me to do an honest work."

"Yes Gorbat, your work is good."

"So please understand this is important. I need that helicopter only for a few hours."

"I am sorry Gorbat, I cannot do that."

"Why sir? You once said that national security is our highest priority. What's the real reason?"

The IGP look around to ensure that they were alone. He then spoke in a low voice. "The Chief Minister will commandeer the helicopter tomorrow for a trip to Gwadar."

"The Chief Minister? But why are we giving him our own helicopter? The helicopter is assigned to the Counter Terrorism Department. What happened to his own?"

The IGP said, "The Chief Minister gave his helicopter to his son as a wedding gift."

"What!" The words stopped in his mouth. Gorbat had never come to terms with the politicians. "The helicopter was given to serve his post. It was assigned to a designation, and not to an individual. How can he think of it as his own?"

The IGP shrugged his shoulders. "Its best we don't get into it. The Chief Minister told me to get a helicopter ready for his visit to Gwadar tomorrow. I couldn't say no to him."

Gorbat hung his head. He wanted to be in Makran tonight and get to the root of the issue. He had hoped to inquire around and then take the helicopter back home to Quetta in the morning. But now that didn't seem possible. Quetta was around eight hundred kilometres from Makran. It was an eleven hour journey by road. By helicopter it took three hours. He looked up as an idea formed in his head.

"Sir, if I take the helicopter tonight to Makran and have the pilot drop me there and return to Quetta, the helicopter should be back well before the Chief Minister needs it. Please understand, this is important."

The IGP thought for a long time as he weighed the pros and cons, and he finally said yes. But Gorbat wasn't enthused. Even if he completed his inquiry by morning it meant that he would return to Quetta by road. He wouldn't be able to spend much time with his son on his birthday.

A sudden jolt due to an air pocket brought Gorbat back to the present. The night was dark and the only illumination came from a nearly full moon that peeked through intermittent clouds. The wind swirled through the windows and buffeted his body threatening to tear off the seat belt that secured him. But Gorbat's face was set in dogged determination. His colleagues used to say that once he started a case, he wouldn't let go till he was able to resolve it. He had been pensive yesterday after the bombing had taken place and he couldn't secure any leads, but now with the Indians dead he could relax.

The case was almost resolved. But there were still some unanswered questions. Who killed the Indians? And if they were armed how were they killed?

"We are there." The pilot said.

Gorbat watched as the dark grey shape of the Arabian Sea materialized in the distance. He hoped he would have the answers soon enough.

Gorbat was out of the helicopter as soon as it touched the ground. He thanked the pilot and the helicopter took off immediately. As he stood on the ramp, the coastal humidity engulfed him. The night was warm and within a minute, his clothes were drenched in sweat. Inspector Bugti was waiting for him at the helipad. They had met each a few times over the years on both formal and informal occasions.

Bugti waved him over. Gorbat was happy to see him. Bugti was one of the rising stars of the police force. He was dedicated to his work and was good at investigations. The only problem with him was that he had no scruples in asking for commissions for his work. He would demand money for services rendered as a police officer. Gorbat had learned to ignore this aspect of Bugti. He got straight to the point.

"Did you get custody of the bodies?"

"Yes, I did. The forensic guy is looking over them."

Gorbat was pleased. Bugti understood that Gorbat would want the details of the case and had already involved the forensics in it. "Did we get any clues as to how they died?"

"Yes," Bugti hesitated. "I will let the forensic person explain it to you."

After a few minutes ride they arrived at the Makola Police Station. It was a two-storey building with a couple of vehicles parked in front of it. They entered the place. Gorbat looked at a couple of police officers conversing in one corner. He followed Bugti as he ascended the stairs.

"Nisar is our forensics expert." Bugti pointed at the man. "He will brief you."

The introductions were made quickly and then Gorbat settled into a chair as Nisar started talking.

"Here are the photos of the victims." Nisar handed a score of photos to Gorbat."The first thing you will notice is that all of them were shot in the head. Ballistics testing have revealed that all four bullets were from different guns and they were fired upon from close quarters. I have taken the DNA samples. We will look for missing persons in the vicinity and hopefully have a match soon."

Gorbat looked up from the photos. "Missing persons? Bugti must have given you the background of this case. These are Indians, not locals."

Bugti spoke, "The bullets that killed them don't match any of those that are used locally. All victims were killed via a headshot, indicating that their opponents were professionals at killing. It appears that the victims were our own people and they were killed by an unknown professional group that you assume to be Indian spies."

Gorbat's heart sank. The Indians were still at large. If they weren't killed, then...

"But, who are these victims?"

"All four were exceptionally fit with toned bodies, their ages range from mid-twenties to thirties. They could only be law enforcement personnel or Army people. I checked around and all the police in the neighbouring districts are accounted for. That leaves the Army. I have asked that any reports of missing persons be brought to my notice immediately."

Just then Bugti's phone rang. He picked up the phone and listened for a few minutes and then hung up.

"We just got a report of four Army men missing."

"Army men?"

"Yes. The call came to us downstairs. My man has

gathered the details and is coming up to report."

Gorbat thought about how the scenario could have unfolded. It appeared that the Indians had beached on the shore using the inflatable dinghy, and then shot the Army men. It still wasn't clear why they had killed the men. Based on the accuracy of the headshots, it appeared that the Army men didn't get a chance to retaliate back or they hadn't even realized that an attack was imminent. They had probably all been shot simultaneously, Gorbat surmised. A standard operating procedure of special forces worldwide. Go in and knock them hard before they even had a chance of knowing what hit them.

One of the policemen Gorbat had seen below came up with a file in his hand. Bugti said, "What did you find?"

"We have the names of the Army officers and the Jeep number. The four Army officers had departed at four am for a routine patrol, but didn't return back. They were to report for an important assignment at seven am, but they didn't turn up at the appointed hour. A search was conducted by the Army but didn't yield any results. They are asking for our assistance in the search."

"Okay, call them back and inform them that we have four bodies that need identification. It may well turn out to be their missing officers."

Gorbat interrupted, "Did we find the jeep at the site of the bodies?"

"No, only the bodies."

"Okay, run a country-wide alert for the Jeep number. If they locate the jeep, they should not take any action, and just report it to us."

Bugti turned to the junior officer. "You heard him. Do it."

The man left and then Bugti said, "It appears the Army men were killed by your unknown Indian spies."

"The Indians must have used the jeep to make their exit. If they are still using it, maybe we have a chance of catching them."

"So we wait till then?"

"No, we have to proactively search for them. If the assailants are Indians, and I am betting on that, then this is not your usual counter-terrorism operation. Take me to the site where the bodies were found."

Half an hour later Gorbat was crouching on the ground next to the N10 highway as he examined the tread marks of vehicles. He spent some time walking around and observing the surroundings. But it was in a dilapidated garage that he stopped and beckoned Bugti.

"Look at this." Gorbat pointed at the floor. He had finally found what he had been looking for. On the ground were four empty cartridges. "They must have hidden here and shot the Army officers from this position."

He continued looking around the garage. Cobwebs strung across the roof in unbroken strands and a layer of dust covered the walls and open shelves, but the ground was undoubtedly disturbed with multiple footprints. He looked around but couldn't find anything else.

Gorbat walked out of the garage, "There were three vehicles here. Two of them look to be vans, and I am guessing the third was the jeep. The jeep went east from here."

"Do you think they were headed for Karachi?"

"It's possible." Gorbat thought for a minute. "Here's what we will do."

"There's a check-post up ahead. What do you suggest?" Roshan asked.

He was driving the Army jeep. It was still early morning and they had traversed more than three hundred kilometres on the N10 National Highway. They had slowed down on the outskirts of Karachi as they joined in the early morning trucks that were bound for Karachi and Hyderabad. They had queued up behind one of the colourful trucks that were ubiquitous on the Pakistani roads, and further up Roshan had glimpsed a check-post with a sentry noting down the license plates as the vehicles came to a stop in front of an imposing looking barrier spanning the road.

"Pull off the safety's on your guns." Armaan responded. "I don't think they will stop an Army vehicle, but be ready to make a quick exit."

Roshan's heart hammered wildly as they closed in

on the check-post. He counted the guards. There were six of them. He glanced at his team. They displayed their guns prominently in front of them. It was a subtle cue if the Pakistanis knew who they really were. *Don't mess with us.* But they were still outnumbered two to one. With Roshan at the wheel, it left only three men against the six guards. If they already knew the presence of his team, Roshan couldn't begin to comprehend the complications in their mission.

It was going to be a bloodbath. And then an open run among the survivors, if any.

The truck in front of him passed the gate; it was their turn.

Taking a deep breath, Roshan eased the jeep to a stop. He gave his best smile to the sullen guard, who glanced at him with envy. He noted down the number and was about to say something when the supervisor in the guard house called out.

"Aziz, come here for a minute."

Roshan watched with bated breath as Aziz walked over to his supervisor. A moment later the supervisor and Aziz came out and walked over to Roshan. The supervisor smiled at Roshan and said, "I am sorry for the delay Lieutenant. I was just telling Aziz here that he should never stop anyone from the Army. I apologize on his behalf."

The supervisor gestured to Aziz and he opened the barrier. The supervisor passed them through.

As they passed the check-post, Roshan breathed a relieved sigh, echoed by the other three. "Done."

The check-post supervisor kept looking at the men in the Army jeep till they vanished out of sight. He had no idea who they were, but the license plate of the jeep had been flagged. The flag had a note that the occupants were not to be stopped, but to report the find to a phone number in Counter Terrorism department.

He picked up the phone and dialled the number.

Gorbat's mobile rang. He picked up the call. The voice on the other end spoke.

"Is this the CTD?"

"Yes, it is."

"We were told to contact this number for a vehicle alert."

Gorbat narrowed his eyes. "Where are you calling from?"

"We are at the Karachi western check-post. A jeep bearing the corresponding number just passed through."

"Thanks for letting me know. I will be there in a few hours."

Gorbat looked at Bugti. "I just got a call from the security officer in charge of the Karachi check-post. The Indians passed through."

"Karachi, eh? Your assumption that they are going to Karachi was accurate. But what is their mission?"

"I am not sure." Gorbat said.

"I think we will come to know after we apprehend them."

"Right, we will. Bugti, I will need to borrow your car. I'm going to Karachi."

"Sure. Just drop me off at the police station."

They had just got into the car when Gorbat's mobile buzzed again.

"CTD. This is Inspector Gorbat Khan."

"This is the security in charge for the Karachi North check-post. The jeep number highlighted in the circular just passed our check post."

"Thank you for letting me know."

Gorbat looked at Bugti with a hint of frustration. "Karachi is not their destination. They just exited north of the city."

"Where do you think they are headed?"

In response Gorbat picked up his mobile phone and scanned through his contact list and then tapped on a number.

"Inspector Mehdi speaking." The voice on the other end answered.

"Inspector Mehdi, this is Inspector Gorbat of the Quetta CTD," Gorbat said.

"Yes sir."

"You saw the vehicle alert that I sent?"

"Yes, we did. The local authorities have been alerted on it."

"They need to be more than alert. The jeep is on its way to you."

Chapter 14

Shafiq greeted the dawn with a smile. The lure of the unknown thrilled him. The day had finally arrived. Today they were going out to an unknown journey to an undisclosed location. It was everything they had been preparing for weeks. He looked around and saw that most of the men were already up and about. The training and discipline had strengthened the men's resolve and they were now eager to prove themselves.

As the men assembled out of their tents, Malik greeted them. Normally grim-faced, Shafiq thought he detected a hint of a smile on Malik's face as he addressed the crowd.

"Brothers, we are moving out in two hours. We have been told to move north to the outskirts of Jalalabad where some friends will join us and then we will be given further instructions."

The crowd shouted in excitement to his announcement. Malik waited for the din to die down and then continued.

"We will now need to wind down the camp and retrieve everything we have and pack it into our truck. Start loading the weapons first. Time is of the essence."

The men dispersed off to collect the armaments. Numerous crates of weapons were picked up one by one and loaded into the two trucks they had. Both trucks were nearly half full by the time they finished.

After the weapons, the men focused on the food supplies. They considered the weapons their number one priority. If they were caught in a precarious situation, they would prefer to be hungry, but not unarmed. It was better to die a hero's death painted in one's blood, than a slow one from hunger. And of course with a weapon you had a chance to take revenge if your comrades died.

The food supplies consisted mainly of dry fruits. It didn't take up much space and was very useful in case they were pinned against enemy forces in a siege-like situation. A dozen large containers stored up to a month's supply of nutrition; and they had replenished their stock only a few days back.

After the food supplies were lugged to the truck, the only thing remaining was to gather the bunk beds and dismantle the tents. Shafiq went inside and folded the blanket and bed and tucked them under one arm. His eyes fell on the chest, and he picked it up and emerged out of the tent.

"What's that you got?" It was Zia standing a few feet away pointing at the chest.

"Just my personal belongings." Shafiq didn't want to speak with Zia. Most of their discussions ended with arguments and sometimes fist fights. With his both hands occupied, he didn't want to confront Zia. Shafiq moved on.

"Wait up." Zia laid a firm hand on his shoulder to stop him. "Nothing in our group can be called personal. We are all brothers here and everything belongs to the group. We share everything we have with everyone. So what's in it? Food?"

Shafiq tried hard to restrain himself, but blood was boiling inside him. He knew that there was nothing to be gained by bickering with Zia, but the guy had an uncanny knack of getting under his skin. He turned towards Zia with angry eyes.

"That's none of your business."

"Oh! Is it? Open it up. Now!"

Shafiq looked around. Everyone's eyes were on him. They had all stopped working and were watching the spectacle. None of them gave an indication that they would either support him or go against him. He was on his own.

"I won't open it." Shafiq said in a firm voice.

"What?" Zia was momentarily stunned by the response, and then his expression hardened. "If you will not; then I will."

Zia reached out and grabbed the chest. Shafiq pushed him away. Zia stumbled backwards and then screamed maniacally as he advanced upon Shafiq. "You insolent dog, I will show you..."

"Stop it." A voice echoed nearby, and both of them halted on hearing their commander's order. Shafiq turned to see the dour expression of Malik. He was positively fuming and looked angrier than Shafiq had ever seen him.

Malik marched towards them. "I tell everyone that we are on a tight schedule, and instead of helping us, you both engage in a brawl. What is the meaning of this?"

Zia spoke before Shafiq had a chance. "It's Shafiq here. Instead of helping others with the loading, he was busy packing up his personal belongings." Zia pointed at Shafiq carrying only a chest. The bed under his other arm had fallen off when he had pushed Zia.

Malik's eyes narrowed and Zia continued, "I asked him to open his chest, but he refused."

Malik walked up to Shafiq and looked down on him. "I won't tolerate this insubordination. Open up your chest."

Shafiq couldn't disobey his commander. He inserted the key and opened the chest. The commander rummaged through the handful of contents and found nothing worthwhile.

"This is all junk."

"Yes sir." Shafiq said.

"Are you a dutiful soldier, Shafiq?" the commander asked.

"Yes, I am."

"Good, then the next time Zia gives an order, you better follow it." The commander turned to Zia. "Keep a close eye on him, and ensure that he is not lazing around."

There was a sadistic gleam in Zia's eyes as he looked at Shafiq. Shafiq tried to ignore it, but a dull ache throbbed through his forehead. Zia would now be all over him. He would not let him rest easy. And would gleefully report any transgressions he did.

Shafiq shook his head and quietly picked up his bed and blanket and proceeded to the truck. There was no sense dwelling upon it. Kismet didn't seem to be on his side.

The two hours passed quickly and it was time for their departure. Shafiq looked around and saw that the entire camp had been dismantled. The tents had been packed; the campfires were gutted and covered up; and a pit had been dug and the garbage had been dumped into it and filled with pebbles and rocks. The camp site now matched the desolation of the surroundings and it didn't look as if anyone had ever been there.

They were gathered in front of the two trucks that would take them to their destination. Everyone around was in an upbeat mood. Malik stood on top of the truck and fired a single shot to get everyone's attention. They all looked up.

"Brothers, we are now bound for Jalalabad. We will move first to Lashkar Gah, then Tarin Kowt and try to reach Ghazni before sundown. We will rest overnight in one of our safe houses in Ghazni. The next morning we will continue our journey to Jalalabad. Any questions?"

"Why aren't we going via Kandahar? That route is quicker." One of the men asked.

"We won't be going via Highway 1 or through Kandahar and Kabul; the roads are teeming with police and they could stop us for any reason. Now once we reach Jalalabad, we will meet up with our leaders and they will let us know what our mission is. Now hop into the trucks all of you. The sun is burning out the day."

Everyone scrambled to get into the trucks. A couple of them moved in next to the drivers; while the others squeezed themselves in the back of the truck. Shafiq got in next to the driver. He looked out of the window. A few stragglers were still determining which truck to fit into, and Malik was shouting at them. Finally everyone was aboard, and the trucks started on its long journey.

It was still early morning and the sun was out but there was no warmth as it shone down through the window. The air was chilly and the wind swept through the open windows.

Shafiq looked at the truck driver. "When do you think we will reach Ghazni?"

The driver kept his eyes on the road. "It will take around nine to ten hours. I am hoping that we reach there without any incident."

"What do you mean?"

"You remember, when we came to Dasht-e-Margow, we had travelled in the middle of the night?

"Yes, I remember. We moved under the cover of

darkness." Shafiq said.

"Exactly. Now, we are driving in broad daylight. It worries me."

"I am sure that Malik has his reasons." Shafiq looked ahead. They were passing through a narrow path at the base of two mountains that ended into a blind turn.

The driver slowed the vehicle as he took the turn. "Yes, he has his reasons. Malik said that the police are more inquisitive of people travelling in the night. They don't think we would risk travelling in the daytime. So by a twisted logic he thinks we would appear as just another goods truck among a hundred others on the road."

Shafiq thought back to the numerous times he had seen traffic on the roads held up by a row of trucks waiting to pass and he nodded. "He does have a point. I only hope that it works."

The driver looked at him, "We will know one way or other, by the end of the day."

Ormara Naval Base, Balochistan, Pakistan.

Hatim peered intently at the screen in front of him. The screen showed a dozen rectangular videos that formed a collage filling the whole screen. The videos on the screens appeared to have been paused. They showed full-colour images of gates, trees, oceans, lighted paths, docks, etc. They appeared to be portraits. It was only when someone walked across on the screen that one realized that it was a surveillance motion video and not a static picture.

The young man was looking at security videos with unblinking intensity.

Hatim stifled a yawn. It was mundane work, but it was extremely crucial. And it was the reason he was in this particular post. He had a keen eye for detail and a photographic memory and he never made mistakes. His friends mockingly called him 'Google'. It was said that once Hatim met someone, he could recall their names and facial features in his sleep. It was an envious skill set that had led him to be selected for this work.

He was the security analyst for the Ormara Naval

base affiliated to the ISI, Pakistan's Inter-Services Intelligence. And his job was to look for anything out of the ordinary.

The ISI was the intelligence agency of Pakistan. Tasked with gathering and analyzing Intel, its agents were spread all over the country as well as over the world. The organization was held in part dread and part awe by the Pakistanis. Its recruits were mainly from the Army and Hatim was one of them.

"Hey Hatim, need your help," his colleague in the next cubicle spoke.

Hatim pushed his legs and slid the chair a few feet to the adjacent cubicle where his colleague pointed to one of the screens. "Do you know who they are?"

Hatim wasn't surprised by the question. The moniker 'Google' meant that he was a walking database on people, events and things that others would forget in a day or two.

Hatim looked at his colleague's screen. He recognized the video feed. It was coming from Camera number 21. It showed the PNS Khalid. A number of crew members were working on the submarine. His colleague's finger pointed at two men who were talking to one of the officers.

Hatim's eyes narrowed as he observed the men, only the sides of the two men showed but nothing registered in his mind. "Zoom the image."

His colleague complied. The focused image showed the two men more clearly, but still Hatim didn't recognize them.

And that was a problem. Because Hatim knew by sight every person who was involved in the Ormara Naval base project.

"When was this taken?" Hatim asked, his eyes still on the screen.

"Yesterday afternoon."

"Give me the time-stamp. I will check it out myself."

His colleague gave it to him and Hatim slid his chair back to his cubicle. He entered the time-stamp and selected Camera number 22 which he estimated would give a better viewing angle. The image appeared on the screen and he hit Play.

From this angle, he could see the two men more clearly. They spoke to the officer at the dock for a few minutes and then the officer escorted them to the submarine. Hatim fast-forwarded the recording. After about forty minutes as per the time-stamp, the two men came out of the submarine. Hatim still couldn't figure out who the men were.

He was wondering what to do when an idea struck him. He could check the security logs. It should have an entry of who the men were. Hatim tapped a few keys on the keyboard and the log files for yesterday displayed on the screen. Thankfully, it had been a quiet day. There were only three entries. Hatim looked through all three entries. All of them had come in the morning, and the security logs indicated that the last person had left the naval base before noon. He looked at the video of the two men again. The time-stamp in the top right corner of the screen showed 17:02:11. There were no logs of two unknown persons entering into the Naval base at around five in the evening, nor were there any records of their exit.

So where does that leave us, Hatim mused. Two unknown men with no entry or exit records to their name. It either meant a system malfunction, or the two men found a way to bypass security. Both scenarios looked ominous.

Hatim drummed his fingers as he looked at the phone on his desk. The PNS Khalid's officer knew him and wouldn't say no to his questions.

Hatim picked up the phone and connected to the dock operator. Five minutes later he placed the phone down, more confused than ever. The officer had said that the men were part of the security team from Karachi. It didn't make sense. He knew the people in the Karachi department. These weren't them. Hatim leaned back in his chair and absentmindedly drummed his fingers on the desk. It was a reflex mechanism to jog his memory to solve the riddle that was consuming him.

But he was drawing a blank.

Hatim leaned forward and watched the video again. He watched as the two men approached the officer next to the docked submarine. They conversed for a few minutes and then the officer guided them towards the submarine. Forty minutes later the two men could be seen exiting the submarine. Hatim paused the video wondering what it meant. He pressed Play and watched the men climb down the submarine, reach the dock and go off-screen.

It suddenly hit him. He could check the entrance gate to see if the two men had exited. He pulled up the feed from the corresponding camera and checked the video. After two minutes, he doubled the video speed and after another minute he quadrupled it. No men exited the gates. Hatim upped the speed to 16x and continued watching. After forwarding through an hour of video feed, he stopped.

Hatim was flummoxed. Where did the men come from and where did they go?

He went back to Camera number 22 and watched the video again. As the men went off-screen he realized they would have been picked up by another camera. He checked the adjacent camera feed and right on cue they came into picture and walked alongside the wharf that outlined the side of the base. As Hatim watched them, he frowned. They were not going towards the exit of the underground base; they were going in the opposite direction deeper inside the base. He watched as they walked off-screen again.

Hatim noted the time-stamp and pulled out the video from another camera. This one showed the men walking towards the fuel station. As he watched, he saw the men don diving suits and plunge into the water out of sight.

Hatim's eyes widened. Their top-secret naval base had just been infiltrated. His hands shook as he dialled his superior's number.

Chapter 15

Sohail Akthar, Divisional Director of the ISI attached to the Ormara Naval base smashed the paperweight against the glass-topped desk in anger. A thin crack formed on the glass-top but Sohail was too preoccupied to care. He stood up and paced around his office clenching and unclenching his fists in uncontrollable rage.

It had all started when Hatim had rushed into his office after requesting an emergency meeting. And with every word that he uttered, his blood pressure kept spiking upwards.

It couldn't be true!

Two spies had infiltrated their naval base and escaped with no one being the wiser. It was only when he had seen the videos of them emerging from the water next to the diesel station that he felt a dull ache in his chest. And his pulse had been throbbing ever since.

He had contacted the submarine officer as well as the Captain, and the picture had become immediately clear. They were after the Babur-3 missiles currently being reconfigured in Sargodha. It was obvious that the spies would go next to Sargodha. He had to secure the missiles first, and then take care of these intruders.

"What should we do, sir?" Hatim asked in a tremulous voice.

Sohail had forgotten that Hatim was still in his office. He looked at him with an ominous gaze.

"First contact Sargodha and secure the missiles. Then we are going to take my plane and hunt down these spies. You and I are going to Sargodha."

Outskirts of Hyderabad, Sindh Province, Pakistan

The man stood next to his car on the side of the highway. He looked down at the car. He had removed one of the tyres and it lay on its side. To any of the vehicles passing by on the road, it would look like he was fixing a flat tyre. And that was the perception he wanted to create.

The agent from the Counter Terrorism Department

had arrived at that spot an hour ago. The place was twenty kilometres south of the city of Hyderabad in the Sindh Province in south-east Pakistan. While he appeared to be working on the flat tyre, his entire concentration was on the road, on the lookout for an Army jeep with four occupants. Based on the Intel he had, he estimated that they would pass by him in the next five minutes.

He didn't have to wait long. The jeep was visible from far off, and as it approached, he could see the four occupants with weapons on their sides discreetly observing the highway.

The man focused on the tyre as the jeep approached and then raced past him. He waited for a couple of seconds and then looked at the vehicle. The profile of the four men receded in the distance.

The man whipped out his mobile phone and spoke. "Get ready. The target just passed by."

"I wouldn't want another check point." Roshan said. It had been two hours since they had exited out of Karachi. They had driven non-stop at the highest speed the jeep could manage. But he couldn't shake the foreboding feeling that the Pakistani authorities were after them. A board indicated that the city of Hyderabad was twenty kilometres ahead. And he was sure that they would encounter another scrutiny of their vehicle. Baldev had took over the driving an hour back from Roshan. Roshan had thought of taking a nap, but he was too keyed up to fall asleep.

"Neither do I." Armaan said, "But they are actually toll plazas rather than check points. They are primarily set up to collect money, and not to check for guys like us."

"That may be the case," Baldev chipped in, "But don't forget the security cameras. If they connect the dots, we will come in the limelight. Our job requires that we should be camera-shy."

"What's that up ahead?" Hitesh asked.

Roshan looked up ahead. He could see a couple of big construction vehicles covering the span of the road. Big barriers were erected blocking their way.

Construction crews were all across the road. It was early morning and there was no traffic except for a solitary truck ahead of them. A traffic policeman pointed them to a diversion on a road that veered off the highway.

They exited the highway and turned into a smaller road behind the truck. Roshan watched the highway they were supposed to be on receding in the distance.

"Now where does this road go to?" Armaan muttered.

"I hope it connects back to Hyderabad somewhere." Roshan said. "Can one of you check the GPS? I don't want –"

A loud screeching sound from the truck in front of him cut his words. Baldev swerved the steering wheel, nearly colliding in the back of the truck as he evaded what could have been a ghastly accident. The tarpaulin covering the rear of the truck opened and a gun materialized.

Roshan grasped the situation immediately. "Get down." He screamed as a barrage of bullets nearly missed them as they swerved parallel to the truck. The driver's window swivelled down and another gun popped out. But Armaan was quick. He fired off three shots and the gun clattered down the road.

"How did they know?" Armaan huffed. No one had an answer.

A stream of bullets whistled past them. Roshan looked back and saw that another truck was bearing down upon them fast. Baldev had already seen it in the rear-view mirror and he slammed down on the accelerator. As they came adjacent to the first truck's cockpit, Roshan glanced inside. He noticed the driver's bloodied hand as he looked daggers at them. The driver swung his hand on the wheel and the big vehicle veered sharply towards them.

Baldev noticed it, but not too fast. "Brace for imp–"

The truck smashed sideways into the jeep.

Roshan's entire body jarred from the shock of the collision. His body crashed like a rag doll against the frame of the jeep. A wave of excruciating pain rippled through his shoulder and legs as he hit the frame. The shock of the pain resonated and vibrated through his bones. A shattering sound rend through the air as metal crumpled against metal with incredible velocity. Roshan moaned as he clutched his body fighting to stay conscious. He focused his eyes on the sight before him. Their jeep had gone off the paved road, and was hurtling along the side of the road strewn with pebbles and gravel. Baldev was struggling to get the jeep back on the road. The front passenger door was crashed in, and Armaan flopped motionlessly on the seat, either unconscious or dead. Roshan had no time to find out as a blur caught the corner of his eye.

The truck was making another pass at them. It accelerated as it reared to the opposite end of the road ready to smash into their jeep. Roshan looked ahead. A tunnel was coming up. The intentions of the truck driver were clear. Their jeep would get sandwiched in between the truck and the tunnel wall. Baldev had the accelerator pressed to the floor, but the truck was still speeding alongside them.

"Hold tight." Baldev yelled as they entered the tunnel. Roshan gripped the seat in front of him with one hand, while he pointed the handgun at the truck driver as he swerved again towards them. He had only one chance at making the shot.

He fired three shots.

A split second later he realized that all three rounds had missed the driver. The truck kept accelerating towards them ready to crush them into pulp.

"Baldev!" Roshan turned to Baldev to warn him. Baldev's eyes were not even on the road. His entire focus was on the truck as it came within striking distance. Roshan saw a movement of Baldev's feet followed by a screeching sound. His body jolted forward as Baldev hit the brakes and then pulled the hand brake hard.

Roshan watched as everything moved in slow motion. The truck's bulky profile loomed over them as it overshot past them and closed the area in front of them. The rear corner of the truck scraped the front of the jeep as it streaked to their side of the road.

Roshan looked at the rear of the truck. The tarpaulin was wide open and four soldiers had them in their sights ready to fire at them. Roshan watched with a blank expression as the men leaned in their guns making last second adjustments as they prepared to fire. They had avoided getting crushed by the truck, but he had forgotten about the men inside the truck.

There didn't seem to be any escape.

Roshan watched the men in the truck, paralyzed with fear. He knew his gun was at his side but he would be dead before he could even raise it against them.

"Move." he urged Baldev and then realized that their jeep had screeched to a standstill. The hand brake had worked too well for their own good.

They were a sitting duck.

As Roshan looked at the men about to kill them, the truck slammed heavily against the tunnel wall with a resounding crash. The men in the rear lost their balance and toppled off the truck. Roshan pulled out his gun and he watched Baldev do the same as they took advantage of the changed situation. He brought the FN2000 assault rifle in front of him and pointed it at one of the fallen men. He was grievously injured from the fall. A squeeze of the trigger and the man was put out of his misery. Roshan moved his barrel in the direction of another man and squeezed off a couple of rounds through the man's body. The man died instantaneously. Baldev in the meanwhile had neutralized the other two.

"We need to get out of here." Hitesh said. It was the first word he had spoken since the crisis unfolded, yet his tone was steady. He glanced back. "Now." His tone became high-pitched.

Roshan looked behind them. The second truck was coming straight for them. Baldev had already unlocked the handbrake and moved the vehicle into first gear. Roshan reloaded his gun as he took another peek behind him. The truck had covered the distance between them rapidly and was almost upon them. He looked in front. They were behind the first truck that had crashed into the wall. The intention of the second truck driver was unmistakable. The truck was going to ram into them, crushing them against the rear of the first truck.

Their jeep was moving but not fast enough. In a flash, Roshan brought around his gun and pointed it at the driver and pulled the trigger, unleashing a hail of bullets. He watched the windshield of the truck shatter into a thousand pieces. The driver slumped back into his seat, dead. The truck slowed a fraction, but the momentum was unstoppable as the truck barrelled into the rear of their jeep.

Baldev hastily turned the steering wheel as the jolt threatened to pummel them into the crashed truck in front of them. He furiously changed gears trying to outpace the rear truck which was still barrelling ahead right in line of the first truck.

Baldev swivelled the steering wheel hard as the truck loomed in front of them. The jeep started steering sideways, but it was going to be close. Roshan reached out and gave a sharp tug on the steering wheel. At the last moment, their jeep whisked out of the way. The trucks crashed behind them sending splinters of glass and scraps of torn metal in all directions.

Roshan sighed in relief but the relief was short-lived. A figure raced across the road and a bloodied hand clamped itself onto Baldev's neck. Roshan realized it was the driver from the first truck. Baldev instinctively tried to free himself but the driver swung the steering wheel with his other hand. The jeep swerved off the road and hurtled straight into the tunnel wall. The impact of the crash loosened the grip on Baldev's throat and he swung his massive elbow into the driver's face. The blow knocked the driver unconscious and he fell on the road.

Shots whistled past them. Roshan turned around and watched as six men emerged from the rear of the second truck and raced towards their vehicle. A jeep with more soldiers was approaching from behind the second truck.

They were going to be overwhelmed in half a minute.

"Give me covering fire." Baldev yelled as he switched into reverse gear. Roshan and Hitesh started firing and the men scurried around as they tried to avoid the hail of bullets.

Their jeep picked up pace and the men became more desperate as they came out of their cover to unleash a fury of bullets at the rapidly escaping jeep.

"I am out of bullets." Roshan said as he reloaded his weapon.

"So am I." Hitesh said as he ducked his head in the leather seat of the jeep as another relentless fusillade of bullets shot overhead.

"We are almost there." Baldev pointed to the exit of the tunnel. He had pinned the accelerator to the floor.

Suddenly, a loud pop sounded as one of the incoming bullets punctured the rear tyre. Roshan gripped his seat with white-knuckled fingers as the jeep careened out of control at high speed and flipped on its side. Roshan could see the ground coming fast at him.

His head struck something and everything turned dark.

Chapter 16

Inspector Mehdi looked at the four unconscious intruders in the jeep and swore. He had lost a lot of good men today. *Curse these Indians.* As the head of the Counter Terrorism Department for Hyderabad, he had put in an elaborate trap to snag them. Two trucks and a dozen men to capture four men, and they had nearly escaped. He was going to make them pay for what they had done. He pulled out his mobile and tapped a number.

"Inspector Gorbat, I have captured the intruders."

He heard Gorbat's relieved voice on the other end, "Thanks for letting me know. I will be in Hyderabad in three hours."

Inspector Mehdi disconnected the call and looked at his men. "Handcuff them and confiscate their weapons. I don't want them to pull another trick."

The pain felt like small waves lapping up a beach. Receding and coming, receding back and coming again. He could bear the small waves, it were the intermittent big waves that he dreaded. They rushed in, the wave of pain as it approached unmistakable from the others. It was rising up towards him. He could sense it clearly. It was bigger than the others. He gritted his teeth as the wave of pain approached. It was already hurting, and then the wave splashed all over his body swamping him in intolerable pain.

Roshan woke up.

He saw the untiled cement floor with its rough texture cover his area of vision. He realized he was lying face down. His tongue was sticking out and pressed to the floor. His mouth was dry and tasted full of cement powder. He coughed, the movement sending a spasm of pain through his shoulders and feet. It was then that he realized his hands were handcuffed behind his back, and even his legs were manacled. He managed himself into a sitting position and looked around.

They were in a jail. Four barren walls greeted him. A row of vertical steel bars made up a solitary door on one end. Roshan glanced at Armaan who was lying next to him. He had regained consciousness and was looking outside beyond the bars. Hitesh and Baldev were at the other end of the wall talking in low whispers. All of them were bound the same way he was.

"Isn't there something that our government can do to get us out of here?" Hitesh tugged with futility at his cuffs.

Baldev shook his head. "You knew the consequences when you signed up. This is a black op; the government will disavow any connection to us or our activities. We are persona non grata."

"So what do we do when they start interrogating us?"

"We are not sure how they were alerted to our presence. We have to first figure out if they suspect we are Indians."

"And what if they do?"

Armaan interrupted, "Shh, someone's coming."

Hitesh and Baldev broke off their conversation and nudged themselves away from each other. A moment later, the key clinked into the lock, followed by the sound of the bolt sliding open.

Roshan watched as a heavyset tall man entered and glanced at them one by one. His eyes finally settled on Armaan. He roughly pulled Armaan to his feet.

"Are you the leader?" Inspector Mehdi asked.

Armaan didn't answer. He stared straight ahead.

Mehdi paused for a moment and then brought his fist crashing into Armaan's stomach. Armaan's knees buckled and he doubled down in agony collapsing on his feet.

"I have very little patience for spies. You Indians think you are so smart. But we are better."

They know who we are; Roshan felt a wave of nausea engulf him.

Mehdi grabbed the hair at the back of Armaan's head and pulled him up. Roshan saw Armaan grimacing in pain. "You are going to die a slow and torturous death. There's no point being brave about it. Everyone eventually succumbs and tells all."

Armaan still kept quiet. Roshan saw the

commander's eyes redden with fury. He pushed him back and walked to the others. He pulled Hitesh to his feet.

"A young face. Do you want to die today?"

Hitesh looked at Armaan for guidance but Armaan's face was impassive. Mehdi noted the glance. He smiled. "So this person is indeed your leader."

Mehdi pulled out a gun and walked over to Armaan and placed the barrel against his temple. Mehdi looked at Hitesh. "You have three seconds. Tell me everything or watch your leader die."

Roshan's heart sank. Things were going from worse to horrible.

The chain of command of the Pakistan Counter Terrorism Department was efficient. After Mehdi had informed Gorbat, Gorbat in turn reported to his boss that they had caught the Indian spies. Within a few minutes the news had reached Islamabad.

To the Prime Minister.

It wasn't every day that one caught spies. The Inspector General of Police had phoned the PM and informed him of the developing situation in Hyderabad and the definite possibility that they had entrapped a team of Indian spies.

PM Mian Fateh nearly choked on his tea. "Indian spies?"

"Yes, Mian *sa'ab*. They were caught just a few minutes back. We are yet to interrogate them but I thought you would like to be made aware of the situation. They could be the ones behind the Gwadar blast."

"Get all the information that you can extract from them. I want names, places, mission details, their local supporters, everything."

"Yes sir." The IGP hung up the call.

Mian resented what he had to do, but his position required him to take a strong action. And he knew that he would.

Jagdish Inamdaar. How he hated the man. Mian knew when he heard of his candidature for the Prime Ministerial post, that he would sweep the elections and become the next Indian PM. When he had called in to congratulate the new PM, Inamdaar had been cold to his effusive praise. It wasn't unexpected, given the vitriolic speeches against Pakistan he had given during his election rallies. He claimed multiple times that if he were elected PM, he would put Pakistan in its place. And the electorate had lapped up his words with glee.

These Indian spies were undoubtedly the malicious handiwork of Inamdaar. Mian had to tell Inamdaar that his game was up with the capture of the spies. He looked at the phone, resentment spreading through him. Inamdaar was an impossible man. Arrogant and rough. Mian didn't like dealing with him.

Mian shook his head and furiously dialled the numbers on the phone. Someone had to tell Inamdaar off.

In New Delhi, Prime Minister Inamdaar looked at the incoming call on the hotline. He smirked. *Mian Fateh. Probably calling to request more of our surplus grid power.* He picked up the phone. PM Mian Fateh came straight to the point.

"We found out who is behind the Gwadar blast."

It wasn't what Inamdaar was expecting the Pakistani PM to say. He wasn't sure why he would call him personally to share this information. "I am glad to hear that."

"No need to be so happy. It was your men behind the Gwadar attack."

My men? The call was going completely off script. Inamdaar wasn't sure where he had got the information, but his allegation was baseless. "Mian *sa'ab*, you have been misinformed –" Inamdaar began.

"Oh, have I? We just caught your spies in Hyderabad. The truth will be out soon."

Inamdaar was fast losing his patience. He tried again. "We had nothing to do with Gwadar."

"Lies. Your spies are terrorising and killing my people."

"Enough!" Inamdaar exploded. "I will not listen to a person who heads a country which has a history of fomenting terrorism in our lands. You think we kill your people. Your extremism is of your own creation. Your people are killed by Pakistani terrorists. Stop blaming us."

"I'll know soon. And if I find you've sent in spies, then –"

Inamdaar had enough of this talk. He butted in. "Then what? What can you do? Nothing. You searching for my spies? All right, I have five thousand spies all over Pakistan, okay? If you open the door of your cabin, you will find a few outside watching your every move. Find them and hang them. Good day."

The apoplectic shrill reaction of Mian was still echoing in the receiver as Inamdaar slammed the phone down.

That's that. Inamdaar told himself. *Now to get back to work.*

But first, he had to call General Singh. He wanted to make sure that it wasn't really his men that Mian had reported as caught in Hyderabad. Inamdaar had shown bravado in dismissing Mian's claims, but if it was true, it would turn to be an uncomfortable situation.

"What!" General Singh felt like a clammy hand had gripped his heart.

"That's what Mian said," Inamdaar's angry voice poured through the speakerphone.

"I'll contact my men and check out for myself. Though I doubt it. My men have gone to Ormara and not Hyderabad."

"Okay, keep me informed." Inamdaar hung up.

Singh stared at the speakerphone wondering who the Pakistanis had caught in Hyderabad. Armaan periodically updated him on the status during his missions. He was already due for an update. He should have called back hours ago. But Singh wasn't too worried. He completely trusted Armaan. Armaan had delivered on countless missions against impossible odds. If he was late, there would be a reason for it.

But the doubt still lingered. What if it were his men that were caught?

And what were they doing in Hyderabad?

"So, you have decided to be difficult, eh?" Inspector Mehdi glowered at Hitesh.

Roshan watched Hitesh turn pale under the inspector's steely gaze. The commander had evaluated Hitesh as the most inexperienced of their group. Roshan looked around to see if they could make a hasty escape. There were two machine-gun slinging sentries just outside the metal door. Their unwavering eyes were ready for any eventuality and their guns were pointed right at the group. Moreover, they had no idea how many other policemen were present in the building they were detained in. Their hands were tied behind their backs; Armaan had a gun pointed to his head, and he had a few seconds to live.

Their situation was hopeless.

"One." Mehdi smirked maliciously as Hitesh turned green in trepidation. The inspector seemed to be enjoying himself. Armaan's head was bowed and his face was an impassive mask. Roshan wondered what was going through his mind.

"Two." The inspector intoned. Hitesh looked at Baldev for an answer, and Baldev gave him an imperceptible shake of the head. Was this how they were going to die? Roshan wondered. He watched as the inspector pulled back the safety catch of the gun.

Footsteps echoed in the corridor outside followed by a voice. "Sir?"

One of the officers of the CTD stopped outside waiting for a response from his superior. Mehdi turned to him and grunted impatiently, "Yes?"

"The Divisional Director of the ISI is here. He wants to speak with you ASAP."

Mehdi didn't respond. He stared for a long time at Armaan, and then at Hitesh, and then put his handgun back in its holster.

"When did he arrive here?" the inspector asked.

"Just a few minutes ago, sir." the officer said.

Mehdi walked out of the room, and gestured to the sentries. "Lock the door and keep a close eye on them."

As soon as the inspector left, Baldev kneeled next to Armaan. "You all right, buddy?"

Armaan looked into his eyes and smiled. "Just

another day at the office." He then turned to Hitesh. "I know what you are thinking. There is nothing to apologize to me. You stayed mum like you were supposed to. My life isn't in your hands or that inspector's. It's in my hands."

Hitesh nodded solemnly. "Thank you."

Armaan continued. "I don't think it's a coincidence the ISI Director is here. The ISI must have heard about our capture; they may want to take custody of us."

Baldev looked around at the cell, "That's sad. I was just starting to enjoy the hospitality of this wonderful suite."

Armaan said, "Things are sad indeed. Our comms, weapons and other assets have been confiscated. We have no way of contacting HQ to let them know of our situation. Our hands and feet are bound making our movement very restrictive. We are surrounded by at least thirty armed personnel of the Counter-Terrorism Department making our escape impossible. And finally, it looks likely that we will be taken to an unknown ISI facility where we will be slowly tortured to death and all the classified information in our heads will be extracted."

"An apt summary of our misfortunes." Baldev made a wry chuckle.

"Like I said, just another day at the office."

Chapter 17

Sohail Akthar, Divisional Director of the Inter-Services Intelligence, took a deep breath forcing his mind on the air that slowly entered and exited from his lungs. He repeated the exercise four more times ignoring the hub of activity that surrounded him in the Hyderabad branch of the Counter Terrorism Department. He had been cruising at forty thousand feet on his private plane en route to Sargodha when a notification had popped up on his mobile screen. One of the advantages of being an ISI top dog was that one had their eyes and ears everywhere. The message informed that a group of four suspected spies were caught by the CTD on the outskirts of Hyderabad.

It didn't take long for Sohail to come to the conclusion that these were the same spies he was in search of. He had immediately ordered his plane to be rerouted to Hyderabad. He then asked his assistant to ready a transport when he reached the Hyderabad airport; his destination being the CTD office in Hyderabad.

Now as he waited in the foyer of the CTD office, the dull ache in his chest had receded. It had been replaced by quiet optimism. If he played his cards well, this could be the biggest moment of his career. He would be known as the person who caught four spies red-handed. The only problem was that of jurisdiction, and that was the reason he had wanted to be the first person on-site in Hyderabad before the news spread like wildfire.

Sohail wanted custody of the spies.

"Director Akthar, welcome to our office." He heard a voice address him.

Sohail rose up and shook the hands of the inspector. "Inspector Mehdi, it's a pleasure."

"How may I help you, sir?" Mehdi came straight to the point.

"I have come here to take custody of the spies. My men will transport them in secure vans to our ISI facility. Thank you for apprehending them. They were on our watch-list for some time. We will take it up from here."

Sohail saw Mehdi's brow darken. He was expecting the reaction. The captured spies were the CTD's achievement and now the ISI would take them. The Inspector's next words were predictable. "Director sir, this was a routine counter-terrorism mission. We successfully executed it and captured the terrorists. I am not sure what role the ISI would have in a counter-terrorism exercise. As terrorists, the prisoners are under the jurisdiction of the CTD."

Sohail glared at Mehdi, "Inspector, the terrorists are not Pakistani nationals. They are foreign terrorists, and as such come under the purview of the ISI."

Mehdi was quick to refute his point. "I don't think that it has been established that they are anything but Pakistanis. Our team is still interrogating them. Our department has captured them, and we will follow the standard protocols for bringing these terrorists to justice. If and when we need your help, we will let you know. I wish you a good day, sir."

But Sohail was not one to be easily brushed aside. He leaned in close against Mehdi's face and growled in a low voice. "Do you know who I am and the power I command?"

Mehdi didn't flinch. "Yes sir, I do. I know your time is important and I do not wish to waste your time. If it's determined that they are foreign nationals, you'll be the first to know."

Inspector Mehdi left without a backward glance at the ISI Director. Sohail watched him leave as he seethed with rage.

The impudent upstart. What does he think of himself? I will show him.

Sohail pulled out his mobile and tapped a number.

Gorbat arrived three hours later at the CTD office in Hyderabad. The long drive had made him cranky and irritated. He had fought sleepiness and exhaustion while driving Bugti's car and the slow moving traffic had frustrated him. He adjusted his collar and smoothed the wrinkles on his uniform. Satisfied, he entered Mehdi's office. Mehdi stood up as he came in and the men shook hands.

"Have the Indians revealed anything so far?"

Mehdi looked down at the floor. "I am afraid there has been a complication."

"Complication? What complication?"

Mehdi looked back at Gorbat. "The Divisional Director of the ISI got wind of the capture of the spies. He personally came here to escort the spies. I refused citing that there is no evidence that they are foreign nationals. He then called my boss, and then my boss gave me a dressing down. An hour later, the four terrorists that you refer to as Indians were taken away in one of ISI's security vans."

"What?"

"Yes. We did the hard work of capturing them, and the ISI simply walked all over us. They will now also take credit for apprehending them, and portray them on national media like a World Cup trophy."

Gorbat felt the room closing around on him. This wasn't what he had expected when he had first started on the hunt. He had followed the scent from the Makran coastline to Karachi and then to Hyderabad. He had always felt like he was one step behind the culprits but Mehdi's words completely deflated him. Now the ISI had swooped in like an eagle, and the prey that was rightfully his had been seized from him.

It was something that he had seen multiple times in his fifteen year career. Opportunistic colleagues and superiors would claim his victories as their own, but he had never complained thinking that others also deserved their moment in the light. But over the years, the pattern became all too clear. When he would ask for reciprocal help, there was none to be found.

It was a difficult career for a person of integrity like him. He had never accepted a bribe in his life. He used to ignore colleagues around him who did, thinking that they had a financial need that justified taking money for providing services. He had steadfastly remained incorruptible hoping that his work would speak for itself. But he had seen junior after junior surpassing him; people who would shamelessly lick their supervisor's boot as well as pay money to get promoted. Gorbat was rarely promoted, but whenever there was an unsolvable case, everyone remembered him.

The motto of their department was 'Serve and Protect' and Gorbat had served and protected the common Pakistani people all these years without any expectation. To the extent that today was his son's birthday, and yet, instead of spending time with his family, he had spent the day in a wild-goose chase through half of Pakistan.

He hadn't slept in forty-eight hours hoping that this would be the chance to prove himself. After the capture of the spies, his supervisors would see fit to give him a much deserved promotion. But instead he had failed.

Gorbat sunk his head in his hands, full of despair.

Armaan's entire focus was riveted on his hands bound behind his back.

The bumpy road was making things difficult for him. They were imprisoned in the rear of a security van travelling to an unknown destination.

Armaan discreetly looked around. Hitesh and Roshan were sitting on either side of him. They were quiet, lost in their own thoughts. Baldev sat on the other end of Roshan. He wondered if Baldev had the same idea as he did.

Two guards sat opposite them, machine guns in their hands staring at them intently. Armaan tried to put up a nonchalant face, while his fingers worked furiously behind his back out of the guards' line of sight. In any case, the light in the container-type van was dim. Two small windows protected by a tightly meshed net were the only source of light. It was a steel enclosure. No one could get in or out without the keys. And the guards in front of him didn't have the keys. They were there just to make sure that Armaan and his team didn't do anything unexpected.

And the unexpected was exactly what Armaan had in mind.

Armaan looked at Baldev; he knew Baldev had also been trained in picking handcuffs. It was a skill that their trainers had made sure they regularly practiced. They would be handcuffed, and then told to escape. Armaan had a record of unlocking his handcuffs in under a minute using a miniature pin.

Concealed on the web of his hand, between his thumb and index finger was a strip of ultra-thin silicon layer that was indistinguishable from his skin. The silicon layer was around an inch in length and stuck to his skin with a special adhesive. The only function of the silicon layer was to conceal and camouflage an inch long pin made of high tensile steel.

Armaan probed with his fingers and found the silicon layer and gently peeled it to expose the pin underneath. He removed the pin and then positioned it against the keyhole of the handcuff concentrating hard as he felt the levers of the lock push against the pin.

The van lurched violently as they passed over a pothole and the pin nearly slipped from his fingers. Sweat started to form at his hairline. Armaan took a deep breath as he commanded himself not to panic.

During his practice runs he would work calmly and quickly knowing that it was a test. But now, seated in a semi-dark moving van with two gun-wielding hostiles staring coldly at him, it was hard work. Armaan kept repeating to himself that he was doing a mechanical task that didn't require his nerves to be so high-strung, but the ISI soldiers in front of him were making it hard for him.

Armaan looked at his colleagues, they were staring in space. Hitesh was looking down at the floor and Baldev was looking at the rectangular mesh window. Armaan picked the polished black boots of the soldier in front of him and stared at it while he worked furiously behind his back. The pin slipped off the levers a couple of times, but he forced his mind to keep it fixed on the texture of the lever. He kept twisting and probing with the pin till with a silent jerk, he felt the handcuff unlock.

Now what?

He assessed his chances. There were two policemen armed and with their weapons pointed at him. He was unarmed.

Chances of survival? Single digits.

He needed a better option.

Armaan caught Baldev's glance. Baldev pointed his

eyes at his rear. Armaan's gaze must have been questioning, because Baldev again flitted a quick gesture with his eyes towards his back. Armaan's eyes widened. *Did he interpret Baldev's gesture correctly?* Was he saying that just like him, Baldev had also removed his cuffs?

Armaan gave an imperceptible nod to Baldev indicating that his hands were also free. He then looked at the guards; they hadn't caught on to their silent conversation. Things were looking much better than they had a minute ago.

Chances of survival? Fifty percent.

Now the only thing left was to pull back the curtains.

It was showtime.

"Officer!" Armaan's voice had a surprised tone.

Both soldiers turned their gaze to him. Hitesh and Roshan sat straight, curiosity registered in their faces. The soldier next to him tightened the grip on his gun. "Yes?"

"My handcuff has come off. See this." Armaan slowly brought the open handcuff forward using his left hand; his right hand still behind his back. "You will need to handcuff me again."

He dangled the open handcuff right under the nose of the soldier. Now both soldiers were staring at him and their guns were pointed at him.

Just the way he'd expected.

A blur of motion passed from the side of his eyes as Baldev rushed at the soldier opposite him and gave him a well-directed punch that knocked him out cold before he had a chance to respond.

But the soldier opposite Baldev had a split-second longer time as he took in the scene of his comrade falling, and instinctively realized that things were getting out of hand. He moved his gun away from Armaan, and swung it towards the apparently more imminent threat of Baldev.

It was a mistake.

Now!

Armaan rushed forward at the soldier; his fists clenched and turned into battering rams. He swung them with lightning speed, the blow catching the soldier's jaw. The shot misfired and Armaan landed another blow behind his ear that pummelled him senseless.

Armaan looked at their handiwork. Both soldiers were unconscious, slumped down on the floor. He took the handgun and the machine-gun from one of the soldiers and gestured Baldev to do the same. He then walked over behind Hitesh and Roshan and fired two shots freeing their handcuffs. Then he did the same with the manacles tied to the feet. They were now free.

One of the soldier's radio squawked, "Number Seven, report status." The caller waited for an answer; when none came, he repeated the message.

Roshan picked up the radio to answer it, but Armaan stopped him. "They will immediately know it's not one of their men. They must have heard the shots and hence are trying to check if everything is all right."

A moment later, the second soldier's radio crackled to life, again asking for a status update.

"This doesn't look good." Roshan said. "They are now sure their men have been overpowered."

"They already know." Baldev peered through the mesh windows. "The van is stopping."

Chapter 18

As Armaan listened, he felt the wheels under him crunch to a stop, followed by the sound of the engine turning off. A sharp command was heard, followed by the sound of running boots. Armaan had tagged the number of soldiers in Hyderabad before entering the van. Two in the rear with the prisoners, two in the van's cockpit, and four in the accompanying jeep. Eight in all.

Two down, six to go.

They had two handguns and two machine guns between the four of them. But it still would not be much of a match against six armed men who assumed that their two colleagues in the van were dead, and were coming to avenge them.

"Hitesh and Roshan, prop these two soldiers in a standing position facing the door, and stand behind them holding them upright. When the ISI goons barge in, I want them to first see their colleagues. They will be coming in from the ambient outside light and looking into the relative darkness of the van, so it would take their eyes a moment to adjust before they realize their colleagues are not standing by themselves." He handed them both a handgun each. "Shoot at them from behind the cover of these guys."

As Hitesh and Roshan picked up the two men, Armaan gestured to Baldev, "You and I will be the primary firepower. We will lie prone on the floor next to our guys and fire at anything that moves outside the door. Roshan and Hitesh will be the backup. They will fire from behind these soldiers. The high and low angles of fire should make life difficult for the hostiles outside."

Armaan heard the metallic clink as the door was unlocked. He looked around to make sure everyone was in position. They were. Hitesh and Roshan were standing in the centre propping the unconscious soldiers with one hand and holding the handgun with the other. On either side of them, Baldev and Armaan were flat down on the floor with their machine-guns pointed at the door. When the soldiers would open the door, they would see their colleagues and hesitate to fire at them.

The split-second hesitation was all that Armaan needed.

The sound came of the bolt being swung across. *Anytime now*, Armaan mused, as he pointed his gun at the crevice between the two doors. The door opened a couple of inches and he saw a hand materialize. But it wasn't holding a gun, but something that Armaan recognised all too well.

"Stun grenade!" he screamed as he pulled the trigger. The ISI soldiers weren't dumb to open the door wide and risk annihilation. They would pop a non-lethal stun grenade inside the close confines of the van. The resulting flash and sound would disorient and temporarily blind them while the soldiers would advance inside and mow down the opposition. And since the soldiers had opened the door only a fraction wide, they wouldn't see their colleagues.

Armaan's elaborate deception was now useless.

Armaan wasn't the only one who had discerned the threat. The other three had come to the same conclusion. If the grenade landed inside the van, they were finished. They all started shooting at the hand carrying the grenade. Spurts of blood erupted followed by a scream. The grenade fell on the ground outside the door. A moment later a blinding flash and explosion rocked the ground outside. The impact of the shockwave on Armaan and his team was significantly reduced by the nearly closed door of the van.

"Move!" Armaan roared as he scurried up and kicked the door wide open. The blinding sunlight outside the van dazzled him, but he forced his eyelids open. They had only a few crucial moments. He levelled his gun at a soldier nearest him and pumped two rounds into his chest. The man shuddered momentarily and then stiffened in death. He looked to his right, two men were staggering from the effects of the stun grenade, both were in the process of training their guns at him. But Armaan had a split second lead over them. He swung his barrel and pulled the trigger twice. One man's head blew up; the second got hit in the shoulder. *Not good*, Armaan criticized his lack of reflexes. But it saved him, as the man's shot whizzed past his head. He pulled the trigger again and the man's head jerked back. It sported a bullet in his temple.

"Armaan!"

He heard a scream right behind him. Armaan looked to his left and saw one of the soldiers only a few feet away. His hand was on the trigger. Armaan was a second away from death. He immediately felt a presence nearby as Roshan rushed all his weight against him and tackled him away from the line of fire. As they fell down, a staccato of gunfire pierced the air above them. Armaan watched as Roshan trained his gun in mid-air at the assailant and shot three rounds. The automatic fire stopped; the assailant slumped to the ground.

"You all right?" Roshan lent him a hand.

"I'm all right." Armaan mumbled as he got up.

He looked into Roshan's eyes, they were full of concern. He turned his gaze away as he realized that Roshan cared deeply for his comrades, while so far, Armaan had only cared for the mission. He had dragged them to Hyderabad and the team had uncomplainingly followed him. They had accepted his arrogance as his leadership. He shook his head. Baldev was right. This wasn't how he had been earlier.

"Four dead." He heard Baldev's voice. "Where are the other two?"

The sound of a jeep's motor answered him.

"They are trying to get away." Armaan yelled as he and Roshan raced to the front of the van.

He saw two men accelerating away from the spot. They could escape and alert others. He couldn't let that happen. Roshan had already come to the same conclusion and was scoping the two men. Armaan levelled his own gun.

"I am targeting the one on the left. You take the guy on the right." He squinted his eyes at the target and pulled the trigger.

Both shots exploded almost simultaneously from their guns killing Sohail and Hatim instantaneously. The jeep slowed down and meandered to a stop.

"Clean up the mess. Check if they have something useful on them." Armaan gestured at the others.

He looked at the road they were on. It was a dusty

brown environment with a narrow strip of tarmac that made up the road. There were no buildings around and the road looked in poor condition. He estimated that it had been an hour since they left the Hyderabad CTD office which meant that they were around forty kilometres from Hyderabad. But he didn't know where they were headed. He observed the jeep in front of the van; tempted to use it, but he wasn't sure if it was the Makran jeep that had given away their location last time. They had been under surveillance twice as far as he knew. Once at the naval base and the second time at the Karachi check-post. One of them had been their undoing.

Armaan kept looking at the jeep, as he made his decision. The ISI used to keep a closed shop; nobody outside knew what they did, and only a few within knew the full picture. With the entire security team of the ISI eliminated, there was just an outside chance that their disappearance would not be noticed for a few hours. They could retrace their way back to Hyderabad, and dump the jeep outside of the city.

Armaan couldn't see any alternatives. They had to get away from the place as fast as possible. He saw Roshan glance at him and smile, happy to be alive. Armaan watched as Roshan rummaged through the pockets of the dead ISI men and saw a soldier happily following his leader's orders. A few moments ago, Roshan had saved him from certain death. Most people would have been paralyzed with indecision, but Roshan had heedlessly thrown himself in danger's way risking his life to save Armaan's.

Armaan remembered labelling him as a novice. No novice could display a killer instinct like Roshan had in the face of gunfire. He remembered before the Bangladesh mission, he had looked over Roshan's record and had been impressed. Maybe he had been too critical with Roshan's one lapse in Bangladesh, and had judged him since then solely on the basis of that event. No, Roshan deserved to be on his team. If not for him, he would have been dead by now.

"A Pakistani Rupee for your thoughts." Baldev stood next to him.

Armaan looked at Baldev and his cheeks burned. Baldev was jovial as always in contrast to Armaan's morose and curt behaviour. He had told Armaan that he would stick by his side because he was concerned by his craziness. Armaan felt a constriction in his throat. Maybe he had been crazy. Crazy enough to believe that he could focus on the mission and ignore his team members. But it couldn't work that way. No team, no mission. Only the support of everyone involved could make the mission work.

Armaan looked at Baldev in the eye. "I am sorry. I mistreated you and everybody else. And my foolishness jeopardised everyone's lives."

He couldn't hide his guilt from Baldev. In fact, Baldev knew it from the start, but he had let Armaan carry on hoping that he would come to his senses.

Baldev patted his side and smiled, "It's good to have you back."

That was it. There was nothing else to add. No rebukes. No I-told-you-so. Just gratitude for seeing his friend returned to his normal self. Armaan told himself that he would do whatever possible to protect Baldev, his brother-in-arms should any disaster befall them.

But first, they had to get out of here.

"I am thinking of using the jeep to return back to Hyderabad." Armaan said.

"It's a risk, but better than walking around in the dark. We should do it."

Armaan looked at the empty road that stretched to the horizon. "We don't have options, it's a bad situation. Our guns, equipment, and comms are gone. No money and no idea where we are."

"Well, on the bright side, our situation is much better than what it was five minutes ago in the van. We can't do anything about our equipment, so we are borrowing our ISI friends' guns. We found some money and a mobile with GPS that shows that we are west of Hyderabad." Baldev handed a mobile to Armaan.

Armaan's face broke into a grin. Baldev's perspective on the situation was better than his. "All those days of endless analysis of worst-case scenarios have made me a pessimist. So the team found guns and money? That's good."

"But there's still one problem."

"What's that?" Armaan asked.

"How do we contact home base?"

"Leave that to me." Armaan replied.

Armaan tapped a number on the mobile that he recalled from memory. It was answered in one ring.

Armaan introduced himself, "Home base, this is Markhor, actual."

Armaan's call sign was Markhor, a species of wild goat with distinctive coiled horns that was the national animal of Pakistan. He included the word 'actual' to indicate that it was the leader of the team on the line.

"Markhor, this is Home base. What's your status?"

Armaan spoke for a few minutes with the General, going over everything that had happened since their infil in Makran followed by the events at Ormara Naval Base and the absence of the missiles. He then talked about the lead on the missiles in Sargodha, and how they were caught on the outskirts of Hyderabad. He concluded with their escape a few minutes back.

"Our mission has suffered setbacks. We have lost mission-critical assets and are pursued by hostile elements. Recommend future course of action."

General Singh said, "Our original mission was to infiltrate Ormara and secure the missiles. It was to be an in-and-out mission with the team returning back to the sub."

"Yes, sir."

"So, what made you decide to chase the missiles instead of returning back to the sub?"

Armaan said, "I wanted to complete the mission, sir."

"Really?" The General's tone was sarcastic. "And I think that it didn't occur to you that your unilateral actions were a complete breach of protocol?"

"But, isn't the mission critical for you?"

"Are you trying to cross-question me?" General Singh smirked. "Yes, the mission is critical, but it doesn't mean that you are free to play cowboy. You were chosen because I trusted you. I believed you would let me know if things fall apart. You've seriously dented my faith in you through your actions. This mission is doomed."

Armaan said, "We can still salvage this, sir."

"How? The mission is dead and buried."

"We can go to Sargodha and complete the mission. I know what's at stake. Please give me the permission to proceed."

"You believe you can still do this?" The General's voice was thoughtful.

"Yes sir."

"Are you sure you understand the risks of continuing with the mission?"

"Yes sir, I do."

"Be advised that Sargodha comes in the northern half of Pakistan. It is quite far from your current location. The further you move north, the farther you are from the coast and an emergency exfil."

"Yes sir, I understand the risks."

"While we won't be able to provide direct support, you will get logistic support from one of our contacts. He is an LTRA in Sukkur. Here's how you will get in touch with him..."

Armaan was surprised that the General had nurtured a Long Term Resident Agent so close to their location. He shrugged off the thought as he focused on the General's instructions for contacting the agent.

"Good luck, Markhor." General Singh signed off.

"What did the General have to say?" Baldev asked as soon as the call finished. Hitesh and Roshan had also joined them.

"We are at a decision point. If we move north, it will be difficult for the support group to assist us in real-time. The General asked me if we would like to continue the mission."

Roshan said, "We should continue the mission. Let us finish what we started." The others nodded in agreement.

"I told the General that we would like to continue the mission. But on a sombre note, you have to understand that it won't be easy, and our risks multiply exponentially with every hour we take to fulfil our mission."

"We have been together on all the missions,

Armaan." Baldev said. "You can count on me."

"I am in too." Roshan said. "Just give me the orders."

Hitesh chuckled, "Without me, there will be no one to manage the technical aspects. Of course, we are in this together."

Armaan smiled listening to their responses. "The mission is a go."

Chapter 19

"We have arrived."

Roshan woke up instinctively. He was sleeping in the back of the jeep after having driven north till two am. Hitesh had taken up the driving and Roshan had immediately fallen asleep. He peered around. The sun had just risen in the east and he could see a town a few kilometres ahead beyond two bridges crossing over a river.

"Is that Sukkur?"

"Yes." Hitesh replied.

Roshan shivered in the early morning chill as he tried to remember what he knew of the town. Sukkur was three hundred kilometres north of Hyderabad on the banks of the Indus River in Sindh province. It wasn't on their list of must-memorize locations, and especially not for this mission. The only other thing Roshan remembered was that Sukkur was close to Pano Aqil, a forward base missile launch site. Roshan rubbed his arms wondering how many unknowns they had to contend with before their mission was accomplished.

An hour later they were in front of a Dry Cleaners shop. Roshan watched as Armaan took out a trouser they had purchased from a nearby store, wrote a message on the inside of its pocket and handed it over to Roshan.

"Come. We have to launder this pant." Armaan walked to the shop followed by Roshan.

The shop was small with ironed clothes arranged in one corner, and bundles of messy clothes in another corner. In the centre of the shop was a table and an old man was meticulously ironing the clothes on it. Armaan waved to the man.

"It's not even 8 am and you are working in the shop?"

The old man looked at him and smiled. "I have been up since 5 am. My worker is on leave and I have to do the ironing by myself."

Armaan took the trouser from Roshan and placed it on the counter. "I have an interview today. Would it be possible for you to iron this urgently?"

The old man took the cloth. "Urgent orders cost double. Are you okay with that?"

"Yes, that's fine by me. When can I get it back?"

"Come back at 11 am."

As they exited the shop, Roshan asked, "What was that about?"

"The proprietor of the shop is the intermediary between our contact in Sukkur. The General gave me the address of the Dry Cleaner shop. The conversation we had was a coded sequence that validated both parties. I have written a message on the inside pocket of the trouser requesting contact with the Long Term Resident Agent. Either the proprietor will send the message, or the LTRA will come to check if he has messages for him. Once he receives the message, he will write a reply on the other pocket. The process is almost foolproof. Let's see how the agent responds."

They took up accommodation in a rundown hotel and paid in cash. Armaan ordered everyone to sleep. They hadn't had much sleep the past couple of days, and Armaan knew the value of a rested and refreshed unit.

Roshan lay down on the bed and as he closed his eyes, he heard Armaan admonishing Baldev for still sauntering around. By the time Baldev was ordered to his assigned bed, Roshan had already fallen asleep.

When Roshan woke up it was already afternoon. He heard Baldev talking with Armaan.

"The graveyard at three pm?"

"Yes, that's what was mentioned in the reply. It is an open area. Very difficult to conceal oneself, both for him and for us. If there's a deception, it can be spotted easily. It's a sign of trust as well."

Roshan glanced over at his watch and cursed. His watch was no longer there, courtesy of the CTD. He didn't know the time. He got up and looked at the wall clock. It was noon. He had been asleep for four hours.

"Having said that, we need to be alert." Baldev continued talking.

"Yes, we will be there by two pm and scout the area first." Armaan noted that Roshan was awake. "Roshan, you and Hitesh will be the backup team for today's rendezvous. Let's get moving ASAP. I will explain the details on the way."

The old man straggled with heavy steps as he walked alongside Shikarpur road, dragging his broomstick behind him. People passed by him in their daily routine ignoring him. And why wouldn't they? He looked like just another common labourer that was earning his daily bread. His clothes were unkempt and torn in few places, his hair was dishevelled and he had an air of lethargy around him.

But for Sultan, it was just another day in a well-rehearsed role of espionage. Sultan had trained himself to hide behind multiple facades; from a seasoned angel investor to a lowly wage earner, he knew how to fit into the role that was required for the moment.

Sultan visited the Dry Cleaner shop every day, and the proprietor gave him 'messages' when they were available. The messages were in the form of clothes that he would take home. Usually stitched on a piece of cloth, or directly written on them would be messages that would tell him of his next steps. Even if the authorities put a tab on him, they would never be able to know that the Dry Cleaners shop was the dead drop.

Today's message however was different.

It involved an actual 'contact'. It was quite different from the one-way instructions that he received. He wasn't sure if it was genuine. It was unconventional and risky.

But Sultan couldn't ignore it. If it was a genuine request, it must be really important for the other party to directly contact him. Eventually, he had decided he would go undercover; the role of a graveyard sweeper wouldn't attract any attention.

As Sultan walked across the innumerable *chawls* that crisscrossed through the locality, the space in front of him widened out revealing the expanse of the Sukkur graveyard. At two hundred metres in width and nearly a kilometre in length, it was the biggest open space in Sukkur. Sultan walked on the periphery of the graveyard with satisfaction. It was exactly like he remembered. There was no place to hide here. He bent down and started sweeping the ground, occasionally stretching his back as he looked at the roads that led into the ground. There were only three routes to the graveyard and he intended to keep an eye on all of them.

Sultan immediately spied them. Two men who were a bit too muscular to be anything other than military. As he watched, he saw the men make a furtive glance behind them. He looked at where they were looking and espied another two men taking shelter in the shadows of one of the *chawls* at the edge of the graveyard. He looked to see if there were any others, but there weren't.

Now, the only question that remained was whether these people were genuine or a threat? Sultan used his broom and languidly swept the ground inching closer to the men, observing them. He saw that the men were looking warily around them every few minutes. It wasn't the look of a hunter, but rather the hunted. They were worried about being out in the open. And that reassured him. Law authorities wouldn't act the way these men did.

He relaxed and approached them.

"I am Sultan, your contact in Sukkur."

One of the men replied, "I am Armaan, and this is Baldev. We were told you could help..."

Gorbat hung up the phone with a heavy heart. He glanced around the almost deserted foyer of the Hyderabad CTD office as he debated on calling back. It was eight o'clock in the evening and his son had refused to speak with him. And his wife had been equally vocal. She chided him for being absent for his son's tenth birthday.

"How could you? All my friends were asking about you? I had planned for his birthday weeks in advance, and you promised you would keep your duties aside. And it wasn't just any other birthday, it was his tenth birthday. All I had asked was for one day, just one day to spend with your family, and this is what I get. Forget about me, you even broke the poor child's heart. Now, what are you going to do?"

Gorbat had no answer to the barrage of criticism

raining upon him. He understood her point of view; he hadn't been present for his little boy's birthday. He tried to reason with her and that's when she had hung up.

His wife was right. It had been all for nothing. He decided that he would take the next train back to Quetta. He checked the railway train schedules. The next train to Quetta was the Bolan Mail from Kotri junction at 9:05pm, but it had been delayed by three hours and would leave at midnight.

Gorbat shrugged. For whom am I doing this? Trains never run on time. Electricity is unavailable for many hours every day. The department is short on resources. Our leaders are corrupt and are unofficial billionaires while we struggle to make even a millionth of what they make.

For whom am I doing this? He asked himself again. Gorbat knew the answer. It was the undying integrity within him that refused to make him surrender to the temptations of corruption and injustice. He did what he did for himself; and for the common Pakistani people. It was the hope for a better tomorrow that directed his actions. And it had been a frustrating fifteen years wait for the ideal tomorrow.

He only hoped that tomorrow would come soon enough.

There was a TV in the foyer tuned to one of the news channels. He wondered what the media would make of it. They would have had a field day. But to his surprise, the news headlines were full of innocuous and boring stuff. He switched to other news channels; there was nothing. No news about captured spies.

Gorbat was surprised. He was familiar with Sohail, and they had worked together a couple of times during his career. The man was brilliant but self-obsessed. He would take any opportunity to toot his own horn. He had been the guest speaker on multiple news shows. It was very unlike him to keep a news like this quiet.

Gorbat called Sohail's office. His secretary picked up the phone.

"This is Inspector Gorbat Khan of the Quetta CTD. I would like to speak to Director Akhtar."

"I am sorry, sir. But he left for Sargodha in the

morning."

"Sargodha?"

"Yes, he took his private plane to fly to Sargodha."

"Okay, please leave him a message to contact me."

"Sure, sir. I will do that."

A few minutes later the secretary called him back.

"It's strange. I have been calling him all afternoon for various appointments, but he didn't pick up the phone. I called the ISI office in Sargodha and they say he didn't come. I will let you know as soon as I get in touch with him."

A germ of doubt began to grow in Gorbat's mind. Sohail had said he would be going to Sargodha in the morning, yet a few hours later he was in Hyderabad overseeing the custody of the Indian spies. Maybe he was still here in Hyderabad. He picked up the phone and dialled the local ISI office in Hyderabad and spoke for a few minutes.

As Gorbat listened, he realized that something was wrong. Very wrong.

One of the things that Gorbat prided upon was his ability to pick up random set of events and merge them into a meaningful whole. It was the ability along with his doggedness that had helped him solve countless cases.

As the disparate pieces of information collided into his brain, he tried to stitch together a narrative that would make logical sense. The Divisional Director of the ISI had left in a plane bound for Sargodha. He didn't go to Sargodha, but stopped at Hyderabad two hours later. The Director's plane was still in Hyderabad, but the Director was missing. And no news was broadcast about the Indian spies.

It all pointed to one thing. Gorbat realized that only one scenario could explain all the facts. The Indians had killed the Director and had escaped.

Gorbat rushed out of the foyer. He had to take Bugti's car and follow the trail.

The chase was on again.

Chapter 20

"You had a plan for Ormara." Roshan said, "Do you have a plan for Sargodha?"

Sultan had taken them into a safe house in Sukkur. The safe house overlooked the Indus River. Sultan had provided them refreshments and Roshan had been glad for once. Now that his growling stomach had ceased howling, he could focus on the question that was burning in his mind. He wanted to know what Armaan had planned.

"I am still thinking about it."Armaan replied. He looked at the team. "I would be happy to hear your inputs as well."

Hitesh spoke up, "We first need to determine where the missiles are kept. The Kirana hills have numerous missile silos. We will need to figure out which silo is hosting the SLBMs. If you can get me close enough, I will be able to tap into their database and find out which silos have the missiles. The next step will be disabling the security systems for a limited time while we infil into the compound. If everything goes well, we should get access to the missiles without anyone being the wiser."

"We will need an exfil plan after our objectives are completed."

"I will drive you to Sargodha and return you to the coast." Sultan said before anyone could speak.

Armaan shook his head. "No, its best you don't get involved in this."

"I am already involved. So why not go all the way?"

"But you are a deep asset, not a black ops operative like us. We can find our way."

"I don't think so. There are scores of checkpoints on the route, and I have a valid driver's license with my photo. You don't have an ID because your papers were taken away. Plus you don't have a vehicle. I own a Land Rover. I have put a government label on the car, and everyone thinks a political big shot is travelling around."

"All right." Armaan conceded.

"Once the mission is completed, you will exfil the same way you came in. I will drive you back to the coast and ensure that you return safely to the sub."

"Thanks. A question. Do you have any weapons and tactical gear that we may be able to use?"

"Yes." Sultan walked over to the far wall and pressed a button under the shelf. A hidden door popped out. Sultan slid the door wide open.

"Here are your toys. Let me know if you need anything else." Sultan said.

Roshan stared with disbelief at the array of weapons. Every type of gun, rifles and small arms was on display along with various tactical gears. "Seriously, where did you get your hands on these?"

"If you have the right contacts, you can literally walk into a place in Karachi and buy them off the counter. How do you think the terrorists get their weapons?"

"You have a Vidhwansak?" Armaan's tone indicated he was impressed.

Roshan looked at the massive ultra-modern gun that dwarfed all the guns around it. He was familiar with the Vidhwansak, an anti-materiel rifle with a stupendous range of two thousand metres. Roshan had never figured out why they spelled the word 'materiel' incorrectly; a term to distinguish the gun as something that could destroy material like barricades and walls; which was different from all other guns which were designated as anti-personnel guns, that is, for killing people. At six feet in length, the Vidhwansak was as tall as a man. It was used by the Indian Border Security Force for counter-sniping infiltrators on the border. It packed such a punch that it could blast a hole through a cement wall even at a distance of two kilometres. It was the perfect answer for terrorists hiding inside terror launchpads.

"Yeah," Sultan nodded, "you want it?"

"Yes, and also the Night Vision Goggles, M4A1 carbines, the SVD Dragunov, Glock 17 pistols and the F2000 assault rifles with red-dot scopes."

Sultan picked out the weapons and started to hand them over to the team. He also handed a GPS set, miniature radio earpieces and a tablet to Armaan.

"Yep, these are my kind of toys. Looks like we are all set."

"Great. We move out in ten minutes." Sultan declared.

"Let's go over the plan once again." Armaan said. "Hitesh, you start first."

Roshan leaned in close to Armaan as he watched the others join in. They were hidden in a grove of trees two kilometres northwest of Kirana Hills in Sargodha. It had taken Sultan around twelve hours to traverse the seven hundred and fifty kilometres from Sukkur to Sargodha. Luckily, it had been an uneventful ride. They had stopped at a safe house on the outskirts of Sargodha. Armaan had made a brief call to the General and informed that Sultan had brought them safely to Sargodha.

They had already gone over the plan a couple of times on the way here, but Armaan had made them repeat the details to make sure that each person knew their role. Sultan had driven them within ten kilometres of the facility. From there they had walked stealthily staying away from the main road and keeping to the shadows. Now sitting in the darkness of the trees, Roshan could see the barbed wire fences outlining the border of the facility. He focused his attention back to Hitesh who was speaking.

"Do you want me to start with the overview or just the plan?" Hitesh asked.

"Start from the overview. It's best if everyone is synced in."

"All right," Hitesh said, "The Central Ammunition Depot on Kirana Hills is one of Pakistan's largest munitions and missile storage base. The location of the hills in close proximity to the PAF Base Mushaf makes it ideal for quick weapons loading, deployment and maintenance. The missile silos are not kept at a single location, but rather they are stored deep underground in bunkers spread all over the hill."

Roshan remembered the satellite images of the Central Ammunition Depot. It looked like a collection of concrete tents spaced hundred metres apart on the foot of the hills.

"Right. What's the evaluation of the security?"

Armaan asked.

"We have double-fenced security perimeter with guard towers every two hundred metres. Plus we have search lights that crisscross over the perimeter that will highlight anyone attempting to get in. If we get past that, there are guards roaming inside the compound plus two guards at the entrance to each bunker. If we find a way to reach the bunker without coming to the attention of the guards and having the entire garrison firing a hailstorm of bullets, we will still run into a roadblock. The bunker entrance requires a swipe-in access card and a biometric fingerprint." Hitesh inhaled deeply. "That's what we are up against tonight."

Armaan shrugged. "Just another day at the office…"

Ijaz Ibrahim gazed at the panel of sixty inch LCD screens in front of him. He wondered if the Intel he had been provided was wrong. It couldn't be; his gut told him.

Ijaz was the Security head of the Central Ammunition Depot at Sargodha. He had been inducted in this role just a few months back. He had joined Sargodha as one of the deputy security officers in charge of perimeter security. He had come to the notice of his supervisor when he had started unconventional yet effective security drills, brutal training regimens and frequent mock drills. It wasn't long before he was promoted to his designation as Head of Security.

Yesterday, the Divisional Director of the ISI had sent an alert to Sargodha indicating that Indian spies were in pursuit of the Babur-3 missiles and they would soon reach Sargodha. The alert ordered that the Babur-3 missiles be shifted immediately. And when the Indian spies reached the Ammunition Depot, they were to be captured.

Ijaz had duly followed the Director's orders and the missiles were safe; now the only thing left was to capture the Indian spies. He had told his men to be on the lookout for intruders and to report anything unusual to him immediately. He further gave explicit instructions that any intruders be captured alive.

Now, as he scrutinized the activity on the LCD

screens, he had only one question in his mind.
When would the Indians attack?

Chapter 21

Roshan crawled in slow motion along the ground, his eyes roving everywhere, ears attuned to the slightest sound, and his nerves on edge. The night was warm and sweat poured down his neck. The olive-green jacket camouflaged his body among the trees, but a metre ahead, the trees ended and then it was an open clearing till the perimeter fence.

Roshan took in the scene in front of him. On either end of him, one hundred metres away to his left and right stood the two guard towers, the sentries atop the towers were barely visible as they stood motionless, but Roshan knew that their eyes swept the area in sync with the searchlights. He would have to stay out of range of the lights. He looked at the barbed fences. The inner and outer fences were spaced five feet apart. He assumed that the fences were electrified barriers electrocuting anyone who touched it. Beyond that, he could see the Weapons Storage Bunkers. As warned by Hitesh, two men manned the entrance to each bunker. The bunkers were arranged like grid points equidistant from each other and continued on barely visible in the distance.

"Markhor One, this is Three. I am in position." Roshan whispered. A micro radio-cum-mic was embedded in his ear, courtesy of Sultan. The cutting-edge comm piece fit easily inside his ear canal and was virtually undetectable. Everyone had synced in to the secure frequency in advance.

Armaan's voice came clearly as if he was standing next to him, instead of the hundred metres that separated them. "Three, this is One. I see you. Stand by till Four gives the green signal. Four, are we ready?"

"A few minutes more," Hitesh replied. "I installed a network sniffer and have taken over one of the sentry's mobile phone. I then masqueraded as a mobile network operator for the mobile and installed a special over-the-air update turning the mobile into a zombie. Now I am using the mobile to piggyback onto the security network."

"Whatever…" Roshan had never figured out the

geek language of computer nerds. "Just let me know when the security system is down." He scanned the perimeter once again, making sure that no guards were alert to their presence. Armaan had told him to take the lead today and he couldn't afford to fail him.

"I am in!" Hitesh declared in an emphatic voice. "Three, get ready."

"Ready to the point of boredom, Four."

Roshan watched the pattern of the searchlights as he crawled out of the grove. Now, he was in the open and every second mattered. He knew that Armaan had his back. If either of the sentries on the guard towers detected him, the team's scoped silencers were trained on them, and they would be killed before they could raise an alarm. On the other hand, if they were detected they had their escape plan in place.

Sultan had stayed behind in the car five kilometres away. He would be their getaway guy. If everything went as planned, they would not need him to come dashing in like a Formula One racer to extract them out.

Roshan raised himself into a crouch. In a few seconds from now, the search lights would swing away from the fences and sweep the areas further away. It would give him thirty seconds to run the fifty feet to the fence. Hitesh was monitoring the search lights and would give him the green signal to take off.

"Three, this is Four," Roshan heard Hitesh, "Counting down. Three, two, one, go."

Roshan dashed forward making a beeline for the fences. He took a quick peek at both towers, but he couldn't see anything in the dark. He would have to trust the team who had their eyes on the sentries. He focused ahead at the fence; his job was to cut through the fence without being detected. As he ran, he pulled out a laser gun in one hand and a roll of canvas cloth in the other hand. He counted off the seconds in his mind as he reached the fence.

I have another ten seconds; Roshan huffed as he unrolled the canvas cloth. The texture of the cloth was brown matching the colour of the ground. He lay down on the ground and covered the cloth over him like a blanket. He hoped that when the search lights passed over him, he would be indistinguishable from the ground around him.

"I am at the fence under cover." Roshan whispered.

"Copy that, Three."

He waited panting heavily under the cloth for the next update from Hitesh. A piercing light lit up the cloth like daylight and Roshan fought against the urge to move or fidget as the searchlights probed the ground in front of the perimeter.

Roshan slowed his laboured breath and clenched his fists in an effort to master himself as he glanced at his body that was illuminated under the cloth. He felt alone and exposed. It's only for a few seconds, he told himself. It was virtually impossible for them to detect him under the cloth at a distance that the tower was.

After an interminable wait that had his heart thudding in his chest, he saw the light sweeping away leaving him in darkness. A moment later, Hitesh spoke in his ear. "Three, you are clear. Get to work. You have twenty seconds."

The signal indicated that Hitesh had disabled the security alarms on the perimeter fences. Now he had to cut through the fence.

Roshan got up and swiftly went to work, cutting off a small hole using the laser gun. He just reached the inner fence when Hitesh's voice chirped in his ear.

"Get back under cover."

Roshan again lay down on the ground and spread the cloth over him. He reminded himself that there was no hurry and he just had to be patient. The light shone down on him once again scrutinizing the camouflaged cloth like a lab specimen under a microscope. Once the light passed off him, Hitesh gave the signal and he now focused on shearing through the inner fence, sweat pouring down his neck. He was almost done when Hitesh shouted in his ear.

"Get back in cover."

The stress had made him forgot to count the buffer time he had before the search lights was upon him. He didn't even look behind as with a single motion he laid himself flat on his back and scurried to cover himself under the camouflage. In his hurry, he pulled the cover too high over his head and his boots slipped out from under the cover.

Oh bother. He reached down to adjust the cover, but the beam of the powerful flashlight was immediately upon him. He could feel the blood throbbing in his neck and ears; but couldn't suppress it. The boots would give him away. They would look like a pair of dark green patches against the brown soil. He expected a hail of bullets firing over him piercing through his body and killing him. The long seconds passed but the light didn't move at all. Perhaps they were already onto him. He half-expected to hear shouted commands ordering his death, but they didn't come.

Eventually, the flashlight went away, but Roshan's body had gone rigid with fright.

"Move." He heard Hitesh, but he felt too exhausted. He slowly pulled off the cover gasping audibly. He was completely worn out with the ordeal. He straggled the couple of steps to the inner fence and cut the remaining portion of the fence and then dragged himself lethargically through it. Once inside he collapsed on the ground trying to catch his breath.

"This is Three." Roshan huffed. "Breach complete."

Armaan replied, "Acknowledged. Two is next."

Roshan watched as Baldev ran to the edge of the grove and waited in the shadows. He would also dodge the search lights to cross into the perimeter followed by the others.

Five minutes later, all of them were huddled together inside the compound. Hitesh was already working on his tablet.

"Can you locate the goods?" Armaan asked.

"Trying that now." Hitesh replied, his eyes on the screen. "I am accessing the Inventory database."

Roshan looked around. After the blazing bright light at the exterior side of the fence, it was pitch dark inside the compound. He pulled down the Night Vision Glasses attached to his helmet over his eyes; the world around turned into green. He could see a lone sentry far off to his right. Two hundred feet in front of him was one of the many bunkers that dotted the landscape. Two sentries walked across it, unaware of their presence.

Now the only question was which one housed the Babur-3 missiles. After a few minutes, Hitesh pointed on his tablet.

"This one."

Everyone peered to get a closer look.

Roshan looked at the Weapons Storage Bunker that Hitesh was pointing at among the multiple others that surrounded it on the map, and tried to get his bearings in relation to their destination.

"It's five hundred metres east of our location." Hitesh said.

"Okay, let's move." Armaan said.

Roshan crept slowly behind the others. They walked cautiously in a half-crouch keeping a wide berth from the bunkers and the sentinels posted there. The Night Vision helped. They could see the guards pacing the grounds in a predictable routine. They waited for the guards to pass and continued their way forward.

Fifteen minutes later, they were in front of their target. The Weapons Storage Bunker looked no different from the others they had passed. It had two sloping roofs on either side that extended down to the ground making it look like a concrete tent. The door was recessed deep inside as a precaution against an air attack. A neon-lit square on the right of the door indicated the biometric readout. To his surprise, there were no guards patrolling in front of the bunker.

"I don't like this." Armaan said. "Where are the guards?"

"Probably on a loo break," Baldev smirked. "Let's get inside before they return."

"Hitesh," Armaan said, "Can you get us inside bypassing the biometric access?"

"Yes," Hitesh held out a card, "I already added my profile and this card to the security database. My fingerprints will get us through."

Armaan looked around. "Then let's get in ASAP."

Roshan followed Armaan and the others to the bunker. He looked around but there were no guards around. His silenced Glock 17 was out of its holster and ready if anyone was going to spring a surprise. But no one came as they walked the length of the open ground and reached the door of the bunker. Hitesh had already pressed his thumb on the glass panel and swiped the card.

Roshan watched as a green LED lit up and the heavy reinforced door opened with a click. Hitesh was all smiles. "Piece of cake."

Baldev took up the rear and looked around. Armaan led the way. They were going into a dark opening. He could see steps going down for quite a distance. They stealthily walked down as Baldev closed the heavy door behind them. Roshan held his Glock 17 upright, ready to fire at anything that moved.

The steps suddenly ended and they looked out in front. The room was long, rectangular and filled with crates of various sizes and shapes. But the crates were small and didn't look like a missile could fit in them. *They could probably be in the far end*, Roshan thought.

"I found a switch." Hitesh said. "Take off your NVGs."

Roshan slid up his Night Vision Glasses, and a minute later the room was flooded with the luminescence of the overhead lights as Hitesh switched them on one by one. Roshan blinked his eyes accustoming his vision to the stark layout of the bunker. On either end of him, the crates he had seen earlier were piled in neat columns that extended right up to the ceiling high above them. There was a wide aisle in the centre through which one could move the inventory around. At one side parked along the wall was a customized forklift. There were a couple of large metal housings at the far end that he hadn't noticed before.

"The goods look to be in the far end." Armaan said. They moved systematically forward checking for hostiles hidden behind each row of crates, but the place looked devoid of life. They made their way to the end towards the metallic behemoth that took up the entire rear wall.

"It's a Weapons Storage Vault." Hitesh stood next to him. The vault had multiple weapon pods for storing the missiles kept in hardened cases that isolated one missile from another. But the cases were empty. Hitesh stopped as the realization hit him. "Where are the missiles?"

Armaan gave a hard stare at Hitesh. "Are you sure

we are in the correct bunker?"

"I am positive. The inventory log stated Bunker B36. The nameplate above the biometric panel said B36. This is the place."

"Then where are the missiles? Show me the tablet." Armaan ordered.

Hitesh gave the tablet to Armaan and pointed to the inventory log.

"Yes, it says B36." Armaan looked around. "So where did the missiles go?" He glanced again at the tablet. "There is an inventory number tagged with the missile. Search using the inventory ID for today's date. It may be possible they moved it to another bunker today."

Hitesh tapped the tablet and searched for the information. "There is no entry under that inventory ID for today."

"What?" Armaan peered closely at the tablet confirming what Hitesh had claimed. "Tap on the Inventory ID. It should give us some information."

"It's not here." Hitesh said with finality.

Roshan walked up to Hitesh. "What are you talking about?"

Hitesh pointed to the tablet screen. Roshan squinted his eyes as he tried to read the small text. It read. 'Outbound. Destination: Classified.'

Roshan looked in Hitesh's eyes for confirmation. Hitesh nodded. "The missiles were relocated yesterday to an unknown destination. It's not here in Sargodha."

A sickening emptiness filled Roshan's stomach. He had looked forward to executing the mission and he knew how vital it was. They should have completed the mission in Ormara itself, but fate hadn't been with them. Deciding to travel to Sargodha had been a risky venture, even leading to their capture. But somehow they had escaped, resolute in their decision to neutralize the missiles.

Now, as he looked at the empty weapons pod in Sargodha, far away from the coast and with no idea of where the missiles were, he felt deflated. It had all been for nothing. He looked up at Armaan wondering if he would give the order to fall back and abort the mission.

A low hissing sound emanated from somewhere.

"What was that?" Baldev whispered.

"I don't know." Armaan whipped out his gun.

Roshan looked around but the bunker was still. If someone had come through the door, he would have heard them long before they reached the foot of the stairs. He suddenly felt a gag in his throat. He was having difficulty breathing; his eyes were rolling all over the bunker walls, unable to focus in front of him. His knees buckled and he saw Hitesh collapse in front of him. A second later he fell on top of Hitesh, and darkness engulfed his vision.

Chapter 22

These Indians are good, but not good enough, Ijaz smiled devilishly.

An alert had just come up on the screen. Barrier Three had been breached. Ijaz looked at the data. There were no reports of Barrier One and Two being compromised, but the surveillance cameras he had installed two months ago on a separate network showed four men crossing Barrier Three. The only thing the Indians hadn't realized was that they were crossing an invisible fence.

Barrier Three was a motion detecting laser fence. An invisible laser light ran along its length and the moment anyone passed through it, the laser light got blocked triggering an alert.

The phone on the desk rang. Ijaz picked it up.

"Sir, we found a car parked in the middle of nowhere a few kilometres from here. As soon as we went closer to investigate, the car bolted."

Ijaz's eyes widened. This was not something that they encountered in their daily routine. "It could be related to the alert we received. Did you give chase?"

"Yes sir, we did but the driver started shooting at us. We shot in retaliation and the car lost control and crashed into a wall. The driver was found dead."

The chair fell to the ground as Ijaz stood up with a jerk. "You idiot." He screamed, "I told you that I wanted the intruders alive."

"Yes sir," the man stammered. "It was only one person. We are trying to find if there were any others."

Ijaz's eyes went to the LCD screen. The four men had made their way to Bunker B36. "Don't bother," he spoke into the phone. "Search the car for Intel and submit a report to me in sixty minutes."

"I already searched the vehicle before calling you. It's a Range Rover. Preliminary search yielded nothing substantial. We are now checking the registration number of the Range Rover. I will submit the report."

"Yes, do that ASAP." Ijaz would be surprised if the background info on the vehicle didn't lead to a dead end.

He focused back on the flat-panel screen. The Indians had arrived at the entrance to the bunker. He had purposefully kept the guards off duty as he prepared to spring a trap on them. A few moments later the bunker door swung open and the Indians went inside.

Ijaz reached into a wall shelf and picked up his trusted Heckler & Koch MP5K. He toggled the safety selector from S to E on the sub-machine gun. S denoted safe and E indicated single fire. He looked at the third option F. F meant continuous fire. He held the safety selector between his thumb and index finger as he debated between E and F. E was redundant, he finally decided. F would be the best option. He switched the toggle to continuous fire.

The forecast for tonight was blood.

Lots of it.

Ijaz stood in front of Bunker B57, fingering the trigger of the MP5K. He hated B57. He had been inside only once and the musty air and the dirty floor had repelled him, not to mention the perpetually putrid smell that hung in the air.

B57 was an abandoned bunker no one dared to go into. Many years ago, a crate of spent fissile material from the nearby Khushab reactor was stored in B57 enroute to its disposal as radioactive waste. While handling it, one of the pellets had fallen to the floor sparking a panic among the workers. Since then, the bunker had been shut down as a potential risk, even though the radiation levels were not that high.

The door to the bunker opened from inside revealing one of his guards. He walked up to Ijaz. "It's done like you said."

"Good. Let's go inside."

"Yes sir." The soldier replied but his voice was uneasy. Ijaz could see that he didn't like going into the contaminated bunker.

Ijaz went inside the bunker with the guard. A few minutes later his wrinkling nose had adjusted itself to the stench of the stale air. At the foot of the stairs, a solitary light illuminated the four Indians lying unconscious on the floor. Three guards stood sentry next to them and the fourth guard that accompanied Ijaz joined them. The prisoners had been tied up, and their weapons confiscated from them.

It had been Ijaz's idea to use the gas in the bunker; an easy way of rendering them out of action without long-drawn standoffs or casualties on either end. The Pakistani soldiers had moved the unconscious Indians from Bunker B36 to the abandoned B57. The effect of the gas would pass any time soon. He had some questions for them.

"They are stirring." One of the guards said. And sure enough Ijaz could see one of the prisoners open his eyes slowly and then blink wide open as he found himself tied and saw four men who had their guns pointed at him.

"Don't even think of doing anything smart." Ijaz warned.

The others also came to their senses and the realization that they were bound. Their reaction was predictable. Confusion followed by surprise and shock. His guards were ready; each had a gun pointed to one of the prisoners. They couldn't escape.

One of them spoke. "What do you want?"

Ijaz laughed. "I suppose that's a question I should be asking." He stopped pacing. "But then, I already know the answer."

The man didn't reply. Ijaz continued, "I am the Security commander here. Nothing escapes my notice. You are here for the Babur-3 missiles, aren't you?"

Another guy spoke; he looked the youngest of them. "If you know, then why do you ask?"

"Quiet." The first man commanded. He seemed to the leader of the group.

So, it was true, Ijaz mused. The ISI Director had been correct when he alerted him that Indians would come to Sargodha. It was rare in their profession to get such precise Intel.

Ijaz had been reserved in his reaction when he had received the call as Head of Security about the alert. In most cases, he would follow standard operating procedures and the alert would turn out to be false, but this time something told him that things would be different. He had carefully chalked out his plan. And the result was in front of him.

"You were fools to come here. As you see, it was a futile quest to search for the missiles. The missiles have been relocated far away from here where you can never reach them."

Ijaz watched the faces of the Indians droop under his words. He had completely outplayed the Indians. It was time to inform them of their colleague's death.

"I also know about your fifth colleague." He immediately saw their eyes on him, wary and surprised. "You guys came in a Range rover." He saw the dejected expressions change into resignation. The car must have been their getaway vehicle. Now they knew that he knew about the car too.

"I am sorry to inform you, that your colleague in the Range Rover is no longer with us. He died." Ijaz considered himself a good reader of faces. The resignation had turned into shock and anger on hearing their colleague's death.

"I am sure you are aware of the rules of engagement as spies. Now that you are captured, the Indian government will disavow all links to you. They will deny your existence. As of now, your only safety is in cooperating with us. Do that, and we may be able to come to an understanding."

"Never, we would rather prefer to die." The response was defiant.

The evidence was conclusive. These intruders were indeed Indians who had come for the missiles.

"Death serves no purpose. Tell me, how is your friend's death helping you?"

The leader spat at Ijaz. In response, one of Ijaz's guards smashed his rifle's butt into the leader's shoulder and shrieked. "You will be sorry for what you did. All of you are going to die like pigs in here with no one to hear your screams of pain." The guard kicked him in the ribs.

The man on the floor winced under the blow and then glared at the guard, the pain apparent in his muffled voice. "Go to hell."

Ijaz had heard enough. He swung his MP5K gun and aimed it at the four men. A deafening fusillade of gunfire

echoed in the sound-proof underground bunker.
Then all was quiet.

Chapter 23

PM Jaqdish Inamdaar felt his cheeks grow hot as he watched the news on the television. There had been yet another terrorist attack in Srinagar; the casualties included both Army soldiers and civilians. He fumed as he picked up the phone and called his National Security Advisor.

"Navnath, report to my office ASAP." He slammed the phone down.

A minute later Navnath Shah entered. He was followed by the three Service Chiefs and the Defence Minister Dayanand Mistry.

"I was about to come to your office. Our on-ground investigators found evidence on the terrorists that conclude that they came from Pakistan."

Inamdaar smashed his fist on the wooden desk. "They have gone too far this time." He stood up and proclaimed, "They will pay heavily for their misadventure." He paced the room, anger coursing through his body clamouring for an outlet. "I authorize a military strike ASAP on all terrorist camps in Pakistan-occupied-Kashmir and Gilgit-Baltistan."

Navnath looked at him. "But sir, consider the implications. You are in effect proposing war."

Inamdaar stopped pacing and glared at Navnath.

"Tell me who is already engaged in a war that killed our people? Those cowards from across the border can never win a face-to-face war against us. So, they supply money and guns to these terrorists and then deny that they sent them. It's time we exterminate these pests once and for all."

General Singh stepped in. "There is a challenge here, sir. We have the capability to strike at the camps in POK, but what is the probability that we will terminate any high value targets?"

Inamdaar looked at the General. "I am not sure I follow you."

"Let's say we strike across the border at the camps that harbour terrorists. What if we kill only a few terrorists, or kill no one important? We get in a lose-lose situation. Not only do we not root out the source of terrorism, but now we also face a potential backlash from Pakistan, and an escalation of war."

Inamdaar resumed pacing as he mulled over what the General had said. He looked at the news broadcast on the television. Already the media were asking the government spokesperson on how they were going to respond to this act of naked aggression.

Inamdaar's anger simmered down. He was walking on a political tightrope. He had to satisfy the common people who were crying out for a fitting response against Pakistan, and at the same time he had to protect the very same people by not risking a war with Pakistan. It was a paradox and no one understood it at the moment better than Inamdaar.

"Are you proposing I do nothing? These terrorists attack us with impunity, and you tell me that I if attack back, I lose. There is a limit to my patience."

"An attack is best, when there is a sure chance of success." The General said. "I am looking at this situation unemotionally and I see no good coming out of it. I am not proposing we do nothing, I am just saying that we need to eliminate the terrorist leaders rather than their minions."

"So how do we do that?"

The General looked at the gathering and hesitated. "I am working on that. I will provide a report in the evening."

"I will be waiting for that, General." Inamdaar stood up, indicating that the meeting was over. "We need to give out an unequivocal and strong response to both the terrorists and the Pakistani civil-military establishment. They should cower with fear before they even think of attacking us next time."

The three Service Chiefs and the NSA left. The Defence Minister Dayanand Mistry stayed in the room. Inamdaar stared at him. The man was from the second largest party in his coalition government and Inamdaar had given the post to him in exchange for the party to support his government. Dayanand was good at politics, but Inamdaar wasn't sure how good his administration skills were for a crucial post like Defence. He wondered what the man had to say.

Inamdaar leaned back in his chair, "I know you resent me. You don't have to pretend otherwise."

Dayanand said, "Yes, I hate your politics."

"Good. I thought you would deny that too. I am happy to see that my Defence Minister has a spine."

"I am not a bootlicker that will do anything you please to keep my post. First, you send a covert ops team; now you talk about a military strike. Your warmongering views will only lead us to grief."

"Since when did safeguarding our sovereignty become warmongering? Do you want me to simply sit quiet and wait for more Kasabs to kill my people? As PM, it is my responsibility to ensure our citizens are safe now and in the future."

"And the best way to do that is by initiating black operations that will exacerbate the fragile situation between our countries? Are we ready for war? We can only fight a war for maximum of ten days before our supplies dry up. We don't have the budget to fight a proper war."

"That's because it's called a Defence Budget, not an Attack Budget. And I am not exacerbating the… what did you call it?… fragile situation. They send brainwashed youths to our country. I am sending lethal professionals who will show them how it's supposed to be done. Two can play this game, and the onus will be on Pakistan to escalate from here."

"It will take only a small spark to start a war, and then the very real possibility of nuclear armageddon. As PM, are you prepared for the death of millions?"

Inamdaar leaned forward on the desk and closed the lid of his laptop. He glanced in the direction of Dayanand, but he had a faraway look in his eyes. "A hundred years ago, in 1913, people thought that a World War was impossible. They couldn't comprehend a global war involving multiple countries in which millions could die. But the War happened and millions did die. And then in 1939 it happened again. With even more devastating consequences. Today, people naively think that no one is fool enough to start a nuclear conflict. They forget the test bombs proposed for Hiroshima and Kokura. Kokura escaped but its good luck turned out to be Nagasaki's downfall. The cities were nuked just to evaluate the extent of devastation that could be caused by the atomic toys. The nuclear scientists requested the politicians not to test it out on humans, but the power-drunk politicians still went ahead. Loss of lives didn't matter with the justification that the only good Jap was a dead Jap. That's humanity for you. We forget history very quickly."

"What's your point?"

"The point I am trying to make is that the law of probability and the ignorance of humanity is against us. We cannot comprehend the horrors of a nuclear war, and the scale of its destruction. Just because we cannot comprehend the magnitude, we naively assume it will never happen to us. But history has shown that it has happened, and probability tells us that it will happen again. We conveniently ignore the lessons from history."

"So, you think we may have a nuclear war in the future?"

"Sixty million died in the Second World War. Two hundred million will die in a nuclear conflict with Pakistan. It's not a question of *if* it will happen. It's only a question of *when*. You asked if I was prepared for the death of millions. I am not. No leader can be. But at the same time, my self-respect wouldn't allow me to stand mute while our neighbour keeps bleeding us through a thousand cuts. As Prime Minister, I have my duties to execute. I will perform my karma fearlessly."

"What's the meaning of this?" Roshan finally found his voice.

He surveyed the bullet ridden bodies under the solitary light of the bunker. The security commander had been so quick, that Roshan hadn't even ducked when the bullets flew around him. Armaan and Baldev were looking at each other and Hitesh was still rooted to the spot in shock.

"Hold your questions," Ijaz looked down at the bodies ensuring that they were all dead. The four guards lay in a heap on the floor, their eyes open in death. "This was necessary; otherwise they would have killed you."

"But why did you kill your own men?" Roshan stared

at the dead Pakistani soldiers.

"Because, they are not my men."

"Not your men?" Roshan couldn't believe it. "Who were they then?"

"The question is not who they were. They were Pakistani soldier pigs. The question is who am I?"

"Who are you then?"

Ijaz smiled for the first time. "I am a member of the *Sayeret Matkal*."

The name triggered a recollection in Roshan's mind. The *Sayeret Matkal* was a secretive group within an equally secret government organisation, *The Mossad* of Israel. Deployed as a special unit of the Israel Defence Forces, the *Sayeret Matkal* operated in shadows all around the world, spying on hostile governments and exposing their plans.

"You are an Israeli!" Shock was plastered on Roshan's face.

"I am surprised you recognized the name. Not many of our own countrymen have even heard about us."

"But what are you doing here?" Roshan pointed at the surroundings. "In Pakistan? In their army weaponisation facility?"

"What does it look like? Pakistan has made its agenda to make a sworn enemy out of Israel. In fact, these illiterate lowlifes go as far as making it a political statement even on their passports." The Israeli spat. "Their passports specifically mention that it is for travel everywhere except Israel. But they don't realize that by naming Israel on a Pakistani passport, they unwittingly give recognition to the existence of our state and its power."

"But why their weapons storage depot?"

"A few years back we were concerned about the nuclear powers of Pakistan. Once a country has nuclear weapons, they get into a different level of warfare altogether. We heard rumours of a dirty bomb being used against Israel. We assembled our men, came to Pakistan and infiltrated into the army and bureaucratic positions to check the veracity of the threat. The rumour didn't turn out to be legitimate, and then we settled down and the mission changed to a long term infiltration campaign. With my induction in Sargodha's Central Ammunition Depot, I get to know all the movement of all missiles, weapons logistics and new technologies. If a military action is thought of, Tel Aviv will come to know of it long before the Army commanders here in Pakistan know about it."

"Are you saying you monitor everything that comes and goes from this facility?"

"Yes, I do."

"Then you must be aware of the Babur-3 missiles?"

"Yes, it was moved out of the facility yesterday."

"Oh! Then it's true of what you said earlier." A sudden realization came to Roshan. "And Sultan?"

"Your friend in the Range Rover? I am sorry about him. His was an unneeded casualty."

"How did he die?"

"I don't have all the details, but I was told that he lost control of his car while escaping and crashed into a wall. When the soldiers arrived there, he was already dead." Roshan had seen his comrades dying in conflict. He was no stranger to losing combat brothers, but the pain never subsided. It still hurt him. He looked at his team. The sombre expressions of their faces matched his.

Unlike a soldier in war, a spy dying in enemy territory never got the accolades or attention they deserved. Army *jawans* would be cremated with full honours. But a spy dying behind enemy territory could only muster the ignominy of an unmarked grave. Roshan knew that Sultan had chosen this kind of life. They had chatted briefly on the way to Sargodha and Roshan knew that this work was a matter of pride for him. Now his family wouldn't even receive a body to mourn upon. It was what Sultan had signed up for. Roshan shook his head. Even he had also signed up for this.

As a soldier, his duty was to follow orders. It wasn't his prerogative to question his leaders and their decisions. He trusted his superiors and knew that whatever mission he was sent to would be a carefully thought-out move in the eternal war to guard India's sovereignty.

This mission had gone south from the moment they

had landed into Pakistan.

"So what are you boys doing here?" The Israeli asked.

"We were after the Babur-3 missiles. Only after we reached here did we realize it was moved out."

"Yes, it was done yesterday. As the Head of Security, I authorized the exit request and verified the goods. They loaded a couple dozen missiles in a van and left."

"Just a solitary van? They didn't provide any cover to it?"

"No, the Pakistani Army doesn't provide any security cover to their weapons." He looked at the shell-shocked expression on Roshan's face and continued. "I know what you are thinking. What if a terrorist got hold of the missiles? But you have to understand the Pakistani mindset first. Their priority is not the safety of the missiles. They are more concerned that US spies don't get wind of their plans. America is their biggest threat, even though they won't admit it ever. They share a love-hate relationship with the USA. They want the grants and monetary bailouts, but at the same time they hate the guts of the Yankees."

"But still, why not transport the missiles in a proper Army deployed unit?"

"A big contingent of army vehicles travelling through the roads will be conspicuous. The Americans already have their eyes everywhere in Pakistan. They have ground assets as well as satellites to monitor anything out of the ordinary. A dozen vehicles will naturally attract more interest than a single lonesome van."

"Do you know where the van went?"

The Israeli smiled enigmatically. "The destination on the form was listed as Classified."

"But you do know where it went." It was a statement, not a question.

"Yes. Courtesy of the CIA I do know. It went to Project S25 in KP."

Roshan plumbed the depths of his memory but couldn't recollect anything. He looked over at Hitesh, who nodded. "It is an abandoned mine project in the province of Khyber Pakhtunkhwa. The Pakistan government abandoned it in a few years ago when they didn't have funds to sustain the mining project."

"Oh, but they didn't stop the project." The Israeli interjected. "The project was publicly terminated, but in reality Project S25 continued to receive secret funding from the National Command Authority."

"The NCA? Isn't that the Pakistani nuclear deployment team?"

The Israeli nodded. "Here's how the CIA came into the picture. In 2010, when the terrorists were creating havoc on the army and taking over vast swathes of land under its control especially in FATA and Gilgit-Baltistan, the CIA sent a high-level delegation to visit the Pakistani Prime Minister. They expressed their serious concern about the terrorists running amok throughout the country, and wanted to know what steps the leadership had taken to lock down its nuclear facilities so that it didn't fall in the hands of the extremists. To their shock, they discovered that the security at the nuclear facilities was rudimentary. The American team offered to provide state-of-the-art security installations to protect the nuclear warheads. The Prime Minister readily agreed and soon after received the high tech security systems to guard the warheads against theft and deployment. But what the Pakistan leaders didn't know is that all of the security systems had micro-GPS trackers installed in them. Once the security systems were installed at all the secret nuclear facilities, the CIA immediately had the locations of all of them. How's that for a double whammy? Not only were the installations secured, but the CIA also knew where they were located."

"That's brilliant."

"Yes, it was. One of the installations was at the so-called abandoned mine at KP. And when the CIA learned that we already had a team in Pakistan, they were ready to provide us with info so that we could dig deeper into their schemes. They wanted to nurture assets in the facilities, and our existing team was perfect for them. The destination of the Babur missiles was classified, but our sources reported that the missiles are bound for Project S25. It's located in Karak district of Khyber

Pakhtunkhwa. We have a contact there. I assume you want to check out the missiles?"

"Yes, something of the sort."

"If you are interested, I can speak with my contact there. He would be able to give you access to the facility."

"Is your contact any good?"

The Israeli smiled. "I believe so. He's the head of the military detail stationed in Project S25. Everyone there reports to him."

Chapter 24

Shafiq woke up with the first light of dawn. It had become a regular habit with him wherever he was. A faint light was peeking through the window. He didn't remember the last time he had slept so soundly and comfortably. The beds and blankets were clean and it felt warm sleeping inside a house, unlike the open where the freezing wind would tear through your insides all night long.

They had reached Ghazni the previous evening and had gone straight up to the safe house. The safe house was on the outskirts of the town. The neighbourhood had sparse buildings dotted around. The buildings looked like warehouses of some sort. He realized that their safe house was also an erstwhile warehouse. The ceilings were higher and the room larger than those in typical homes.

Malik had told them not to venture outside, so, Shafiq had simply retired to a room that had been converted into a bedroom and laid himself on one of the beds. Sleep had come instantly; his body tired from the trials of many weeks had welcomed it immediately.

Shafiq rose from the bed and walked over to the window. It had been dark when they had reached yesterday so he hadn't got to see much of the area. Fog had descended over the area and he couldn't see the horizon. Only a dull light indicated that morning was on its way.

Zia came into the room. He ignored Shafiq and spoke with the other men who were up and about. "Malik says we are to move in ten minutes. Everyone should join him in front of the garage in five minutes.

The men bustled about. Most of their stuff was in the trucks and hadn't been offloaded. For Shafiq, it was a matter of simply going down to the garage. The two trucks were lined next to each other, ready to leave. Some of the men had already hopped into the trucks. Malik was busy talking with a couple of men, their contacts in Ghazni who had welcomed them yesterday. Shafiq decided to sit in the back of one of the trucks.

A few minutes later Malik peeked into the rear of the trucks. Satisfied that all the men were accounted for, he gave the order to proceed to Jalalabad.

It was just after noon that they reached Jalalabad. Instead of stopping at a particular place, they passed through the city and took the road east. A few kilometres out of Jalalabad, they stopped at a small settlement which had camels for sale. Malik spoke to the owner while everyone in the truck watched with mild curiosity. The owner left, and Malik turned around to the truck and spoke just two words.

"We wait."

Thirty minutes later, the owner returned. This time he was accompanied with two men. They were bearded, tall, well-built and each carried an AK-47 under his arm. Their eyes were alert and were constantly roving around. As they approached the trucks, Shafiq found their faces familiar. He gasped as he recognized the duo. They were the Kunduz brothers named after the town where they came from. Their names were Nadeem and Nazal. Their tales were legendary. They had been inducted in the war against the Soviets as kids of eight and nine years old; wielding guns too heavy for their frail bodies and ordered to fight against a professionally trained enemy.

Miraculously, they had survived, and over the years, the two of them had fought in almost every major war that had raged through Afghanistan. They had been one of the first to join the Al-Qaeda, and had grown through the ranks. Each devastating assault on their enemies had increased their reputation and their incredible feats spurred on their followers. It was said that they were one of the few remaining core members of the disbanded Al-Qaeda.

Shafiq wondered what the brothers were doing here. As he evaluated the scenarios in his mind, only one thing seemed possible. The Kunduz brothers were going to assist or lead them into the mission. Which meant their mission was going to be a major one.

He wasn't the only one who had reached this conclusion. Excited murmurs had broken in the group around him. They were all sitting on their haunches in the truck, discussing their mission and the presence of the legendary brothers. Everyone eyed the conversation taking place between the four men and wondered what they were talking about.

After a few minutes, Malik broke away from the group and went to the front of the truck. He beckoned the drivers of both trucks. They stepped out and spoke with Malik and nodded at his instructions. Malik told the co-passengers in the front to disembark and sit in the back. He then invited the brothers to sit next to the drivers.

After everyone was settled in, Malik thanked the camel owner and then told the driver to move on.

They had been travelling for few hours. Jalalabad was now behind them. Malik hadn't spoken of where they were going.

"I think we are going to Kabul." Hafeez conjectured. "We will confront our old enemy. It will be the final assault on the traitors of Afghanistan, and the rebirth of our nation. I am happy that the Kunduz brothers chose us for this mission."

Some of them nodded. Pasha shook his head. "I am not sure…"

"Why?" Hafeez asked.

"The Kunduz brothers have their own men who have sworn their lives to them. Why aren't they using them? And where are they?"

Shafiq thought about Pasha's questions. And it made sense. The veteran soldier had an uncanny common sense. It was unusual for the brothers to not use their own men. He wondered if his group was going to be used as a suicide squad. The possibility seemed quite likely.

He was about to air his thoughts when the truck rumbled to a stop. They had gone off the main road half an hour back, and had traversed through open fields, followed by a rocky ride along the foot of a mountain, and had even risked going across a small rivulet. Shafiq wondered where they were.

"Everyone out." He heard Malik's voice.

Shafiq got out along with the others. Once on the

ground, he stretched himself as he looked around. The trucks had been parked in a narrow gorge between two hills hiding it from view. The peaks of the hills cast a long shadow over the gorge. The entire scenery was beautiful. However, Shafiq's eyes were drawn to two strange looking vehicles that were next to their trucks.

The vehicle had the basic frame of a truck. But that's where the similarity ended. The exterior was painted in a garish sprinkle of bright colours. Red, green, blue, pink; all of them competed for space from the cabin in the front to the wooden sides that made up the cargo compartment and till the rear bumper.

The Kunduz brothers walked up to the colourful truck. "All right. Everyone listen up."

The men gathered around the Kunduz brothers eager to listen to what they had to say. Nazal silently observed the group for a moment before he spoke.

"Brothers, we just crossed the Afghanistan border and are now in Pakistan…"

Chapter 25

"I am sorry, boys." Armaan said. "I failed you again."

They were in the safe house on the outskirts of Sargodha. Roshan watched Armaan slumped on the sofa, his face was drawn, his shoulders hunched and his gloomy eyes stared at nothing in particular. Roshan felt an ache in his throat. He turned his head away, a wave of sympathy rushing through him. He couldn't bear to watch Armaan in this state.

They had been glad to find the destination of the submarine missiles. But the elation had quickly turned into a sombre reality-check as they realized that they had lost one of their men in the process.

Armaan continued, "First Namit, and now Sultan. I've been a terrible leader."

"No, Armaan." Roshan said. "You are a good leader." Roshan wanted to say something, anything that would pull out Armaan from his defeatist thinking. "You cannot control what happened. It was just one of those situations."

Armaan looked at him. "You have been blind to my faults, Roshan. You have followed my orders because you thought I am right. What if I am not?"

"I am not a fresh face like you assume me to be." Roshan said. "I have been in the warzone and I know a good leader when I see one."

Armaan shook his head. "Look at the results. The mission has failed. I have failed."

A quiet voice spoke, "The Armaan Ahmed I know would never have uttered those words. Failure is not a word he would have understood. He would have professionally taken it on the chin, and figured out a solution."

Roshan looked at Baldev who had just spoken the words. Baldev was looking intently at Armaan. Armaan looked at Baldev and Roshan could see a glimmer of life in his eyes.

Armaan said, "But I have led you all in this mess."

Baldev scoffed, "I don't see Armaan Ahmed in this

room. Instead I see a man down on his luck complaining about the odds he's against. A soldier fights on the battlefield. He doesn't grieve on it. He grieves only after the battle is over. Our battle is still not over. We are in hostile terrain. And we await our leader's orders. Armaan Ahmed's orders. Don't expect any sympathy from me. If you think you've led us into a mess, it's your responsibility to lead us out of it."

Armaan straightened at Baldev's words. He glanced around at the men. They were looking at him for guidance.

Roshan said, "We trust your decisions, Armaan."

Baldev stood up and walked over to where Armaan was and placed a firm hand on his shoulder. "Quit whining and order me around. I really like the plans you make."

Armaan looked at Baldev and in an instant pulled him close in a tight embrace. "You are right. I don't know what I would have done without you."

"Probably something stupid," Baldev's muffled voice came through the embrace.

Armaan released him and looked at the group. "What do we do next?"

Roshan said, "We do what we came here for. We complete our mission."

"Agreed," Baldev said. "We should follow the lead the Israeli gave us."

"You need me for whatever you are planning." Hitesh chuckled. "So I have to drag myself along."

Armaan looked at each of them in turn. His eyes acknowledging their commitment to the mission. "I'll inform the General about what happened."

Roshan winced. He was grateful he wasn't the one to be sharing the bad news with the General. He wondered how the General would react to a second failure. They knew where the missiles were relocated, but the bottom line was that their infiltration into the missile base was a failure.

The Pakistanis had proactively relocated the missiles and they had returned empty-handed. The Israeli had given them the details of the location the missiles had gone to. Armaan had said that he would contact him if he needed more information. But Roshan understood that they would have to inform Homebase of the latest developments. Armaan walked towards the conference phone and dialled a number. The call connected immediately.

"Homebase, this is Markhor, actual."

"Markhor, this is Homebase. SITREP please."

Armaan gave the situation report. He kept it brief and to the point speaking about the absence of the missiles and the loss of the LTRA followed by the Israeli's help and the destination of the missiles.

"Markhor, your mission has been an unmitigated disaster. I order you to abort. Clean up and exfil." the General's words boomed on the speaker.

"Negative sir." Armaan said. "We know the location of the missiles and the head of the facility is a friendly."

"Markhor, you will follow orders. We already had two failures and one casualty. I wouldn't risk losing additional lives."

"Sir, we are very close to a breakthrough. You yourself reiterated how critical this mission is. I insist that you give us the green light."

There was a pause on the line. Roshan pictured the General in his office thinking about the mission. The General had been realistic when he had described the mission to them. They would be going inside enemy territory and would accomplish their mission with skill and stealth. So far the stealth part had failed. They had been chased through half of Pakistan, and it had been a combination of luck and skill that they were still alive. He still wasn't sure if their escape from outside Hyderabad had been discovered; he hoped not.

Roshan didn't harbour any delusions that what Armaan was proposing would make things potentially worse for them. And by going north, the challenge of returning to the coast for an exfil increased exponentially. Sultan had offered to escort them back to the coast, but with his death that was no longer an option.

But he knew the importance of the mission. They were professionals and the mission came first. They would think about their exit options only after the mission was accomplished.

The General came back on the line. His tone was brusque. "What are the chances of success?"

Armaan replied, "Given that the friendly will help us gain access to the facility, I would say ninety percent."

"I won't approve this just on the basis of your recommendation. Is the team there?"

"Yes, they are here."

General Singh said, "Team, do you agree with going ahead? Responses please."

Baldev spoke. "I am in."

"Me too." Roshan said.

Hitesh said, "Yes from my end."

"Everyone is ready, sir." Armaan said. "We just need your permission."

The General paused for a moment and then spoke. "Permission granted. Make sure that we meet our objectives. I don't want another Charlie Foxtrot this time."

"Thank you, sir." Armaan gave a thumbs-up signal to everyone and then continued. "Sir, request SAT eyes for this mission. Would that be possible?"

Roshan was surprised by the request. Armaan was asking for satellite surveillance for their mission. He wondered if the General would be willing to grant his request. Satellite surveillance required the trajectory of the satellite to be changed from whatever it was currently monitoring. Plus satellite time was an extremely precious commodity and there were a ton of government agencies that 'borrowed' satellite time for their own projects. Such a request would not only require top-level approval but it would also need justification for the prioritization.

"What do you need SATs for?" General Singh was apparently as surprised as him.

Armaan pressed on. "And also we will need someone that can coordinate the SAT Intel with us in real-time."

"You are asking for a lot." General Singh said. "I don't have the bandwidth for this."

"But sir, we will need all the support we can get. This mission was originally planned to be a quick in-and-out from Ormara. We have failed twice and having someone help us will help raise our odds of success. I don't know if we will get a better opportunity than this."

"The opportunity is there, but I recommend you make do with existing resources."

Armaan looked at the others as he shook his head. "At least, can we get satellite imagery of the facility in KP so that we know the terrain, number of hostiles, and exit options?"

"For that to happen, we will have to make a satellite pass over the target. I will have to run this by the PM. It would be best if the approval comes from the top."

"Thank you, sir."

When the General spoke again, his voice had softened just a bit. "I was a field agent and I know how the perception on the ground differs from the operation centre. Having said that, we also have to follow the chain of command. I will speak with you in a few hours."

"PM sir, we need a few minutes of satellite time for our operation." General Singh knew that Inamdaar liked to come to the point straight away.

"How are the boys doing?" PM Inamdaar asked.

General Singh had informed Inamdaar about the impending infiltration in Sargodha yesterday. Now he would have to talk about its failure. He quickly went over the facts of the mission, and ended with the team's resolve to follow the missiles into Khyber Pakhtunkhwa. Inamdaar didn't interrupt, but listened to him closely. When he was done, he only asked one question.

"What was our agent in Sukkur involved in? How will his loss affect us?"

"He was part of HUMINT monitoring the Tactical Nuclear Weapons kept by the Pakistani Army in Pano Aqil. Pano Aqil has mobile TEL launchers for launching their Nasr mini-nukes against our army if we invade. Now with our on-ground resource gone, we will have to use SIGINT from our satellites to rely on providing us with Intel of any military build-up in Pano Aqil. We will eventually have another HUMINT agent in place."

"Do you think the boys can accomplish this mission?"

"Yes PM sir. They are the best we have."

"What do you need the satellite for?"

"We can make a pass over the area the team is going to and understand the risks and opportunities of the target beforehand."

General Vishwajeet Singh watched as Inamdaar walked over to the window and looked outside. Singh could see the magnificent dome of the Rashtrapati Bhavan from the visitor's couch. He walked up to the window and stood next to Inamdaar and admired the Mughal Gardens in all its splendour. He had to admit that the view from the PMO was the best in all of South Block. Finally Inamdaar spoke.

"Right now, in this moment we are creating a legacy. A leader is judged not just by the actions he takes, but also by the actions he fails to take. In the military, guns and bullets can be replaced, but men can never be replaced. The soldiers are the real assets of a country, not its missiles or tanks. And if among our soldiers, these are the best of the best; then I want to ensure everything possible for the boys to get the mission done and make a safe exit out of Pakistan."

"Yes sir. What do you recommend?"

"I recommend that dedicated satellite time be given to this mission till its conclusion. Use the Cartosat satellite that we just launched. I want you to do everything possible to make sure we succeed in our mission. You have complete autonomy. Assign and redirect whatever resources you need. I only care about the results."

General Singh smiled. "Yes PM sir." The Prime Minister had given him a carte-blanche; he had instinctively understood what the team would require and had given the General the authority to get everything addressed.

Armaan had requested for satellite monitoring and coordination; the General had rejected his suggestion. Now, not only had the PM given them the much-needed permission, but he had gone ahead and ensured that they had a dedicated satellite till they accomplished the mission. This op was important for Inamdaar and he wanted results. Singh appreciated the decisiveness of

Inamdaar on all matters.

The Prime Minister had delivered, now it was up to him to deliver.

But would he be able to deliver, Singh wondered. Armaan was his most reliable operative, and he had seen him succeed in numerous missions. Usually when he sent Armaan on a mission, Armaan would contact him and tell him that the mission was accomplished. He didn't even have to oversee the mission or get into the finer details.

But this time, not only had the mission bombed, but Armaan hadn't even bothered to let him know. Instead of giving him the update and asking for a course of action, Armaan had foolishly decided to move ahead. And he had got himself captured. General Singh snorted. *The imbecile*. He should have refused to allow Armaan to go to Sargodha.

That was still an option. He could still refuse to send them to the KP facility. He rubbed the back of his neck. They could return back to the coast and count the mission as a loss. But it would mean that they wouldn't have a viable solution to counter a nuclear threat from the sea. He shook his head. The stakes were too high. Millions of lives would hang in the balance in a future war. He had to see the mission through and ensure it was successful.

He would appoint one of his guys to keep an eye on Armaan and make sure that he didn't screw up. That way he would get regular updates even if Armaan didn't tell him anything. Armaan had gone too far this time. He was no longer the reliable leader he once was. He had turned into a liability. General Singh hated liabilities.

Once this ordeal was over, he would ensure that this was the last mission Armaan led.

Chapter 26

General Singh said, "Markhor, I have some good news."

Roshan looked at the speaker phone, the words filling him with optimism. It looked like they would finally get the much-needed satellite images of the KP facility. Once they had that, they would get detailed information on the facility and would be able to evaluate their infil and exfil options.

"Good to hear that, Homebase." Armaan replied as he sat opposite him. Roshan looked at Baldev and Hitesh who were eagerly waiting for what the General had to say.

"You will get dedicated satellite monitoring till the mission is completed, plus I have reassigned one of my men to coordinate the satellite Intel with you in real-time."

"Excellent news, sir."

"Yay!" Hitesh pumped his fist in the air.

"My resource will help you with the SAT stuff. He's here with me. Code name Eagle."

"Hi there, Markhor, this is Eagle," an excited voice was heard next on the speaker.

Armaan said, "Eagle, this is Markhor. How soon can we get the Intel?"

"Give me ninety minutes." Eagle replied, "I will have everything you need."

The General joined in. "I have given the details on what we are looking out for to Eagle. We will talk in ninety minutes."

"Copy that, Homebase."

"Homebase, signing off."

Armaan smacked his hand on the table in exhilaration as the call ended. "That calls for a toast, eh brothers?"

Baldev said, "Let me check the menu. I am sure they have a wine barrel in there somewhere."

Roshan looked around. Everyone was in smiles. For the first time since they had landed in Pakistan, there was a lightness in everyone's manner. Once they got the imagery, they would be able to plan their approach to the facility. The biggest advantage this time would be that their entry would be facilitated by an insider. As far as he was concerned, the mission was in the bag. Maybe it was what everyone else felt too. Once this mission was completed, they would get a couple of days to rest, maybe a week if they were lucky.

Ninety minutes later, Eagle gave them the ultra-high resolution schematics. He had done a great job capturing every possible angle of the facility.

Armaan said, "Excellent work, Eagle."

"You have to thank the guys at ISRO for this." Eagle's voice poured over the speakers as they flipped through the dozen images of the site on a wall projector. "These shots were taken by the satellite from a height of five hundred kilometres. The satellite passes by every ninety minutes, so we have almost real-time information on the sentries posted, their strength and formation."

"Great. Walk me through this."

"The facility is surrounded on three sides by mountains and a river on the fourth side. There are no civilian buildings for miles around. The only approach as you can see is via a bridge that crosses over the river. High walls of around ten feet surround the facility on all sides. On both corners of the front perimeter there are two guard towers that monitor the entry road and the bridge. The access road ends at the gate. The gate is at the southern end of the facility. The U-shaped mountain acts as a natural shield on its north, east and west sides."

"Got it. Mountains on three sides. Sole access via a road from the south. Are there any entry or exit paths through the mountains?"

"I saw some goat trails when I zoomed in on the mountains. But nothing man-made. Like I said the mountains act like a natural barrier. Once you get inside the compound, on your right is a parking lot. Adjacent to the parking lot is the barracks for the guards. Next to the barracks is a flat structure that houses multiple missile bays. Further ahead is the main facility. It is a rectangular behemoth of two stories taking up the entire area—"

"One question." Armaan interrupted. "I also noticed that's its only two stories tall. That seems a little small for a missile facility."

"Yeah," Eagle said, "That is where things get interesting. But having the latest cutting edge satellite technology helps. Not only can our satellites give crystal clear images even if the place of interest is under cloud cover, but with the breakthroughs in Synthetic-Aperture Radar imaging technologies, we can get to see right through the roof and walls of the facility."

"And you found something." Armaan probed.

"Yes," Eagle's voice was full of pride. "Not only were we able to see through the two stories, but I discovered four additional floors beneath the two visible stories."

It took a moment for it to sink in. "The facility has four floors extended under the ground?" Roshan asked. What were the Pakistanis doing in this facility? Four underground floors built such that no one could observe it from afar, except for the technological miracle they had on their side. A place surrounded by mountains and a river, isolated and impregnable. It seemed ominous.

"Yes." Eagle replied, "Also, the site has missile launch pads as well which means they can manufacture and deploy the missiles from a single location. I will try to gather any other piece of information that I can get. This Eagle will keep an eagle eye on the target. Talk to you soon."

"Copy that, Eagle."

"Things seem to finally going well for us." Armaan said. "We have the imagery. The facility does look curious. Eagle has given us the overview. Hitesh, you study the images that Eagle has given. I would like to hear your thoughts as well once you are done."

"Sure." Hitesh replied.

"Good," Armaan turned to the others. "Next, I will contact the Israeli and tell him we will need an entry into the Karak facility. He should be able to work with his agent to give us the access."

Roshan watched Armaan move into the other room. He heard Armaan speak with the Israeli on the phone. Now the only thing left was to decide when to infiltrate the facility. The sooner the better. He wondered if their escape had been noticed. Hitesh had checked the news websites; he hadn't seen any information that related to their capture or subsequent escape. It was best that they finish the mission ASAP and exfil. He still didn't have any idea of how they were going to traverse the entire length of Pakistan and reach the coast without getting caught at the routine check-posts or avoid the CTD and the ISI who by all indications were actively pursuing them.

"*Shalom.*" Roshan's mind was immediately riveted to Armaan as he expressed his goodbye to the Israeli on the phone. A moment later Roshan heard Armaan's voice from the other room.

"We have a problem."

Armaan came out of the room and answered the questioning stares. "The Israeli's contact will be going to Rawalpindi for a conference the day after tomorrow."

"Why is that a problem?"

"We were going to lie low for a while. Well, we cannot do that now. We have to move to KP, because Tahir is the only person who can give us access."

"Tahir?"

"Mohammed Tahir. He is the Israeli's contact. Once he leaves the facility, it will be impossible for us to gain access so easily. We will have to move ahead on our plans."

Roshan thought about it. This was unravelling a little too quickly. He looked at Hitesh. The analyst didn't look too pleased. "How are we going to get out of here? We don't have a ride."

"I will look around for a local rental. Be back soon."

"You do that." Baldev said. He turned to Hitesh. "Get me all the details you can of our destination. I don't want to be caught unprepared."

Hitesh took out the tablet. "I'm on it."

Baldev squeezed next to Hitesh, and gave instructions as they waded through the data that populated on the screen.

Gorbat blinked his eyes rapidly. It didn't help. He still felt sleepy. The morning haze on the highway made driving difficult. He wasn't sure if it was his sleepiness or the fog. He lowered the window of the car that he had borrowed from Bugti. The blast of air that rushed through the window helped. The fresh air cleared his head a bit.

It was early morning and the N-5 highway was nearly deserted save for a few trucks. Gorbat was driving at ninety kmph. He again blinked his eyes, a slight headache developing. He had driven till two in the night, and had only stopped when he had suddenly woken up and found an incoming truck frantically honking at him. He had swerved to his side of the road just in time, his heart thudding in his chest. He had promptly braked to a stop at the side of the highway and had told himself that he would sleep if only for a few hours. He couldn't remember when he had last slept.

Gorbat had parked on the side of the highway and dozed off immediately. It had been a fitful sleep that had ended when the early light of the dawn had pierced the sky. He had woken up freezing in the open plains.

Gorbat wanted to reach Sargodha at the earliest before the Indians. He wasn't sure how they would be coming to Sargodha, but he was pretty sure they would follow the road, just as he had. They wouldn't go by air. When they reached Sargodha, he would be ready for them.

He saw a signboard up ahead on the road and turned off the highway. He made his way to the Central Ammunition Depot. He knew that there were only three places around Sargodha that the Indians would be interested in. The air-force base, the Central Ammunition Depot and the Khushab nuclear plant.

He stopped in front of the barricade and showed his Counter-Terrorism Department ID card to the guard manning the entrance.

"Inspector Gorbat Khan of the Quetta CTD. I am here to meet the Security Head."

The guard made a call and spoke for a few seconds. A moment later he beckoned Gorbat. Gorbat leaned into the narrow guardhouse as the guard handed him the phone. He held the phone to his ear.

"Inspector Gorbat Khan, this is Major Ijaz Ibrahim. I am the Head of Security here. How may I help you?" Ijaz spoke from the other end.

"Major, I need to meet you. There is an emerging threat that we need to discuss."

"Inspector Khan, could you be more specific? Maybe I can help you."

"Yes, I have credible intelligence that spies may try to attack installations in Sargodha. I am not sure which one, but I thought that it's best that every facility in the area is alerted."

"You are too late, Inspector." the voice turned mocking. "Our men neutralized the threat you speak of."

"What?" Gorbat grabbed the phone tighter. The Indians had already reached here? "Where are they? The spies I mean."

"They are dead. Our security forces killed them as they attempted to infiltrate the facility."

"I need to see the bodies and take custody of their belongings."

"I don't think that's possible. They were caught in an Army facility, so this matter is not under the jurisdiction of the CTD. We will be completing the necessary formalities. Till then I request that you keep the matter quiet and don't raise it. It is a matter of national security and prestige."

"But, shouldn't we work together? We can pool our intelligence and learn more about why these spies were here."

"Yes, we will. You know what, if I need your help, I will call up the Quetta CTD and ask for you. Have a good day."

The line disconnected.

Gorbat looked at the receiver in disbelief. The Security head had refused to even allow him inside. Moreover, he hadn't given him any information on how the Indians had died. The Security head had completely dismissed his presence.

Gorbat stomped back to the car in anger. The Army had always been cagey about their facilities. He knew that Ijaz wouldn't call him again. As he turned on the ignition and backed the car out of the premises, he realized that his chase was over.

The Indian spies were killed by the army. Gorbat

supposed he should be happy.

But instead he felt empty.

Ijaz watched the video feed that was streaming in from the camera installed at the gate. He watched Gorbat drive away. A smug satisfaction crossed his face.

The enemy of an enemy is my friend.

Ijaz had anticipated that someone would come questioning in about the Indians. It was virtually impossible that they would not create a trail. The trail had ended at his door and he had smudged out the footprints.

Now the CTD couldn't do anything but seethe in anger. The CTD was a powerful force in Pakistan, but none matched the authority of the Army. Even the PM couldn't influence what the Army could or couldn't do.

Pakistan was a strange democracy, Ijaz smirked. There were four factions in Pakistan and everyone thought they had the power. They were the politicians, the terrorists, the army and the common Pakistanis.

Each of them were deluded into thinking they were the most important faction, when in reality, only the Army had the true power. Being a part of the Army, Ijaz would do his utmost to use that power and influence to reach his goals.

Chapter 27

Shafiq looked at the winding roads passing along the mountainside. They were surrounded by lush green fields that reached up to the snow-clad mountains on both sides of the road. The road was narrow and ascending slowly upwards. The Kunduz brothers had said that they would go north to a secret location in the mountains.

He was sitting with the others in the rear of the truck. It was nearly dark inside except for streaks of light that escaped between the wooden planks making parallel beams of light on the faces of his comrades. The roof of the truck was covered with tarpaulin. The truck creaked as it negotiated the twisted roads and the engine groaned on the bumpy road that kept ascending upwards. The vehicle slowed to a stop forty minutes later.

A small slot at the front of the cargo area that connected to the driver's cabin slid open. A voice whispered from the slot.

"Everyone, stay quiet."

The mood in the back immediately tensed. Shafiq gripped his weapon close, finger on the trigger. He saw others sit up straight and gather their weapons. Shafiq peeked through the wooden walls of the compartment. The walls were beams nailed together and one could see the outside through the thin spaces between the beams.

They had approached a sentry check point. The sign next to it read *Mattani Check-post* followed by the words: *Please be ready with your identity papers.*

He looked at the guards. Two of them were patrolling the road and one of them was sitting inside the guardhouse. Nazal had said that there would be checkpoints along the way, but they would not be a problem. Shafiq wondered what Nazal would do.

As he dwelt upon it, he saw Nazal get down from the cabin and approached the guard with a smile. He reached into his pocket and surreptitiously handed the sentry a wad of cash. The sentry nodded at him and waved to his colleague in the guardhouse to let them through. Nazal climbed back into the cabin and the vehicle started.

Shafiq watched the guards as they passed through the check-post. They looked bored and didn't give their vehicle a second glance, but he stared at them warily till the truck turned a corner and the check-post went out of his line of sight.

They reached their destination two hours later. As Shafiq exited from the truck, he took a deep breath and inhaled the ice-cold air. They were on a high plateau surrounded by mountains. The mountains in front of him were grey, and the ones far off were white with snow. A sprawling resort had been constructed on the plateau with around a dozen cottages. The ground was covered in a thin layer of snow. In the middle of the plateau was an enormous villa. He looked down at the valley they had come from. The place was isolated for miles around.

A couple of persons were waiting for them, obviously their hosts. The Kunduz brothers and Malik greeted them.

"Welcome brothers." The hosts embraced them.

"This place is beautiful," Nazal said.

"Yes, it's a legitimate resort, exclusive and private, but no one knows it's ours."

The hosts led the group to their cottages. The cottages were spacious with all possible luxuries the resort could boast of.

"This is where you will make your accommodations." As Shafiq and his colleagues glanced around, the host said, "Don't get too cosy in here. It's a temporary stop."

"When is the meeting set up?" Malik asked their host.

"You are the last group to arrive. We start in a few minutes at the villa."

Fifteen minutes later, Shafiq joined Malik and the others as they made their way to the villa. He trudged through the snow taking in the natural beauty of the place. Zia was already in the lead exhorting others to hurry. They entered the villa. Inside the villa was a huge open square. They joined the throng of people that sat on the outskirts of the arena. There were around a hundred people already. Most of them were unfamiliar to him.

A hush suddenly descended on the audience as three men entered. Shafiq craned his neck to see the newcomers over the jostling and shouting men around him.

The newcomers greeted the crowd, "*As-salaam Alaikum!*"

"*Walaikum Salaam!*" The crowd thundered.

Shafiq's eyes widened as he looked at the speakers. It was unbelievable. He recognised Majid Al-Abadi, one of the numerous sons of Osama Bin Laden and the current leader of the Al-Qaeda. The second man was Najib Mushtaq, leader of the Tehreek-e-Taliban Pakistan, and the third was Muhammed Akbaruddin, the leader of the Jamaat-ul-Ahrar.

It was even inconceivable that their group had been invited to this gathering. Shafiq wondered how the varied groups had come together. Someone had done a lot of rapprochement to get all these diverse groups together. He wondered what it meant. It seemed he wasn't the only one surprised. Others were also talking in hushed whispers.

Majid Al-Abadi, Najib Mushtaq and Muhammed Akbaruddin appeared pleased as they watched the gathering.

"Brothers, welcome." Al-Abadi said. "First of all I thank you for your support in the fight that we are battling against the enemies of Allah. Today will go down as one of the most important dates in the history of our Islamic brotherhood. And you, my brothers in blood will strike a decisive blow in the heart of the enemy. Amongst all our successes, perhaps September 11, 2001 is the most highly acclaimed day in our history. But now, today will be marked as a red-letter day surpassing the deeds that our valiant brothers accomplished many years ago."

Al-Abadi paused as his words were received with cheers and shouts from the crowd. He continued, "Yes, my brothers. You will be the new heroes, the warriors that will take part in the holiest of wars against the infidels. Your names will be inscribed on the tablets of history. Mark my words; today will be the day of reckoning for our enemies. In fact, September 11 will pale in comparison to what you are going to do."

Shafiq tried to make sense of what he had just heard. The crowd around him went delirious with joy. The crescendo of voices roused up, deafening in its pitch. The vibes of exultation from the crowd were contagious. Shafiq focused on the words of Al-Abadi. His words still echoed in his ears.

September 11 will pale in comparison...

He mulled over it. Around three thousand people had died in the Twin Tower crash. What were they looking at? Five thousand dead? Ten thousand? He wasn't sure.

If Al-Abadi was right, this would be the biggest terrorist attack of the decade. If that was the case, he would be involved in the biggest mission since he was recruited. Curiosity gnawed at him. He had to know more about the plan.

Al-Abadi continued, "Brothers, we are the chosen ones. We will have a few senior people to lead the teams. We will divide the teams into smaller units, and each unit will have its own commander. You will be notified what to do next by your designated commander. Remember, if you die in today's jihad you will get to experience the pleasures of heaven. Fight with all your might."

Al-Abadi raised his hands in the air. "*Nara-e-Takbeer!*" He roared.

"*Allah-u-Akbar!*" The response from the gathering was deafening.

Al-Abadi and the two leaders turned and exited to their quarters. The crowd started to disperse. Shafiq snaked his way through the crowd in the direction of Malik. Malik was speaking to someone but Shafiq interrupted him.

"Malik, I want to be one of the commanders to lead the units."

Malik looked at him, distracted. "Oh, I have already shortlisted four people for leading our units. You will report to Zia's unit. Go find him and he will give you your orders." Malik turned his back on him before he even had a chance to say something.

Shafiq turned around stiffly and walked at a fast pace, fuming to himself. He exited the villa. A cool breeze wafted through the air, but it couldn't dissipate his anger. Zia would now make life hell for him. Malik had told him to report to Zia. He hoped that Zia would be in a good mood.

Shafiq saw his men in front of the cottages. They had grouped into four units. Zia was talking to one of the groups.

Shafiq walked up to him and said, "Malik told me to report to you."

Zia nodded at him and then continued to address the unit. "I am no coward to sit behind while my brothers fight the enemy. Rest assured that I will be fighting from the front, shoulder to shoulder with my valiant comrades, ready to sacrifice my blood for Allah. Just observe and learn from me. We will devastate and destroy all those who come in our paths. There will be no stopping us…"

Shafiq tried to stifle a yawn as Zia went along in his monologue. At the first pause of Zia, he edged in.

"Zia –"

Zia looked at Shafiq with displeasure. He didn't like being distracted in the middle of his speech. "What is it?" he snorted.

"Al-Abadi said that this will be our biggest mission ever?"

"Yes, it will be. It will be bigger than the destruction of the Twin Towers. People will talk about it for decades; our enemies will whisper about it with fear in their hearts, and our friends with pride. We will be honoured on earth, and blessed in heaven…" Zia started another torrent of words.

"Zia –" Shafiq interrupted him again.

Zia glared at him. "What is it? Why do you keep interrupting me?"

"I just have one small question."

"Yes?" Zia asked bluntly.

"What is our mission?" Shafiq asked.

Zia opened his mouth as if he was going to let go another torrent of words describing the mission. His mouth stood open and stuck for words. "Er, I don't know."

Shafiq kept a straight face, but the crowd laughed. Zia's face turned red and he looked to explode like a sizzling stick of dynamite. He turned towards the group, "What's so funny? We are on an important mission here. I am told to report in some time to Al-Abadi. They are going to brief the unit commanders on the mission."

"Oh, I see," Hafeez chuckled. "The way you were droning on. I thought you had created the entire plan for the mission."

The laughter was more pointed this time. Even Shafiq's lips escaped a suppressed smile.

"I will be back in some time. Al-Abadi needs my help. I have more important things to do than slouch here like you all are doing." Zia brusquely excused himself and left.

"Well," Hafeez slapped Shafiq on the shoulder, "you certainly put a lid on that empty vessel."

"I didn't mean to. I was just asking a valid question."

"No, you did well. You should have listened to him earlier. He was already in full swing with his praises about the mission before you came in."

Shafiq winked. "It's good I missed it." He then turned serious. "Hafeez, my brother; what do you make of Al-Abadi's speech today?"

"I am surprised that he brought together three different groups, in fact four, counting ours. It means that the leaders have patched their differences for now. They are working together on this new mission, whatever it is. And the most satisfying aspect is the promise that it will be bigger than 2001. I can't wait to learn what they have planned."

Shafiq nodded quietly. "Even I have been thinking the same thing. We will find out soon enough."

Hafeez left. But Shafiq's mind still burned with a thousand questions. He had to know what was being planned.

Shafiq went over to his room and pulled out the chest. He knew what he had to do.

Chapter 28

"You have the plan against the terrorists ready?" PM Inamdaar asked the General.

"Yes," Singh replied. "I didn't talk about it during the meeting because it's a private project I was already working upon. I am not ready to disclose it to the others."

Inamdaar looked at him with a keen gaze. "You were already working on a plan to eliminate the terrorist leaders. This was before today's attack in Srinagar?"

"Yes. We are already working on a classified mission for many months now."

"What is the mission about?"

"We are using HUMINT assets in Afghanistan and Pakistan to track terrorist threats in India. Our assets are deep undercover in some of the terrorist organisations. The assets will assimilate and rise within the ranks till they understand the organisational hierarchy and locate the key leaders. The eventual goal is to eliminate all high value targets in the terrorist organisations."

"Why didn't you inform me about this earlier?"

"Plausible deniability, sir. This is a black op. If someone would have asked you, you would have straightaway denied the existence of such a mission, simply because you didn't know it existed. And the questioner would have been satisfied because the answer came from the top."

"Are these assets our men?"

"Some are, some aren't. From dedicated undercover professionals to dissidents, we are using every trick in the book to scourge out this rot of terrorism."

"Have we had any success so far?"

"It is a game of patience. If the hunt for Osama and Mullah Omar has taught us anything, it's that the leaders rarely show themselves, even to their own gangs. But when they do, our men will let us know."

Shafiq knelt down and picked up the Quran from the chest. He flipped through until the end till he found what he was looking for. Nestled between two pages was a bug. It appeared to be squashed between the pages, but Shafiq knew that it was a marvellous feat of engineering.

The bug was grey in colour with stripes of dark green. It could be easily camouflaged anywhere. He looked at the thin, transparent wings that actually were rotor blades able to lift the bug and fly it anywhere. A micro camera was mounted atop the bug along with a highly sensitive microphone that could be used to remotely observe any ongoing event.

Shafiq carefully placed the electronic bug in his palm and kept the book back in the chest. He then pulled out one of the spare magazines and slid out a fake cover to reveal a thumb-sized joystick that controlled the bug.

As Shafiq glanced at the bug and the controller, he was reminded of a time long back when he had been given the devices. It seemed like it was in another lifetime.

A lifetime that he had left behind forever.

He was born as an orphan in a rural town of Haryana in India. He had grown up among scores of other abandoned orphans in a rundown NGO's basement. They provided him with rudimentary education and craftsmanship skills.

He moved to Shimla in his early twenties hoping that the tourist city would help him carve out a meagre living. He started selling trinkets to the tourists. But only a few months in, he found himself almost out of money as the local police asked him for *'hafta'*, a weekly protection money to allow him to sell the trinkets on the roadside. After the cut given to the policemen, he found that he was barely making a profit.

Disgusted with the ill-treatment, he vowed to get even. He donned a Senior Inspector's uniform and walked in to where the policemen were counting their illegal cash. He admonished the policemen for their corrupt ways and confiscated the money.

But the policemen were not fooled for long. Three days later he was caught and the Senior Inspector whom he had impersonated looked at him across the table. Another person who looked like a government official accompanied the Inspector and he looked at Shafiq with curiosity. Instead of being offended, they were amused.

The government official had a job for him. It would be dangerous and it required skills that he had. Would he be interested? If he would be willing to do it, they would let him off without any charges. For Shafiq, the choice was clear, and four months of training later, he found himself in the Indian embassy at Zahedan in Iran. The Iranian city, strategically located at the westernmost tip of Pakistan, was an ideal infiltration point into Pakistan.

His job was to go across the border from Iran into Pakistan and gather intelligence on the government activities, exploit the social fault lines of Pakistan and recruit the local Balochi people. He proved to be good at his job. He spent months at a stretch engaging with the local folks, understanding their needs and expanding his influence right up to the Naval base of Ormara, where he posed as a rich Pakistani businessman who had contacts with international defence companies. The naval elite naturally flocked around him, eager to curry favours with him, hoping to get a cut out of any defence deals that he could garner them.

The deception was perfect, and the trap was set. Over a period of two years, he asked probing questions about the naval capabilities under the guise of tendering naval contracts. It was such an unprecedented success that as soon as a new naval project was started, within a couple of days, the complete details were available in New Delhi.

But the utopia didn't last long. Spies were present on both sides of the border, and soon the Pakistani establishment realized that their secrets were being leaked almost on a zero day basis. Rather than being exposed and burned, Shafiq's bosses told him to return to Zahedan. They would give him a different assignment.

When Shafiq heard about the new mission, he almost balked.

Go into Afghanistan and join a dreaded terrorist group, his superiors told him.

This was worse than the Pakistan mission. If the terrorists got wind of who he really was, he would be tortured mercilessly. There would be no Geneva conventions to protect him and no consular access if he was captured. He would be on his own.

But Shafiq finally took it. The Pakistani mission had given him a confidence boost that he could impersonate and deceive anyone. Not the least, the illiterate terrorists. The General himself arrived in Zahedan to brief him on his mission. His presence indicated to Shafiq how critical the mission was. General Singh informed him that he would be a deep cover agent and his mission would be to identify the organizational structure of the various terrorist groups, gather actionable intelligence and eliminate their leaders at an opportune moment.

Shafiq was flown into Afghanistan where he met the top brass of the National Directorate of Security; NDS for short. The NDS was the covert intelligence agency of Afghanistan. There he spent a couple of months with the NDS agents familiarizing himself with the various rebel groups peppered through Afghanistan. After the formal training was completed, a dissident rebel helped his induction into the Lashkar-e-Jhangvi group.

He had been content to spend at least three years to discover his way to the top terrorist masterminds. Now only nine months in the mission, he had found them all together in one place. As he looked at the hi-tech bug and its controller, created in the DRDO labs; he realized that today was the reason why he had dedicated his past few months.

After taking out the bug and its controller, he closed the chest and kept it back in its place. He got up making sure that no one had observed him and he quietly exited the room.

It was time to gatecrash a meeting.

He would be the literal fly on the wall.

Shafiq placed one hand on the villa wall and glanced up at the open balcony on the mezzanine floor that had been designated as Al-Abadi's suite. He was at the rear end of the villa. The sentries had been kept at the front; none were stationed in the back. The leaders were speaking in hushed tones. But the pitch of quiet excitement reached his ears. He couldn't overhear them without getting close enough, and without risking being detected. Detection would mean being ready to field all sorts of unpleasant questions about his presence in the sacred space of their leaders. He had anticipated the challenge and hence he had brought over the miniature bug.

Shafiq pulled out the bug from his pocket and pressed an almost invisible button on its underside. The artificial wings started rotating. The activity caused him to smile. It felt as if he had revived a dead insect. He took out the controller and pressed a button. The bug started flying in the air.

Quieter than the real bug, it moved in the direction Shafiq directed it to. He slowly directed it upwards towards the balcony. The bug flew through the open balcony into Al-Abadi's room. A one inch square video screen embedded onto the controller showed him the room had a tall ceiling. He saw the three leaders were huddled together on a sofa. He discovered a small closet on one side of the room and gently landed the bug on it. The voices were clearer now. He leaned forward and listened intently.

"Are you completely sure this will be a success?" Shafiq could see Akbaruddin ask.

Al-Abadi answered, "Yes, there's no doubt in my mind. We should go ahead. All the preparations are done. We captured the engineer and brought him over. Initially, he was reluctant, but once he realized who our target was, he was only too happy to see our mission realized."

"That's good to know." Akbaruddin turned to the third person in the room. "How are we going to take control of the missiles?"

Mushtaq said, "We are going to use suicide bombers similar to how we operated at the Wah cantonment a few years back."

"But wasn't that mission a complete failure? Once the suicide bombers killed the guards, they responded immediately. You couldn't even get past the outer security."

"We have learned from our mistakes. Moreover, this facility is not as well-guarded as Wah. We have a definite advantage here. They won't be expecting us. The facility is thirty minutes away. Our brothers will rush in, kill everyone and launch the missiles. We will stay here and await the good news. Once our brothers return, we will announce to the world the biggest attack they had ever seen."

Shafiq's heart dropped in his stomach. *What abominable plan were these terrorists hatching?* And it involved launching missiles? He listened closely, dread rising in him with every word spoken.

"The engineer will accompany the group. He will help launch the missiles. And once the missiles strike its target, our enemies will die."

Shafiq felt the trepidation grow within him. He wondered who they will launch a missile against.

He continued listening.

"So it's settled then, we will launch the missiles and completely destroy New Delhi. The Indians will be headless once their power centre in Delhi is wiped out. Soon we will celebrate the victory of our soldiers against the infidels."

Chapter 29

... completely destroy New Delhi.

The words clanged inside Shafiq's head. He felt the bile rising in his stomach making him sick. It was a nightmare scenario. A barrage of missiles to be launched on New Delhi. But how? Where could the terrorists get access to those kinds of weapons? He racked his brains trying to figure out the terrorists' modus operandi. They had mentioned an engineer. Probably, they had abducted him and now based on what he overheard; the missile engineer was now willing to work for them.

It made sense. The engineer would be happy if the target was Pakistan's arch enemy India. Who wouldn't want to launch a missile that will take down the enemy? And once the missile launched, there would be no way to destroy it. Missiles didn't come with an Undo button. They were of the fire and forget breed.

Shafiq had to figure out a way to stop these madmen. A missile attack would be an unambiguous and unprovoked act of war. India would retaliate strongly, couldn't the terrorists see that? Or were they so engrossed in hurting the adversary that they didn't realize it would hit back?

He couldn't sit still. He had to do something.

As he evaluated, his actions, Shafiq realized he had only two options left with him. One was to invoke an unprecedented call into HQ. The second was to stop around hundred terrorists from launching the missiles and foiling their plan. But he realized he couldn't act unilaterally. He would have to call into headquarters and tell them what he had discovered.

Shafiq exited the area and made his way to the entrance gate of the resort from where they had arrived earlier today. A couple of guards were there but they barely looked at him. They were only interested in people coming in.

"Are you guys not joining in the celebration today?" Shafiq asked.

"No, we are on guard duty tonight." One of the men replied.

"Oh, sorry to hear that. Well someone has to be alert while the others are not. You are doing a good job. I appreciate it."

Shafiq knew that the guards would question anyone that would be coming inside. Now that he had a brief chat with them, he knew that they would remember him and wouldn't ask any questions when he returned. It would only take him a few minutes anyway.

He turned right at the entrance and walked along the compound wall to a cropping of boulders around two hundred metres from the entrance. He looked back, the entrance wasn't visible. The guards wouldn't be able to observe him here. And the snow was undisturbed. No one had come in here since the last snow fell.

He sat down and pulled out the pseudo magazine. It had one more function that he was grateful for. It was also a powerful communication device. He pressed a button and the one inch screen displayed a set of controls. He initiated the communication with a special number that was to be used only in emergencies.

His mission was one of the pet projects of General Singh. The number that he entered would put him right through to the General. Within one ring, the phone was picked up.

A voice said, "Identify yourself."

"Immortal Chief, this is *Tazi Spay*." Shafiq said, using the project's call sign for Afghan hound.

There was a silence for a moment, and then the General said. "I hope you have something mission-critical to report, otherwise you wouldn't have called me."

"Yes sir." Shafiq replied. He then proceeded to tell the General everything he had learned about the terrorists' plans. "I am in Khyber Pakhtunkhwa. You will see my coordinates on your console. All the major terrorist leaders that we have been searching for are here."

"Do you know from where they will get their hands on the missiles?"

"No, I only know that they plan to execute the mission today."

"Okay, find that out. What are your chances of

eliminating the HVTs without being detected and escaping?"

"There are over a hundred terrorists here. Guards are present at the outer entrance as well as in the villa where the leaders reside. I would consider my chances to be less than one percent."

"But, this is a valuable opportunity. Not sure if we will get another one like this."

Shafiq understood that the General wanted him to eliminate the High Value Targets all by himself. If he was captured or killed, he would be completely disavowed. It was the standard protocol of espionage. "Yes sir, I will do my best." He paused and then continued, "Sir, if I am not able to..."

"I have been thinking of that. The other option is an overt strike on the camp. But since the camp is in a foreign land, that will be the last possible recourse."

"Thank you, sir."

"In the meanwhile, you move forward as decided. If you get in a fix, call me."

"Will do. I will send a status report every hour. If you do not hear from me even after three hours, assume the worst."

There was a pause and then General Singh replied. "I will be here, waiting for your next update. I know you will do well."

"Thanks Chief." Shafiq terminated the call.

Zia walked as if he was in the air. The slight he had faced a few minutes ago was forgotten. *Malik gave me an important job. I am indispensable.* It was time for him to show them who was the boss around here. They doubted his potential and his killing abilities. He would show them once and for all.

They would understand that Malik evaluated his abilities and found him deserving enough to lead his own unit. *Today, they will know that Zia is the true hero of Allah. A fearless warrior.*

Suddenly a figure caught his eye. It looked like Shafiq and he was talking to the guard at the entrance to the resort.

Is that Shafiq? Zia couldn't be sure. The entrance

was far away, but his profile and mannerisms resembled that of Shafiq's. The man passed the gate and disappeared beyond the compound wall.

What is he doing talking with the guards? He should be with the rest of the team. If it's Shafiq, he's going to have it from me. Its time he understands that I make the decisions around here.

Zia walked towards the entrance wondering if he was still right about his hunch that it was Shafiq. It could have been anyone.

Zia gave the guards a contemptible stare. "Who was the person who just went outside?"

"I don't know. Probably out to get a smoke." One of the guards replied.

"You incompetent fools, your job is to question anyone who comes in or goes out." Saying so, he moved past the guards and looked outside. But beyond the white expanse of snow on the plateau, it was deserted.

Now, where did he go? Zia muttered.

Zia took a left from the entrance and kept walking around. His eyes roving across the white plains trying to locate the unknown stranger who had inexplicably vanished. The wind was picking up, inducing a biting pain in his ear. In a few minutes it could start snowing. He turned back to the resort entrance hoping to shelter himself. As he reached the entrance, he espied a track of footprints made by someone recently. Zia smiled an evil grin.

He had found his man.

As he followed the track, he could pick out a faint voice through the wind that was sweeping the plains. Intrigued he walked cautiously. It appeared that two people were in a meeting. He wasn't sure what they were meeting about, but if this was the place that they had selected, far away from the others, it meant that it was private. Zia loved snooping on other people and discovering their secrets. He inched closer. The sound was coming from beyond a clutch of rocks at the base of the cliff a little ahead. He reached closer, and inched his head over the boulders.

He couldn't believe it. It wasn't two persons speaking, but only one. And he couldn't miss the familiar back of the head that was visible in the midst of the small clearing.

It was Shafiq. It appeared that he was communicating with someone.

But who?

As he stood at the edge of the boulders wondering, he heard Shafiq say, "Thanks Chief." and it went quiet after that.

Zia's mind did a double-take. Shafiq had just called someone as Chief.

It could only mean one thing.

He was working for someone else.

Zia pulled out his sub-machine gun. He wanted some answers.

Shafiq shut down the communication device within the magazine and placed it in his pocket and took a deep breath. He knew the task the General had given him was a tall order. Kill three terrorist leaders and exit from the camp without any of the other hundred terrorists around knowing about it.

It was not just impossible. It was an invitation to certain death.

But Shafiq wasn't a stranger to death. He wasn't afraid of it. He was a professional. He would perform the task unemotionally with no regard for his safety. If need be, he would kill as many people as he could before he died.

He wrapped his arms and slapped his shoulders. It had started to get chilly. It was time to return to the relative comfort of the cottage. He was about to pick up his gun, when he heard a voice.

"Put your hands up, Shafiq."

Shafiq froze in surprise. He twisted his head and found Zia, wielding a submachine gun pointed at him.

"No sudden moves or it will be the last thing you do." Zia pushed the barrel of the gun into his chest. "Now, you will answer a few questions. Who were you talking with?"

Shafiq wondered how long Zia had been listening to his call with the General. He guessed that he hadn't heard much. If Zia had understood that he was working for the Indian intelligence agency, he would have directly shot him. Maybe he listened to the last few words and gathered only enough to know he was working for someone else. Shafiq kept quiet, his eyes locked into Zia's, waiting for him to make a mistake. But Zia's gaze never wavered.

"So you won't answer me. Well, if you don't tell me I will have to kill you."

Shafiq's lips curled at one end in a wry smile. Zia was threatening to kill him if he didn't reveal everything. *Who did Zia think he was fooling?*

Shafiq knew how it worked. Once he told the truth, he would be killed anyway. Shafiq kept a stoic silence knowing that it would madden Zia.

But Zia was unperturbed. "Looks like we will have to do this the hard way." He circled Shafiq and poked the barrel of the gun in his back. "You will come with me inside. And there I will expose you as a traitor in front of our brothers. Now move it."

Shafiq's mind raced as he was pushed ahead at gunpoint to the resort entrance. Once he got inside, he would be outnumbered and at a disadvantage. Whatever he had to do, he had to do it in the next few seconds.

He twisted his head to glance at Zia.

"Eyes straight ahead or I will shoot you." Zia growled.

Shafiq side-stepped suddenly and twisted his torso out of the line of fire. Zia let loose a round of shots. Shafiq winced with pain as one of the bullets tore through the side of his stomach.

But he didn't have time to glance at it. Zia was reloading his gun, and the next volley would be fatal. He swung around his fist hoping to knock his skull, but Zia was faster. He dodged out of the way and gave a rousing kick to Shafiq in the crotch.

An intense pain rippled through Shafiq's abdomen as the kick struck hard. His knees buckled and he instinctively clutched his hands between his legs. It was a mistake. He had lowered his defences. His eyes were blurry with tears of pain, but he could see the butt of a gun rushing fast towards him encompassing his entire vision. Zia had wasted no time in taking advantage of the situation.

The butt struck his face with a resounding thud, and Shafiq's vision changed to a painful dazzle of exploding white lights.

Then everything turned dark.

Chapter 30

"That high-end tablet really looks incongruous lying among the rocks." Eagle's cheerful voice hummed in Roshan's ears.

They were at the top of a tiny hill ten kilometres from the KP facility. From this vantage point Roshan could see for miles around. The narrow road they had just used to drive down here was completely devoid of cars or traffic. Nobody could have followed them in the deserted stretch that marked this part of Khyber Pakhtunkhwa.

"Now that's what I call real-time." Roshan heard Armaan's voice twice. First, directly from a few feet across, and secondly from the secured communication earpiece that was unobtrusively inserted into his ear. The earpiece was a technological marvel. It was extremely small and fit snugly into his ear canal. The earpiece was virtually undetectable. The team and Eagle were all tuned on a secure satellite relay that would allow them to communicate with each other from anywhere in the world.

"Not quite real-time, but very close." Eagle said. "The satellite goes over you every fifteen minutes. We get a time-lapsed view here at HQ."

Armaan said, "I find it very reassuring that I have got an eye literally looking over me from above, sitting in judgement over my every action."

"So be it, my child." Eagle's tone had a touch of derision.

"Don't tell me you can zoom in on everything that we are doing." Roshan echoed Armaan's sentiment. "It's like I am being stalked. I feel naked."

"Not sure about being naked but I can even tell the colour of your underwear from here." A shrill cackle emitted in his earpiece. It looked like Eagle loved his new role of playing God over them.

Roshan looked north. The hill they were on was just the starting point of a mountainous range that stretched adjacent to the target facility and continued beyond. They were on a ridge and the mountains ahead were capped at their peaks with snow. He looked at the satellite image of the area on his tablet and tried to understand his relative position with respect to the facility. Hitesh was watching him and he pointed at a jagged peak of a mountain.

"It's on the foothills of that mountain."

Roshan nodded impressed with Hitesh. He had precisely determined their location from the myriad hills and vales that he was seeing on the screen. Roshan looked at the mountain and back at the tablet. He peered at the multicoloured depressions and elevations that made up the contours on the map. They all still looked the same to him. He panned and zoomed the map alternatively and then raised his hands in frustration and gave up trying to figure it out. Hitesh laughed looking at his confusion.

"You are better with weapons. Let me handle the technical side of things." Hitesh picked up the tablet and spoke to Eagle. "What do you see up ahead?"

"The path over the mountains is a mixed bag. At some places it's a steep climb, and at other places it's a level walk. You should reach the observation point within three hours."

"How about weather?" Armaan asked.

"It may snow tonight. Wind is steady, but not threatening."

"Roads?"

"The roads ahead are deserted till the facility."

"Any patrol on the mountains?"

"None."

"Copy that." Armaan said. "Roshan and Hitesh will be at the observation point, while Baldev and I will get inside the facility."

Before leaving for Karak, they had discussed their approach to the facility and had eventually decided that Armaan and Baldev would take the role of visiting scientists and Hitesh and Roshan would act as their lookout from an adjacent mountain that gave a clear view of the facility. Roshan hadn't been sure what their role entailed, but they had all agreed that it was best that they split up with two people getting inside the facility, two outside on a mountain and Eagle monitoring them from headquarters.

Roshan looked at Armaan and Baldev. They had both donned white suits and white trousers; Armaan had said it made them appear like scientists, while Baldev had frowned that his tie would cut off his air circulation.

The Israeli had said that Mohammed Tahir, their contact at the facility had informed security that he was expecting guests today. So their entry would be pretty smooth. Hitesh and Roshan would reach the lookout spot before Armaan and Baldev, and set up an observation post overlooking the facility.

"All right," Armaan declared, "it's time for a buddy check." They made pairs and faced each other. Hitesh and Roshan double checking each other's equipment while Baldev and Armaan did the same between them. The difference being Armaan and Baldev checked to make sure they weren't carrying any weapons. Once they had completed the buddy check, Armaan walked up to Roshan.

"We make plans, but it is rare that plans are executed perfectly. Keep an eye out for any patrols in the mountains, though Eagle has said that there are none. And most important, don't get caught."

Roshan nodded solemnly. Armaan and Baldev would be taking up the car that was currently parked at the foot of the hill and drive it to the facility. They would leave once Roshan and Hitesh reached the observation post. It was a thirty minute drive to the facility and Eagle had informed them that the road ahead was devoid of traffic.

Roshan looked at their destination. A far-away peak clad with snow. There appeared to be four mountains between them and their destination. The wind picked up conspiring to fight against his will, but he ignored the biting chill on his cheeks and started to trudge through the rocks, balancing the Vidhwansak that was strapped to his shoulder. Hitesh followed close behind him.

"Good luck, boys." Roshan heard Armaan call out behind his back. He raised a thumbs-up sign as he walked forward.

Roshan was happy to be trekking the mountain ridge. Even though it was strenuous, it was better than being cramped in a tight space like he had been for the six hour journey from Sargodha. He was glad to be out in the open and be able to flex his arms and legs.

He had seen Armaan and Baldev venturing down the hill when they were leaving. They would stay in the car waiting for them to reach the observation post and then move out once they were ready.

Roshan looked at Hitesh. "It's a good day to be out in nature, isn't it?"

Hitesh simply grunted. Roshan realized that as an analyst, Hitesh didn't have the same gruelling training that he had. He could endure harsh environments. It looked like Hitesh had never experienced anything like this.

"Have you been trained for cold mountainous region?" Roshan asked.

"No, we only went through the standard training. As desk analyst designates, we never received advanced training."

"You are getting that training now." He heard Armaan's voice in his ear. They had decided to keep the communication lines open. That way they would keep in touch with each other in case they were suddenly ambushed, which was a very real threat this close to a military outpost.

"I guess I am." Hitesh had a wry smile on his face. "Though I would have liked if I had got advanced notice about this so called involuntary training."

Roshan chuckled. He remembered when they were doing the Advanced Level training, it had seemed inhumane. The level of physical and mental stress had been insanely high. He had joked to a colleague that the training could be probably the worst thing he would endure during his career.

"Maybe they are doing it on purpose." Roshan had quipped at that time. "To see if we can withstand this brutality."

"It's possible," the colleague had remarked. "Only the best of the best graduate through the training."

A few days of training later, the colleague had not reached the benchmarks required for the next level and had been told to return to his existing team. Roshan had ploughed on. Every day he got to see more and more soldiers being dismissed. When their trainer informed them that the training had finished, Roshan had been in such a stressful grip that he couldn't believe it and thought of it as another test for them. When the commanding officer told them they were now part of an elite unit, Roshan had looked around; only a handful remained out of the hundreds he had seen on the first day of training. He had somehow made it through with grim determination.

"Someone once said, what doesn't kill you makes you stronger." Armaan's words brought him back into the present. "Let us see if we can survive through the day."

"We will," Hitesh replied. "We are well prepared."

Roshan smiled. "We are always well prepared, but eventually all hell breaks loose."

"We will know in some time." Armaan said. "Let's be on radio silence till you boys reach your destination."

Roshan and Hitesh trudged through the snow. They were now only a mountain away from their designated location. Further up, he could see the mountain rising high up in the sky. This was the toughest part of the trail, Eagle had warned them.

"There's the goat trail." Hitesh pointed towards it. Eagle had informed them that there was a small trail that cut through the penultimate mountain and they slowly made their way to it.

Roshan looked at the trail and his heart sank. It was narrow and only two feet across on the face of the mountain. A high wall on one side and a sheer drop on the other.

"I hope you were trained in mountaineering." Roshan said peering down at the foot of the hills far below. Any sane person would have got vertigo.

"I have got this." Hitesh replied and effortlessly started tiptoeing across the narrow trail. Roshan watched Hitesh; he seemed to be comfortable balancing himself as he used his hands to grip the clefts in the mountain face. Roshan watched him for a moment and then followed him.

The duffel bag dug into Roshan's shoulder as he

shuffled behind Hitesh.

The narrow trail expanded into a small clearing fifty metres ahead. Roshan tried to focus on one step at a time, but the weight of the duffel bag topped by the Vidhwansak cutting in his shoulder distracted him. He leaned into the mountain face telling himself to imagine that he was just playing a slow step shuffling exercise in the army camps, but the biting breeze reminded him of where he was. He wasn't afraid of heights but the situation was debilitating his logical response.

"We are almost there." Hitesh said.

Roshan looked at the clearing, just ten feet away and he was tempted to jump across, but he held himself back. He watched as Hitesh sensibly and slowly made his way to the end of the trail and lightly stepped on solid ground. Roshan followed closely behind him and eventually they were both on the other side, safe and not worse for wear.

They were on a narrow plateau that was one of the three mountains that cradled the facility. They looked around cautiously and made their way to the other end of the plateau.

The facility suddenly appeared below. It was exactly like they had seen in the satellite images. A flat rectangular two storey building centred inside a wide compound. The sentries at the gate appeared like specks from this height. There were a few vehicles in the parking lot. The missile launch silos were adjacent to the main building.

Roshan looked around and found a boulder that jutted out at the edge of the mountain. He beckoned Hitesh to follow him and made his way to the boulder. The boulder was perfect for their needs. They could hide behind it and observe the on goings without being detected. Hitesh and Roshan positioned themselves behind the boulder. It was time to let the other know.

Roshan initiated the communication. "Markhor One, this is Three. We are in position."

"Copy that, Three. I presume the journey went well."

"Yes, it did. I see multiple hostiles in here, but nothing looks out of the ordinary."

"How many are there? I need to know what we are getting into."

"We are too far away to find out with any reliability." Roshan said. "I assume at least twenty hostiles guarding the perimeter."

"The exact number is twenty-six." Eagle's smug voice boomed in their ears. "I already counted them while you were on the way."

"Thanks Eagle." Armaan said. "It's nice to know you are not spending your time checking the colour of our undies and actually doing something useful."

"I try to be of service, One."

"Three and Four," Armaan spoke to Roshan and Hitesh. "We are moving in. Keep us covered. If they start shooting at us, give them hell."

"Roger that, One." Roshan replied.

"I will contact you once we have reached near the gates."

Chapter 31

"Kill him, I would say." One of the voices intoned.

"But, we need to know who he is working for." Another voice spoke.

The voices were sometimes indistinctive and sometimes clear. They floated in and out of his head.

"It doesn't matter. He's a liability and a traitor."

"Yes, but if we know who he is working for, we could know which of our enemies turned him against us."

"Okay, once he wakes up, question him. If he's uncooperative, kill him."

Shafiq struggled to open his eyes and found the ground staring up at him. From deep within his consciousness, an instinctive voice told him, *you are captured*.

A dim light illuminated the room; the walls were grey in colour, the shadows darkened the room in a gloomy hue. A chair creaked somewhere and then footsteps echoed on the floor moving out of the room.

Shafiq tried to focus. There were two people talking to one another as far as he had understood. One had left; meaning somewhere around him the second person was nearby. He didn't want to let the person know he had come to his senses. He discreetly stretched his hands and legs. He couldn't move them. His hands were bound behind his back. There was a creaking of another chair and footsteps appeared in his line of sight as the person walked across him.

Shafiq quickly stole a glance at his captor. It was Zia.

Zia said, "So, you are awake?"

Shafiq didn't know how Zia could see that he had come to his senses. Zia kneeled down in front of him and grabbed his jaw in his hand and shook it. "You know, I wanted to torture and kill you. But it looks like you are going to be dead soon anyways." Zia ran his finger down Shafiq's side and then poked at the bullet wound in his stomach.

Shafiq yelled as an excruciating pain sizzled through

his insides. He glanced down and saw with horror that his robe was sodden red. He remembered that he was shot in the stomach when he tried to evade Zia outside the resort.

"Where am I?" The place didn't look familiar.

"I will do the questioning around here. But I will satisfy your curiosity. We are in a basement room of the villa. You have been unconscious for two hours. I was supposed to go on the mission, but I let my team move ahead with the others. Malik and I stayed because of you. For all intents and purposes, you are a prisoner. And I am your executioner." Zia's face was filled with glee. "And since you are my guest, I will have the pleasure of slowly torturing you if you don't answer my questions. Now tell me, who were you speaking with?"

Shafiq coughed, "None of your business."

Zia's eyes glowed like red-hot coals. He reached into his pocket and brought out a switch-blade. He kept looking at Shafiq as he brought it over to his stomach and slowly twisted it in the open wound.

Shafiq felt the painful jarring travelling from his stomach all through his body. His nerve-endings were on fire. The pain reached a crescendo with every twist to an unbearable level. He let out a long, tortured, agonized scream.

Zia looked pleased to see a response out of Shafiq.

"Tell me," He almost shrieked. "Who do you work for?"

Shafiq shuddered in pain. He tried to compose himself. Zia was a maniac who didn't know the subtle art of torture. When torturing to extract information, there was a fine balance between pain and death, and it looked like Zia would likely finish him off before he would gain any information. He glanced down and could see that the blood was flowing freely.

The life was ebbing out of him.

He had to do something. This couldn't go on for long. Shafiq knew that Zia didn't realize who he was truly working for. His only safety lay in the fact that he could bluff his way to gain a few minutes. Zia was impulsive and jealous by nature. He could use his flaws against him.

"Okay," Shafiq spluttered. "I work for the Jamaat-ul-Ahrar."

"The Jamaat-ul-Ahrar?" Zia frowned. They had been present today as one of the groups. "It doesn't make sense."

"Yes, it's true. We in the Jamaat were the ones who first conceived the idea of this mission. It was a lofty mission and we pitched it to Al-Abadi. Al-Abadi loved it but he said that we needed an army of terrorists to execute this mission. It was then that we decided to bring other likeminded groups together. But what if there were dissidents and rebels, or even worse spies and traitors who would report our every move to our enemies in the government. It was then a few of us were tasked to join other groups and check if there were any spies in the groups. It was a top-secret mission and we wanted to ensure there were no leaks. I was chosen to join Lashkar-e-Jhangvi. Over the past few months, I observed every member of the clan and I was satisfied that there were no threats to the mission. It was then that your leaders were told by Al-Abadi to join the mission."

Shafiq hoped that Zia would take the bait. He continued, "I am a trusted veteran in the Jamaat. We appreciate the role Malik's group is going to do. It's going to be a difficult mission and I knew that you brothers will help us. Especially you, Zia."

Zia's eyes betrayed his thoughts. Shafiq could see his expression widen when he informed Zia that he was a senior member of the Jamaat. For long Zia had abused him thinking him as just another person in the group. He could see the hatred spiral out when Shafiq appreciated Zia as a true warrior. Zia obviously didn't like the patronizing tone in which Shafiq talked about Zia's achievements. It seemed to instigate him even more. He could see the struggle on his face as the realization dawned that his captive was in fact a veteran member of another gang.

"I don't believe you," Zia managed, his tone unconvincing.

Shafiq knew his only chance lay in unbalancing Zia for the moment so that he could buy time. The members of the Jamaat were here and his secret would be out once they walked up to him and identified him as a stranger.

Zia's slow brain reached the same conclusion. "The Jamaat leaders are here. They will tell me if you are telling the truth. And if you are not..." Zia left the words hanging.

Shafiq appeared unperturbed. "Yes, that's a good idea. They will be horrified to find one of their senior members tied up and being tortured. They will ask who did this. And once they find it was you, there will be serious consequences."

Shafiq didn't know if Zia would be afraid to own up to his deeds, but he wanted to see if there was a chance he could delay Zia going over to the Jamaat group.

Zia looked at him and then at the door. He wavered for a few moments and then came to a decision. "I will ask Malik. He will know what to do."

Zia walked up and went to the door. He slammed it behind him and Shafiq could hear the bolt being latched tight. He appraised the locked door. The door was reinforced with steel rods. Zia had chosen a good place to interrogate him. Probably it was used as a storage room.

He had to escape. But that seemed impossible in the state he was in. Shafiq twisted his body sideways. The white hot pain deep inside his stomach burned like lava. But Shafiq clenched his jaws tight against the pain. He slowly rolled around. Each roll was an agony. His insides were on fire. Blood oozed out at the slightest movement of his body. He kept rolling till he was at the door. He then twisted himself into a foetal position.

If his understanding was correct, Malik would listen to Zia and guess correctly that Shafiq was bluffing his way out. Malik would go to the Jamaat to confirm if Shafiq was one of them. Once they told him that Shafiq wasn't one of them, they would return and the torture would start.

Again.

This time in earnest.

"Approaching target in sixty seconds." Roshan heard

Armaan speaking.

"Copy that. We are in position."

It had been twenty-five minutes since they had last spoke. While Armaan and Baldev made their way to the facility, Roshan had scoped the area using the Vidhwansak. As he had observed earlier, nothing looked out of the ordinary. The sentries were patrolling the perimeter in a systematic pattern. There wasn't any unusual or sudden activity that would cause them to feel disconcerted about going in the facility.

"Now, the only thing left is for the Israeli's mole to let us in." Armaan said.

Roshan watched as Armaan's car swung in view from behind a mountain and made it to the bridge at a sedate pace.

"I am approaching the entrance."

"I have you covered. Good luck."

Roshan peered through the scope of the Vidhwansak and focused it on the guard tower in front of the gate. He estimated his distance at around one and half kilometres. Yet the guard's head in the powerful scope appeared as if he was only a few metres away. Roshan could clearly see his profile as the guard's eyes fell on the incoming vehicle. The guard rose and walked over as Armaan's car stopped.

It's the moment of truth. Roshan whispered to himself as he saw the guard peering down the window of the car speaking with Armaan. His finger gently touched the trigger ready to pull it; he would know instinctively the moment things went awry.

A moment later, the guard waved at his colleague to open the gate. Roshan exhaled in relief as the gate swung slowly open and the car passed through the entrance.

The Israeli's agent had come through.

They had penetrated the enemy's liar.

Chapter 32

"That is the second delay in a month." Mohammed Tahir's voice boomed across the conference table. There were five men sitting at the long table. The conference room was relatively empty, it could seat twenty people.

Jamal, the recipient of his anger squirmed in his seat. "Our apologies sir. We faced some logistic issues but they are now sorted out. We promise the shipment will come in a week." Jamal flustered.

But Tahir would have none of it. "That's what you said last time as well and the time before that. Meanwhile, my men," Tahir pointed outside the glass windows of the building where one could see the soldiers moving around purposefully intent on their work, "my loyal soldiers are struggling bravely against the cold."

Tahir had enough of this snivelling nonsense. He had ordered thermal jackets for his team to protect them against the harsh environment. He always dealt with another gentleman, but that person had been transferred to a different department, and now he had to contend with Jamal who never seemed to run out of excuses.

The person was from Central Trade and Logistics, who supplied them their military equipment and gear. If Jamal had been reporting to him, Tahir fumed; he would have fired him on the spot.

"This is your last chance." Tahir blasted. "If I don't hear anything by Wednesday, your supervisors will get a nasty feedback about their new recruit."

"Yes sir." Jamal stammered. "You will receive your order."

The meeting was over. Everyone dispersed from the meeting room. Tahir stood up and walked over to his office, his anger dissipating with each step. He had long ago learned to control his emotions, and use his emotions to his benefit. The angry tone was meant to convey his opinion about the non-shipment of the consignment. The additional threat of escalation to Jamal's supervisors was a way to reinforce Jamal's commitment. In truth, Tahir felt nothing.

He felt emotionless.

Empty.

In fact, he no longer cared much about anything. He was just doing his job, without hope, without expectations.

It had all started with the death of his son.

On 16th December, 2014 he had received a call informing him that his son was gunned down by terrorists. The terrorists had entered his son's school, the Army Public School in Peshawar and had fired indiscriminately at everyone. Along with his son, one hundred and forty innocent children were killed.

The loss had been devastating. Tahir had felt a sickening pit in his stomach. What kind of cowards targeted children? He was overwhelmed with grief and rage. For Tahir, the culprit was clear enough. The terrorists were just a symptom. The real virus was in the system itself. It was the ISI which had harboured and armed the terrorists for decades, and now the terrorists roamed around Pakistan with impunity and terrorized the citizens.

Mohammed Tahir wasn't just a cog in the Army ranks. He was a much-decorated Colonel. As such, he vehemently expressed his rage against the ISI and publicly condemned the ISI's good terrorist, bad terrorist policy.

It was a skewed policy wherein terrorists who crossed the border and attacked in India and Afghanistan were called good Taliban, and those who attacked Pakistanis in Pakistan were treated as bad Taliban. Tahir knew that all terrorists were the same. They had no creed and no honour. Once their means were attained, even the so-called good terrorists wouldn't have any qualms killing the friendly Pakistanis who harboured them.

A lot of people shared solidarity with him for his pragmatic opinion. Since he was a top-level Army officer, even some people quoted him in the media for his outspoken thoughts.

But his opinions didn't find any quarter in the ISI camp. He got a few calls from unknown officials to keep a low profile. But the spark had already lit up the hay, and now a lot of voices joined his in unison.

Soon enough his commanding officer called him. "Tahir, you have created a controversy with your remarks." his superior said bluntly.

Tahir was unmoved; he was still mourning the loss of his son, "I have spoken only what a true Pakistani should. These terrorists should have no place on our soil or in our policies."

"I am sorry for your loss, Tahir." His superior said, "But this is a time for you to focus on your family and not get into these affairs."

"What family are you talking about, sir?" Tahir could barely restrain himself. "I had one son and one wife. Now, I only have my wife who is sobbing her way to death. She is neither eating nor drinking and lamenting her loss all day long. What was the fault of my kid that the terrorists killed him in cold blood? Who do you think is responsible for the loss of so many innocent lives?"

But his supervisor didn't want to see his point of view. "I think you need a break. The stress of work and your personal loss has unhinged your beliefs. I have been ordered to give you a posting which will be relaxing and less stressful."

And just like that, Mohammed Tahir had been transferred because he stood up for what was right and humane. It hadn't been the first time it had happened, but it was the first time he realized that in a country ruled by corrupt and self-serving leaders, a voice of sanity had no place.

Two days later, Tahir had been moved into the Karak facility as the head of the facility. It had been a demotion for him and he had stoically accepted it. His wife had joined him and they had their quarters a few kilometres away from the facility. But the place was isolated, and his wife was lonely as he spent long hours learning the responsibilities of his new assignment.

Two weeks after he had been transferred, he came home one day to find his wife lying face down on the floor, dead. She had committed suicide by consuming an overdose of sleeping pills. A letter left by her expressed her grief at being lonely without her son, and asked for forgiveness for her extreme step.

Mohammed Tahir was inconsolable. He raged at the unfairness of life. First his son, and now his wife. He was left all alone. A victim of terrorism and state policies.

But he decided not to protest. He felt numbed by the vicissitudes of his circumstances. Complaining against anyone wouldn't lead to any results, nor would it bring back his family.

Tahir threw himself headlong into his work. Nothing mattered to him and nothing made sense to him. He lived on a day to day basis, immersing himself into his work so that the pain of loss couldn't touch him. He dreaded going back to the house that had been allotted to him; it would be empty and forlorn. He started sleeping in his office and rarely went home, working eighteen hours a day, and sleeping only because of exhaustion.

A month after his wife's death, he was contacted by a person who called himself Ijaz Ibrahim. Slowly over two or three meetings, he realized that the person was an Israeli and he had a job for Tahir.

Tahir wasn't surprised by his offer, and accepted it. And so far Ijaz had been pleased with all the information Tahir had provided.

Ijaz had told him that he should be expecting visitors today and to provide them with the Intel that they wanted. Tahir as usual had agreed to the Israeli's request.

"Sir," his subordinate entered the office, "there are a couple of visitors who say they have an appointment with you. Shall I let them in?"

Mohammed Tahir looked at the clock. It was ten-fifty am. The appointment was scheduled for eleven am. He was pleased with his visitors' punctuality. He had wondered about the visitors that Ijaz would be sending. He wasn't sure who they were or what they wanted but Ijaz had desired to give them a free reign in the facility. And since he was the head of the facility, all his subordinates would follow orders without questioning him.

"Have they been cleared by security?"

"Yes sir."

"Good, give me five minutes and then send them

in."

The subordinate left. Tahir got up from his leather chair and walked over to the window. It showed a panoramic view of the area. Snow had fallen yesterday and the mountains glistened like fluorescence in the morning light. The clear blue sky offered a dazzling contrast to the snowy mountains. It was going to be a good day after all.

Tahir looked at mountains that shielded his facility from three sides. He felt reassured by the natural cover that the mountains provided. *No one can breach us from three sides and the southern bridge is impregnable.* He felt like the king of a small kingdom.

He thought about his wife and son and the path he had taken since their deaths. Would they approve? He shrugged. He had lost his faith with the loss of his family. He didn't believe there was an after-world where he would be judged by a higher being.

It's all here and now. Whatever I have to do, I have to do it now; there is no tomorrow.

In fact, Tahir had stopped thinking of tomorrow. He didn't see any future for himself.

"It's good we decided not to bring our guns in here." Baldev whispered to Armaan.

Armaan nodded silently and looked around. They were sitting in the ante-room of the facility. They had just been frisked by the guards who checked if they carried any weapons.

It had been a point of a big debate when they had discussed their infiltration strategy into the facility. Roshan and Hitesh hadn't understood why Armaan would risk his life going unarmed into hostile territory. Now they would understand why, he told himself. They had kept the secure comm channel active so that Roshan and Hitesh could listen into their conversation. The guards hadn't discovered their miniature communications earpiece and now they used subtle words to describe the facility to Roshan and Hitesh.

"This ante-room is small compared to the lobby outside." Baldev said to Armaan in a low voice.

Armaan nodded. Their conversation was not for

themselves but for their colleagues so that they could understand the layout and personnel inside the facility. If anyone overheard them, they wouldn't find anything unusual. He continued their charade. "Yes, those ten security guards in the lobby looked bored doing guard duty all the time. It's as if they don't expect anything to happen in here."

"I would be happy if we get to see more of the facility. We need to complete our inspection so hopefully we won't be delayed for long."

They didn't have to wait for long. An officer entered the ante-room. Armaan looked at his uniform and deemed him to be a Major. Probably one of Tahir's next-in-command. The Major gestured at a door in the far end.

"You can go in now, gentleman."

They stood up, thanked the officer and proceeded to the door. As they entered the door, Tahir looked up and greeted them.

"Good morning, gentlemen."

Armaan took a close look at the Israeli's agent. He was huge. At around seven feet in height, his body was muscular with not a shred of fat. His persona filled the room such that you could ignore everything in the surroundings when he was in the room.

"It's indeed a pleasant morning, Colonel."

Tahir gestured to the chair in front of him and they sat down. An attendant came in with three cups of coffee. After he had left and there were only the three of them in the room, Tahir finally spoke.

"I would like to get straight to the point. Ijaz Ibrahim told me that you need my help. Tell me what you want?"

Armaan looked at Baldev for a moment, Baldev nodded and then Armaan spoke. "I need to inspect the Babur-3 missiles which are stored in this facility."

"Why do you want to do that?"

"It's best that you don't know. You won't get into trouble if anything happens."

"Listen, *mister*," Tahir spoke in a low voice stressing the word 'mister', "you couldn't have entered this facility if I hadn't given you permission. If I am putting my neck on the line here, I need to know what it is I am risking it for."

Armaan said nothing, and Tahir continued, "Don't you think I know that you are up to no good when I am told to give you access to the facility? So why hide? If you don't answer, you can leave."

Armaan replied, "We are going to program kill switches in the Babur-3 missiles."

Tahir looked at them with keen eyes, but didn't comment. Armaan felt as if tumblers were rotating in Tahir's brain, figuring out the various implications of what he had just revealed.

Armaan waited for a few beats and then asked, "So, are you going to help us?"

"The missiles are stored four floors below the ground." Tahir replied. "I will show you the way."

Chapter 33

They walked along a wide corridor. Tahir led the way and Armaan and Baldev followed him. At the end was a door. Tahir swiped his ID on a sensor at the side of the door. The sensor turned green and the door opened revealing a wide hall filled with rows upon rows of cubicles, not unlike a corporate office. It seemed to take almost half the floor.

"This is Level 1, Research and Development. This is where our team tests existing missiles and develops designs for new ones. We use an advanced VR system to create ballistic solutions and test the results. There is a lab there." He pointed to a double-door at the far end of the cubicles. "That's where we create simulations on a micro-level. It gives us great insights as we look forward to create more indigenous missiles. The missile technology has come a long way since the Kettering Bug."

"The Kettering Bug?" Armaan wondered what Tahir was talking about.

"Oh, you don't know? That was the world's first cruise missile. In 1918, almost at the end of the First World War, a scientist by the name of Kettering conceived an idea wherein a bomb would be made to fly and crash into enemy territory. Though we like to call it a cruise missile, technically it was an aerial torpedo powered by an unmanned conventional biplane."

"The Kettering Bug must have been quite a hit at that time. No pun intended." Baldev chuckled.

"It never saw active service. The war ended a month after it was manufactured. But it did pave the way for innovations in long-range alternatives to artillery."

Tahir kept walking and made his way to a lift. "Let me show you Level 2."

They went inside the lift. Armaan noted that the button indicators of the lift were in inverted order, starting with 1 at the top and 6 at the end.

"These are the six levels of our facility," Tahir answered his questioning look. "Two floors are above the ground and four floors are underneath."

The lift dinged a sharp bell and the doors opened. "On Level 2, we manufacture the nose cone and the cylindrical main body of the missiles." Tahir pointed out to two technicians standing close to them. "We have multiple stations as you can see across the floor. Half of them are for creating the nose cones and the other half for creating the rocket bodies." The arena in front of them was filled with dozens of stations positioned at regular intervals. The station was equipped with an LCD screen and a long horizontal platform that held the nose cone between two ends. One of the technicians was rotating the nose cone and the other technician was checking the information on the flat panel screen.

"Missile engineering is a very delicate science and the manufacturing tolerances are in fractions of a micron." He pointed at the technician rotating the nose cone. "It is rotated to check if the nose cone circumference is precisely symmetric or not. At the speed of eight hundred kmph, even a difference of a few microns can cause disastrous results in the missile's aerodynamics."

Mohammed Tahir pointed further ahead to another station where the cylindrical rocket body was spinning on its axis. "Each part must fit precisely with the other. It is a shame that we work on this so hard, yet a missile's productive lifespan is a handful of minutes. Imagine all these weeks and months we spend manufacturing it, only for the missile to work just once, and that too for a few minutes. It's a real shame if you ask me."

Tahir guided them through a stairway and they walked down one level. "This is Level 3 where the missiles are assembled together. All missiles from the Ghauri to the Babur are made here." He walked over to one of the assembly stations where five technicians were assembling the various pieces of the missiles together.

"A typical missile has various parts that need to be fitted together." He pointed at the components. "A standard missile has the booster rocket at the end, followed by the turbofan jet engines that connect to the fuel chamber. The front end contains the communications and navigation system. The Babur-3 uses the GLONASS, the Russian version of GPS, though we are looking to replace it with BeiDou GPS from our Chinese friends. Even if the GPS is blocked during wartime, it contains a Terrain Contour Matching technology, which can allow its onboard sensor to map the topology of the ground it is flying over and compare it with the onboard master map so that it can confirm its going on the right route without the aid of GPS. The body is titanium metal and the insides are made of composite to reduce its radar signature. At the top, we install the warhead. Let me show you that."

They walked down another level.

"This is Level 5. Here we install the warhead and complete the fuelling." The floor consisted of multiple large pipes that criss-crossed along the floors and walls of the level. Contrary to the previous levels, the stations here were devoid of manpower. The missiles were automatically loaded from a docking station onto the fuelling platform where they were fuelled by nozzles guided through levers. Once the fuelling was completed, the nozzle retracted and then the missile moved across the floor on a mobile carriage to another platform where the top door was unscrewed, a warhead was inserted and fixed inside the missile, and the cover was screwed tightly again.

Only a couple of technicians were monitoring this level. Armaan watched as the missile carrying carriage moved to one corner where the floor was open at the ground level. The missile was slowly lowered down and it vanished out of sight.

"Once the missiles are fuelled and weaponised, they are ready for deployment to the missile launch facilities across Pakistan. Let's go down. I want to show you the last level."

Tahir led them down the stairs and they entered a level where they were surrounded by missiles. Unlike the previous floors which were open and accommodating, this floor felt claustrophobic. The missiles were stored in racks that touched till the ceiling. The missiles blocked the view and it was difficult to gauge the size of the room. It could have been as large as the others. Armaan felt as if he was in a library except that the rows of stalls were filled with missiles instead of books.

"This is the storage level. It is purposefully kept at the lowest level to protect it from bunker-busting missiles. No missile can penetrate four floors below the ground, so this is the safest place in Pakistan to be during wartime. Let me now show you what you came here for."

Armaan followed close behind as Tahir led them through labyrinthine passages. On both sides, they were dwarfed by columns of stacked up missiles ominous in their design.

"Are these the Ghauri missiles?" Armaan looked at a stack of long missiles with a red cone and an olive green patched body.

"Yes, they are. We manufacture and store all kinds of missiles in here."

Finally he stopped at a rack that contained twenty missiles. The missiles were painted in white with a red cone at the top.

"Gentlemen, I present to you, the Babur-3 missiles."

Armaan looked at the missile and inhaled deeply. He had travelled more than a thousand kilometres with a couple of dead ends, only to now look at his objective in front of him.

Tahir extended his hand. "It's all yours."

Armaan and Baldev walked ahead; there was a toolbox in one corner. Armaan rummaged through it till he found a couple of screwdrivers. He handed one to Baldev and they started unscrewing the panel that housed the communications component. Armaan knelt down and gave a twist to the sole of his boot to reveal a hidden cavity in it. He pulled out an electronic device. Baldev did the same from his boot. The device would program the kill switch on the missiles. He plugged the device into a port on the cruise missiles circuit board and waited for the device to reprogram the missile. A few seconds later an indicator beeped on the device indicating that the kill switch was installed.

Armaan closed the panel and screwed it shut. He looked at Baldev who had already started working on another missile.

Armaan went over another rack and worked quickly reprogramming the missiles with the new programme. Within ten minutes, they had both completed reprogramming all twenty missiles that were present.

"Are you done?" Tahir asked.

"Yes, we are done here." Armaan replied.

"Good," Tahir whipped out a handgun and pointed it at them. "Now, it's time to put an end to your arrogance."

"What!" The word escaped from Armaan's lips.

"Surprised?" The Colonel spat. "You fools always underestimate us."

"But the Israeli told me you had turned."

Tahir smirked, "The Israeli is a blockhead. We have been spreading disinformation through him for months now. He has turned into our most valuable disinformation agent."

"But, you publicly accused the ISI of killing your family."

"Yes, I did. I am disenchanted with the ISI. It doesn't mean that I will become a willing traitor to my country. The Israeli made the same wrongful assumption that you are making. There is a lot I dislike about my country and its leaders, but I can never betray it. When the Israeli first contacted me, I reported the incident to my supervisors. They told me to bite the bait and see where it leads to. We have been feeding a lot of carefully constructed crap to the Israelis. Our supervisors are so happy with the Israeli that we are going to give him a promotion so that he can pedal even more high-level disinformation that will convince the Israelis that their best men are traitors in the pay of Iran." Tahir made a throated laugh.

"If you knew the Israeli was sending us, why did you let us in your facility? And why did you allow us to sabotage the missiles?"

"The Israeli hadn't told me why you were here, but I had my doubts. When you told me you were here to sabotage the missiles, I wanted to know exactly what you were doing. We will reverse engineer the program you installed on the circuit board and will use it against you. We are going to have the final laugh."

"What if you are unable to undo the programming we did? That's a risky proposition."

"Not when you compare it to the benefits. Hacked components can be replaced; but enemy designs and counter-strategics, that is really valuable."

Armaan looked around. They were two of them and Tahir was alone, but the gun in his hand tipped the balance in his favour. He had smartly stepped back when pointing the gun at them. Armaan couldn't make a dash at him without being gunned down. Plus his seven-foot frame made any confrontation a dead contest.

"I know what you are thinking. Give up your thinking. You cannot overpower me. With or without gun. But just to be clear, my gun is ready and pointed at your head. And know that I am a good shot." He pulled his mobile to his lips and spoke. "Level Six, ninth row, come ASAP."

He pocketed his mobile and then smiled. "My men are coming. You have a few seconds to try something rash. The rules are simple. Move and you die."

Tahir waited as if he expected Armaan and Baldev to make a move. Armaan found Baldev looking at him for guidance. He looked at Tahir's massive bulk standing guard in the middle of the aisle blocking their way to the lift. His gun was levelled on them, his eyes alert and the finger on the trigger.

A moment later Armaan heard the trample of boots indicating the incoming guards. His breath caught in his throat. There was no way they could escape.

They were trapped.

Chapter 34

"We've been suckered into an entrapment."

Roshan watched through his scope as Baldev and Armaan walked out of the main entrance of the facility. They were easily distinguishable from the others. Their white suits were in contrast to the green khakis of the soldiers. Four guards flanked them, their guns pointed at Armaan and Baldev. A couple of minutes earlier, Roshan had been shocked when he heard Tahir calling in his guards to arrest their colleagues. He had heard every word of Tahir's conversation with Armaan and Baldev. The bile in his stomach rose up to his throat. He felt sick at Tahir's duplicity.

Hitesh looked through his binoculars. "Why didn't they listen? I told them to be armed before getting inside the facility."

"It wouldn't have made a difference. They would have been caught at the security checkpoint. Tahir already knew about us. Once we decided to enter the facility, we simply walked into his trap."

"What do we do now?" Hitesh asked.

"Eagle, did you hear that?" Roshan asked on the secure frequency. They had decided to be on open communication throughout the mission. It meant that everyone on the mission team along with Homebase would get the updates in real time.

A sombre Eagle answered them. "Yes. I heard everything. I will try to contact the General. He should have some ideas on how to get out of this predicament. Though being all alone in Pakistan, don't get your hopes too high."

"Thanks Eagle. But I am not sure he will be able to do anything. We are on our own."

"I don't like surprises." Armaan heard Tahir speak behind him as he and Baldev were marched towards the barracks. "So please don't spring one on me. It will be a waste of time."

Tahir hadn't even bothered to handcuff him. Maybe he was overconfident about his prowess and skill,

Armaan thought. Though so far, Tahir appeared to read the situation well. Armaan and Baldev were Defenceless and they were being escorted by four armed guards and the giant Tahir. He evaluated his possibilities and quickly came to the conclusion that they were at a disadvantage.

Armaan shrugged, "The surprise element has been from your side. Currently my predicament is that of a mouse trapped in a cage guarded by cats. I will have to wait for the right opportunity to escape."

"Good that you see it that way." Tahir said, "I know you can't escape. Do me a favour, when you find that opportunity to escape, inform me first so that I can tell you if it will succeed or not."

"That makes sense."

They walked up the steps to the barracks. Tahir continued talking, "This job is so mundane and routine. Thank you for spicing up my day. I'll be honest; I have not yet decided what to do with you gentlemen. Till the time I decide, you will be my guest. We Pakistanis are famous for our hospitality."

"Thanks. I look forward to see what you've to offer."

Tahir hailed one of the men in the barracks. The man walked swiftly towards them. "Sir?" he asked.

"Keep a close eye on these gentlemen. They will be spending time in your quarter. Make sure their needs are catered for." Tahir turned to Armaan, "You both must be hungry. I will ask the chef if he can cook something unique for our guests." Thus saying, Tahir left them.

"This way, sirs."

Armaan and Baldev followed their new escort to his quarter; two guards were still with them. He entered the room. It looked like a typical barrack room, except that there was only one bunk bed in the room instead of the four bunks they saw in other rooms on the way. The person appeared to be the leader of the soldiers.

Apart from the bunk bed, there was a rudimentary desk and two chairs in the room. The room was frugal and clean.

"Make yourselves comfortable."

Armaan shrugged, he wasn't sure what fate held in store for them. He walked in the room and sat on the bed, all the while looking for points of opportunity within the room.

There were none.

The room was made up of the four walls and the ceiling; it had no other connecting doors or a place to hide in. The only break in the wall was a small window at one end. It was barred with thick iron bars. Armaan walked up to the window. Beyond the window, he could see a guard, arms at the ready staring at him. Tahir had done his homework well. He turned his gaze back inside the room. The owner of the room looked at him. He stood in the doorway casting an intent eye on Baldev and Armaan. The two guards flanked him, making no indication that they were to leave.

Armaan sighed. He was under house arrest.

Tahir walked across the length of his office deep in thought. He reached the window and looked out at the scenery. It was just as beautiful as it had been in the morning. There was something about the snow-capped mountains that seemed to soothe the nerves.

But today Tahir wasn't feeling the magic. He should have felt exulted, he told himself. The plan had worked perfectly and flawlessly and the Indians were now under custody. But he wasn't happy. He realized he hadn't thought farther ahead. He had only been concerned with capturing them.

Now that he had captured them, an apprehension started to get hold of him. So far, he hadn't let anyone in his plans within the facility or with his supervisors in Rawalpindi, but now he realized that the plan could backfire upon him.

When he had been transferred to this facility, there had been voices within the Army fraternity that had called him a traitor for questioning the ISI. Tahir bristled with rage. A traitor? Him? There were few men who had served their nation so faithfully over so many years. Even fewer who had risen through the ranks of a Colonel by spilling their blood in numerous battles against the Indians and the terrorists.

How dare they question his love for Pakistan? These people fit only for bootlicking were now labelling him as a worthless traitor. After his wife's death, he had been driven to work by only one desire, to clear his name and get back the dignity he had lost.

Tahir had carefully plotted the trap and the Indians had walked right into the trap. This was his chance at redemption. He had come back to his office to make the call to his supervisors to give them the good news. Their 'worthless traitor' had captured two Indian spies on his own.

But he had stopped himself as a possibility rankled in his mind.

What if the ISI came in between and took over his trophy? Tahir was familiar with the modus operandi of the ISI over the years. He had experienced enough incidents where the ISI would meddle into Army and police detainees under the garb of national security and would whisk the prisoners away. In a significant number of cases, the prisoners were never heard about again. Probably killed or incarcerated in a dank cell known only to them.

The ISI would jump up at the opportunity to interrogate the Indian spies. They wouldn't bother crediting him for the capture. His honour would not be redeemed.

Tahir stopped pacing and looked out of the window at the barracks that held the Indian spies. A germ of an idea was forming in his mind. There was only one way he could claim the capture in his name without the opportunistic ISI fanatics getting in his way. The only way he would be able to regain his dignity would be if the ISI couldn't get any mileage out of the spies. He walked behind his desk and pulled out the drawer. Inside was his trusty handgun. The idea had now completely formed in his head. He cocked the safety back on the handgun and smiled.

The ISI would have no use of the Indians if they were dead. Dead people couldn't be imprisoned or tortured. The dead were of no use to the ISI.

But the dead spies would prove most useful in clearing his name. He could picture the news already. *Legendary Colonel shoots two spies as they try to infiltrate his facility.* Tahir pocketed the handgun and exited his office. A few minutes earlier he had been unsure of what to do with the Indians. Now he knew their fate.

The Indians would have to die.

And he would redeem himself by claiming their kill.

Chapter 35

"What are our options, One?" Armaan heard Roshan's voice in his ear.

Armaan looked through the barred window at the gate. There was freedom, only two hundred metres away. But between him and the gate stood numerous guards ready to gun him down. He looked at the sentry guarding the window. He stared unwaveringly at Armaan, as if telling him to get away from the window. Armaan turned and looked at the door. The door was open, but three men guarded it, again staring at him. He knew that if he walked in the direction of the door, the guards would stiffen and get ready to shoot him. He lingered a moment longer near the door and then sat down on the bed.

"You guys stay put. Do not attempt to rescue me. That's an order." He spoke in a low voice looking at Baldev. The guards at the door would mistake him for speaking with Baldev.

"Acknowledged. But how are you going to get out of there?"

"I am not sure. I am looking for chinks in the armour, and so far I don't see any. There are hordes of guards within the barracks as well as outside. Our chances of survival are in single digits."

Baldev spoke, "I think we have reached the end of the proverbial tether. This looks to be our swansong."

Armaan placed a hand on his shoulder, "There is no need to be pessimistic. We have been in bad situations over the years. Somehow, we always survived."

"Yes, you had your rules and because of them, we never failed in any of our missions. What do you think of our situation now?"

"I ignored my rule number one."

Roshan asked, "I have been meaning to ask you, what is rule number one?"

"Never underestimate the enemy. Your perception of your enemy is your weakness. Whether you underestimate an enemy to be weak, or believe it to be strong; in both cases, they are perceptions and will lead to an incorrect decision chain."

Baldev nodded, "Yes, we never imagined that Ijaz Ibrahim was being fed the wrong information all the time. I think he will be crushed when he finds out the truth. He was taken for a ride for so long."

"Before, we can warn him, we need to get out of here. So far I don't see a route out. This Tahir is more dangerous than the others. He hasn't even handcuffed us, as if he is flaunting his strength and the impregnability of this place."

"I think we should admit," Baldev said, "that our situation is hopeless. If we are lucky, we will get a quick death. If not, it will be months of torture and pain in our destiny. I vote for making a suicidal escape bid. At least we will die quickly. Who's with me?"

Armaan said, "I am with you, but it's the last option we should consider. Our mission is not yet done. Tahir knows that we have tampered the missiles. He says he will undo our sabotage attempt. We will leave this place only when we are sure that our mission objectives are complete."

Roshan said, "How can you be thinking of the mission when your life is at stake? You are seriously not thinking of going inside the facility again?"

"I will go there if I have an opportunity. As far as I know only Tahir knows that we have sabotaged the missiles. He will have to be killed before he tells anyone."

"So what's the plan again?"

"No plan. I will just have to wing it. Like Baldev said, it is a suicidal mission."

Armaan walked over to the window and took a good look at the bars and the metal framework. It was solid and meant for durability. He grabbed the bars and tugged at them. The guard beyond the window gave a terse shout.

"You! Stay inside. Don't come near the window."

"Is that guard pestering you?" Roshan asked Armaan."He is in my sights. Should I take him out?"

Armaan smiled involuntarily at Roshan's offer. "No. One guard won't make a difference. Besides we will only attract other guards who will wonder how he was killed.

It will make things worse for us."

"There's some commotion going on at the gate," Hitesh interrupted.

What? Armaan wondered. He looked in the distance at the gate. Sure enough, he could hear some of the guards shouting and moving in the direction of the gate.

Boom!

The sound of a thunderous explosion rocked Armaan's world. He looked in disbelief as a powerful bomb exploded in front of the gate. A second later, the shockwave hit him. The incredible energy pent up inside the bomb knocked him off his feet, and he tumbled to the floor, his forehead and cheeks hot with the heat of the explosion, as the warm air swooshed through the windows. A ringing sound filled his ears drowning all other sounds. He saw Baldev looking over him, his lips were shouting something, but Armaan couldn't hear anything other than the ringing sound, and in a corner of his mind, he realized that the shockwave had caused temporary deafness.

A couple of seconds later the ringing in his ears ceased, and he heard disjointed words and shouts stream into his consciousness.

"...exploded in front of the gate." Armaan heard Hitesh's words through the earpiece. Hitesh had an eagle eye view of the place. He should have seen what happened. He craned his neck towards the door. Two of the men had left, and only one guard remained, but instead of the relaxed position earlier, he had trained his gun directly upon them. Armaan and Baldev were the outsiders in the facility and would be the first under suspicion.

But what had really happened at the gate?

Armaan turned his head away so that the guard wouldn't see him speak. "Hitesh, what happened? Tell me."

"A man ran in. The guards gave him a warning, but by that time he had reached the gate. He blew himself up. It was a suicide bomber. The gate got mangled due to the force of the explosion. I see multiple guards down in front of the entrance. Other guards are converging onto the gate. They are assessing who is dead and who is wounded. They seem to have a lot of work on their hands. It seems to be a terrorist attack. Terrorists have tried to attack military sites before this. I remember the previous attempt at the Wah ordinance factory –"

Armaan digested the information Hitesh had provided. He remembered the suicide bomber attacks on Wah, as well as other locations. The terrorists selected such locations for their high profile attention that they got. He knew that the terrorists would know that attacking a closely guarded military facility was ultimately going to fail, but they still did it to highlight that no place in Pakistan was safe from them.

Armaan was lost in his thoughts when he felt a hand grab his shoulder. "Get up."

He saw that it was the soldier guarding them. He was accompanied by Tahir. Tahir looked quite composed considering that a horrific attack had just happened in his facility. The only difference was that he was no longer smiling. His words to Armaan were also brief.

"I will ask only once. Who is behind this attack?"

"I have nothing to do with this. It looks to be a suicide bomber."

Tahir pulled out his handgun. "Don't play games with me. You two come in, and a few minutes later my men die in a bomb explosion. I don't believe in coincidences."

"I repeat, we have nothing to do with this. Besides blowing up things is not our style. I think you know that."

Tahir was about to say something when another explosion rocked the room they were in. This one seemed to be of a lower intensity but seemed to be closer. Armaan walked over to the window and looked outside. Smoke billowed in the parking next to the gate. A car had been blown up. The soldiers who had converged on the entrance were screaming shouts.

Did another terrorist get inside the facility? Armaan wondered when he saw an unexpected sight.

A dozen streams of traces streaked from the top of the western mountain. The white streams whizzed in a straight line leaving a white line of smoke behind them that was barely visible against the snow-capped mountains. The traces seemed harmless till they landed all around the entrance where the soldiers were.

A cacophony of explosions erupted as the streams hit the tarmac, pulverising steel and ripping flesh in its wake. It rained death. He watched the soldiers run helter-skelter; racing across the compound desperate to shelter them from the overhead onslaught. One of the streams landed right atop a soldier and tore him to shreds.

"RPGs! Take cover." He heard one of the soldiers outside scream.

Armaan looked high up in the mountains where the traces had originated from and could see small moving specs. The terrorists were ensconced in the mountains and used Rocket Propelled Grenades on the soldiers below. Their strategy had been effective. Start with one explosion by a suicide bomber in front of the gate killing a few. When other soldiers come in to help the wounded, pound them with the RPGs.

"There are hostiles in the mountains." Armaan heard Tahir shouting behind him. Tahir had also watched his men routed by the multiple RPG explosions. More soldiers were rushing in the compound; they had watched their brothers in arms die and immediately opened fire at the intruders in the mountains.

Another explosion was heard; another suicide bomber had raced up to the gate and blew himself up. A moment later the loud staccato of machine gun fire sounded. Armaan looked through the window; he could see the soldiers moving towards the gate firing at someone beyond. A loud siren reverberated through the area. Shouts were heard and orders were issued.

The second in command rushed in the room, "Colonel, we have had two attacks on the gate. The gate is bombed out. A handful of terrorists are engaging with our men outside the perimeter. We have had multiple casualties due to the RPG assault from the mountain. An alert has been sounded. Our guards from inside the facility and the reserves in the barracks are on their way to provide support. Based on the attack pattern, it appears to be a full-fledged terrorist attack."

The colonel barked, "We will grant these scum their

death wish. They will know the force of the army." He turned towards Armaan and said, "I'll deal with you later."

Tahir left the room.

Tahir rushed outside and saw the barricades around the facility swarming with his soldiers taking cover against the barrage of RPGs. He looked up. He could see the terrorists spread out in a one-eighty degree arc high up in the mountains. Every other minute, an RPG was being launched at the facility from a random point on the mountain. The height gave the terrorists a tactical advantage, and his men were being caught in the cross-fire.

We are completely exposed.

"Target the RPGs." The second-in-command shouted.

The men were already doing that. The challenge was that the terrorists were deeply ensconced in their positions giving the soldiers a small target. And they had spread out wide enough to minimize their casualties.

There was only one other group apart from the Al-Qaeda that could organize such an attack.

It's the bloody Tehreek-e-Taliban Pakistan!

He watched his men targeting the terrorists. They were well concealed making it difficult for his men to kill them. The kills were few and far between. But his men were putting on a brave fight. The RPGs relentlessly pounded the facility, injuring the soldiers and killing a few. Smoke billowed all over the place.

"Keep firing. We will murder these dogs today." The second-in-command exhorted.

"No, stop firing." Tahir ordered.

"Why?"

"Because, this is exactly what they want. Don't you understand we are playing into their hands? They will wait out in the mountains till our ammunition is depleted, and then come down and launch a frontal attack."

"But, the RPGs are killing our men."

"That's because we are out here in the open. Do we really need to be out here? We have four underground levels that can withstand heavy artillery. Two can play this game. Let us make them sweat."

"You are right Colonel, as usual." Turning to the others, the second-in-command ordered, "Everyone fall back. I need some men near the entrance to observe the enemy movements. Inform me the moment they make any moves. Everyone else, take cover. I want one group in the barracks and the other in the facility. Await my further orders."

More grenades pounded the compound, but now the compound was deserted. A few minutes later it was quiet outside. Apparently, the terrorists had understood that there would be no retaliation.

"Some of the terrorists are gathering together." The sentry on the west checkpoint shouted.

"That's okay. I would be interested to know what they will try next."

The Colonel was reminded of one of the stories from Aesop's Fables. It involved a one-eyed deer who lived on the shore, keeping the good eye towards the land, looking for hunters. The blind eye was turned towards the sea, since no dangers were expected from that direction. A hunter came to know about this. He sailed in a boat and shot the deer from the boat. The Colonel wondered if he had also turned a blind eye to the so-called impassable mountains.

It seemed too late to dwell on it.

Minutes passed with no activity. "They are still gathered together."

"Instigate them. Fire indiscriminately."

A couple of soldiers rushed outside, took cover against the building and started firing at the group huddled high up in the mountain. The terrorists cowered and ducked for cover. But there was no returning fire.

Tahir understood that the terrorists would not draw themselves out in the open. "Stop firing. Get back to your positions."

"What are they doing? This is most unusual."

"And that is what worries me. They have a plan and they are working based on that. And we have to figure out what their plan is." Tahir turned to his office, "In the meantime, I will contact the airbase in Peshawar and tell them to hightail a couple of helis in here. We are at an impasse, but not for long. Terrorists always have a Joker in their deck."

"What does that mean?"

"It means they are insane enough to run in here and blow themselves up. If they can't get through using firepower, they will try something unconventional. And that worries me. With the helis, we can flatten the terrorists in no time."

Tahir marched up to his office and contacted the Peshawar air base. A minute later, he hung up the phone, satisfied. They would be sending a couple of attack helicopters immediately. He was given an ETA for thirty minutes. He walked out back into the open sunlit mountains and looked at the ledges where undoubtedly the terrorists took refuge secure in the knowledge that they couldn't be shot at from ground level.

From ground level, no chance of shooting them. From an attack helicopter like the Cobra, their hideout would be pulverised into rubble in seconds.

Tahir smirked. The terrorists were in for a nasty surprise.

Chapter 36

"Why aren't we going down, Nadeem?" One of the terrorists asked.

"We will, eventually." Nadeem Kunduz looked down from the mountain at the facility below. The compound was deserted, except for the numerous dead bodies at the gates. His suicide bomber had succeeded in breaching the gate open. They had bombed out the soldiers who had rushed in to help. The casualties on the mountains had been minimal. They had scouted the mountains for deeply entrenched ledges from where they could shoot but not be shot at.

Only with proper preparation comes success, and they had prepared well. He looked at the group. Till yesterday, they were from diverse factions, but today they were united in a common fight. Their goal was in their sight. He estimated that within an hour the facility would be in their command.

An hour was more than enough for what they had planned.

"It's been half an hour since they have shot back at us. They have now retreated to a safe place and aren't making any moves at attacking us."

"Oh, but they have already made the move." Nadeem patted the weapon in his hand. If he understood the Army response, the weapon in his hands would come in useful.

"What move?" The terrorist said. "I don't see them doing anything."

And as if in answer, they heard the powerful rotors of two helicopters approaching from the south.

"Get ready, brothers." Nadeem said to the other unit commanders.

He lifted the weapon in his hand and propped it on his shoulder. It was a surface-to-air missile. He looked through the scope and targeted the broad frame of one of the helicopters. He knew that there were four other commanders in their group doing the same thing.

The helicopter was a Bell AH-1F Cobra, the most common attack helicopter in Pakistan. It was still far in the horizon, but was rapidly approaching. He knew that they hadn't been detected yet, or else the helicopter would have started targeting them. It didn't matter. In a few seconds, the helicopter's pilot would realize he was locked on by a SAM missile. Nadeem flipped on the activator, the missile immediately locked onto the helicopter. He pressed the button. With a shudder, the SAM ejected out at a furious pace, reaching the target in seconds. Nadeem watched in satisfaction as it hit the target precisely.

A deafening explosion sounded. The helicopter exploded in smithereens casting the flying debris everywhere. A second later, the second helicopter also blew up. His friends had synchronised the twin attacks precisely.

"Now." He yelled, and half of them leapt down the trail to the base of the mountain.

The explosion of the Cobra helicopter was so powerful that Tahir felt like a knife had stabbed him straight through the heart. A fraction later he watched in disbelief as the second helicopter also exploded as it was shot by a SAM missile. The remorse stung even harder. This was all his fault. He had sent the pilots on a suicide mission.

As he scurried under cover to evade the raining debris, anger coursed through his body. He would send out his soldiers directly to the mountains. And he himself would lead them. His logical mind told him that he couldn't win against a high altitude enemy, but he was beyond caring. This was a question of honour. As a soldier, he had to avenge his fallen brothers. He couldn't shirk his responsibility. They would fight till the terrorists were flushed from their hideouts. He was about to give the order, when he watched an army of terrorists racing down the mountain towards the gate.

Their intentions were unmistakable.

"There are multiple terrorists attacking the facility. Suggest course of action, One." Roshan said.

Armaan looked through the window at the gate. He could see the terrorists approaching the gate.

"Do not engage." Armaan said. "I repeat, do not engage. This is not our fight."

"But, it will soon become our fight." Roshan replied. "The terrorists have thinned the ranks of the soldiers guarding the facility. I see only a few at the gates; and few others outside the barracks and the facility entrance. Once they reach the barracks, you may get caught in the crossfire."

"Looks like we are in the wrong place at the wrong time." Baldev said. "Weaponless, defenceless and caught by the Pakistani army. Imagine the irony if we are rescued by terrorists."

Tahir's soldiers were already taking covering positions and were shooting at the terrorists. But the wave of terrorists was unstoppable and the men at the gate were few. They were going to be overwhelmed soon.

It was going to be a bloodbath.

The guard who had been stationed outside the window was no longer there to monitor Armaan. He had already left, and was fighting the enemy. Armaan glanced at the door. To his surprise, the man at the door was also absent. He walked through the door and looked at the entrance of the barrack. The man was propped against the wall and taking out enemies using his sniper rifle. Armaan could see around twenty guards in position outside the barracks. No one was paying them any attention.

Armaan went back in the room where Baldev gave him a questioning look.

Armaan spoke, "Boys, we may have an opportunity to escape. Right now, the enemy soldiers are distracted and will not pay much attention to us. This is our chance to escape."

Roshan's voice spoke in his ear. "There are around twenty soldiers outside your barrack. You two are unarmed. You cannot simply escape from there without someone gunning you down."

"I know it's downright suicidal, but an opportunity like this won't come again. Use the Vidhwansak and provide covering fire as we try to escape."

There was a pause and then Roshan's reluctant

voice came in, "Yes, Armaan, I will do my best."

Armaan nodded silently. It wasn't the best plan, but it was the only plan they had. He walked out of the room with Baldev at his side. He glanced at the windows of the barracks. All of them were barricaded with iron grills like the one in his room. The only way out was through the door. He could see it twenty metres away. Just beyond the door, he could see two soldiers shooting at the terrorists. Their backs were turned to him.

Armaan walked towards the door, debating whether to make a run for it, or to incapacitate the soldiers nearest the door and take their weapons. It would alert the others, but at least they could fight their way out of the area, instead of being defenceless like they were now.

Just then, Tahir walked through the door, a handgun in his massive palm. "Thinking of going somewhere, my friends?"

Armaan and Baldev stopped in their tracks.

"We Pakistanis are known for our hospitability." Tahir said. "It's a shame if you are thinking of leaving so quickly. Anyways, I have decided what to do with you spies."

"What's that?" Armaan asked in an even tone.

Tahir was about to reply when a powerful explosion rocked the barracks. This one was closer; the impact bursting the glass off the windows. Outside Armaan could see a massive hole in the west wall. Smoke was billowing out of the wall. A moment later a horde of terrorists swarmed through the opening in the wall.

Tahir rushed out screaming at his number two. "Spread out and shoot the terrorists."

As Armaan watched, a stream of RPGs exploded outside the barracks. One of them landed just outside the door where the guards to their room had been. As the smoke cleared, he could see their bodies metamorphosed into burnt flesh and dismembered remains. Both the guards were dead.

Armaan raced outside. The terrorists were only a couple hundred metres away shooting indiscriminately at the remaining soldiers. He saw Tahir lying on the ground; one of his legs had been blown off due to the shrapnel from the grenade. He was crouching behind one of the numerous corpses and was returning fire with manic frenzy.

"The terrorists have surrounded the barracks from three sides." Armaan heard Hitesh's panicked voice.

Another wave of RPGs rained near the barracks. Armaan hastily ducked inside the door. The terrorists were attacking from the gate at the south and they had breached the wall on the west. Plus, the terrorists on the mountains were pounding the facility with their RPGs. It was a murderous three-way crossfire and they were trapped in the middle. Armaan saw the soldiers outside bravely fighting off the enemies. Numerous terrorists had died at the hands of the soldiers, but they still approached the barracks relentlessly.

Armaan looked towards the gate. There were less than five guards fighting against some thirty terrorists. In a few minutes the terrorists would overwhelm the guards and gain access to the gate. In front of him, the terrorists that had breached the west wall were spreading out in a wide arc and closing in. They were taking whatever cover they could muster, intending to kill as many as they could before they died.

Hitesh was right. Armaan and Baldev were trapped. Armaan squirreled his way to the door followed closely by Baldev. He needed to be armed. He took the assault rifles besides the dead guards and handed one to Baldev.

They had to fight their way out of here.

"Get in cover!" He heard Hitesh's voice. Armaan and Baldev didn't wait. They raced back into the safety of the barracks as another RPG blasted the spot they were at a few seconds ago.

"Three," Armaan ordered. "Use the Vidhwansak and blast the terrorists in the mountains who are firing at us."

"Roger, that." Roshan said.

"Baldev," Armaan said, "take position against the windows. Our first priority is to push back the terrorists on the west side. Weapons free."

"Weapons free it is." Baldev immediately crouched under cover of one of the windows and started shooting, his rifle on automatic fire.

Armaan took shelter under one of the windows and peered high up at the mountains where he knew the terrorists were ensconced. He could see sporadic streams of RPGs flying down to the compound.

But not for long.

Roshan peered through the Vidhwansak's scope. He had already highlighted the terrorists hiding on the opposite mountain a few minutes ago, but he had been waiting for Armaan's permission.

Now he would go all out.

The Vidhwansak was side-loaded with a round of 20mm ammo and was ready. *The Destroyer*. That was the meaning of the Vidhwansak. And the terrorists would soon realize what it meant.

Roshan selected a group of four terrorists hiding behind a rock, firing RPGs down at the facility and laughing at the devastation they were causing. He held his breath and squeezed the trigger.

An explosive crack echoed in the plateau they were on. The gun shuddered in Roshan's hands as it jerked back with a powerful impact that threatened to shatter his shoulder bones. A dull pain spread through Roshan's shoulder, but he smiled. He was on the safer end of the rifle. He watched through the scope to see how the terrorists on the wrong end of the barrel fared.

The Vidhwansak's powerful large calibre rounds were on display. The momentum of the massive palm-sized ammunition was huge. The first shot tore through the boulder as if it was brittle glass. The boulder exploded into a thousand pieces on impact, the pieces acting like shrapnel for the terrorists around it. The terrorists crouching behind the border had no chance to escape, no place left to hide. They were peppered with granite and their mangled insides splattered on the cliff face.

Roshan could see the other terrorists standing up from their positions wondering where the shot had come from. But at a distance of one thousand five hundred metres, they would have no idea that it came from the mountain opposite to them. Plus the muzzle brake at the end of the Vidhwansak suppressed the flash of the escaping bullet. He swivelled the gun and picked out another target and pulled the trigger again.

Armaan didn't hear the shot from the ground but he could see half a dozen terrorists fall around simultaneously, dead. Armaan continued watching as he saw the muted explosions of the rocks high up in the mountains every few seconds. With each blast multiple terrorists around it died. The terrorists were now panicking and trying to search for cover. But Armaan knew. No cover could hide a terrorist against a Vidhwansak. Soon the terrorists were running helter-skelter.

Armaan smiled grimly. *Metal death*.

But the smile didn't last long. Apparently a leader shouted at the fleeing terrorists. The terrorists stopped. A moment later they regrouped around the leader and trooped rapidly down the mountain.

Towards him.

Chapter 37

"Terrorists at nine o'clock." Armaan heard Baldev shouting at him.

He looked at the western wall. The narrow hole had turned into a bottleneck, causing most of the terrorists coming out from the hole to be an easy target to hit. Scores of terrorists with their blood-sodden bodies lay in front of it. He counted around twenty terrorists remaining based on where they were shooting from.

But it wasn't just the terrorists among the fallen; he could see an equal number of soldiers dead in front of them. The RPGs had been stopped, but by then it had taken a heavy toll. Armaan continued to fire at the terrorists; the situation was precarious and could go either way.

"Three," Armaan said, "you will have a better viewpoint from there. Shoot the terrorists outside the gate."

"I am already doing that." Roshan said. "The problem is that there are too many of them."

A grenade exploded near the gate. Armaan watched in horror as the few remaining soldiers at the gate were overrun by the horde of terrorists. The soldiers were mercilessly gunned down. An entire contingent of the terrorists swarmed through the gate and raced across the open compound. Some going towards the facility entrance, others towards the barracks. Armaan started shooting at the ones closest to the barracks.

"The gate has been breached," Hitesh reported. "They will reach the barracks in no time."

"I am trying to snipe off as many as possible," Roshan said.

"Me too." Baldev said. He had shifted from shooting at the terrorists in the west to the larger contingent of terrorists at the gate.

Armaan watched Tahir in front of him outside the barracks taking shelter behind a pillar. He was surprised that Tahir was still alive with all the shooting and bombing happening around him. Tahir was prone on the ground firing at the terrorists like a maniac.

Armaan remembered his story. His son had been killed by terrorists. The intensity on his face was full of hatred, yet he aimed and fired with mechanical precision taking down the terrorists a hundred metres away. Two of Tahir's team members called to him to take cover, but Tahir ignored them, almost in the open with barely enough cover. He was living with a death wish.

Armaan watched through the windows as the two soldiers rushed out and picked Tahir's heavy seven foot frame and brought him through the door and laid him down. Tahir didn't protest, but resumed his firing from behind the door. The two soldiers crouched next to him and continued shooting.

Lying a few feet away, Armaan watched Tahir's blood splotched uniform and realized that Tahir was grievously wounded. An ordinary man would have died by now, but not this massive bear of a man. Armaan watched Tahir let off a round of bullets till the click of the empty chamber sounded. He reloaded a fresh magazine clip and smiled weakly at Armaan.

"My friends, I fought against your army many years back in Kargil. Today, it is strange that we have both picked up guns and yet we are not fighting against each other, but fighting together side by side. It is said that soldiers understand the difference between right and wrong." Tahir pointed outside. "We both know that they are wrong."

"Terrorists are always in the wrong." Armaan levelled his gun and squeezed the trigger twice in rapid succession. Two terrorists approaching near the barracks had their heads blown off. "These illiterate fools are no match for a trained soldier."

The terrorists at the west side had been completely eliminated by the soldiers at the facility entrance; but only two soldiers had survived the encounter. In the meanwhile, the terrorists at the gate had crossed the compound. They were now only fifty metres from the barracks. They were throwing grenades in their direction.

"You know," Tahir spoke with a wry laugh, "my only son was killed by terrorists. Today I will avenge his death and rejoin him in heaven. I was once called a traitor by my people. Today I will sacrifice my life and everyone will know that I was a proud soldier who gave his life fighting the real traitors of our country."

Tahir gripped the gun tightly as it recoiled with the barrage of bullets that spewed from it targeting the terrorists with precise accuracy.

Armaan kept his head low against the window sill as he continued to pick the terrorists that came close. There were now less than twenty terrorists that he could see. They continued to hurl grenades around the barracks. He wasn't sure how many soldiers had survived outside, but he didn't have time to figure it out. The terrorists were approaching the barrack doors as if no one stood in their path.

A clink.

It sounded very close. Armaan instinctively knew what it was. A grenade had fallen close to where he was. He looked around him trying to locate it. Baldev had also stopped firing and looked at him. It wasn't in the room. Which meant it was right outside the window.

"Take cover." Armaan yelled. Armaan and Baldev stood up and ran only a couple of steps when an ear-shattering explosion happened right behind them, tearing off the wall and window. They were slapped forward by the force of the blast; the gun slipped off Armaan's hand. He landed heavily on the tiled floor. A fraction of a second later, he felt a block of the broken wall hit the back of his head, and he went out like a light.

Shafiq pushed his shoulders and haunches against the door to prop himself into an upright position. He had just observed something that could help him. As he got into a kneeling position he stared at the lowermost hinge of the door. It had been torn halfway off the door. The thin metal sheet protruded perpendicular to the door; the edges were sharp, perfect for what he had in mind.

Shafiq backed himself against the door and brought his hands that were bound behind his back parallel to the door. He positioned his wrists against the sharp metal protrusion and slowly moved his hands back and forth rubbing the ropes that bound him against the sharp hinge using it as a makeshift saw. He estimated that he had fifteen minutes to make his escape.

He breathed heavily, the pain from the wound in his stomach a chronic agony. He still wasn't sure how bad it was, but based on the seeping red blotch on his cloth, he had lost a lot of blood. A normal person would have fallen unconscious by now, but Shafiq was as strong as a bull. He kept his focus on sliding the rope back and forth over the jagged edge hoping that the strands of the thick rope would splice and eventually weaken enough for him to shear apart the ropes that bound him.

Shafiq felt the rope strands tearing under the friction. He grunted with each swipe of the rope. Beads of sweat poured down his face, and his breath became laboured, but he carried on resolutely knowing that he had very little time. Zia and Malik could return at any moment. The thought gave him wings, and he hustled on unmindful of his body weakening against the loss of blood with a single-minded intention to cut free.

Eventually, he felt the rope's grip on his wrists slacken. He forced his hands apart and they jerked free. Shafiq took a deep breath and rubbed his sore wrists. He then untied the bounds on his feet. A few seconds later he was free and he gripped the handle of the closed door to support him as he straightened himself to a standing position.

He pulled up his clothes and looked at his wound in the dim light. A deep black hole oozed dark red blood from the side of his stomach. He tried to plug the hole with his fingers, but the wound didn't look to be clotting fast enough. He looked around hoping to see a piece of cloth in the room, but beyond a table and two chairs, the room was empty. There were no windows, and a solitary bulb illuminated the room.

Shafiq rummaged through his pockets. His fingers felt the magazine. They had taken his gun. He looked at the door and appraised it. It looked sturdy and it was the only exit out of the room. There were no windows or hiding place anywhere.

It appeared that he had to bulldoze his way through. He backed up to one corner of the room, and then dashed towards the door and hurtled himself at the door raising his arms at the last minute to shield his body from the impact. There was a loud crunching sound of metal and wood as the door shuddered against his weight, but the door was impregnable and Shafiq rebounded against the door like a rag-doll. He fell on his side and the shock tore through his wounded body like a tremor igniting all his battered nerve ends.

Shafiq writhed in agony and the pain refused to subside. Outside of the door, he heard voices shouting. "The prisoner is trying to break free. Arms at the ready. Go and alert Malik."

There were guards posted in front of the door. Shafiq realized that he hadn't accounted for the fact that there would be tight security for him. He hadn't heard the guards maintaining vigil outside while speaking with Zia. He was unarmed and they could enter inside and gun him down if required.

He was clearly trapped, and there was no escape. He was severely wounded and his chances of surviving were dwindling with every minute.

But what anguished Shafiq the most was that he was so close to realizing his mission, yet he couldn't execute it. The terrorist leaders were here and he could do nothing against them.

He raised himself and bolted the door from the inside. If he couldn't get out, they couldn't get in either. Maybe for a few minutes anyways. He had run out of options.

He closed his eyes and took a deep breath willing his mind to focus. There had to be a way; that was how they were trained to think.

There is always a way. I just have to find it. His hands suddenly clamped on the magazine inside his pockets. The magazine that was in fact a communication device.

The General. He could tell him what happened.

He pulled out the magazine, and slid off the hidden cover. A minute later he was speaking with the General.

"I have been burned, sir. Unable to execute mission."

If the General was wondering why Shafiq was unable to complete his mission, he didn't mention it.

The General's reply was quiet and measured. "Are the leaders still at the location?"

"Yes sir, they are here."

"I can authorise a strike subject to one hundred percent confirmation of location of the High Value Targets. We needed HUMINT on the ground before we could go ahead with this. Since, you verified the presence of HVTs, I want to know what is our success percentage."

Shafiq remembered that the leaders were in Al-Abadi's suite and he had seen them discussing the mission. They wouldn't get another chance like this.

"Target is hot. Success probability at one hundred percent."

"Excellent, give me the coordinates."

Shafiq hesitated. A strike would mean a handful of one thousand pound missiles strafing the area. If one of them missed their mark and fell near his vicinity, he could possibly die.

As he dwelled upon it, he heard voices growing louder outside the door. One of them was the manic screeching of Zia. He sounded very angry.

Shafiq's mind was up. He spoke into the communications device.

"Here's the GR." He gave the Grid Reference he could see on the small screen. "Use this with a circular error probable radius of one hundred metres. Bomb it as hard as you can. *Tazi Spay* out."

Shafiq hung up the call as he heard the guards making futile attempts to open the door. He laughed at the irony.

He had just called an air strike on himself.

Chapter 38

"This guy is still alive... He's twitching..."

There was darkness everywhere. Armaan's entire body was on fire. It felt like his body had been smashed into pulp. He heard the words spiral up and down through his consciousness. The volume went from high pitched to mute in his eardrums.

A sudden staccato of gunfire pierced his conscious. But it stopped only after a moment. "There," someone said, "he's dead now."

Armaan could hear the jeering laughs of victory. Another round of gunfire cast its shrill resonance on his ears, and he finally returned to consciousness. He slowly opened his eyes, the darkness in his mind giving way to the bright sunlight reflected off the snow-covered hills streaming through a big hole in the barrack wall. He blinked, trying to focus his sight.

The dark, unblinking eyes of Tahir stared back at him from a few feet away. He was stone dead. Armaan felt a momentary sadness for the Colonel; but he was now with his son, hopefully at peace.

"Kill all soldiers that you find." Armaan heard someone ordering. "They killed our wives and children. It's time to avenge their deaths. They launch their *Radd-ul-Fasaad* on us, but the real *jadd-e-fasaad*" – root of the problem – "are these uniform-clad barbarians who launch airstrikes on our homes, hoping to kill us, but instead kill our families."

Armaan looked up to see the barrel of a gun pointed right at his head. Behind the gun he could see the cold eyes of the terrorist. His face was veiled behind a black cloth. Armaan waited for him to shoot. The seconds passed by, but the terrorist didn't shoot him.

Why doesn't he shoot me like he shot the others? Armaan wondered.

Armaan looked around. While he was no stranger to death, the number of bodies piled around him made his insides twist. He felt the raw taste of bile on his tongue.

Baldev! Armaan remembered and turned to look at him. Baldev was on his knees in a corner, alive but another terrorist had his gun to Baldev's head. There were around half a dozen terrorists in the barracks.

Armaan heard sporadic shooting outside. He assumed that the remaining soldiers were getting massacred. The fight had been even for a long time, and now it had tilted in the terrorists' favour. The casualties on both ends had been heavy, especially on the terrorists' side, where they had gained access to the facility only by the sheer strength of their numbers. He estimated that there would be another dozen terrorists fighting inside the facility.

A few minutes later the firing stopped. Armaan watched as around a dozen terrorists joined the others in the barracks. Most of the terrorists were wounded. One of the terrorists, a heavyset bull of a man spoke, "The soldiers are all dead. Gather up all the scientists and herd them into one of the offices. We can use them as hostages if needed." He appeared to be the leader of the group. The terrorist looked around, "Where is our friend Abdul?"

A scrawny bespectacled man moved forward from the group. He was dressed like the terrorists but unlike the others, he wasn't armed; and he gave the appearance of a college fresher about to be ragged by his seniors.

"I am here." Abdul spoke quietly. Armaan watched the man look around in repulsion. He didn't look like a terrorist; he seemed more of the geek kind who sat behind keyboards and played digital god. Armaan wasn't sure what he was doing among the terrorists. *Maybe he is being coerced?*

"You know what to do?" The terrorist asked.

"Yes, my ID badge has Level 3 authorisation for the Missile Control Room. Once we get in, I will program the coordinates and launch the missiles."

Launch the missiles? Armaan did a double-take. *What was this guy about to do?*

A gun poked down into Armaan's shoulder. "Get up." The terrorist meandering over him said. "You are to join the other scientists."

In an instant, Armaan understood why he and Baldev hadn't been shot. He looked down at his white civilian suit and realized for the first time, that all of the Pakistani soldiers were in uniform. When the terrorists had reached the barracks, they had gunned down everyone in uniform, but spared them as they lay down unconscious on the floor noting their civilian dress and assuming them to be part of the administration staff.

Armaan stood up without resisting and looked at Baldev who was also getting up. The terrorist behind him poked his gun in Armaan's back again. Armaan started walking towards the facility entrance with Baldev and another terrorist. The two terrorists prodded them through the entrance and up a flight of stairs which Armaan remembered from Tahir's conversation housed the R&D lab.

The place had metamorphosed into a mess. Computers and monitors were strewn around; the chairs had fallen in the aisles. Armaan pictured a chaotic scene of the terrorists storming the floor and herding the panicked employees under the threat of a gun. They walked past the rows of empty cubicles to the lab room in the far corner. One of the terrorists knocked on the door and announced, "More hostages."

The door opened and Armaan and Baldev were butted through. Armaan looked around. A terrorist signalled at Armaan with his barrel, telling him to join the others. It was a spacious section divided by glass partitions that housed various equipment. He saw the facility employees bundled together in one corner. Their expressions were resigned and tired. Another gun-toting terrorist hovered over them.

The terrorist at the door unceremoniously pushed them at the group of hostages sitting in the corner. Armaan heard one of the employees from the group ask, "Are you going to kill us?"

"If we wanted to kill you, we would have done that already. Now keep quiet and don't bother me. We have a mission to complete and will leave you unharmed if you follow our orders."

Armaan looked up at the terrorist, a realization forming in his mind. Till now he hadn't consciously thought about why the terrorists were here, but when he heard the word 'mission', he understood that the terrorists didn't just want to kill the soldiers, there was more to it.

The terrorist guarding them continued talking, "Today is a great day for us. We will be remembered for orchestrating the largest terrorist attack ever. Everyone remembers 9/11. From now on, today's date will be carved in history and our leader will become more famous than Osama Bin Laden."

Armaan's brow darkened with each word that the terrorist spoke. He looked at Baldev. Baldev shook his head. He too was completely clueless about the terrorist's intentions. Armaan suddenly remembered that the thin man with the terrorists had said that he would launch the missiles. It conjured all sorts of foreboding in Armaan's mind. Maybe he could get more information about the mission.

The terrorist kept gloating. "I don't understand why you are so sad. Rejoice. Your Army employs you to create weapons, but doesn't use them against the enemy. Today, we will show you how to use the weapons that you created."

Armaan knew he had to know the terrorist's intentions. "You are going to launch the missiles, aren't you?"

The terrorist stopped and looked at him, "Yes, what use are missiles, if they aren't launched at the enemy?"

Armaan ventured, "Who is the enemy? What is your target?"

"New Delhi. We will strike a decisive blow and cut the head of the snake."

The blood froze in Armaan's veins as the realization swept all other thoughts from his mind.

They are going to launch a missile attack on New Delhi.

Armaan looked at Baldev, the shock in his face was visible. They had to do something and prevent the terrorists. He nodded at Baldev. Baldev gestured with his eye at the terrorist near the door. Armaan silently indicated he would take down the terrorist next to the group. He looked at the terrorists. They were walking on the floor in a repetitive pattern. He waited till the terrorist at the door walked close to them and then turned around.

Now! He gave the hand signal to Baldev. Baldev sprinted towards the terrorist, while Armaan charged at the terrorist who looked in surprise at Baldev. As a terrorist, they had been brought up with the belief that if they wielded a gun, the common civilians would submit to their will. They hadn't counted on the probability that one of those civilians could be a Covert Ops commando with thousands of gruelling hours of training under his belt.

Armaan swivelled in mid-air and landed a brutal kick at the terrorist's shin knocking him off balance. The gun clattered to the floor. He gave a powerful chop on the man's neck and he went limp immediately. He looked over at Baldev. Baldev gave him the thumbs–up; the terrorist in front of him was lying motionless on the floor. Armaan looked at the captives. They looked at him as if they had met a real-life comic book hero.

"Don't go out. You are all safe here." Armaan advised the hostages. He looked at Baldev. "Grab their guns. Let's go."

They opened the lab door and raced through the empty cubicles and reached the exit that went down to the lobby and paused.

"What now?" Baldev asked.

"The geek named Abdul said he was going to the Missile Control Room. It's on Level 3, two floors below us. We have to stop him before he launches the missiles."

Chapter 39

Abdul looked at the screen in front of him. It had been a long time since he had sat in front of the console. He still remembered the evening in Hunza Valley when he was abducted by the terrorists. He had feared for his life then. But the terrorists hadn't harmed him. In fact, they had treated him well.

During his captivity, Nadeem Kunduz, the leader of the terrorists had explained his bold plan of a missile attack against New Delhi. Even though Abdul wasn't too warm about the Indians, he had been shocked by the proposal. But over time, Abdul had realized that it was either his life or his enemy's life. And the choice for him was clear. He would save himself rather than some thousands of Indians who viewed Pakistan as an enemy.

"How much time will it take?" Nadeem Kunduz asked him. He stood next to Abdul and watched him operate the console and enter the commands on the screen.

"Only a few minutes more. The coordinates for Delhi have been programmed. We have locked onto the Parliament, Secretariat Building, Rashtrapati Bhavan, and other major targets." Abdul looked up at Nadeem and saw a malicious smile on his face.

"The infidels will die by our hand. I can't wait. Make it quick."

Armaan and Baldev crept quietly down the stairs. Level 2 was deserted. Armaan looked around and signalled downstairs. They tiptoed down, their suede-leather shoes making no noise on the polished tiles of the stairs. They reached the entrance door to Level 3. Armaan peered around the corner. Twenty feet away, a young terrorist stood admiring the stations that were loaded with missile components. The automated machines were still working. No one had bothered to turn them off. The components were being loaded in the stations; the nose cones were manufactured and were then deposited on an assembly line. It was probably the first time the young teenager had seen such an advanced technology. Armaan wanted to ensure it was his last.

Armaan looked around. There were no other terrorists in the vicinity, or if they were, they were out of sight. He couldn't shoot the gun he had taken from the terrorists in Level 1. It would create a lot of noise and alert everyone. He had to be discreet.

Armaan raced forward, quickly covering the distance between the terrorist and himself. He clamped his hand on the terrorist's mouth and with a swift jerk pulled the terrorist's face towards him. The terrorist's neck snapped and he slumped to the floor.

Armaan looked around. No one had witnessed the incident. He beckoned to Baldev to join him.

"I think the Missile Control Room is in the far corner." Armaan said, "We passed by it without thinking much about it, but I think I saw a narrow corridor that leads up to a locked door."

"We don't have a moment to lose."

They scurried swiftly past the row of stations using them as cover, but couldn't see any other terrorists. They reached the corridor and Armaan took a peek. A massive imposing door stood at the end of the narrow corridor complete with an iris scanner and a biometric console for access. But that wasn't what bothered Armaan. In front of the door stood two heavily built terrorists, their eyes on the corridor. Armaan backed his head out of their sight, but he wasn't quick enough.

"Who's that? Hamid, is that you?" one of the terrorists had already sighted him. He started walking down the corridor towards him.

"Oh bother," Baldev uttered. He brought his gun to his chest. Armaan nodded. They had been discovered. The time for discretion and stealth was gone.

It would now be replaced by violent force.

"What are you doing down here?" Armaan heard a startled voice behind him. He turned around. A terrorist was walking towards them. Apparently he hadn't seen the guns in their hands and mistook them for employees who had escaped. He would be Hamid that the other terrorist had referred to. The terrorist's eyes widened as he saw the guns in their hands. He brought his own up, but Baldev was quicker. A short burst of gunfire arced through the man's chest and he was down in a flash.

"Who's there?" The voice in the corridor grew closer. Armaan backed up against the wall while Baldev raced to safety behind one of the missile stations, his gun pointed at the corridor. Armaan could hear the terrorist's footsteps bounding across the floor echoing through the corridor. A moment later, the terrorist came into view. Armaan let loose a quick burst that ripped through the terrorist's body.

One left.

The second terrorist had stopped. No sound came through the corridor. He would have seen the fate of his companion. He would probably be backing up to the door. Armaan wasn't sure how many terrorists were in the Missile Control Room, but he could take his chances with one terrorist.

Armaan gave a quick signal to Baldev and then sprinted towards the corridor and dived sideways, his gun pointed towards the passage. As the opening of the corridor came into the view, he saw the terrorist crouched in the far end next to the door. He squeezed the trigger and let loose a hail of bullets. As he landed on his side, he realized that all his shots had missed.

The terrorist was now aiming at him.

Armaan thought of rolling out of harm's way when he heard a burst of gunfire behind him. He saw the terrorist slam back against the reinforced door due to the impact of the bullets and then slide down on the floor, lifeless.

Armaan looked back at Baldev who offered him a hand, "I have your six."

"Thank you." Armaan nodded gratefully.

Abdul's hand stopped instinctively on the console as he heard the sound of gunfire. He was almost done uploading the coordinates into the system. He looked up at Nadeem. The gunfire sounded quite close. He wondered if there were still soldiers out there who hadn't been caught by the terrorists.

"Keep working," Nadeem ordered.

"Should I go and check?" Nazal walked over to the

closed biometric door and asked Nadeem.

"No. There are two guards outside the door. And no one can come inside bypassing the security."

"So, we stay put in here?"

"Yes, our mission is to launch the missiles, not to fight the soldiers. As long as the door is sealed no one can stop us from carrying out our objective. If anyone does come, we shoot them down. Am I clear?"

"Yes, brother." Nazal took position in front of the door.

Abdul felt Nadeem's eyes upon him. He answered his unasked question. "We are done. The missiles are programmed for launch."

Abdul walked up and went to one end of the console. He pulled out a key from his pocket and inserted it inside a hole. He looked at Nadeem. Nadeem walked to the other end of the console and inserted an identical key into the keyhole on the other end. They had taken the keys from Tahir and the second-in-command.

"On my mark," Abdul said, "One, two, three."

They both simultaneously twisted the keys. A minute later the information on the large screen changed to a single sentence.

Press red switch to initiate launch sequence.

Abdul walked back to his seat and looked at the red button. He lifted the transparent switch cap and his finger wavered over the button. Once launched, there would be no going back. There was no way missiles could be recalled or diverted once they were in the air. They used to call the missiles 'fire and forget.' It was time to fire and forget.

Abdul firmly pressed down the red button.

Armaan looked at the reinforced door with the biometric security. He was totally at a loss. "There is no way we can get past this."

"An iris scanner, a biometric fingerprint and an access card." Baldev counted. "We cannot force our way through. We will need an employee who already has access to this place."

"Let's go to Level 1 and see if someone works in the Missile Control Room."

They raced up the stairs and ran across the cubicles on Level 1. Armaan opened the Lab door and was relieved that the employees had followed his advice and were still there.

"Does any one of you work in the Missile Control Room?"

Armaan waited, but no one said anything. He spoke again.

"This is an emergency. The terrorists will be launching missiles. We have to stop them."

One of the men spoke up. "I am from Level 3. There are only a handful of employees that have access to the Control Room but I don't see any of them here."

Armaan felt a froth bubbling in his stomach. "There has to be another way to get inside."

"There is none. It's completely secured from all sides. Only authorised personnel have access to it."

The froth in his stomach threatened to burst. The terrorists would be inside and they would launch the missiles any time now. "We have to get inside somehow…"

Suddenly a deep rumbling noise echoed from the depths of the earth.

"What was that?" Baldev walked over to a nearby window. A moment later he yelled, "Armaan!"

Armaan rushed over and looked at where Baldev was pointing. The missile bays were open and he watched in incredulous disbelief as thirty missiles whooshed out of the launch pads and raced into the skies heading east.

Armaan watched the missiles till they disappeared in the horizon. He roared in a fit of impotent rage. He had failed to stop the launch.

New Delhi was about to burn.

Chapter 40

"Eagle! Did you see that?"

Roshan's voice was frantic. He had just seen the missiles zoom over their heads. Roshan had been worried for Armaan and Baldev when they were trapped inside the barracks, but he had overheard Armaan's conversation with the terrorists and had quietly hoped that they would be able to shut down the launch. But then Roshan had seen the missiles eject from the launchpads. They were in a no-win situation. Based on where the missiles would hit, Delhi would face casualties running into tens of thousands up to a million. And he hadn't even taken into account the political implications.

All hell is going to break loose.

"No. The SAT is not over the area. But I heard." Eagle said. "I have been trying to contact Homebase for the past five minutes, ever since I learned the terrorist's plan, but Homebase hasn't responded. Let me try to get the Delhi GES or BMD team on this."

"Okay, but make it quick. We have literally only a few minutes."

Five hundred kilometres over the earth, the Cartosat series of satellites moved in a sun-synchronous orbit. One of their jobs was to look out for ground based threats and analyse them. A few seconds after the missiles were launched; the infra-red sensors on one of the satellites detected a huge thermal footprint over a pre-designated coordinate in Pakistan. The coordinates matched the list of threat sites in its database. As per the program coded on its software, it sent out an alert to all the ground based ELINT systems.

The Ilyushin IL-76 aircraft hovered at a height of thirty thousand feet above the Pathankot air base in northern Punjab. Atop the IL-76 aircraft was fitted the Phalcon Airborne Early Warning and Control Systems called as AWACS in military slang. Hovering right at the edge of the international border, the job of the AWACS was to detect incoming aircraft or missiles and coordinate the information to the Ground Exploitation Stations. With an impressive radar range of 400km, it immediately picked up the missiles hurtling towards India.

Shikha stifled a yawn. She tried to focus on the computer screen but couldn't. Documentation was the most boring part of a project. She loved the creativity of working on a project, but hated having to document everything that she did. But today she felt unusually sluggish. She had taken her work home last night and had slept quite late. She wasn't sure if she was sleep-deprived or just plain bored penning down the documentation.

I need to get a cup of coffee.

Shikha rose from her desk when a sharp beep emanated from her desktop computer. Her heart skipped a beat. She couldn't remember the last time she had received an unexpected alert. She immediately sat down and looked at the notification message that had popped on the screen.

It was an automated alert from the Cartosat satellite. It had detected a massive thermal gradient change that corresponded with a missile launch, plus the location of the thermal spike corresponded to Facility Project S25.

Shikha stood up and walked out of her cabin and looked over at her team sitting in the cubicles. Everyone's eyes were on her. They all had received the same alert and everyone was wondering what it really meant.

"Do you think it's a false positive?" Shikha asked.

"No," Tanmay replied, "We will need separate evidence before we can confirm this is indeed a missile launch." He paused, "In fact, multiple missile launches. We have received thermal signatures in the past, but they were of a single missile during test launches, but nothing on this scale."

"Yeah, the thermal difference is what unnerves me. We –" Shikha was about to say something when another beep sounded simultaneously on everyone's computer. She quickly walked around to Tanmay's desktop and viewed over his shoulder.

The new notification was from the Phalcon AWACS. Shikha read it and her heart spiked up in her throat. The AWACS had detected the launch of thirty missiles. They were headed east, towards India.

It was impossible!

"Did Pakistan issue a NOTAM?" Shikha tried to reassure herself that this couldn't be happening.

The NOTAM or Notice to Airmen was an announcement made prior to any missile tests that informed aircraft pilots everywhere to not be in the vicinity when a country was conducting a missile test. Pakistan had always issued NOTAMs before testing their missiles. Maybe she had missed out on the notification due to her workload.

Tanmay shook his head, "There were no NOTAMs." He looked at her and spoke in a low voice. "It's really happening."

Shikha's mobile buzzed. It was an unknown number, but it couldn't be a coincidence. She picked up the call, dreading whatever she was going to hear.

"Multiple missiles are headed for New Delhi. Please take evasive action." The voice on the other line didn't even introduce himself, nor did he elaborate on his outrageous claim. But Shikha knew immediately that he was speaking the fact. There was no way anyone could have known about the alert so quickly.

"How…" She left the question dangling.

"Please trust me." Eagle replied. "We have HUMINT on the ground on Facility S25. Thirty missiles were launched. The target is New Delhi."

"We will follow the protocols. Thank you for letting us know."

"Thanks." The unknown caller hung up.

Shikha squared her shoulders. They had trained multiple times for such an eventuality. Only this time, it was for real. She couldn't afford to fail. Shikha went back to her desk and initiated the Crisis Response program on her computer. It had been live tested only once before when the system was introduced and was demoed in front of the PM and the NSA.

The program loaded immediately and Shikha swiftly

executed the commands. She pulled the headset over her ears. The program was designed to create a teleconference bridge and it immediately dialled the hotlines for the Prime Minister, Defence Minister, National Security Advisor and select members of the National Security Council. The software would emit a distinctive ringtone on the group member's phone and keep dialling till they picked it up. A few seconds later, all of the members were on the teleconference and Shikha informed them of the alert.

Prime Minister Inamdaar spoke first, "The Ballistic Missile Defence are programmed to automatically respond to incoming missiles, is that correct?"

"Yes, sir," Shikha said.

"How much time will it take for the missiles to reach us?"

"The Ghauri missiles are travelling at a speed of 6 Mach. The launch site is nine hundred kilometres from New Delhi. Not counting the parabolic path of the missiles, the minimum time we have is seven minutes, twenty one seconds. Two minutes have already crossed since launch time so the current ETA is five minutes."

Inamdaar said in a calm voice, "We have prepared for such eventualities. Vishwajeet, Rabindra and Dharamveer," the PM addressed the Chiefs of the Army, Navy and Airforce, "we initiate Operation Rapid Revenge. We have gone over the second strike doctrine multiple times and I am sure we can adequately respond to anything the Pakistanis can throw at us."

The Defence Minister interrupted, "Sir, there is something wrong with their attack pattern. If Pakistan wanted to attack us, they would have launched their missiles on all our cities and from multiple launchpads all over Pakistan. This attack is just from one site to only one of our cities. I suspect it's a rogue attempt."

Inamdaar fumed. "Undisciplined fools. They can't even control their rank and file. I will speak with the Pakistani PM on his hotline. Vishwajeet, you speak with the Pakistani Chief of Army Staff."

General Singh said, "Sir, I just got an update from my subordinate. We have HUMINT at the missile launch site as well as SAT. This launch was initiated by terrorists and not the Pakistani Army. We aren't sure if they are conventional warheads or nukes. I would suggest we call off the decision on Operation Rapid Revenge and inform the Pakistani counterparts on what happened."

"We will decide that later. First, we will focus on our BMD response. Can we ensure that we can eliminate all the incoming missiles without letting any of them fall through our defences?"

Shikha hesitated, "Sir, no Ballistic Missile Defence is one hundred percent foolproof. It is like stopping one bullet with another. We have our S400 BMD systems located a few kilometres north of here for such a situation. But we've tested it with only single missiles and not with multiple incoming missiles. We have thirty incoming missiles. Considering that we may not be able to reload the missiles and fire in five minutes, it's too close a call."

"Let's have faith in our systems." Inamdaar said. "I approve all methods necessary to neutralize the threats."

Shikha watched the action on the large LCD screen. It seemed like a video game. Thirty red streaks were mapped on the left side of the screen, and she could see multiple blue streaks on the right that rose up to meet them. She had mentioned that Ballistic Missile Defence was like stopping a bullet by firing another bullet at it. The comparison wasn't off. She watched as the first blue streak reached the closest red streak and then both vanished indicating that the missile had been demolished in mid-air. A moment later, the second blue streak touched a red streak and the red streak disappeared. The third and fourth streaks also did their work.

It's working. We can get this done. Shikha looked around at the team. Most of them were watching the screen and inputting their commands to the BMD system. She looked at Tanmay, he was on the phone speaking with someone.

"Tanmay, we are in a crisis here." Shikha said, "I need you to focus on your job instead of being on the phone."

Tanmay spoke a few words and then hung up the phone and then looked at his computer screen. "I am doing my job."

"Good." Shikha couldn't believe that Tanmay could shirk his responsibilities at such an important moment for them when she wanted all hands on deck. She turned to look back at the screen and realized that a few of the BMD missiles had missed their mark. As she watched another couple of BMD missiles missed their targets. She looked at the remaining BMD missiles and compared them with the incoming missiles. To her shock she realized that both the numbers were the same.

They had reached missile saturation point.

It meant that each BMD missile had to hit its target with one hundred percent accuracy.

There were twenty missiles still incoming. She watched as the two streaks collided and vanished. Then another. She started to exhale now. Maybe it might just work.

The next BMD missile missed its target. Shikha watched in horror as the red streak continued its path. *Oh dear God,* she uttered. Even one missile could kill thousands of people. She couldn't take her eyes off the screen as she watched another BMD missile miss. And then another.

A few BMD missiles still hit their targets, but Shikha's dread notched up as each blue streak missed a red streak. She watched as the final blue streak hit a red streak, but her breath had caught in her throat. She watched ten red streaks hurtling rapidly towards New Delhi.

Towards her.

We are going to die! The dire realization pierced through every cell of her body.

Chapter 41

High above the earth, ten Ghauri missiles dove down into the final leg of their journey. Unemotional and logic-based, the internal computer counted down on the ETA to its destination. It had less than sixty seconds left. The missiles didn't care how many thousands of casualties they would inflict. They were programmed to just do their jobs.

And the ten missiles were highly efficient at it.

"What?" Shikha couldn't take her eyes off the screen. The red streaks were very close now. Tanmay was saying something.

"- is ready for deployment."

Shikha finally looked at him. "What?" she repeated.

"I am deploying the KALI 5000. Let's see if that works."

Shikha suddenly realized why Tanmay had been on the phone. He must have talked with the KALI team. The KALI or Kilo Ampere Linear Injector was an experimental High Power Pulsed Electron Accelerator weapon that could send a powerful pulse against enemy aircraft or missiles. It was still in beta mode and hadn't been fully tested. She looked at the incoming red streaks. They had nothing to lose.

"Do it."

Tanmay pressed a few keys on his keyboard and looked up at the LCD screen. "KALI 5000 is live."

A few kilometres away, the KALI 5000 manufactured by the DRDO and the BARC tracked the ten missiles. It emitted an invisible yet powerful burst of gigawatts of electron pulses on the incoming Ghauri missiles. The pulses seared through the missile control boards and fried the onboard circuits. With the onboard computer dead, the missiles were rendered useless. The missiles turned into duds and fell harmlessly to the ground.

Shikha looked at the screen and her jaw dropped. The red streaks were all gone. The KALI 5000 had done its job killing all the incoming missiles in one go.

New Delhi was safe.

A barrage of gunfire followed Armaan as he raced for cover behind the facility. He ducked down behind a wall and the bullets whizzed past him. Armaan waited for the terrorist to foolishly expend all his bullets. When the gunfire stopped Armaan scoped his target from behind the building and fired a single shot hitting the man square in the head.

"Three, I need supporting fire. Two and I are going to be surrounded in minutes."

"I am almost out of ammo, One." Roshan replied. "I am trying to conserve my rounds. I will fire only if I am sure of a hit. Sorry."

"No apologies needed," Armaan replied. He knew that only the Vidhwansak could reach at the distance they were at, effectively ruling out the conventional rifle that Hitesh had. "I am also in the same situation. I have only the ammo that is currently loaded in the rifle, nothing more. Same for Baldev."

After watching the missiles leave their pads, Armaan had been seized with a fit of fury. He couldn't get inside the Missile Control Room, but he could ensure that the monsters inside wouldn't survive. He went to Level 3 and lined up a set of booby-traps using a string connected to grenade pins in front of the door. The moment the terrorists opened the biometric door, the pins would be pulled leading to their deaths. Once the trap was set, Baldev and Armaan used the lift to go down to Level 6 to ensure that the kill switches for the Babur-3 missiles were still activated and not tampered with.

The kill switches were undisturbed. It appeared that with the terrorists attacking the facility, Tahir hadn't got any time to investigate and fix the sabotage done on the missiles. They were about to leave the floor, when they heard three grenade explosions one after the other. Armaan laughed with a sadistic satisfaction. The terrorists in the Missile Control Room had died. They took the elevator to Level 3 and Armaan looked at the open door to the Control Room blocked by the dead bodies of the geek and two other terrorists. He nodded to himself. Justice had been served.

Suddenly gunfire erupted around him. Around half a dozen terrorists had converged on the floor hearing the grenade explosions. They had to escape. With gunfire blazing on their heels, they quickly raced up the stairs to the facility entrance on Level 2.

Once out in the open, a couple of terrorists at the gate detected them and fired. Armaan and Baldev took refuge behind the facility building, their escape route to the main gate blocked by terrorists. More terrorists spilled out from the facility entrance. Baldev and Armaan popped one terrorist each forcing the others to crouch behind cover.

But this couldn't go on for long. As far as he could see, they had killed around six terrorists in the past few minutes which meant that there were around a dozen terrorists left.

"Spread around the building," he saw one terrorist shout. Immediately the terrorist fell to the ground shot by a long range rifle.

Roshan. Armaan was grateful for his comrade. Even with the lack of bullets, Roshan was trying to increase their odds of survival. They could yet make out of this one alive.

The thought died in his mind as he saw the terrorists divide in two groups and approach the rear of the building from both sides.

We are going to be outflanked, Armaan realized.

Khost airfield, Khost province, Afghanistan.

Rustom paced back and forth on the wide expanse of the Khost airfield. Located one hundred and fifty kilometres south of Kabul, the Khost airfield was strategically located near the Durand Line, the line that demarcated the border between Afghanistan and Pakistan. Just twenty kilometres separated Rustom from Pakistan and he looked east wondering if the mission was going to be successful.

After a discussion between the Indian R&AW officials and the Afghan NDS, the Afghan government had generously allowed the Indians the use of the airfield for a limited time. Rustom knew that his experience of flying in hostile territories was going to be critical for today's mission.

Rustom took a slow, deep breath to calm his nerves. He was going into Pakistan for a crazy rescue mission. He had listened to the report on the way to the airfield. The friendlies were surrounded by terrorists. And they were almost out of ammunition.

It was going to be a hot landing.

"Don't worry." His boss walked over to him. "General Singh called in. We took some contingency measures. Hopefully you won't get much heat." He pointed at the chopper. "The refuelling is done. The Landing Zone is in Karak, one hundred and fifty kilometres from here. You will fly low and stay under the radar. ETA to LZ is forty minutes."

Eagle's voice echoed in Armaan's ears. "You will be picked up in forty minutes. A chopper is on its way."

"Forty minutes!" Armaan shouted as he sprinted to the corner of the rear wall of the facility, "We barely have four minutes before these pigs kill us."

Armaan and Baldev had pinned the terrorists on both sides. They had decided to hold both corners of the rear wall, one at each corner so that the terrorists couldn't outflank them.

But time and ammo were against them.

Roshan was helping them; picking off the terrorists, one by one but the terrorists seemed to have wised up to the existence of a sniper in the mountains and were now moving forward under shelter. The other terrorists had joined them and it seemed that all of them had come together to avenge the death of their leader.

"Tell that pilot, he will only pick up our dead bodies forty minutes from now." Armaan yelled.

"… will help. … coming soon…" Armaan could barely hear Eagle over the burst of gunfire.

What good can one pilot do against so many terrorists? Armaan wondered.

"I am out of bullets. One," Armaan heard Roshan declare.

"Oh boy." Armaan muttered.

A moment later Baldev announced. "I have only one

bullet left."

Armaan heard a shot.

"Target down," Baldev said, "Now, I have none."

Armaan saw a terrorist racing across the open towards another cover a few yards away. *This is the moment.* He quickly scoped on the running target and pulled the trigger only to hear the sickening finality of a metallic click. Even he had run out of bullets.

"Boys. Even I'm out."

It would be a fight to the death, Armaan realized.

There were only a handful of terrorists left. Armaan reached down to his ankle and realized that his trusty knife wasn't there. They had come in unarmed to the facility and now Armaan was weaponless and defenceless.

The terrorists were backing up. He wondered how long it would take them to realize that they were out of bullets. A minute at most. Eagle had said that the rescue heli would come in forty minutes. A minute from now, he and Baldev would be dead.

So be it. Armaan told himself.

"We are coming down the mountain to help." Roshan said.

"Negative, Three." Armaan ordered, "It will take you ten minutes to reach here. We won't survive till then. Wait for the heli and rescue yourself."

"No, I can't sit still and watch you die." Armaan heard a trace of emotion in Roshan's voice. "We are coming down."

"Negative Three. Stay put. That's an order. Two dead are better than four dead."

There was a long pause on the line. Armaan wondered if Roshan was thinking of the Bangladesh incident where he had defied his orders. Finally Roshan said, "Copy that, One. Good luck."

Armaan peeked around the corner. The terrorists were peering from their shelters more frequently. They were evidently getting restless, but weren't sure of going ahead to attack. He overheard their disjointed conversation and pieced together that they were deciding to attempt a blitz attack.

Armaan looked at Baldev and gave a hand signal.

Baldev ran to an alcove in the middle of the rear wall and crouched there. A moment later, Armaan joined him.

"They will come for us any moment now." Armaan whispered.

Baldev's face stiffened. "It will be a fight to the death. No retreat. No surrender."

"Agreed." Armaan's resolve was absolute.

"Boys," Armaan heard Eagle's high-pitched voice. "Help is here."

What? How did the heli get here so quickly? Armaan wondered.

A moment later he heard a massive explosion on either side of him. More explosions rocked the area. The terrorists' hideouts were being relentlessly pounded. Armaan looked up in the sky to see the silhouette of an ugly looking small plane with no windows, doors or cockpit. Armaan immediately recognized the strangely designed aircraft.

Of course. Ghatak UCAV.

The Unmanned Combat Aerial Vehicle manufactured by DRDO was equipped with the powerful Nag anti-tank missiles specially modified for the drone and renamed as Helina missiles. The Helina missiles screamed down to the ground bombarding the terrorists and pounding them to rubble. The drone circled around the building ensuring that all the terrorists were dead. It made two more passes flying low over the facility and finally flew away.

Baldev watched the skies, his mouth wide-open in shock. "Did I just dream that?"

Armaan laughed and slapped him on the back in exultation.

They had survived.

Chapter 42

"Sir, it was a terrorist attack with no connections to the Pakistani government or their Army." General Vishwajeet Singh spoke up on the conference bridge.

They had just watched the Ghauri missiles almost destroy New Delhi. When the missiles disintegrated in mid-air, there was a muted celebration. Inamdaar wanted to know who was behind the attack.

"It doesn't matter if it's official or not," Inamdaar boomed. "The attack came from Pakistani soil. The Pakistani establishment, whether they were directly involved, or just innocent bystanders is beside the point. We will use our full military force against them."

"PM sir," General Singh said. "There is a way to punish the perpetuators without going into a full-fledged war. Our HUMINT asset has informed me that all the major terrorist leaders came together for the strike on New Delhi. We know their exact location at this very moment. I suggest it's time we give them a dose of their own medicine. You remember you wanted to strike at the terrorist camps to eliminate the leaders? We were worried about how the Pakistanis would react. Now, we have a way to do this without tipping our hand."

"Okay," Inamdaar drawled, "I'm listening."

"Boys," General Singh said, "I am really proud of what you have done?"

"Thanks Homebase." Armaan said. "We are happy to have completed the mission."

"I have news, Markhor," the General replied, "Your mission is not completed. You have one more assignment."

"Sure sir, what do you have in mind?"

"A counterstrike on our enemies. They launched a missile attack on us. It is time we launch one on them."

Armaan gave a blank stare at Baldev. He wasn't sure what General Singh was saying. He replied, "What are your orders, sir?"

"Markhor, here's what you will do…"

Roshan watched the missile launch on the flat panel screen inside the Missile Control Room. He looked at the faces of Armaan, Baldev and Hitesh. They were solemn and determined. It had taken Roshan ten minutes to climb down the mountain to reach the facility along with Hitesh. He had heard the General's idea of bombing the terrorist hideout on the way down. It would be a fitting response to their terror attack on New Delhi.

The General had the coordinates and Hitesh guided Armaan to initiate the launch sequence. Eagle monitored the resort via satellite. Hitesh had said that the missiles would reach the destination within two minutes.

Shafiq looked at the men around him. They had finally broken through the bolt that he had used to lock himself in the room.

The leaders of Al-Qaeda, TTP and Jamaat-ul-Ahrar stared at him. They had come in to watch him die. He knew that they would try to torture him to extract information out of him, but he chuckled silently as he looked at the blood that still seeped through the hole in his stomach. They wouldn't have the pleasure of slowly torturing him.

He would be dead in a few minutes.

Suddenly, he heard ear-splitting explosions around him. He laughed heartily as he looked at the panic-stricken terrorists. They had no idea what was happening. They looked around each other as they heard missiles screaming all around the place. A moment later, a missile pierced through the ceiling into the room.

There was a blinding flash of light and his pain was wiped off in an instant.

Armaan heard Eagle's voice on the line. "Multiple hits on target confirmed. I am checking if there are any survivors, but the entire area is completely demolished and I can see nothing but smoke and fire. Switching to radar imaging... No movement detected. Confirm area secured and hostiles have been eliminated."

"Thanks for the confirmation, Eagle," the General replied, "Good job team. Your mission is now officially over. Eagle has informed me that your pickup will come any minute. Take a break, boys. You have earned it."

The sound of a chopper broke the silence of the facility. Armaan walked out in the open and saw a dark blue Light Combat Helicopter hovering a few feet above the ground. The pilot waved to them to climb aboard.

"I am Captain Rustom." He surveyed the damage around the facility. "I was told about a contingency measure, but this is overkill."

"Overkill is good enough for me."

As Armaan rested his back on the seat cushion, he realized how tired he was. He looked at his team members and nodded. They had been through a lot, and they had survived. He reached out and hugged his team members.

Armaan pulled on the safety belt as the chopper rose in the air. He looked down at the facility nestled in the lap of the snow-capped mountains. As the helicopter took speed, the facility reduced in the distance, till they passed beyond a mountain and the facility disappeared out of sight.

Epilogue

"I'm very pleased with your prompt action, Mian *sa'ab*" PM Jagdish Inamdaar spoke to his Pakistani counterpart."

"I am sorry, my friend," PM Mian replied, "I don't understand what you are referring to."

"I heard that terrorists attacked a military facility in Karak and tried to launch missiles against New Delhi. Your soldiers bravely fought them and defeated them."

"Oh, I apologize. I am not aware of any such event."

"Moreover," Inamdaar continued as if he hadn't heard, "your soldiers even launched missiles against the terrorist headquarters and destroyed it killing all leaders of major terrorist groups."

"What?"

"Yes. I am very pleased that your government is working towards positive policies and confidence-building measures between our countries."

"Huh?"

"I would go on to say that this is a new chapter in India-Pakistan friendship. Thank you for everything you are doing. Have a wonderful day."

Inamdaar hung up the call leaving Mian speechless.

Armaan quietly sipped his wine and sighed contently. It was a time to celebrate. He was finally back in his quarters. The return journey was via an Indian Air Force plane that took a circuitous route through Afghanistan, Iran and the Arabian Sea before they reached India. He had slept through most of the journey; the exertions of the past few days had exhausted him.

He looked at Baldev, Roshan and Hitesh and raised a toast. The glasses clinked and he took a deep sip. The liquid burned down his throat and he felt good. The General was supposed to contact them on their return but he hadn't yet. Anyway, Armaan mused, they deserved a break.

There was a knock on the door.

Armaan rose to answer it. He was surprised to see the visitor. The General had come in person.

"Sir."

The General ignored Armaan and strode into the room. He still hadn't forgiven him for his hasty behaviour. The men stood up as he entered.

"How are my boys?" He looked at the gathering.

"Excellent sir," Roshan replied.

"Great, let's get straight to business. Something has come up."

Armaan smiled, "A new mission?"

General Singh looked at Armaan. He remembered his resolve to not let Armaan lead a covert op again. The mission had been eventually accomplished but he still wasn't sure if Armaan was a fit after what had happened. He turned and gazed at Baldev.

"You boys are to leave ASAP."

"Where?" Baldev asked.

"Xinjiang."

THE END

CPSIA information can be obtained
at www.ICGtesting.com
Printed in the USA
BVHW091548090522
636559BV00011B/619

9 781976 202407